ETERNAL DREAMS:
THE CURSE OF MEMORIES

WRITTEN BY CHRISTOPHER COMPTON

This book is a work of fiction. Any resemblance to actual events or persons, living or dead, is entirely coincidental.

"Eternal Dreams: Cures of Memories," by Christopher Compton. ISBN 978-1-62137-278-3 (softcover); 978-1-62137-284-4 (ebook).

Published 2013 by Virtualbookworm.com Publishing Inc., P.O. Box 9949, College Station, TX 77842, US.

Manufactured in the United States of America.

LOOKING FORWARD

"When you woke up from your dreams this morning, did you ever think you would wish they had lasted forever?" He asked this question without any malice, without any passion, without any heart. He knew the answer; he just wanted the question to stick in my mind as much as it was in his.

"Time and memories. Dreams and escapes. That is all we have now. How could I wish for something that can no longer be possible?" I asked this question with malice, with passion, and with heart. Could he really not remember? Had his memories fallen into the same darkness that I now faced?

"You were always one with words, ya know that?" he said, smiling, an unfamiliar twinkle sparkling in his eyes.

"Yeah, well, I got pretty good with them getting you out of messes," I replied hesitantly. I stared at him intently, noticing a subtle change in his stance. I still refused to let down my guard, thinking his sudden change in mood was merely a trap. It wouldn't have been the first time.

"I don't think of times before this. This is where I belong: Away from messes; away from the weight of the world. Nothing can hold me down here. I'm as free as I could ever dream of." He turned his back to me, his tone becoming more serious, and his voice dropping in volume.

"That's something you were always good at," I said softly, silently and gradually progressing toward him. Maybe I could use this moment to my advantage and end this—or at least come that much closer.

"And what would that be?" he asked in a hushed voice.

I stopped directly behind him. This was my chance. My mind was whirling, unable to come to terms with the fact that I was about to destroy my own best friend. I was to put an end to the trail of our memories together. It was necessary, and yet... all I could do was choke out a single word.

"Pretending."

For all those who have had a dream come true-
and especially for those who had one that didn't.

To Pattie
Burgess,

Dream with your
eyes wide open
Christopher
Gupton

CHAPTER 1: THE BEST INTENTIONS

"You'll *never* believe what I found," a familiar voice whispered to me.

I slowly opened my eyes, having been in a deep slumber and nowhere near ready to be woken up. My eyes took a few moments to adjust to my dim surroundings inside the tent. I rubbed them and let out an obnoxious yawn, ignoring the person standing over me.

"I'm not getting up for some stupid animal you found living inside a tree again," I grumbled, rolling over and closing my eyes, trying to get back to sleep.

My blanket was torn away from me, letting the morning cold seep into my pyjamas. I shivered and reached for the blanket, knowing all I would grasp was air. I reluctantly opened my eyes and groaned.

"I promise it isn't an animal this time," he said with a laugh. His voice did give an edge of excitement. "This is different."

I rolled onto my back and let my eyes adjust to see his face. He had a big smile etched across his face and a sparkle in his eyes. I could tell he wasn't going to let this go until I followed him on another wild adventure that would leave me disappointed.

"Okay, but this better be good, Kanoa," I said, stretching my arms with another mighty yawn.

"Trust me," he said as he ran out of the tent, leaving my blanket at the entrance. "You won't be disappointed!"

I scoffed at him and remained seated inside my tent. I wasn't buying his adventure just yet. Judging from the limited sunlight creeping into the tent, it was still quite early. We had all stayed up late last night telling scary stories and making s'mores, so I was still extremely tired. I had been having that dream again...

Kanoa stuck his head back into the tent with an annoyed look on his face. "Well, are you coming or what, Kail?" I could see he was tapping his foot in anticipation.

"Give me a break," I groaned. "I told you I'm coming. Just give me a second, would you? There's no way it can be that important, anyway."

"You're going to be apologizing to me when we get there." He laughed again and darted back out. I took a deep breath and hoisted myself onto my feet. There was never a dull moment with Kanoa around.

I lazily poked my head out of the tent and looked at my surroundings. As I had thought, it was still very early. There was a little light trying its best to brighten our campsite, but the darkness of dawn still ruled the sky. Six tiny tents encircled a fireplace that now held only ashes. Unless Kanoa had woken everyone else up too, I assumed that the rest of my friends were still fast asleep inside their own tents, possibly having nightmares based on the scary stories we had told the night before. Lucky them.

"Kanoa," I whispered into the trees. "Where did you go?"

I fully emerged from my tent and began wandering around, looking for clues as to where he could have run off. It was rare for him to actually wait for others to keep up, whenever he got this excited.

"Well, if you had gotten up the first time, you wouldn't be having such a hard time!" I heard him shout, sounding rather far away. Despite its apparent distance, it nevertheless was rather distinct in its direction. I spun around to discover an opening in the trees that led to a small path deep within the forest.

"Ready or not, here I come!" I shouted back, momentarily forgetting about my sleeping friends. I clapped my hands around my mouth in embarrassment and mouthed "sorry" at the tents. With that, I began my hunt for Kanoa within the shadowy woods. I just hoped that I wouldn't get lost before I found him.

The sun was lifting higher into the sky, but the area around me remained dim as ever. I constantly brushed up against tree branches and gained my fair share of scrapes. I wasn't sure where Kanoa was anymore and was becoming increasingly disoriented with every step I took. The path I had started on had faded long ago, and I was now walking aimlessly. Saying that I was lost would have been an understatement.

I turned around, thinking about heading back to the campsite, when I realized I wasn't sure where that was anymore. I started thinking that if I just kept walking in one direction, I would eventually pop out of the woods, near a stream or a road or something. A nervous chill crept up my spine and filled me with doubt. Following Kanoa, I remembered, was usually a bad idea.

I heard the sound of a snapping branch from somewhere in the woods. I spun around to see if I could find the culprit, but couldn't see anything. Could it have been Kanoa? Or was it a wild animal? Or maybe it was just my imagination… Then I heard it again, closer.

"Kanoa, is that you?" I asked, trying my best to sound calm. It wasn't working very well as my voice deceived my emotions. "This isn't funny. Just come out. I know it's you!" There was no response.

The crackling of fallen branches grew louder and more frequent. I continued to snap my head from place to place, hoping to find my stalker before he was right on top of me. I picked up a stick by my feet and held it firmly, awaiting my attacker. I spun in circles, trying my best to not leave any spot to darkness. The snapping noise was ever so close now…

"If you knew it was me, what's with the stick?" I heard a voice ask coolly from behind me.

I instinctively jumped and spun around with my stick, only to realize I had just struck Kanoa instead of a wild animal.

"Ah!" He shouted in pain, holding his arm. "What was that for?"

"You sca--" I began, but quickly corrected myself "I mean, that's what you get for sneaking up on people!"

He laughed and massaged the area on his arm that I had hit. "Well, I wish you could have taught me my lesson a little less violently." He pushed me as he passed and began walking deeper into the woods. He turned back toward me with a frown on his face. 'Well? Are you coming or what?"

"Maybe this isn't such a good idea," I said, rubbing the cold spots on my elbows. "Whatever it is can't be all that important for us to get lost over. Can't you just tell me?"

He sighed heavily and walked back to me. He placed his hand on my shoulder and tilted his head. "Why can't you just trust me for once, huh?" he asked. The smile on his face still brimmed with electricity. His eyes still held the same twinkle. Whatever it was he wanted me to see really seemed to have mesmerized him.

"Ugh," I moaned in protest. His stare remained firmly upon me. I knew that if I didn't see it now, he would never let me hear the end of it. "Fine, but this better be really good! And how about you don't run off again?"

He laughed again and patted me on the back. "Good boy! Now come on, we're actually pretty close. I'm telling you, you're going to be so sorry you doubted me."

This time I followed closely behind him. The trees grew thicker and thicker, as if they were trying to block us from something. We were steadily walking uphill, and the further we went, the steeper the incline became. We then came upon a large, rusted fence that had many bends in its frame, probably from years of neglect. It had barbed wire running along the top and the links were very thick. What was such a severe barricade doing out in the middle of the woods?

Suddenly the trees became started thinning out and Kanoa's walk transformed into a jog, and then a run. I tried my best to keep up with him, stumbling up the now-rocky hill. The tree lining gave way to an opening, filled with only large stones and weeds. Kanoa reached the top and stood waiting, looking out into the distance.

A rock beneath my foot slid out of place, causing me to slam my knee into the sharp stones. A cut formed and caused me to seethe in pain. I rubbed it furiously, still scaling the rocks as fast I could. I finally reached the top, still massaging my wound, and punched Kanoa on the back in frustration. He didn't flinch. I looked up to meet his gaze and instantly realized just what it was that was so important to him. Before me was something I had not only never seen before, but something I had not even imagined.

"Sorry," I whispered.

"This will make us legends," he whispered back. Kanoa had always been fascinated with things of legend, or making a legend of himself, but I never thought his words or sayings would ever hold any weight. This was definitely the time.

"Cora, you've got to wake up and see this!" I shouted as I shook her, probably a little too forcefully.

Kanoa and I agreed to return to the camp and wake up the rest of our friends, to go back and investigate what we had just seen. Everyone needed to see it.

Cora and I had been friends for as long as I could remember, just like Kanoa and I. I had always been made fun of for having girl friends, but I never really saw it that way. She was just as willing to go on adventures as my guy friends and never slowed us down. We always studied together and never went very long without seeing one another. Nobody really understood me like she did, and something about that fact always scared me. Other than Kanoa, she was probably my closest friend. We even somehow managed to remain friends after....

"What are you doing in my tent, you weirdo," Cora whispered. She waved her arm sleepily and smacked me a few times on the face.

"Cora, Cora, could you please stop hitting me in the face?" I asked.

"Okay, where else would you like me to hit you for waking me up so early?" she asked as she rolled away from me, still waving her arm around. This was going to be more difficult than I thought.

"Hey," I started, lowering my voice to a more serious tone, "could you just trust me on this one?"

"Trust you!" She scoffed, smacking me even harder than before. "That's a funny one, Kail. You should really think about getting into a specific form of comedy."

"No, I'm telling you, this is important!" I shouted even louder, pinning her arm to the ground and looking her right in the eyes. There was a moment of silence as she studied my face to see my expression. She raised her eyebrow cautiously.

"Important enough for me to have to get out of my tent?"

After convincing Cora, I shifted my focus to Osias. Kanoa had already woken up Adora and was now moving onto Thalia. I always found it kind of funny how we acted as a group. We were all very close, and our lives were more focused on our relationships with one another than facing the world alone. We took every gain and every loss together. However, that fine balance was beginning to shift, as post-secondary education and part-time jobs were drastically changing the paths that had once all been one. Trips like this were becoming fewer and farther between. I often wondered what would happen when the time came that we wouldn't be able to hang out, wouldn't see each other at birthday parties, wouldn't go to the same school, would start to forget each other's names...

"Hey, Osias, you've got to wake up, buddy!" I demanded, kicking the bottom of his mattress.

Only Osias brought a mattress. He was always over-prepared for situations. He left nothing to chance and was a total control freak. Needless to say, he was often ridiculed as the least popular of the group, which did nothing for his low self-esteem. Luckily, we didn't see him that way. He had dissuaded us from many stupid ideas in the past and was always there when you needed an answer. He often told us that we gave his life 'purpose,' whatever that meant.

"No, I think you're confusing what I *have* to do with what you *want* me to do," he said with an irritated yawn.

"Okay, fine. Don't come," I said as I started walking out of his oversized tent. "I guess the rest of us will have to try to explain it to you when we all get back." Osias hated it when someone knew something he didn't.

"Okay, okay, I'm coming," he growled, "but only because I'm sure the rest of you will butcher the description of whatever it is, and it will drive me crazy."

When Osias finally finished combing his hair, which was something nobody else had bothered to do, the entire group had all assembled around the now-flameless fireplace. Kanoa seemed as excited as he had been when he woke me up. Osias looked more than a little annoyed, Cora looked as though she may have fallen back asleep at any moment, despite having a lit cigarette dangling from her mouth, and the sisters Thalia and Adora were leaning up against one another for balance.

Thalia and Adora were fraternal twins, and although they were not necessarily similar in appearance—Thalia was almost a whole foot taller than her sister—or personality, it was impossible to argue that they weren't close to one another. Thalia looked after Adora, who had always been centre of attention with the boys in our school. Adora was very angelic, and things went her way whether she cared for them to or not. Thalia, on the other hand, always seemed to be short-handed. If things could go wrong for her, they usually did. And yet, she never complained and always kept her head up. She was possibly the strongest person I had ever known, or at least was really good at hiding pain.

"Why are you staring at me?" Osias asked, looking over at Thalia.

"I always stare at people," she explained. "Try not to flatter yourself. I promise it isn't just you. I don't know what it is. I just like to stare. I feel that I get to appreciate a person better by really taking in what they look like, rather than just stealing hurried glances. I've heard that staring isn't polite, but I don't really care. I guess that makes me impolite, huh?"

"It sure makes you something, all right," Osias replied with a shrug.

I always found it fascinating when someone else made an observation that I too had made, but actually decided to make it known out loud. It sometimes shed light on long-time idiosyncrasies I had noticed in my group of friends, but never fully understood. Thalia's habit of staring at people, for example, now had a reason I rather enjoyed.

"So are we just going to tell some more scary stories, or do you guys actually have something to show us?" Osias asked irritably between yawns.

Kanoa was basically running in place at this point. "This very well may be the greatest thing you ever lay your eyes on. I'm talking absolutely legendary! Isn't that right, Kail?"

I nodded. "Yeah, he isn't kidding this time. I couldn't believe my eyes when I saw it, to be honest."

"Hey, what do you mean by 'this time?'" Kanoa asked with a wink.

"Well, I've seen everything from the Sistine Chapel to the Aurora Borealis, so that would be quite the claim, guys," Osias said, looking back to his tent and probably wishing he was back sleeping inside it. "So please excuse me if I think you are both full of it.

"Full of what?" Kanoa asked with a little menace in his voice, taking a step towards Osias.

"I'll give you a hint," Osias replied, not backing away. "It's a four-letter word and rhymes with idiot."

Kanoa walked right up to Osias threateningly, a confident smile still displayed upon his face. Osias was unmoved, but looked uncomfortable. The relationship between Osias and Kanoa was easily the most strained within the group. Kanoa didn't like having a shred of authority ruling over him, which was a poor match to Osias's way of making sure everything was always in order. They weren't always at each other's throat, but occasions such as this weren't exactly uncommon.

"Let's not do this, you two," Adora said, gently easing her way between the two, her eyes remained fixated upon Kanoa. "Perhaps we should go on this adventure now? It sounds like fun to me."

Everyone remained still for a few moments, the air around us filled only with the now-waking wildlife and Cora's lingering cigarette smoke. The stalemate between the eyes of Osias and Kanoa seemed unbreakable for a moment, when suddenly Kanoa broke free and let out a laugh. He turned toward the pathway leading into the forest.

"You gotta learn to relax, man," he said as he reached the entrance. "Everyone follow me."

"Kanoa," Cora muttered, keeping her head down. "This isn't going to get us into any trouble we can't get ourselves out of, is it?"

"Oh, come on," Kanoa said, brushing her off. "What trouble have I ever—"

"Kanoa," she repeated, raising her voice, which stopped him in his tracks. She was now staring right at him, and when he turned to face her it looked as though he had run into a brick wall. "I'm serious."

He bowed his head and gave a slight nod. "We'll be fine," he replied. Cora's stare lingered for a moment, considering his pacification, and then she walked toward him. He smiled at her and she shook her head, pushing him as she passed. Kanoa tore off again into the forest without any further interruption, refilling with excitement.

The rest of my friends all gave one last look around at the campsite before making their way down the path. Osias stayed behind for a moment with an annoyed smile on his face.

"Can you believe that?" he asked. "He tells *me* to relax! That guy has some serious problems."

"Yeah, well at least he doesn't cry at the end of Lord of the Rings," I teased, trying to ease the mood. He chuckled and quickly shrugged his shoulders, brushing off the confrontation he had just faced.

"Well, as long as you keep your mouth shut, that occurrence never took place," he said as he patted me on his way to pursue the rest of the group.

I smiled as he began his walk onto the path. I took one last look around the camp and recalled the evening we had. It was almost like a dream now: All six of us trying our best to scare one another, before bursting into laughter at how ridiculous we probably seemed to strangers. Not that we ever really cared what strangers thought about us; the world outside of our group were all strangers to us.

"Hey, Kail!" Cora shouted from somewhere within the forest. "Kanoa says that if you're trying to get yourself lost again, you're off to a pretty good start. Hurry up!"

I nodded and slowly turned away from the memories I was reliving. I felt a slight chill go up my spine. I wasn't sure if it had been caused simply by the cool morning breeze, or the thought of seeing the top of that hill again. Something told me that not even Osias would be able to explain it. And if Osias was unable to explain something, it never boded well for the rest of the group.

"And here goes The Inseparable Six on another wondrous adventure that shall be related to all for generations to come," heralded Thalia as we exited the woods and came upon the rocky hill Kanoa and I had scaled earlier.

"You really like that name, huh?" I asked with a laugh.

She was referring to the title our classmates and the rest of our community had coined for us. It was very well known that the six of us were so close, and instead of having to list off all of our names to describe the many escapades and exploits we had performed over the years, this label was used to reduce the effort. We were famous, or infamous, depending on how a particular individual in town knew us. It had been a while since I had heard the title used by one of us, though.

"Yeah, I always thought it has a nice ring to it," she responded. Cora rolled her eyes, having long ago grown tired of being a member of The Inseparable Six.

"Wow. If I had known that we would be mountain climbing, I would have worn my boots," Osias complained as we trudged up the rocky hill. It was unnaturally cold for this time of the year. There was far more wind than there had been before, and the sky seemed darker. We were almost at the top.

"You would bring mountain climbing boots on a camping trip," Thalia teased, nudging him with her shoulder. Osias blushed, but tried his best to hide it.

"Well it's better to be safe than sorry, and clearly I was smart to bring them," he said.

"Yeah, but not nearly smart enough to use them," Kanoa pointed out.

"And yet I somehow managed to reach the top of this summit the fastest," Osias howled as he quickened his pace. He scurried his way to the top, flinging loose rocks down toward us. He turned around to look down on us with a big smile on his face with his arms raised high in the air triumphantly. "You tell me how!" he yelled as he turned back around. His arms slowly lowered, as did his voice as his eyes befell upon what awaited him at the top. "Tell me how that's possible."

"What, did you forget how to brag or something, Osias?" Thalia joked, almost at the top of the hill. We were all going to see it at the same time. Osias never responded. "Osias?"

The hill and the rocks gave way to the open, barren plane I had seen earlier. The air seemed non-existent; it was as if we were standing in a vacuum. There were no noises—no birds singing, no trees swaying, no people breathing. The sky seemed impenetrably dark and ominous. There was nothing on top of that hill other than the structure before us. There were merely six people confronted with dream's creation.

Towering over us, with its shadowy spires and twisting walls, was a dark fortress. Its murky stone walls stretched on seemingly without end, and its thick, piercing steeples stabbed into the black sky. There were no windows, and yet the castle seemed as though it was emitting a light glow, as if beckoning to be found. It seemed abandoned and yet untouched; forgotten even by time. It remained still, and yet its walls gave off the illusion of movement, as if it were spiralling and churning with unrest. The citadel gave off the impression it had been built with complete disregard for reality. It was the embodiment of the darkest form of fantasy.

"Is this the part where I wake up?" Cora whispered.

Her words were quickly consumed by time and emptiness. It seemed as though it had been an eternity since we had arrived at the summit, and it seemed of equal length before someone finally answered.

"No. I don't think even dreams could pull this one off," Kanoa replied.

"Is it just me, or are there only clouds over the castle?" Thalia asked. It seemed impossible, but the menacing sky seemed to be drawn to the structure. The castle was a magnet for darkness.

"That doesn't make any sense," Osias replied. Nobody seemed to be particularly attentive to what they were saying. Their minds were doing the same thing mine was: focusing on the spectacle before us.

"Maybe the castle is somehow attracting the clouds?" Thalia asked, continually trying to make sense of things.

"That makes even less sense," Osias muttered.

"Any less sense than a magical castle being built on top of a barren hill in the middle of a forest?" I asked with a hushed tone. After no reply from Osias, or anyone else for that matter, Adora began walking toward it.

"Adora, get back here!" Thalia yelled in horror. I had barely even noticed her movement, and nobody other than the two sisters seemed to remember how to move anymore. The castle had rendered us paralyzed.

"What's the matter?" Adora asked, clearly not seeing any flaws in her actions. It was as if she was merely going off to pet a bear that she somehow found cute and friendly, while the rest of us knew it to be vicious.

"You don't know if it is safe, Adora, you can't just walk off like that," Thalia scolded, trying to pull her sister back to safety.

"What do you think, Cora?" Adora asked, ignoring her sister. Thalia winced a little, but acted as though it didn't bother her. Adora often went to Cora for advice instead of Thalia, even though Thalia was the one looking out for her.

"I can't exactly say it looks welcoming," she replied, biting her lip.

"I don't think anyone is here anymore, if there was ever anyone here at all," Adora reasoned, now willingly following her sister back to the rest of the group.

"Well someone would have had to build the damn thing," Osias stated with a hint of worry and doubt in his voice. "It can't have just always *been* here. Right?"

"I guess there's only one way to find out," Kanoa responded, beginning to walk to the large entrance doors of the building.

"Kanoa, what the hell do you think you're doing?" I called after him.

Unlike Adora having Thalia to talk her out of bad decisions, Kanoa didn't have an older sibling, so the responsibility always fell to me. I knew from the moment I laid my eyes on the castle that Kanoa would want to do some exploring. I also knew that I was going to have to do my absolute best to dissuade him.

"I know what I'm doing," he replied. "I'm going to go on the greatest adventure I have ever been on." He stopped and turned around to face us. I had seen Kanoa excited many times, for many different reasons. Sometimes it was excitement before going on a roller coaster, and sometimes it was excitement while sneaking off in the middle of the night. Never before had I seen his eyes sparkle as much as they did now. "Would you like to join me?"

There was another long stretch of silence. Kanoa, although not very far away from us, seemed as though he was being consumed by the dark monument behind him. I was afraid that if I stepped forward, the castle might engulf me in its mass. It loomed over me as if to intimidate me, mocking my cowardice.

"I will join you," Adora said.

Thalia began protesting, but this time Adora was not dissuaded. She walked up beside Kanoa and stood next to him. They exchanged a glance and smiled. Adora always had Kanoa's back no matter what, even if it meant following him into certain danger. I admired their bond without really understanding it. I shifted around uncomfortably. I knew that we were all going to have to go investigate, one way or another.

"How about it, Kail?" Kanoa asked. "What's the worst that could happen?"

I winced at the question and didn't want to think about the answer. Maybe I was overreacting and there really was nothing to worry about. The place did look vacant, and even if it wasn't, I doubted anyone was cruel enough to harm curious teenagers. Then again, worse things have happened...

"Famous last words, Kanoa?" I asked in a sinister tone. I often posed this question to Kanoa whenever he said something that I knew would come back and tear the words right out of his throat.

"No, not this time," he replied wearily, his usual response to my largely repeated question. "And there's nothing that can go wrong."

"Well I'm sure there are plenty of things that could go wrong," I finally answered, walking toward him with a cautious weight to my steps. "But you'd better have *me* to get you out of them."

"Oh, there's no way you're going on this adventure without me!" Cora protested, running to my side. She pushed me light-heartedly with a smile on her face. "If you're going, I'm going."

"Okay," I agreed and added teasingly, "but only if you can keep up with us."

She pushed me again, and her tone became more serious. "You can count on that, Kail."

"And what about you two?" Kanoa snapped, tapping his foot. "I want to go inside and I'm getting a little impatient over here."

"Come on, Osias," Thalia said, turning toward him, slightly bouncing up and down in excitement. "It couldn't hurt to do a little exploring."

"Oh, I strongly disagree," Osias scoffed. "That castle looks like one big trap to me, and I'm not going to be another dumb teenager that winds up dead on the news for falling into it."

"Osias," Thalia said, gently grabbing his hand. Osias's back straightened quickly and his face perfectly captured just how self-conscious he had become at her touch. The whole group laughed. "Do it for me?"

He let out a big gulp and shrugged his shoulders, as if trying to show that he wasn't being affected by Thalia's pleas. "Well, I suppose it couldn't hurt to do a little poking around. Besides, I'd better come along to make sure you guys don't break anything valuable."

Thalia let out an excited squeal and, still holding Osias's hand, skipped her way over to stand with the rest of us, basically dragging him the whole way. The six of us stood together and faced the mighty castle, soaking in all of its reverie glory one last time. We all stepped forward in unison.

CHAPTER 2: INSIDE THE IMAGINATION

Footsteps were all that filled the suffocating air. We remained close, forming a united front against the castle. Six small beings against the reality of a dreamscape. How would we ever be able to explain this to anyone back home? Why would we even bother? Nobody would ever believe us. I didn't even believe it myself.

"Why would something like *this* be *here*?" Thalia asked out loud.

The castle walls seemed to be looming farther and farther above our heads and continued to persist in their moving illusion.

"It seems to have been built in a secluded area for a reason," Osias said, beginning one of his usual analyses of a situation. "That fence also leads me to believe that whoever built it didn't want anyone going in. I have a hunch that although this place looks very old on the outside, the inside will reveal its true age."

"Well, then, it's a good thing we're going in," Kanoa said with a laugh.

We finally reached the door after crossing the barren chasm between certainty and impossibility. We had crossed an invisible barrier into the realm of dreams. Anything was possible at this point.

"Speaking of getting in," Adora said with silky curiosity in her voice, "how are we going to do that?"

The doors before us were monstrous. There was no lock anywhere upon its frame, but that wasn't the problem. There was no handle to speak of, and no other apparent mechanism that opened the door. It was simply two gigantic wooden slabs bolted to the walls of the castle. There was also one last extraordinary thing about the door. It had a symbol on it that weaved intricately in all directions. It seemed to resemble...

"Is that a clock?" Cora asked, seemingly reading my thoughts.

It was true: the design etched across the doors seemed to be a big clock, frozen in place. It had no arms to read the Roman numerals found at its edges, but there was no mistaking its identity. Its carving was deep, elegant, and elaborate. The clock appeared to have wings sprouting out of it. Oh, how time flies, I thought.

“Maybe, but I don’t care what’s on the door,” Kanoa said with a slight hint of frustration. “I just want to know how to open it.” He quickly studied the door before shrugging his shoulders and pushing with all his might upon them. They shifted a little, but did not open. “This is a lot more fun than it looks,” he added. “You guys plan on helping me or what?”

The group all exchanged glances before moving forward and helping our friend. Kanoa, Cora and I pushed on one of the massive doors, while Adora, Osias and Thalia worked on the other. It didn’t seem to be working at first, until an almost ancient sound erupted from the wood. Loud groans and creaks emitted from the doors, as if screaming in agony. The noise sent a shiver down my spine, but it didn’t stop me from pushing. I wanted to know what was inside, even if I did have a bad feeling about it.

The doors continued their protest, but steadily opened. A bellowing, cold rush of wind escaped from the darkness within the castle and rifled through us on its way out into the world. Its sound was bone-chilling and resembled that of a large, dying animal.

“Well, that sounds inviting,” Osias said, shaking his head in disapproval.

“Yeah. I don’t trust this at all,” I muttered, peering into the opaque darkness that filled the castle’s entrance.

“What else is new?” Cora asked.

We were now inside the enormous entrance of the building and staring into complete darkness. The room’s height and length was immeasurable, and unless we could find a light source, we would all quickly be consumed by the abyss.

“I really wish you guys would have told me we were going into the forest to explore a dark, scary castle,” Osias complained. “I would have brought some useful things, like a flashlight, or a camera, or a cell phone so that I could have called my parents to get me the hell out of here.”

Suddenly, the room filled with light, temporarily causing me to shield my eyes from the white blindness. A hallway lay before us, the roof hanging far above our heads and its end reaching almost beyond my sight. Pillars jutted up from the sides, almost like the boundary of where we were to walk in the hallway. Archways of marble and sparkling light fixtures protruded from above. Everything seemed to be made of a slick marble that had lost its polish over years of neglect. Clearly, the inside was going to be just as much a spectacle as the outside.

“Well, whoever built this place knew about electricity,” Kanoa said, moving away from the light switch he had found on the wall near the entrance. “Got any ideas when it was built now?”

Osias was quiet for a moment, still soaking in the information about this new sight. “Well,” he finally began, clearing his throat. “Although it does seem that it was actually *built* many centuries ago, these light fixtures would suggest that it was renovated after Edison's time. My guess is that someone or some company found this castle, and decided to use it as their new base of operations."

"Whatever you say, man," Kanoa said with a disrespectful laugh, beginning his trek down the long hallway.

Adora was right behind him, with Thalia at her side. It was probably a good idea to stick close while within these walls, I thought to myself. I still wasn't convinced that we were the only ones here.

"Then why the hell did you ask?" Osias muttered, walking with frustration in his stride.

Their steps echoed all across the corridor, creating a near musical tune. I couldn't even begin to imagine the work that must have gone into building such a place. Although Adora's theory of it always being here seemed crazy at the time, it began to feel more and more possible with each new discovery.

"I guess that means we're going to walk together, Kail," Cora said, poking me in the back. "Try to keep up, would you?"

We walked down the daunting halls, immersed within our surroundings with great wonder. There were no blemishes or cracks present in the architecture, and other than the lack of sheen in the marble, everything was in great condition. I didn't trust it.

"If this is our last adventure together," she said, keeping her voice low enough that only I could hear it, "at least it'll be an interesting one."

"Just because summer's almost over doesn't mean we're never going to see each other again," I said.

Cora had a habit of looking forward that didn't really sit well with the others. I wasn't as afraid to look to the future as the rest of them, but just as afraid as anyone else. I appreciated anything that got me away from the past.

"You know what I mean," she said, rolling her eyes. "We're all heading in different directions soon. I know we all promised each other to stay in touch, but... The future doesn't really care about words between friends. Don't get me wrong, I'm so fucking excited to get out of this nowhere town—but I can't pretend I'm not going to miss these moments."

"Yeah. Me too," I muttered.

"You're still thinking about university or college, right?" She asked, already knowing the answer. She just liked pressing me on the subject, rubbing my nose in my own indecision.

"I'm just not sure yet," I sighed.

Cora and Osias were the only two that really had a clue about what they wanted to do after high school, and even Osias was cagey about it. We all had the marks, except Kanoa. We just didn't have the courage or ambition. It was a lot of responsibility, and I just wasn't sure if we were ready for it. I knew I was certainly wasn't.

I noticed Cora seemed upset that I was shutting her conversation down and decided to lighten the mood. "It just takes some time," I said, adding a little melody to my words to make it sound like I was singing.

"Don't get me started," she laughed. "You know how much I love that song."

"Little girl, you're in the middle of the ride," I continued, swinging my hips and pretending to hold a microphone to my mouth. She pushed me and I stumbled a bit, pain coursing up my leg from the wound I had inflicted earlier.

"What happened to your leg?" Cora asked. She pointed to the cut that I had received from when Kanoa had first shown me the castle.

"Oh, it's nothing," I shrugged, pretending to not feel the stinging pain in my leg. I tried my best to not limp, showing off to Cora that I could take a hit or two. It still hurt really badly, however. "You know Kanoa. Always getting us into trouble."

"Yeah, he can be quite the handful, huh?" Cora said with a laugh. We looked forward at the rest of the group. Thalia was now walking with Osias, who appeared to be explaining something in great detail. Kanoa sprinted from wall to wall, showing off to Adora the many details of the hallway. "I always told you one day he'd bring you down."

"Yeah, yeah," I laughed. "I believe the exact words you used were 'bring you spiralling down.'"

"Good memory!" She smiled, tapping my temple. Her face then sagged and her eyes dimmed. "And yet I bet you trust him more than me."

"Cora, let's not do this again," I groaned. I hated getting into this conversation, yet Cora insisted it at least once a week when she had me isolated from the group. "I told you it's nothing personal, and I don't want to talk about it."

"Well, when are we going to talk about it, Kail?" Her voice was getting louder and more desperate. Cora was always filled with passion; anger, even, over the seemingly mundane. It was very important to her, but I didn't want to tell her the truth. It would hurt too much.

"There's nothing to talk about, Cora," I insisted, avoiding her stare.

I knew that if I was ensnared in her eyes, I would crack, and that wasn't going to happen. I had made it this far without cracking to the pressure of my friends, and without any end in sight, the promise I had made to myself would remain fulfilled.

"How could you say that, Kail?" she asked with a clear signature of hurt in her voice, but her tone continued to elevate. She loved to use my name whenever she was being serious about something. I hated it. "We all aren't going to be this close forever, and I'm not living the rest of my life without knowing why you can't trust me!"

"It isn't just you, I don't trust an ---" I snapped and began yelling back, staring right at her. I stopped myself and looked around, noticing that everyone was now listening in on our conversation. Cora's face had gone red with embarrassment or anger, I wasn't exactly sure, but my own face probably reflected hers in shade. I cleared my throat and calmed myself down. I lowered my eyes away from hers and began walking away. "I just don't want to talk about it, all right?"

"Yeah, whatever, Kail," I heard her say with pure resentment within her voice. It wasn't resentment toward me, really, but rather my problem with her. She just wanted to know the one thing I could never tell her. It wasn't her fault. Only I was to blame. "Just walk away, like you did before."

My heart dropped into my stomach for a moment and slowed my pace. She had hit where it hurt and she knew it. This was the exact reason I didn't like letting anyone into my heart. All they did was manipulate it. I kept walking and didn't look back, just like I had done before.

"What was that all about?" Osias asked as I passed by. I saw that everyone looked very concerned and confused. It was understandable, but I wasn't planning on opening up, not even to my friends.

"Forget it. Let's just keep going," I said coldly and walked past them.

Kanoa was in the lead and had a harsh look on his face. He didn't like it when I was upset. He always protected me like a little brother whenever I got into trouble. Trouble he usually caused.

"You wanna talk about it?" he asked half-heartedly as I walked by. His lack of enthusiasm didn't come from a lack of concern. It was because he knew he wasn't going to get an answer. And that was exactly what he got.

"Didn't think so," he muttered.

Adora fluttered over toward me in order to cheer me up as her sister blankly stared on. She couldn't stand when a group member was upset. I had never actually seen her anything but happy, or at the very worst, neutral. In fact, of all my friends, she was the only one I had never once seen cry. Even Thalia, her ever-optimistic sister, had cried in my presence due to the collapse of her sister years earlier. I couldn't say that I blamed her for it.

"You should not yell so loud, Kail," Adora said. "You might wake up whoever lives here."

I laughed at the thought of someone actually living in a place like this. Adora was very innocent, but I knew she was merely trying to cheer me up. After she succeeded with me, she would no doubt turn her attention to Cora. I turned around and realized that Thalia was now talking to Cora. Apparently, the sisters now worked as a team.

"I don't think anyone lives here, Adora," I said weakly. It was probably better to have someone to talk to, rather than leaving myself to my own thoughts. My dark imagination could sometimes make situations much worse than they actually were.

"Well then, I guess nobody will mind us exploring it," she said, my sombre disposition doing nothing to defuse her enthusiasm. "I think we are going to find something very special in here." She paused for a moment, as if thinking about what could possibly be in such a place. I didn't think we were going to find anything. "What do you think, Kail?"

"I don't have very high hopes, Adora," I said. She twitched her mouth to the side with disappointment, and then shrugged her shoulders.

"Party pooper," she whispered.

Kanoa sprinted past us with a crazed look in his eyes. I looked up and realized we had reached the end of the hallway. I was almost expecting a dead end, and then we could just leave the castle and go back home. It was an exciting discovery, but something about the whole place didn't sit well with me. It almost seemed as if it had been set up for us.

"Is that an elevator?" Osias asked with a tone of disbelief.

All six of us had stopped in front what seemed to be two metal doors with buttons and lights framing them. Above the doors spelled out the name HUGO in bright golden letters.

"What does that mean?" Adora asked, pointing at the sign.

"Maybe it's the name of the person or company who made the building," Osias answered. "I'll have to do some research when we get back home and see if I can find anything matching a HUGO corporation."

"Why do I have the feeling that you won't find anything?" Cora asked. Apparently she was still a little mad about our earlier conversation. I would have to talk to her later.

"I'll go back if you guys want," Kanoa said.

"You're pretending again," Adora stated. She was never afraid to call Kanoa on one of his bluffs. She called him out a lot, especially as of late. "I don't like it when you pretend."

"I was just trying to be nice," he sighed, brushing off the fact that he had just been caught in a lie.

Kanoa walked up to the panel that held all the different buttons. He studied them briefly before pressing the button with an arrow pointing down.

"Kanoa, I wouldn't just start pressing things if I was you," Osias insisted. "You don't know what they -- "

A loud rumbling arose from beneath our feet, and the walls started to shake. I pressed myself up against a pillar for balance and started looking around. Everyone looked rather frightened; even Kanoa seemed a little uneasy. I began to realize that the buttons on the wall didn't have anything to do with the metal doors at all.

"I knew it! You don't just start pressing buttons inside a forgotten castle when you don't know what they do!" Osias yelled over the noise of the quaking hallway.

To my astonishment, the metal doors rose upward into the ceiling. Kanoa attempted to jump up and hit the control panel again, but it was too late. The look of fright upon everyone's faces once again turned to wonder. I was right—the buttons had nothing to do with the metal doors. We were already inside the elevator. We had been since we first walked inside this twist on reality.

The turbulence in the hallway subsided and the noise quieted. More and more metal doors crawled by up the walls as we slid deeper and deeper into the castle. I had no idea how far down into the earth we were going, but I assumed we were far beneath our campsite.

"I can't even imagine how hard it would be for them to make this hallway move like an elevator," Osias said with wonder in his voice. "Quite the architectural feat."

"Architecture doesn't have feet, silly," Thalia teased. She often poked fun at Osias's diction, which Kanoa especially enjoyed.

"Why would you have pressed the down buttons, of all things?" I asked Kanoa, who had a huge smile on his face. The twinkling in his eyes seemed to be at their peak.

"Well, I figure that in all secret laboratories, the most important stuff is always at the very bottom so it can be hidden," he explained with great eagerness. He had an almost wild look in his eyes. "Well, the secret laboratories in movies."

I looked over to Osias for some sort of response. He looked as though he had completely given up on trying to make sense of anything we were seeing. He shrugged and said, "You know what? Anything is possible at this point. We could find unicorns and Santa Claus playing poker on a couch made out of Bigfoot's fur, for all I care."

I laughed and realized he was right. We really should stop trying to relate this place to reality, I thought to myself. There wasn't, isn't, and probably never will be again anything quite like this that any of us would experience for the rest of our lives. It was kind of depressing to think that we had found something so substantial this early in our lives, but I supposed it was better than most would ever find. I had a feeling that once our descent ended, it was going to get a whole lot more unbelievable. Then again, I was beginning to question the definition of such a word, anyway.

The hallway began to slow in its plunge into the earth, and the final metal doors emerged from beneath the floor. There was a final jolt as we hit bottom, which nearly caused us all to fall.

"Jeez, you'd think they would have made this place a little safer," Cora grumbled.

"Yeah, well I don't think safety was exactly what they had in mind when they were creating a moving hallway, Cora," Osias said.

We all cautiously approached the metal doors before us. I exchanged glances with Kanoa and gave him a questioning look. What did he plan on us doing now? What was he expecting to find down here?

"No matter what's beyond this door," he said quietly, tilting his head to the ground, "we all stick together, okay? I promise that I'll do my best to keep us as safe as I can." He turned around to face us, and I noticed the twinkle had left from his eyes. There was no mistaking his concern this time.

We all nodded in agreement. "I don't think any of us were planning anything different. I promise, we stick together," I said with assurance.

He smiled and accepted my words. He turned back again to face the mysterious doors that undoubtedly held long-kept secrets that a group of six teenagers were about to be a part of.

I was right behind him as he slowly stretched his hand out toward the door. I noticed that it was shaking uncontrollably. He glanced over and realized I was watching him and retracted his hand, shaking off the fear with a laugh. He then focused back on the door and quickly pushed it open. A bright white light spilled out of the room and into the hallway upon us. There was a moment of silence that befell the group as we stared in, not being able to see anything but the light.

"Well," Kanoa said, breathing slowly. "Here we go." With that, he took a step into the light and out of our sight.

I froze up for a moment, unsure if I should follow him. The promise I made him about staying together as a group quickly floated back into my head and I broke free.

"Remember, guys," I said, snapping my head around to face the rest of the group. They all looked just as scared as I felt. "We stick together, no matter what. The Inseparable Six, right?"

They all agreed and hesitantly began moving closer to the door. I faced the dazzling light one more time, took a deep breath, and stepped through the threshold into uncertainty once again. I was beginning to wonder how many times I was going to do that in one day. Hopefully, this was the last.

At first the light overwhelmed me. My eyes just could not adjust to the brightness, and a jolt of terror that I had somehow gone blind temporarily filled me. Fuzzy objects then filled my sight and as time passed, clarity returned to me. I was standing inside a circular room that had been coloured a heavenly white. Wires and machinery cluttered the room, as did desks and stacks upon stacks of paper. Kanoa was standing near a monstrous, blinking mechanism that lay in the center of the room.

"As if we didn't understand this place before," he said.

There were many gasps as everyone piled into the room. The middle of the room held the largest machine, which Kanoa was studying carefully. It resembled an hourglass—wide at the top and bottom, but thinning in the middle. Many wires and cables extended from its metallic frame, which was lit up with many different coloured blinking lights. Surrounding the hourglass machine were many smaller, bed-like stations. All the cables protruding from the center machine connected into these technological beds, as if it were some sort of mainframe.

The beds were tilted at an angle, facing the hourglass machine at an almost standing position. Glass bowl-like instruments were located at the head of the beds and seemed to have the purpose of being slid onto someone's head. There were no straps on the beds, and despite being made of hard, silver metal, they had thin cushioning upon their frames, suggesting that they were made with comfort in mind.

The tables at the far end of the room were fortified by massive amounts of papers and documents. Some had overflowed onto the floor and some stacks had fallen on their sides. Clearly a great deal of work and research was being done before the place had been abandoned—if it had been abandoned.

I could not see any specific light source, and yet the room remained painfully bright. It was as if the colouring of the room was illuminating it. I hadn't realized it at first, but the center of the room seemed to be lower than the rest of the room. The ceiling, too, seemed to become higher the closer I went to the middle. I wasn't sure if the orb structure of the room was an illusion created by its colouring, or by the machine's orientation within the room, but it certainly felt as though we were standing inside a tiny world within our world.

"HUGO INDUSTRIES," Osias read aloud. He had walked over to the paper area of the room and was reading a document he had picked up off the desk. "Where your greatest dreams are our best intentions."

"So this place *is* owned by some sort of company," I said. "Any idea what they made or why they were here?"

"Well, I'm just searching through all this paperwork," Osias said, his thoughts clearly focused on the documents, his eyes scanning them intently. "So far, all I can tell is that they were onto something big regarding sleep technology."

"Sleep technology?" Cora inquired.

I walked over to Osias and began searching through the many piles of paper. There were many drawings of different machines that resembled the ones now in the room. Some were of images of the castle, and some were of the surrounding area. One sketch even looked eerily similar to our own campsite.

"Yeah, it appears that they were working on some kind of process in which they could manipulate dreams to make them more vivid and real," Osias explained.

More sketches presented themselves to me. Many of them were of things that were not of this world. There were people flying over oceans, men and women standing atop mountains, and one was of a man who appeared to be walking across the surface of the sun.

"What does Pons mean?" Adora asked. I looked over and saw that she was inspecting one of the beds. She seemed to be reading a word on the side that I wasn't familiar with.

"What's that, Adora?" Osias asked excitedly as he rushed over to her. I could tell that all this technology and research was whirling within his mind.

"It says 'Pons Version 6.0' on the side of this bed," she clarified.

Osias quickly pushed her aside and examined the inscription with a furrowed brow. He rubbed his hand across his chin and thought for a moment, muttering something to himself.

"The Pons is a part of the brain that controls many functions of dreaming," he finally stated.

All the pieces were starting to fall into place. Everyone else was thinking what I was now. It didn't take a genius such as Osias to put together the clues this room had given us. Whatever this place was, they were very interested in dreams.

"Anyone want to take a wild guess and say that this HUGO company has something to do with dreaming?" Cora asked.

I chuckled and looked over to her. Our eyes met, and she smiled reluctantly. I knew she was getting over our earlier argument, but it was going to take a lot more than laughing at one of her jokes to make amends. I decided I would talk to her once we got out of this place.

"I think I know how to turn these beds on," Kanoa said, pacing back and forth between the central machine and one of the Pons.

He was looking at a large switch that was attached to the hourglass and trying to figure out what it would do if he turned it on. Another bad idea from Kanoa in the making.

"Even if you did, there's no way we're going to do anything with them," I argued. I walked over to him and tried to get him to understand how serious this could be. He wouldn't look at me, as it would only make him doubt the idea he had in his head. That was Kanoa—think after you have gotten yourself into the mess.

"If we all get into one of these machines," he continued, ignoring my plea, "and I flip this switch, maybe they will work. There is no way of knowing how long these things haven't been used, so --"

"Kanoa, stop it. You're being crazy!" I interrupted. He finally started paying attention. "We have no idea what these things could do to us. I know I say that I don't trust the sights or sounds of something often, but this should be so obvious. Maybe they don't do anything at all, but I would rather be safe than sorry."

"No, you listen," he countered. It wasn't a threatening tone, but seemed to be filled with sadness, of all things. "If we leave this place, it's just going to be found by someone else, and then what? The news will pick this place apart until there's nothing left, and we will never get to experience what this place has to offer. Can you really live your life without knowing? This could be our biggest and last adventure we all go on as a group. This is the kind of thing I've been talking about since the first day we met, Kail. Do you really want to take that away from me?"

I looked around and realized everyone had their full attention on us. They all had solemn looks on their faces. We were just kids, and nothing mattered more to us than what we did together; the memories we made. I had far too many memories I could have done without. A few good memories might actually benefit me. I knew he was probably right, and the part of me that wanted to know was overpowering my reason. Could I really live with myself if I passed this by?

"Let's just try, Kail," he continued, putting his hand on my shoulder. "Like you said, maybe nothing will happen at all. But if something does happen, I promise you it won't hurt us." I scoffed at his promise, and he grasped my shoulder harder. "Hey, I promise."

I stared at him and saw the sincerity in his eyes. I knew that it didn't matter whether I wanted to or not. He was going to flip that switch. I decided right then that it was better if I was here to keep him in line, than to just leave him down here. However, his promise meant nothing to me and he knew it. I hadn't trusted a promise for many years now.

"Fine, Kanoa," I sighed. "But I'm not doing this because of any promises you make. I'm doing this to keep you out of any more trouble."

"Yeah, yeah, I hear ya," he laughed, pushing my shoulder and turning back to his search for more clues as to how to make the contraption work. "Anybody else have any objections?" No one posed any. "Osias?"

"No, I actually think this could be a very interesting experiment," he said, stepping away from the papers. "Additionally, I believe I know how to get these things working."

"You do?" Thalia asked, squeezing his elbow. Osias flushed for a moment and lost his thought, but quickly collected himself and continued relaying information.

"Yes I do," he said matter-of-factly. "From what I have read, it seems that we all need to lie down on these Pons and put these glass objects onto our heads, which they have named Interpreters, and then flip that switch. Once the switch is on, the Pons will activate and the process will begin."

"What process?" Adora asked, sounding just as nervous as I felt.

"Well, I didn't read anything regarding what they actually do," he said with disappointment. "However, I could look through that mountain of documents for a few hours and find out what exactly happens."

"No, I think I'd rather just take my chances, thank you," Kanoa replied as he rushed over to a bed. Osias shrugged and walked toward one of the beds. "Everyone pick a bed, and get ready for the ride of your lives!"

"Kanoa, we don't even know if these things work anymore," Cora said as she looked around the room for a bed that she wanted. "For all we know, these things weren't even completed!"

"That is a risk," he said as he jumped into the bed closest to him, "that I'm willing to take."

I shook my head and chose the bed next to him. Cora decided to take the bed next to me, and Osias the one beside her. Thalia laid in the one next to him, and Adora next to her sister. It was at that moment I realized that there were exactly six Pons—one for each of us. We had completely circled the room, so that Adora lay beside Kanoa.

"Anyone else find it a little creepy that there is exactly the same number of us as there are of these machines?" Osias asked anxiously, shifting side to side in his bed.

"Oh, you worry too much," Thalia said, trying to pinch his cheek.

"Yeah, well, my worry is going to save us all one day, and you will all thank me," Osias declared, brushing her hand aside.

I watched as he brought his Interpreter down over his face so that it completely covered his head. Everyone took his lead and brought the glassy object down upon them. The inside was completely clear, and there didn't appear to be anything connecting it to me. Maybe they were broken.

"Who's going to flip the switch?" Adora asked with a yawn. I too felt sleepy at that moment, but attributed it to the fact that we had woken up too early and hadn't had anything to eat yet.

"I got it!" Kanoa volunteered quickly. He jumped out of his bed, ran over to the switch, and flipped it down without a second thought. He ran back to his Pons and slammed the Interpreter down so that he didn't miss out on anything.

Moments went by without any response. There was a slight whirring noise within the hourglass machine, but neither the Pons nor the Interpreters seemed to be functioning. I shifted back and forth in my machine uneasily. I looked around and saw that everyone else was becoming impatient. Seconds aged into minutes without any results. It wasn't going to work.

"Well, Kanoa, I guess that's it," I said, beginning to lose hope. I tried pushing my Interpreter away from my face, but it seemed to be stuck on something.

"Just wait a bit longer, Kail," Kanoa pleaded with me, desperation as clear in his voice as it was in his eyes.

He wanted it to work so badly, but I felt that he was investing in a lost cause. It would be just another disappointment he would have to live with. I tried again to remove my Interpreter, but it wouldn't budge. With my luck it was probably broken, and I would have to get someone to help me out.

"Is anyone else's Interpreter thingy stuck?" I heard Thalia call out.

I heard her aggressively pushing up against hers, remembering that she had a mild case of claustrophobia. Mild in the sense that she rarely got herself into situations where her phobia posed a problem. When she actually got into tight spaces, the results were unpleasant.

"Just calm down, Thalia. You have tons of room," Osias said, trying to remain calm.

I could see he too was trying to push his away from his face to no avail. I sensed something was wrong, and there was no coincidence between our seemingly broken Interpreters. Something was happening.

"What the hell? Mine's stuck, too!" Cora exclaimed.

Everyone except Adora and Kanoa was now fidgeting with their devices to try and get them off. I too was struggling without any progress. I heard Thalia begin to breathe heavily and Osias try to calm her down. Kanoa and Adora were just lying still, smiling together.

Suddenly, there was a flash on the screen of the glass. Everyone must have seen the same thing, as the noise within the room ceased, as if it were sucked into a vacuum. I heard static in my ears and tiny lines began forming before my eyes. The lines were straight at first, but slowly began to bend and twist. Whatever was going on, the machines seemed to be working.

The static became louder and the lines transformed into blurred images. There was a tingling that seemed to be coming from the back of my head, but I couldn't move anymore. I felt very light, and my mind emptied out. All I could think of was the images on the screen and the noise in my head.

The blurred images cleared into still pictures, and the static evened out into words and sounds. Before me were memories of my life. Snapshot after snapshot of different events that had happened to me flashed before my eyes. I could see myself as a child, and my sister too. I could see the orphanage I had spent my childhood in, the day I met my parents, a graveyard, and then all my friends as small children. My first day at school, Christmases, and even my darkest memory all resurfaced on the screen. Laughter, crying and screaming filled my ears. A searing pain tore through my head and consumed me with terror.

I let out a scream, which was met with the screams and laughter of my friends. Real screams and laughter. They too were experiencing the same pain and joy I was. We were all being exposed to a lifetime of memories, all at once. Tears filled my eyes and I tried to close them but couldn't. I stretched out my hand to grab something and found my friends' hands were there to catch me. I felt Kanoa in one hand and Cora in the other. My body felt as if it were free-falling into nothing. I could no longer breathe, yet I was still screaming—or laughing, I could no longer tell.

My grip on my friends tightened and the sensations continued to intensify. I felt that at any moment I was just going to die. The pressure I was feeling was unimaginable and showed no sign of giving up. The memories became brighter and brighter; the sounds louder and louder. I was spiralling into my own life at the speed of sound. There was another flash, brighter than anything I had seen before, and then silence. The last thing I remembered was the promise we had all made to one another. We stuck together, no matter what.

CHAPTER 3: DOWN THE RABBIT HOLE

I was dreaming of the third day of God's creation. The world around me was building itself like a puzzle. The pieces of the ground and the trees and the sky and the clouds all tumbled into one another, looking for their places to fit in. The areas that hadn't been formed yet were of empty whiteness. Soon the entire space around me was complete, and I was standing within a jungle of some kind. Although I knew I was conscious, nothing about me could have been real. I couldn't have just seen the world generate itself around me. No, what I witnessed must have been the offspring of imagination.

There was a slight blurriness in my peripherals that never subsided. I rubbed my eyes, but the haze remained. There was no sound within the jungle, which I found strange, because it appeared as if would contain many buzzing insects and singing birds. As I thought of the anomaly, many different sounds erupted from within the flora, as if to quash my curiosity. Why had they been so silent not a moment ago? Was it due to my presence that they hid?

I surveyed my surroundings and realized that every bit of plant life was surprisingly vibrant, almost to a level of hyper-realism, even with my hazy vision. As I turned and turned to look all around me, I noticed that I felt very light, almost as if my feet were not even touching the ground underneath me. I swayed my head back and forth to soak in the feeling of a weightless world. I grabbed at my leg and realized that the cut I had received earlier was nowhere to be found. There was something odd about this place that I could not yet describe.

A dog suddenly emerged from a bush nearby. It was panting heavily, with what almost looked like a smile on his face. The tail wagged back and forth like a pendulum in excitement. Its fur was well groomed and had a magnificent sheen to it. The dog's innocence filled me with happiness and relief at seeing such a friendly animal in this foreign place.

It was at that moment I recognized the fact that it was rather odd for such an animal to be inside a forest, so far from civilization. The dog then shifted in shape and began to grow and contort. Its legs became longer and thinner, and its fur shrank into its skin. Its tail receded into its body and antlers protruded from its forehead. Where there once stood a small dog was now a full-grown deer. The deer then skittered off into the jungle, frightened by my presence.

My mouth fell wide open and my eyes grew with amazement. It was at that moment I remembered what was going on.

I started running as fast as I could through the jungle, battling against the thick shrubbery and trying not to collide with any trees. I had no idea how deep into the jungle I was or where an exit would be, but I just kept running. It wasn't long before I realized I was passing by the same trees, the same vines and the same flowers, over and over again. Not in the sense that they were similar in nature to the ones I had run by already. They were exactly the same. I stopped running—and then, with the loud sounds of creaking, crackling and crunching the whole jungle shifted, so that the ground beneath my feet was now the exact place I had awakened. I watched as trees the size of houses seemed to slide across the earth to rearrange themselves and put me back where I started. I knew I wasn't crazy. It was the world that wasn't making any sense.

"Kanoa! Cora! Osias! Thalia, Adora!" I yelled at the top of my lungs.

The trees around me physically bent as the sound waves from my voice escaped my throat. Their branches snapped and leaves fluttered to the ground. I rubbed my hands against my eyes to try and make sense of everything. Was I really seeing any of this?

I stopped worrying and collected myself before I completely fell apart. I cleared my head of all the impossible events I had witnessed—or caused, I wasn't exactly sure—and thought of what I was going to do. I focused on getting out of the jungle with all my will. The only thought in my mind was of being on the outskirts of the trees and away from this open patch of ground I was glued to. I opened my eyes slowly, and it was so. I was now outside the jungle, just like I had imagined.

I turned around and saw the jungle that had played as my prison moments before. The trees began to shift again, resembling the bars of a prison cell. Their colours turned from an energetic green to a pale and dead black and white, the same colours I may have seen an inmate wear in a clichéd movie. Branches extended from the trunks like malnourished arms, beckoning me back into their grasp.

I slowly backed away with a look of doubt and shock on my face. I had to wake up soon. This was all just too much for me to handle. I decided that if I wanted to survive in this place, I was going to have to keep my thoughts under control before they became my own undoing. I turned away from the frightening wilderness and set off to try and find the rest of my friends. Maybe they would have some answers.

I looked up into the sky and saw all sorts of clouds comprising all types of different forms. When people said they saw objects in clouds, they had no idea what they were talking about. Moving animals and monsters battled in the sky, fully detailed and highly life-like. Space shuttles launched and fumes poured out from beneath them. People were dancing and singing down upon the earth with smiles on their enormous faces. It was then that I knew I inhabited some sort of fantasy world.

There was no real distinction between day and night. Stars constantly soared back and forth over my head and, the sky faded in and out between many shades of blue, purple and red. Instead of a sun, a gigantic clock filled the sky. I studied it carefully, instantly remembering the engraving we had seen on the front doors of the castle. They struck an uncanny resemblance to one another.

I was walking in a field, the grass extending all the way up to my thighs, swaying to and fro with a nice breeze that tickled my face. Mountains before me reached to the sky, snow forming at their peaks. They seemed to glitter with a sparkling shade of blue. Everything in this place seemed almost too real, like I had walked into a highly detailed painting or digital image.

At the top of one of the mountains, I spotted movement. A tiny speck seemed to be falling down the side at a very fast pace. The snow seemed to be falling with it. A loud rumbling chased after the tiny speck, but then I heard the sound of someone screaming. It wasn't a scream of fright or displeasure, but more of joy and thrill. It also sounded extremely familiar.

I started to run toward the mountain at a speed I wasn't aware I was capable of running. The tall grass around me angled toward me as I passed, being sucked into the force I was creating and causing a wave-like effect within the field. The closer I got, the clearer it became that an avalanche had occurred. The speck became clearer and its form changed into who I had thought it had been. Kanoa had caused an avalanche within the first hour of our adventure.

The snow he rode rocketed to tidal wave proportions. He stood atop the curve and had his arms high in the air, blowing his lungs out with the loudest and happiest yell I had ever heard. I quickly realized that the avalanche would threaten to swallow me if I came any closer, so my run slowed to a jog, and then a walk. I wanted to be close to Kanoa when this ride of his crashed down on him, so that I could save him. I didn't need for both of us to be saved.

To my continued surprise and amazement, the snow slowed down and levelled off the closer it came, until it was no more than a carpet beneath his feet. I began to doubt who the person on the snow was. It appeared to be Kanoa, but something about him was different. He looked as though he had some elements of my friend, but they didn't add to a whole I recognized.

The snow slowed to a crawl and the man riding it stopped just inches away from me. I was surprised that I didn't flinch or try to run away. It probably had something to do with the fact that I had been mesmerized by the scene and forgotten how to move.

"Well, Kail," the man said breathlessly. "I think I just became a legend."

I studied the smiling man with great vigilance. Maybe my mind was playing tricks on me and this man was merely an imposter of my friend. If it was, however, his voice was a spot-on impression of Kanoa. I still wasn't convinced.

"Who are you?" I asked, circling the man.

His hair was a dazzling shade of golden, which was feathered to the side and wild in the back. It looked as though a wind was constantly passing through it, despite there not being enough of a breeze to do such a thing. He wore baggy clothing with a holy hue of white and silver, and a long flowing cape hung around his shoulders. He seemed taller and more packed with muscle than Kanoa had been. A long, sharp and shimmering sword was slung across his back, with a highly detailed, golden handle. His skin seemed to glow, without a single imperfection to be found. I remembered that the real Kanoa had a light sprinkling of freckles on his nose and yet, despite all these discrepancies, he still felt like my friend.

"Please excuse my new appearance," he laughed with a hint of flattery in his voice. "But I assure you that it's me, your friend, Kanoa. Don't act so surprised. You look different too, ya know."

"What do you mean, I look different?" I asked, unable to hide the shade of surprise in my voice.

The man laughed again and held up a finger, as if to tell me to wait a moment. He then pointed down to the snow under his feet and leaned down. He blew with great force upon the snow, pushing it away to reveal a shiny surface underneath. It showed his reflection on it, and he marvelled at his appearance.

"I don't think I'll ever be able to get over that," he said. Clearly he had already done this and was well aware of the way he looked.

"How do I know that you're really him?" I persisted. He jumped back to his feet effortlessly and patted me on the back.

"Oh, Kail, you never were one to trust anybody," he explained, beginning to prove his identity. "Even your friends! You really have to work on that, buddy."

"So it is you," I said, slowly beginning to accept this new discovery.

I reached out and touched him, making sure that he was really there and I wasn't just being tricked by another illusion. He laughed again and brushed my hand aside.

"Yeah, you creep, it really is me," he confirmed again.

He took the large sword off his back and began slicing at the air with it. I didn't ever recall Kanoa being equipped with the skills necessary to use such a weapon, but he seemed to have no problems. He skilfully brandished it, cutting up and down and side to side, causing grass and snow to fly up all around him.

"Why do you look like that?" I asked in a daze. He stopped swinging his sword for a moment and turned to answer me, his eyes gleaming.

"It's this place," he explained. "It changes things. It changes everything."

He motioned me over to the mirror he had created out of snow. I wondered how he was so easily accepting everything that was happening. I still hadn't gotten my head around the fact that a dog had transformed into a deer, and yet he was fully comfortable with riding avalanches down the sides of mountains. I assumed that Kanoa would fit right in with this place.

I slowly knelt down and almost anxiously approached the mirror. I was afraid of what I would look like. Maybe my mind would cause my appearance to become distorted and unrecognizable. My face reflected back, and to my relief, I knew who was looking back at me. I had changed, but I was still me.

My once plain, fair hair had turned dark. It was spiked in all directions, yet layered elaborately about my head like a chaotic and impenetrable fortress. My face, like Kanoa's, had become faultless and radiant. My once-fragile frame had become toned and sculpted. My eyes had changed from a dull brown to an oceanic blue. My clothes, unlike Kanoa's, were packed tightly against my body. I wore a dark vest, with many straps and buttons delicately placed upon it. I thought for a moment how the vest resembled a closed book that had been hidden away. Red sleeves covered my arms with golden chains extending across them, dangling close to the fabric. Thick pants wrapped around my legs, with black vine-like symbols rising from my feet up to my thighs.

"Don't forget your back!" Kanoa exclaimed, still practising his sword lunges.

I hadn't noticed before, but four cylindrical spires extended from my back, one spire in each direction. I felt around on my back for a sword like Kanoa's, but my hands came upon something else. I looked for some kind of sling or strap to explain what was holding the object in place, but came across nothing. It was as if it were just magnetized to me. I pulled it off without any resistance and brought it slowly to the mirror. Weightlessly held in my hand was what would have been a shield, if it weren't for the large gaps in its base between the four spires. No, this object was not used for defending, but attacking.

The four golden, lightning bolt-like spires all converged in the middle and were held in place by a sharp circle that cut through the middle of the spires. It closely resembled a steering wheel on some old pirate ship, only this was far from old. It reminded me of something I had once seen at a museum called a chakram, but far more complex.

I had never held anything like it before, and yet I knew how to use it. I clutched the middle section of the weapon where the bolts all met and stood up, still looking into the mirror. I wielded it at first like a shield, placing the weapon in front of my face, and looking through it to see how I looked. I noticed that my hands had golden markings across them, vein-like in nature. They matched the colouring of the object perfectly, as if we were meant to be paired together.

“I don’t think that thing is meant to be used as a shield,” Kanoa stated, looking over my weapon with a slight twinge of jealousy in his eyes. Although his sword seemed far more dangerous than my own weapon, there was something about the design of this object that made it special.

“Yeah, I know,” I agreed, still looking at my mirror image. “But I could still use it to guard myself.”

“Want to try?” Kanoa asked. He raised his sword before him, directing it at me. I looked over to him and laughed.

“Don’t be ridiculous,” I said. “You know how dangerous these things could be? We don’t even know how to use them properly.”

“Speak for yourself,” he persisted, still maintaining his stance. “I think I can just do fine with this thing, and you looked a little too comfortable a second ago holding yours. Come on, it could be fun!”

“No,” I said firmly. “I don’t feel like getting cut in half, thanks. I’ve never seen anything like this. How the hell am I supposed to use it?”

He sighed angrily and advanced toward me. I backed away, raising my weapon across my body for protection. “Kanoa, put it down. This isn’t funny,” I demanded.

We were now circling one another, staring right at each other without any chance of breaking eye contact. A crazed look was displayed in his eyes, and a sinister grin cut across his face.

“Just because this place doesn’t seem real, doesn’t mean you can’t hurt me!” I pleaded with him. He shook his head and let out a gruff chuckle, waving his sword in the air in front of me.

“Come on, man, don’t be a baby,” he teased with a devious smile. He pretended to strike, causing me to flinch instinctively. He laughed again and shifted his footing. “I promise it won’t hurt.”

He lunged forward with his sword. I leaned back, and with inhuman speed I lifted my weapon to catch his. His sword got caught between two of the spires under the circle of my weapon and stuck for a moment. A look of shock gave away Kanoa’s surprise, and I took advantage of the moment. Almost as if I were programmed to do so, I spun my weapon around rapidly with both hands like a steering wheel, tearing his sword out of his hand. The blade flung into the hard snow on the ground and made a twanging noise as it stuck. The whole exchange took less than a second and it was over. I had won without knowing what I had done.

“Now *that* was cool,” Kanoa said, his eyes wide and captivated with what had just occurred.

He gracefully walked over to his sword and pulled it out of the ground, wiping the snow off the blade. I would have thought that the level of athleticism I had just performed would have caused me to become mildly fatigued, but I didn't feel anything. In fact, I felt more energetic and alive than before.

"You have done some stupid things in the past," I said, "but that had to be one of your worst. What if you had hit me, and I got hurt? Would it have been worth it?"

His steps seemed very precise, yet natural. He patted me on the shoulder and looked me right in the eyes, a look of sympathy in his. "I'm sorry to have worried you," he said, surprisingly sincere, "but I was in control. I wouldn't have hurt you, even if I could. But you're good, just like I knew you would be."

"How do you know that?" I asked.

"It's this place, Kail," he said again, turning away from me and looking back toward the mountains he had descended from. He slung his sword back over his shoulder and crossed his arms. "It's everything I dreamed it would be. We have nothing to fear here."

I tried to place my weapon onto my back, but realized I wasn't sure how it had stayed there in the first place. I pressed it gently against myself and then let go, feeling a slight pressure as it stuck. I released it, and to my surprise—or lack thereof at this point—it didn't fall.

"Well, I wouldn't say that just yet," I said, walking up to stand beside him to view the magnificent mountains.

The snow beneath our feet receded away from us with a slight slurping noise, back up the slope of the mountain, returning to where it had fallen from. The grass grew back up to our thighs within an instant. As if someone had hit a rewind button on our surroundings, everything went back to the way it had been. I assumed that Kanoa had caused the event, as the snow hadn't been on my mind at the time.

"Wouldn't say what?" he asked after a few moments of silence, holding back laughter. Even though he seemed to be fully comfortable with the way this new world worked, it was nice to know that things still astounded him as they did me.

"I wouldn't say that there's nothing to fear," I answered. "If this is some sort of dream world, or whatever Osias was talking about, then where there are dreams, there are nightmares."

Kanoa shook his head slowly, agreeing with me for once. "I can't even imagine what nightmares feel like in real life," he said, no louder than a whisper.

"Yeah, well don't think about it too much," I suggested. "It seems this place is very keen on creating reality out of our imaginations. The less bad thoughts you think, the better."

"The rest of the group!" Kanoa burst aloud suddenly. I stared at him, perplexed. He looked back at me with worry on his face. "We need to find them right now, Kail!"

"Calm down. I'm sure they're just as fine as us," I said, trying not to sound too worried. The grass around us began to swirl violently, as if an invisible tornado were forming around the two of us.

"Come on, let's get going!" he persisted. The wind grew more intense, and I was becoming nervous that Kanoa was going to rip the world apart before we had even settled in.

"Okay, okay!" I agreed, trying to shout over the increasing wind. "Just calm down before you blow us into the sky!"

The wind began to subside as Kanoa calmed, yet he remained restless. We were going to have to learn to control how we expressed our emotions before we accidentally caused some serious damage. He looked around at where we should begin our search. Ahead of us were the mountains where he had come from, and behind us was the jungle where I had emerged.

"When I was at the top of that mountain," he said, looking back at the top, "I saw some sort of building out in the distance. You want to check it out first?"

"What kind of building was it?" I asked, going over our options in my head. Was it possible that there could be other people here? Or was the building merely another creation of one of our imaginations?

"It looked like a church or something," Kanoa explained, beginning to walk past me along the mountains. "Come on, it was this way."

"Kanoa, I didn't say yes yet," I said with a sigh.

Once again, he was acting before thinking. No matter how many times I told him to think before he acted, it never stuck. It was true that he possessed the strongest leadership qualities of our group, and I would have been the last person to deny him such a position, but that didn't mean he wasn't aggressive—and often dangerous. Some things about people are just essential. Without Kanoa's brash behaviour, there would be no Kanoa. And although he did seem to know his way with this place much better than I did, I didn't quite trust him enough to just start making quick decisions.

"Yeah, I know," he laughed, continuing to walk away, "I'm just making the decision a lot easier for you, is all. You know me," he said, turning around to look at me, another adventurous smile on his face. "Always looking out for you."

I tilted my head to the side and pushed out a pained giggle. "You remember our promise, huh?"

“Yeah, I do,” he said. “I plan on sticking to it. Now, are you ready to have some fun or what?” He motioned me toward him with his hand and continued on his path.

I ran up to him and punched him on the shoulder with a laugh. We laughed together as we walked through the grass-covered field on our way to find our friends and keep the promise we had made to them. There wasn’t one bit of me that was certain of anything or worried about nothing. I just had to look at Kanoa, and I would feel that much safer. I was hesitant to trust anything that entered my life, but following Kanoa always held my conviction. Something about his confidence filled me with assurance. While I was unsure of the world around me, I was glad I had him. That’s when I realized there was something I could be certain of—I was sure the promise we all had made would keep us together.

CHAPTER 4: ALL THE RIGHT FRIENDS

We had left the grassy field and were now walking on smooth, shiny stones. The stones seemed to actually be the ground, as Kanoa had dug for quite some time trying to reach solid ground without any progress. After he had given up, we continued on our path to the building he had seen from the mountaintop. He was positive it was fairly close.

“Do you think there are other people here?” I asked him.

He shrugged, picked up one of the stones and threw it. It bounced across the other stones without disturbing their placement, letting the stone bounce well out of eyesight, as if it were hopping across water.

“I guess so,” he replied. “I mean, if there’s a building here, then it’s possible. It could just be something one of us created with our imagination, though.”

“Created with our imagination?” I asked. Kanoa seemed to have figured this place out pretty quickly. Or at least he thought he had.

“Well, yeah,” he explained, skipping more stones off into the distance. “I mean, do you really think I could have done any of that stuff with the snow in real life? You act like you don’t know what I’m talking about, but I bet you’ve done some things here that aren’t possible back home.”

I was instantly reminded of the forest and the dog. Had I really been the one to cause it to change like that? Did my thoughts turn the jungle into a prison?

“See?” Kanoa said with a laugh, seeing my expression turning into one of deep thought. “You’ll get the hang of this place soon enough. It probably just comes naturally to me, as this is what I always wanted home to be like.”

Kanoa had always been a dreamer. When we were kids, he would never pay attention in school and would always be imagining what kind of adventures he could go on when the day was over. He made forts in his backyard and fought wave after wave of invisible enemies, until the sun had long left the sky. When we matured to high school, his aspirations matured very little. He wanted to become an actor so that he could live out his fantasies as best as our world allowed. He loved reading fantasy novels and watched science fiction movies religiously. He never was interested in actual science, however. He said it cramped his style. People on the outside thought he was so cool and relaxed. Only his friends on the inside knew the truth.

"Yeah, well that's another good point," I replied. "Once we find the rest of the group, if they are even here, that is, we'd better start looking for a way to get out of this place."

"Yeah, maybe," he muttered.

"What did you just say?" I asked, fully aware of what he had said. Did he really think we were going to stay here? He had his fun, I thought, and now it was time for us to get out of wherever we were, before something bad happened.

"Look, there it is!" he shouted, pointing directly ahead of us.

At first I was confused, lost in Kanoa's foolish words. I looked to where he was pointing and spotted a large building out in the open. Nothing appeared to be around it. It was just standing, alone and mysterious.

"I guess you were right," I said, more than a little reluctant. I almost didn't want to believe him, as I was becoming increasingly nervous about the fact that we may not be the only ones in this dream world.

"Race you there!" Kanoa shouted, and without so much as a breath from me, he was off and running, spraying stones in all directions behind him.

A shock wave exploded from behind him, temporarily distorting my hearing. Some stones flung directly at me, and I braced for impact as they came to strike my face. I felt nothing. I slowly opened my eyes and saw that the glistening stones were suspended in the air, bobbing up and down as if they were in water. I carefully brushed them aside like curtains and walked on through, causing them to float back to the ground. Here I was, unable to get accustomed to stones floating in the air, and yet Kanoa was fully capable of running at the speed of sound without so much as a question.

I ran toward the building at a normal pace. Kanoa was waiting impatiently before it. I reached him and looked intently at the building. As Kanoa had mentioned earlier, the building did look like a church, just not like a church I had ever seen before. It was made entirely of glass, the doors included; stained glass that seemed to have been created with a specific design in mind that I could not recognize from the outside. The glass was rather foggy, so I was unable to see inside.

Other than its glassy structure, there was nothing incredibly unique about the church. It was quite tall and had an oddly shaped roof, as each tile was slanted in different directions. A tall tower situated behind the main building stored a large golden bell at its peak, hovering freely above the tower without any sort of ropes or pulleys keeping it in place. I wondered what the point of a tower was at all, if the bell was just going to hang there by itself.

"What took you so long?" Kanoa asked eagerly, smiling at my inability to keep up with him. He was relishing the fact that I could not accept this world as he was.

"Sorry," I said, "but I haven't gained the skills to travel the speed of sound yet. Maybe you could teach me sometime?"

"I'll think about it," he said with a laugh. He turned to face the church and walked toward the entrance. "Quite the place, huh? I wonder what's inside."

"Let's think about this first," I reasoned, still worried about what else could occupy this world. I hoped that if we were to run into anything, they would at least be people. Then again, what could possibly be more dangerous than a human?

"Kail, judging from the skills you showed back there," he said, "I don't think we have anything to worry about."

He moved forward and gently pushed open the glass door. It opened swiftly and without sound. He walked in, readying his sword, and was out of my sight. If I had been given a dollar for every time I unwillingly followed after Kanoa, I would have had enough money to buy the castle he had forced us into. I sighed heavily, releasing my weapon from my back, and followed him into the glass church.

The building seemed even larger from the inside, its roof stretching high over my head and its walls extended far off on all sides. Glass pews were layered on both sides, all the way from the entrance to the far end of the church. Eight glass pillars rose from the ground to hold up the roof, which led me to the discovery of what the stained glass had painted. On the walls were painted twisting and bending roses with green, thorny stems producing luscious red blossoms. On the roof was a beautifully illustrated white dove, looking over the roses like their guardian. Its wings were extended in flight, and the slanted construction of the roof led to an optical illusion, or reality, that with each step I took, the dove's wings appeared to actually flap as if it really were flying overhead, guarding those beneath it.

At the far end of the room was a tall, slender woman whom I did not recognize. She was standing in front of a glass statue of a praying angel, its large wings shading the woman with protection. Faint beams of light filtered into the room behind the angel, bathing the woman in gentle sunlight. I looked over at Kanoa anxiously and he brushed me off, transfixed by the woman. He lowered his weapon, but remained silent as he stepped toward her. I followed behind him, still holding my weapon tight. We were about halfway down the middle aisle when I realized a long staff with a blade on the end of it was lying on the ground behind her. I remembered from history class that such a weapon was called a polearm. Judging from what I had learned in school of its deadly abilities, I hoped that the woman didn't know how to use it well—or at least not as well as Kanoa and I could use our weapons.

"You know I could hear you boys since you came in, right?" a silky voice asked. I gasped and brought up my weapon instinctively. Kanoa did the same.

The woman chuckled and turned to face us. It was then that I realized who she was.

“Cora?” I asked, shocked by her new appearance.

She giggled and picked up her weapon, walking toward us while looking up at the dove. Her once-brown hair had turned a stunning shade of red, carefully flowing upward at the top, yet sleekly falling down around her face and back. The hair that had fallen in the front seemed to form a heart. She too glowed with the skin Kanoa and I had been bestowed with, and her fiery eyes shone brightly. She wore a pale pink dress, elaborate and wonderful yet not cumbersome to her movement. It billowed down from her body and swayed as she walked, giving off an almost cloud-like impression. It had neither straps nor sleeves and yet seemed to wrap around her willowy figure comfortably. She was like an angel descended from the very clouds her dress imitated.

“You look...” I trailed off, becoming entranced in her eyes the closer she became. She stopped in front of us and leaned to one side.

“I look?” she repeated playfully. She began twirling her polearm effortlessly in one hand, displaying her apparent mastery of the object.

I cleared my throat, embarrassed by my own gawking. I looked away and back up at the ceiling. “How did you get here, exactly?” I asked, trying to make it seem like I no longer cared about how she looked. I was quite sure the damage had been done.

She giggled again. “I woke up here, actually. I was just about to go look for Osias when you two showed up.”

“You’ve seen Osias?” I asked. Kanoa had walked up to the angel statue and longingly touched its wings with his hands. I bet he wished he had wings.

“Yes, he came in here shortly after I woke up,” she explained, twirling her polearm, shifting from clockwise to counter-clockwise motions in front of her. “He told me to wait here while he looked for the rest of you guys. He hasn’t been back since, and I was getting worried. There’s something very odd about this place.”

“Yeah, no kidding,” I said. “Any idea where he went?”

“No,” she replied, “but I can come with you guys and look for him!”

“Maybe it would be best if you stayed here, just in case we run into any trouble,” I recommended. Cora didn’t seem too pleased, as her stance became more aggressive and her eyes actually seemed to blaze.

“Why?” she demanded. “Because you’re so much better at dealing with trouble than I am? No, I don’t think so! I’m not waiting around for Thalia and Adora to walk through the door and tell me to wait here, too!”

Suddenly Kanoa snapped out of his trance and became aware of our conversation. He walked toward Cora and placed a hand calmly on her back. “Relax, you can come with us if you want to,” he said, soothing things over. “Nice new look, by the way.”

Her smouldering eyes simmered slightly and she settled down. She nodded to Kanoa and said, “You too.”

She strutted down the aisle and brushed past me angrily. She whispered, “I’m not a little girl anymore, Kail,” as she passed by. I stared at her, bewildered, but she didn’t look back. Kanoa followed behind her.

“You really shouldn’t be so strict with her, Kail,” he said. “Although, she does do it to the rest of us, and it *is* kind of funny to see her get a taste of her own medicine... Forget what I said. Be as strict as you want with her.”

I shook my head, and he replied with a shrug as he walked out the doors just after Cora. I took one more look into the glassy church with the dove vigilantly watching over her roses with care. A tear seemed to have formed in its eye, but it may have just been a trick of the lighting. I hesitantly pursued my friends out of the building and back into the unpredictable world we had apparently created.

“Where to now?” Cora asked, observing her beautiful surroundings.

I looked to Kanoa for an answer, but he didn’t appear to have one. He was looking around in all directions, wondering where he wanted to go.

“Did you see anything else up on that mountain of yours, Kanoa?” I asked wearily.

“You climbed a mountain?” Cora asked, her eyes lighting up.

“Well I kind of woke up on one,” Kanoa replied, as if it wasn’t a big deal to him. “But yeah, pretty much. And I do remember there being a pond or a lake around here somewhere.”

“Well, that’s better than nothing,” I said. “Osias never was much of a swimmer, but I don’t think that would matter here for some reason.”

Before I could ask him where he thought the body of water was located, he once against burst into a run and was out of sight in an instant. Cora stared at him, amazed at his speed.

“Did he just—” she tried to ask, but quickly lost her thought.

“Yeah he does that sometimes,” I answered. She looked over to me and laughed incredulously, her eyes still wide with surprise.

“You know,” she said, shaking her head in Kanoa’s direction. “He was the first thing I thought about when I realized what this place was. You can guess why that’s a bad thing.”

“I know what you’re thinking,” I said with a nod, “and I don’t blame you for it. But nothing bad is going to happen, and certainly not because of Kanoa. Not with me around to keep watch. He’s just having a bit of fun.”

“Plenty of bad things seemed to happen back at home, whether you were there or not,” she muttered. “Especially in the name of Kanoa’s ‘fun’.” After a moment, she looked over at me and began to study me carefully with a spark in her eye.

“What’s with that thing on your back?” she asked, hitting it with her polearm. I pulled it off my back and spun it around in my hands, showing off my newfound skills with it. She seemed impressed.

“I don’t know,” I answered honestly. “It was with me since I woke up. I thought it was a shield at first, but Kanoa proved me otherwise. Here,” I offered it to her to hold, “you want to try it?”

She nodded and took it out of my hands. She marvelled over it for a moment, but then it abruptly ripped free from her grasp and flew back into my opened hands. She looked at me, puzzled yet accusing.

“I didn’t do that on purpose,” I stated.

I stared at the object carefully, drawing the conclusion that it was somehow connected with the new and strange markings that had been etched onto my hands.

“Can you try holding mine?” she requested, presenting her polearm to me cautiously.

I placed my weapon onto my back and took hers in my hands. I waited for it to fling back to Cora, as my weapon had done, but was stumped when it didn’t. I threw it up and down in my hands, waiting for some form of involuntary movement, but none came.

“I guess something is different,” I concluded, handing her weapon back to her. She took it with a disappointed look on her face. There was a sudden rushing of wind and Kanoa was back in our company, looking triumphant.

“I found it,” he said, not sounding the least bit winded. “It looks pretty cool. Try to keep up, but it isn’t too far, so you shouldn’t get lost.”

“Okay, okay,” I said, motioning with my hands to calm him. “But do you think you could run at a normal pace this time?”

“Kail, I have spent my whole life trying to be normal,” he explained, the carefree smile leaving his face. “For the first time ever, I actually feel right at home. This is the way things should have always been.”

Heavy conviction was expressed in his eyes and words. He believed in this world, and nothing I could do would stop him. Who was I to crush his fleeting dreams, anyway?

"But I will slow down for you guys this time," he digressed, relaxing his posture and outstretching his hand. "Come on, it's just over that hill."

"Kanoa," Cora said. "You haven't forgotten the promise we all made, right?"

"Funny you should mention that," Kanoa said with a wink. "Kail and I were just talking about that. The answer is no, I haven't forgotten, but your always-encouraging brand of faith in me has been noted. Do you get paid *every* time you pick on me, or is it an hourly wage?"

"Someone ought to pay me for how tiring the job of looking after you is. And yes, I absolutely consider it a job."

Cora scrunched up her face, and Kanoa stuck out his tongue at her. She smiled and looked over at me, and I nodded my head to signify I was okay with the plan. She smiled a little, which caused my heart to beat just a little faster. Kanoa tried to suppress his laughter. I cleared my throat and walked past him defiantly, pretending not to know what everyone was laughing about. I would have to get over Cora's new appearance quickly if I wanted to stop embarrassing myself.

They eventually caught up with me as I climbed the inclining grassy hill. I noticed that the hill seemed to curve in both directions, forming a bowl in the middle. The crater must have been at least the length of a few football fields and just as deep, yet lively green grass covered it wonderfully. Once I reached the top of the hill, I looked down to discover the pond Kanoa had been talking about. It was still as glass and coloured the clearest blue I had ever seen. In the very middle of the water was what could only be described as a cave, except for one small difference—the cave appeared to be made completely of the same water in the pond. It swirled up into the air off the surface, but it was very dark and not see-through like the rest of the pond.

"Is that a cave made out of water on top of a pond?" Cora asked as she reached the top.

"Yeah, it made perfect sense to me as well," I agreed.

"Well, I guess we'd better go see what's inside it," Kanoa said.

He began walking down the hill, but in such a way that it didn't seem like he was walking downhill at all. Apparently he knew how to shift his center of gravity as well as break sound barriers.

"I seriously doubt that anything would be inside that," I said. He kept on walking with Cora right behind him. I was glad to see that everyone cared about my opinion.

"Yeah, well if there is, that makes me two for two," Kanoa replied, recalling the fact that he had been right about the church already. If Osias were here I would have some backup in the reason department, but until we found him, I was among dreamers.

I trudged my way down the hill like a normal person and contemplated just how deep this depression in the land was. The distant mountains faded into the crest of the hill overhead, and I saw less and less of the wondrous sky. Kanoa and Cora had stopped at the outskirts of the pond and waited for me to reach them.

"How should we get across?" Cora asked. "I really don't want to get this dress wet."

"Well I guess we could just walk across," Kanoa responded.

"Um, excuse me?" I barked as I reached them. "You want us to walk on water?"

"I don't want you to do anything, Kail," Kanoa said, taking a few step forward, looking down at his feet. He postured himself and raised his foot over the water. "This is the way I want to do things."

With that, he lowered his foot tenderly onto the pond's serene surface. Tiny ripples pulsated from the impact, but he did not pass through the water. He breathed excitedly and brought his other foot forward to meet the first. He was now standing on water without any assistance. Cora and I looked at each other in utter disbelief. He was performing a miracle.

He continued to put one foot in front of the other until he was well on his way to the mouth of the cave. He turned to face us, a look of great accomplishment on his beaming face.

"Come on, guys!" he exclaimed. "The water's great!"

Cora and I both laughed at just how ridiculous the whole scene was becoming, and at the thought of having to actually perform it. Cora looked over at me nervously.

"Well, here goes nothing," she stated.

She closed her eyes and took a deep breath. With her eyes remaining closed, she stepped up to the water and shakily brought her foot forward. Her foot pressed down, but stayed afloat. She leaned forward a few times, unsure if she had gone forward far enough. She then opened her eyes and realized what she was doing, which was met by a shriek of happiness. She quickly brought her other foot onto the water and began spinning around in circles like a ballerina on ice.

"See?" Kanoa shouted. "It's easy! You just have to pretend it's solid ground, and then it's a piece of cake!"

I shook my head with frustration. It was much easier said than done for someone like me. Unlike Kanoa, and Cora too apparently, I couldn't just forget all about what the world back home had taught me. I couldn't pretend like Kanoa could. I had been holding on to everything the real world had taught me from the moment I had gotten here. How was I supposed to just let go of things so deeply engrained into my life? We were not supposed to be able to walk on water.

"Yeah, well unfortunately," I said, slowly making my way up to the water's edge, "I can't pretend as well as you guys."

I edged up to the glassy surface and hesitantly raised my foot. In my mind I placed my foot down and it soaked into the water, just like it would in real life. I tried to push the thought away, but it just kept on coming back. There was no shaking reality for me. I dropped my foot down and it plunged into the water, just as I knew it would.

I withdrew my drenched foot, embarrassed by my failure. I kicked at the surface in frustration, causing the entire pond's surface to become rough and choppy. The once-still surface grew wild and dangerous. Cora and Kanoa lost their balance and began to reel as the waves crashed around them. So my anger could create storms, but my ambition couldn't even let me walk. Perfect.

"Hey, Kail, think you might want to turn down these waves a bit!" Kanoa shouted as a wave nearly swallowed him whole. After a few moments my aggravation levelled off, and the waves followed suit.

"Sorry," I grumbled. "I'm just a little pissed off. You guys go on and tell me what you find in there."

Kanoa ran back toward me with an accepting smile. I knew he wasn't going to let me give up that easily. If he was going into that cave, I was too. One way or another, we were going to face it together.

"Piggy back time," he stated.

I rolled my eyes and groaned heavily. Back in elementary school there were many moments when Kanoa and I had to work together to complete some sort of task. Sometimes there would be a snack too high up in a pantry, or I would be too afraid to walk across the bug-ridden ground of a forest, and the only way to solve the problem was by Kanoa lifting me onto his shoulders and carrying me. It was teamwork at its finest, but we had long outgrown it. Well, until now anyway.

"You're not giving me a piggy back ride to that cave," I resisted. "Simple as that."

He crouched down and nodded his head onto his shoulders temptingly. I crossed my arms and shook my head, mouthing the word 'no' quite plainly. He shrugged his shoulders after a few moments of futility and stood back up. He looked away from me for a moment and I let down my guard, which was a big mistake with Kanoa. He quickly spun around and grabbed my legs with both arms, swiftly and fluidly raising me onto his shoulders. I had been piggy-backed against my own will.

"I swear, if you drop me I'm going to break your legs!" I shouted as he sprung into a run across the tranquil pond. We blasted passed Cora, who was too busy laughing at us to care—laughing at me, more specifically. I turned around and waved at her.

"Aren't we going to wait for Cora?" I asked as we rushed onward to the cave's entrance. The wind rustled through my hair and warped sound around me. Kanoa was running far too fast again.

"Nah, she can meet us when we get there," he replied. "Besides, I think you were right back there. We should probably make sure it's safe first." Kanoa actually agreed with me for once. Any doubts I had about this being a dream world were instantly extinguished.

We stopped abruptly at the mouth of the water cave, causing me to fall off Kanoa's shoulders and sprawl onto the ground. Luckily for me, there was a thin layer of gravel on the ground of the cave, which caused my body to create a loud thud instead of a splash. I got up quickly and gave him a punch for being inconsiderate. He pushed me aside and equipped his sword. I did the same, composing myself for the possible dangers ahead, and stood beside him as we stalked inside.

The water comprising the cave's walls seemed to be constantly and rapidly washing over it from left to right, yet the pond's surface itself was unmoved. It was as if the cave was merely a wave that had gotten stuck in midair. There was nothing inside that I could see, but somehow there was a great darkness that was only illuminated the farther we walked in. The cave had angled downward from the outside, meaning it led under the pond itself to an unknown depth.

I then heard a rustling from just beyond my sight. Kanoa heard it as well, as he stopped walking and raised his sword. I too brought forth my weapon to face whatever emerged from the shadows.

"Come out slowly," I demanded of the ominous noise.

The rustling ceased for a moment, and then grew louder and more urgent. I took a step backwards, but Kanoa nudged me with his shoulder, begging me to stay with him. I held my ground, my heart beating and eyes fluttering. What could possibly be in such a place?

"Is it gone?" A familiar voice echoed from within the darkness. The noise changed into footsteps and a human form could vaguely be seen.

"Is what gone, Osias?" Kanoa asked, taking a deep breath of relief and lowering his weapon. I did the same. Osias finally materialized from the bowels of the cave and waved at us.

"Um, nothing," he said, clearing his throat. "But if you see a giant, stuffed, cute but highly dangerous lizard running around, I promise you that it wasn't me."

Kanoa and I exchanged amused glances before looking back at Osias, who was nervously smiling and scratching his forehead. He, like the rest of us, had changed. His once spindly build had matured, and he no longer wore glasses, unsheathing his wide green eyes. His skin bore the familiar glow I had become accustomed to, matching everyone else's. His hair, which used to be brown and cut very short, was now longer and a tinted shade of blue, yet still strict and well kept. His hair was hard to see, however, as he wore a heavy hooded robe that fell down to his feet. Constellations were displayed on the dark fabric, which seemed to twinkle and move on its own. It was rather mesmerizing. In his hand he held a long metal staff, which had golden clouds and sparks literally spiralling up its neck. At the top were four golden hands perpendicular to one another, all holding up a floating blue jewel. The small, yet impressive jewel twirled slowly and bobbed up and down within the grasp of the hands. He looked like an ancient sorcerer.

"Pretty neat, huh?" he said, motioning toward his staff. "I don't know how to use it yet, but for now I just like looking at it."

I heard Cora enter the cave behind us and she made her way to us from the sounds of our voices. She still seemed excited from being able to walk to the cave and shot me a look of accomplishment, trying to conjure some jealousy from within me. It worked, but I shifted my focus away from her quickly.

"What took you so long?" Cora asked Osias, who quickly tried to make up a story that didn't involve him being chased by a monstrous toy.

"Oh, I was just exploring the land," he lied, "when I came across this cave. I was just coming back to get you when I bumped into these guys."

"You find anything down there?" Kanoa asked, finding more interest in the cave than Osias's lie. He walked past him and further into the darkness.

"Well actually, yeah, I did," Osias explained, happy that we didn't call his bluff. "The cave seems to go underneath the mountains and leads out on the other side. Unfortunately, the exit appears to be at the bottom of a deep chasm, probably caused by some shift in the tectonic plates."

"Yeah, I wouldn't worry too much about why things are the way they are," I told him, "we're inside of a cave made out of water after all."

"Well then, we'd better get going," Kanoa urged us. "It's going to take us a while to get through this without any light."

"Oh!" Osias exclaimed. "That's something I do know how to do with this thing."

He brought his hand up to the floating jewel and touched it lightly. As he let go, the jewel burst into a small blue star, illuminating the entire area around us. He smiled, impressed by his work, and scurried ahead of Kanoa.

"I think I will lead the way, if you don't mind," Osias stated, proud of himself for once.

Kanoa laughed and pushed him forward so that he would start guiding us under the mountains. I wondered how long it would be before we found Adora and Thalia and were all finally reunited. The closer we became to fulfilling the promise we had made, the closer we were to getting out of here.

"So there doesn't appear to be any rules to this place, per se," Osias said, thinking out loud as he often did. For once, I actually felt like hearing about one of Osias's hypotheses. "However, it seems that the more ingrained something is within our minds, the harder it is to manipulate."

"What do you mean?" Kanoa asked. The last thing he wanted to hear about in this place was rules or limits. Then again, the more supposed rules Osias explained, the more Kanoa would become aware of—and the more he would enjoy bending.

"Well, the water, for example," he explained, pleased that he had even Kanoa's full attention. "We walked across it to come to this place, correct?"

"Some of us did, anyway," I fumed.

"Whatever," he continued, Cora and Kanoa laughing as they reminisced about my failure. "That task only took two simple ideas: The idea of walking and the idea of the water. By ignoring the fact that we shouldn't be able to walk on said water, we were able to bend the rules of physics. It wasn't a complex thought. We just had to bridge the two ideas over what seemed to be an unreachable split within our brains. No doubt more complicated things would require much deeper thinking and imagination."

"What would be considered hard?" Kanoa asked, boldly wishing to test the limits of possibility. Osias thought for a moment, and I noticed a dim light peeking out at the far end of the cave. The exit was within sight.

"Well, creating things that didn't exist before would be rather difficult," he proposed, unsure of his answer. I remembered the dog in the woods once again. Why had I been able to change its shape, but not able to do something as simple as walk on water? "I doubt we would be able to create things we had never seen before, but I could be wrong. I also think that reacting to our environment quickly, without applying logic to said environment, would be tricky. An example would be if I were to turn around and hit one of you with my staff without you anticipating it. It may be too hard to stop me, or dodge it, as we are not expecting to be able to do such a thing."

"I'm surprised you are able to do anything here then, Osias," Cora teased. "Wouldn't a science nut like you find any of this a little too hard to believe?"

"Despite what you guys may think," Osias scoffed, "my love of the sciences is only overshadowed by my wonder of the impossible. I have always wanted to see what would happen if matter could be created, or if gravity could be defied. This place is fascinating."

There was something about his tone that sounded rehearsed or fabricated, like he wanted to believe his words as much as he wanted us to believe them. The real world had been such a series of disappointments for him. Maybe he hoped this world would treat him better.

"Such a dork," Kanoa laughed, dampening Osias's spirits. "I think I see the light at the end of the tunnel."

"I think you should definitely walk toward the light," Osias suggested, turning off his light, as it was no longer needed.

"Very funny," Kanoa shot back. His pace quickened and the ground began to incline to the surface.

As we emerged from under the mountains, it became evident quite quickly what Osias had been talking about when he mentioned a chasm. We were standing inside a deep, narrow orange canyon that dug deeply into the face of the land. Tiny rocks and dust fell from the walls, powdering the ground at our feet. I could scarcely see the tips of the mountains above us due to not only their height, but also the dust that blocked the far reaches of my eyesight. I couldn't see a way out of the gorge. We could just barely walk two by two inside the canyon as the walls threatened to close around us. Thalia was lucky that she wasn't with us, or she would surely be panicking.

"I don't suppose you found a way out of here?" I asked. Without waiting on an answer, I kept walking down the narrow path. Kanoa quickly caught up to me, never a fan of being left behind.

"I would imagine that if we just keep on walking, we will eventually get back to level ground," Osias reasoned.

"Yeah, well keep on imagining, and maybe it will come true," Kanoa muttered so that only I could hear, nudging me with his shoulder playfully.

"You shouldn't be so mean to him," I said, keeping my voice low so that he couldn't overhear us. Kanoa sneered and shook his head.

"I'm just teasing," he assured me. "Besides, did you hear him back there with his rules for this place? *Rules* for *this* place! As if."

"He's just trying to help," I protested. It had always been a constant struggle to get Kanoa to accept Osias to be a part of the group right from the beginning. Although I often didn't agree with Kanoa's decisions, my objections were greatly outweighed by Osias's. The two were polar opposites. Even when they agreed on something, they managed to find conflicting reasons why. "If you just gave him a chance for once—"

"Shhh," Kanoa interrupted. He held his hand in the air and looked intently at the far reaches of the chasm. Cora and Osias stopped behind us.

"What is it?" I asked, unable to hear anything but the stones pouring down from above.

Kanoa waved his hand, motioning me to stop talking. He raised his ear and listened for a moment. After a few seconds, I then picked up on an unusual sound. It sounded like something was trotting toward us very rapidly. And it sounded like there was more than one of whatever it was.

We all raised our weapons, prepared to face whatever was coming our way. The noise grew louder and echoed across the walls of the chasm. The dust made the air thick and hard to see through, meaning we probably wouldn't be able to see what was coming until it was right on top of us. I titled my weapon to block off the impact, hoping to somewhat deflect the blow.

Large shadows formed in the dusty mist, which were slowing down and sounding a lot less menacing. Laughter could be heard accompanying the trotting noises. It was now clear that there were two separate entities, both identical. The dust around them cleared and revealed their true nature.

"Wow, I guess he was right!" Thalia exclaimed.

Adora giggled affectionately and clapped her hands together. The two girls were riding atop two majestic white horses, with long flowing white hair about their necks and tails. Their hooves were a golden colour, as were the horns sticking out of their foreheads. It was then that I realized they were in fact unicorns.

"Where did you guys find those?" Cora asked, incredible levels of excitement in her voice. She walked up to Thalia's and rubbed its nose gently. The animal whinnied warmly and begged for more attention.

"Well, actually," Thalia explained, jumping down from her unicorn and assisting Adora in her descent, "they found us when we woke up."

"Great," Osias said. "Now we just need to find Santa Claus and Bigfoot, and we can have that party I mentioned earlier."

"Hey Osias," Thalia said, trying to get a better look under his hood. "Why is your hair blue?"

"Oh, um," he stuttered, blushing as he pulled his hood up further. "Blue is my favourite colour, and I figured we're in a dream world, so—Shut up, I think it looks cool!"

"Just asking," Thalia laughed.

The two sisters stood in front of their rides, and I studied their appearances. Thalia had also conformed to the perfect complexion and radiant skin the rest of us now possessed. Her gazing eyes flashed a shade of purple, and her wild hair had turned from black, which she had dyed from blond, to a shocking hue of blue with long strips of white. Black lines extended from the edges of her eyes like wings. An intricate golden necklace with tiny dangling orbs rest upon her neck, its glow pulsating on and off periodically. She wore a bright green silk shirt, with flaps covering her arms that swayed a little as she stood. Her silky pants matched her shirt, but she wore large red boots that reached to almost her knees and covered most of her legs. They appeared to be made of nothing more than tinsel and glitter. Strapped to her sides with a thin belt were two glinting scimitars. She looked as random and peppy as I had always known her to be.

Adora, on the other hand, was probably the most interesting looking out of all of us, as she hadn't changed one bit since I had last seen her. Her skin was not perfect, and did not share the same glowing quality as the rest of ours. Her pale skin stuck out among us, as if she was abnormal. Her shoulder-length hair remained the same extreme shade of light blond/almost white it had been before, and she carried no weapon. The only change I noticed was in her attire. She wore a plain white dress that reached only to her knees, but it bore no remarkable features. She was the exact same angelic Adora we had known all along.

"Adora," Kanoa whispered, stepping forward toward her. "You...you look the same."

She looked at him with a perplexed look on her face. "I like the way I look," she stated. "Don't you?"

"Of course I do," Kanoa said. "I wouldn't ever want you to change."

"Then why did you change?" Adora asked.

An awkward silence befell the group as Kanoa could not answer. We all exchanged glances, looking over our new appearances once again. There was a moment of shame among us, brought forth by her innocence. I decided to speak up.

"What did you mean when you said 'he' was right?" I asked Thalia.

"What?" she asked, snapping out of her thoughts. "Oh right. Yeah, we met this old, and I mean really old, man shortly after we woke up, and he told us to go get you guys. He told us exactly where to go and, well, here you all are. Kind of spooky, actually."

"There are other people here?" Cora asked.

An uneasy chill skittered down my spine. If there were other people here, it was probable that we could run into trouble. In my mind, where there were people, there was danger. My memories had taught me that devastating truth long ago.

"Well," Thalia explained, "I wouldn't go so far as to call him a person." A wave of confusion washed over the rest of the group.

"What is that supposed to mean?" Osias asked.

"I guess you'll see when we get there," Thalia assured us with a laugh. "Come on, it isn't all that far from here." She hopped back onto her steed gracefully, and Adora did the same. "Oh and when we get there, try not to stare at him," she advised. "He doesn't like it. Trust me, it's so hard not to."

With Thalia in the front and Adora right behind her, their unicorns began prancing through the cloudy air. Thalia kept her head held up high and took deep breaths while she hummed along to a song playing in her head, looking to the sky to undoubtedly take her mind off her compact surroundings. Kanoa walked next to Adora, deep in conversation as he told of all the things he had been able to do. Osias ran up to Thalia and began questioning her about her ride, which left me and Cora walking together once again. I decided that I would take this opportunity to make amends with her.

Before I began my apology, I thought of all that had already transpired inside this dream world, and what lay ahead for us. We had begun to fulfill our promise to each other by reuniting, and I hoped that whoever the two sisters had met knew of a way out of here. As wonderful as dreams were, there had to be a time of waking.

CHAPTER 5: INTRODUCTIONS

"Sorry for being mean back in the castle," I finally spat out. I didn't necessarily like saying sorry, but I knew when I was in the wrong. Cora smiled compliantly and put her hand on my shoulder.

"It's okay," she replied, accepting my lame apology. She had gotten used to it over the years. "I know you have a hard time trusting people. But we're your friends, Kail. If you can't open up to us, then who?"

"I don't know," I lied. This had been an issue with me for a long time now, and I doubted it would ever subside. It was a part of who I was now. Some memories just dug too deep. My memories were now engraved in me and not just a part of who I was; they *were* who I was. "Maybe I can't trust you guys because I don't trust myself."

The walls around us were shortening as the ground began to incline, meaning we were getting close to level ground. Thalia and Adora had gotten off their unicorns and let them run free, as Adora didn't think it was fair to make everyone else walk. The animals ran off into the distance before fading out of sight. Thalia had told us that we would have to traverse through a forested area before reaching where they had woken up and met the man they spoke of before. From the sounds of it, the man seemed to be friendly, but looks could be deceiving.

"I trust you, Kail," Cora said, her words sounding as genuine as words could possibly be. "We all do. You can't live this whole life by yourself, ya know? You have to let some people into that head of yours."

"I'll think about it," I said, letting the thought fade away instantly.

Our heads were now poking over the tops of the walls, meaning we had escaped the depths of the chasm. Before us was a heavily thicketed forest, except for one straight clearing ahead. There was a dirt path right in the middle, with bending trees on both sides that cast the path in shade. It was as if someone had cut a hole right through the heart of the forest.

"It's almost like it was expecting us," Osias observed. The group stopped to examine the all-too-ideal path. A level of distrust arose from within me. It felt like a trap.

"I'll go in first, if everyone else is too scared to," Kanoa proposed, bravely stepping forward and readying his weapon.

"You don't have to pretend, Kanoa," Adora replied, looking to him tenderly. "We will all go in together."

Kanoa looked to her, clearly restraining the embarrassment caused by his exposure at the hands of a friend. "I'm not scared," he stated through clenched teeth. "And I'd prefer if you stopped doing that."

"Don't worry," Adora said, paying little attention to Kanoa's anger. "This is the way we got here. I promise that it is safe."

"Looks like a trap to me," I said, voicing my concern.

I looked around the forest to see if there was anything waiting to ambush us from within. The trees and shrubbery were heavily bunched together, and I was unable to view much of anything outside the main pathway. A white object caught my attention just off the path. I focused carefully, and then felt my knees buckle when I realized what it was. I fell to the ground hard, my eyes transfixed by what I had seen. It stared back at me for a moment, and then disappeared.

I was then removed from my friends; my body and soul taken from me. I could see myself kneeling on the ground as I was lifted high above my friends. A great pressure pressed down upon me and the air was sucked out of my lungs. The world as I knew it faded into a wisp. The forest, the chasm, my friends and the spaces in between had all been crushed into a small puff of air.

The tiny dark plume reached up to me and hovered before my eyes. It began to swirl around my head, slowly at first, before gaining both speed and mass. Before I knew it, the wisp had formed a new world around me. It was a world I was sadly familiar with. It was the world of my childhood: The Holy Trinity Orphanage.

I was standing in what was once my room. Its dull, red-bricked walls were only large enough to fit a bunk bed, which was just barely large enough for me to sleep in. A small desk with a lamp on it was squished into a dark corner of the room. There were pictures hung all around the room, but they were all blurred out, the faces and places unrecognizable. I tried to move, but I couldn't. I was trapped inside my own body. There was a knock on the door.

"Kail?" A soft voice whispered from beyond the door.

The old wooden door slowly creaked open and a young girl walked into the room, closing the door behind her. She wore her blond hair in pigtails with dull pink bows. Blue faded overalls covered a white long-sleeved shirt, and dirty purple running shoes enveloped her tiny feet. She was poor in appearance, but not in spirit. A hopeful smile accentuated her naive outlook on life.

"We're never going to get out of here," I heard myself say.

My eyes looked around for where the voice had come from, but I then realized the response had come directly from my own mouth, without my will. I was going through the motions of my memory, unable to alter my past. The only difference was that I was still my "dream world" self instead of the young boy I used to be.

"Don't say that, Kail," she said, persistently optimistic. "Someone will find us and take us away from here. We just have to wait for the right people."

I scoffed, instantly feeling terrible for how I was treating her. She was only trying to make things easier for me, despite how bleak things actually were. Back then, I had no hope within me. I only fed off what she granted me. But in this moment, I hoped for the chance to change my past.

"You don't get it," I barked. "Nobody will take the two of us. They would have taken you or me, not both. Either one of us goes, or none. You want to live in this place forever with these people?"

"Someone will come," she said, my negativity rendering her unfazed. "It just isn't time yet."

"Listen to me," I said, finding myself moving forward and kneeling at her feet, holding her hands tightly. "If someone wants to take you but not me, you go with them. I'll be fine here, okay? I'm not leaving you, but I want you to leave me if you can."

"Don't be silly," she replied, immediately pulling her hands out of mine and turning for the door. She looked back, the smile still managing to stay on her face. "We get out of this together, Kail. Kail. Kail."

My echoing name escaped from her lips, but it was no longer her voice. My room shattered into pieces, each piece a sharp reflection of my distraught face. I studied my appearance, thinking of what I had been then and what I had now become; how little things had actually changed. The pieces hung in the air for a moment and then quickly reformed into the dream world I had left moments ago. I had left my memories and returned to my dreams.

"Kail, what's wrong?" Cora asked, kneeling at my side, holding me in her arms tightly.

I began shivering all over, my eyes stuck open. There was no way anything I had seen was possible; not even here. Cora looked right into my eyes, great fear present in hers. Light mist welled up in my eyes. I gasped for air, realizing I hadn't taken a breath for a long time.

"He saw something in there," Kanoa said, rushing to the edge of the forest, holding his weapon closely.

He scanned the area, but was unable to find what I had seen. I didn't expect him to. He walked back and joined the rest of the group in monitoring my behaviour. They looked at me as if I had seen a ghost. They were right.

"It was her," I whispered. "She was standing in the forest, just staring back at me."

"Who was?" Cora asked. "Who was standing in the forest?"

I went over what I had seen once again in my head. She was leaning against a tree with a look of grave concern on her pale face. She had been wearing the same clothes she had been wearing the last day I saw her—a pink t-shirt and blue jeans. Her eyes had been wide and beckoned for me. She looked as if she needed me. Even if I had seen her, what did it mean? Did I actually see her, or was it just another piece of my imagination brought to life? Was this the beginning of a nightmare?

"Delphia," I finally murmured.

Everyone's tone instantly shifted from concern to distress, sorrow filling their hearts at the name. Adora looked confused, unaware of what the name meant. Cora embraced me, trying to help me get over what was now burned into my eyes.

"Who is Delphia?" Adora asked.

She tugged at Thalia's sleeve, not wanting to be left out of the group. Apparently the rumours had never made their way to her. Adora never cared much for gossip, and since that is all there was of Delphia, she was unaware of her existence. Outside of me, Delphia was nothing more than whispers.

Thalia took her sister farther back to try to get out of earshot from me. She didn't go far enough, as I heard their low voices clearly. "Delphia is Kail's sister," Thalia explained in a hushed voice. "Or at least, she was."

"Was his sister?" Adora asked. Thalia was quiet for a moment. "What happened to her, Thalia? Did she die?"

"We don't know," she replied, uncommonly gloomy. "He never talks about her to anyone. But whatever happened, it took place before any of us knew him. Even before he was adopted by his parents."

My adoption was no mystery to anyone who took the time to know me. My real parents had abandoned my sister and me when I had been one year old and my sister had just been born. For whatever reason, they weren't ready for us. We lived in a lowly orphanage for what felt like our entire childhood before we had been finally adopted by my new parents. Well, I had been adopted, anyway.

Adora left her sister and walked up to me, a look of comfort illuminating her eyes. She knelt down before me next to Cora, who was still hugging me. She looked right at me, a slight smile cresting across her face. I felt a tingle of happiness within me, even in spite of what I had just gone through. She always had a gift of healing.

"What was she like, Kail?" she asked.

I felt that she knew something, like she had known of a mystery for a very long time and had only now solved it. At that moment I felt completely at peace. Her words drew harmony within my broken heart. As I thought about it more, Adora was a lot like my sister. I had been too young to change what had happened, but now that I was older, I felt that change was within my reach, even if time separated me from my sister more than anything. For the first time in a long time, I opened up to my friends and gave them the first clues into my dark and hidden past.

"She was all you could ask for in a sister," I replied with a pained smile. "She was what kept me together as a kid in the orphanage. Even when I had given up hope, she would find more for us to live for."

A tear streamed down my face. It reached my chin and fell toward the ground, but was caught by Adora before it reached its inevitable destination. She studied the droplet in her hand and then angled it towards me. My tiny tear had grown into a word, which glistened in her palm. I quickly read the word "Hope" before it faded away. That was what I felt in that moment—the hope that perhaps this place would give me the reunion I aspired for with my long-lost sister.

I looked into Adora's kind eyes and nodded my thanks. Cora held me tightly for a moment and whispered "Good start" into my ear before getting back to her feet. I stared at her thoughtfully, and she offered her hand to me. I took it and stood shakily. That's what friends were for.

"I'll be all right," I stated. "I'll be fine."

"That's good to hear, Kail," Thalia said with assurance, yet urgency tinged her voice. "I don't mean to rush anyone, but we really should get going."

"Are you sure you're okay?" Cora asked. I brushed her off, as all the attention I was drawing was beginning to make me feel weak. As quickly as I had opened up, I closed again.

"Yes, I said," I said, the cold spite re-entering my voice. "I'm not a goddamn child."

I began walking into the shaded pathway, keeping an eye out for any more hallucinations. I heard the rest of the group begin to follow after a moment, unsure of my rapid mood swing. They probably thought I was going crazy. Maybe I was.

Although the branches blocked out any light, the belly of the forest was still packed thick and hot. No animal life could be seen, but ambient noises emitted from all sides, as if there was some sort of soundtrack playing for the forest. Thalia and Adora now held the lead, as I realized that I had no idea where I was going, despite the path being fairly linear. I never was the best at holding a lead.

"I don't remember the path being this long," Adora said. Thalia looked around anxiously, trying to recall where she was.

"We should be out soon," Thalia replied, not letting her sister's worry get to her. She started singing a song under her breath, something she often did to soften any silence that fell over us.

I noticed that I was walking through patches of lively, multi-coloured flowers that were running in a line. I looked behind me and realized they only grew in a very straight path. I looked forward and found the cause of the growth: Wherever Adora walked, flowers came to life.

"Hey, Adora," I said with a laugh, "do you realize that you're making flowers?"

She looked toward me and smiled. The rest of the group studied the same observations I had just made, and all looked toward her incredulously. "Of course I know, Kail," she replied clearly and happily. "I have always loved flowers. Aren't they pretty?"

Before I could respond, the far reaches of the forest path began to vanish away. It was as if it was being erased straight off the ground, causing us all to begin to pace backwards. The trees receded toward us at a startling rate, and the ambient forest becoming silent. The deletion of the forest stopped abruptly before us with a loud whoosh, opening up to a clearing surrounded by the woods. Small huts appeared in the middle, the trees still sticking close to the huts. Apparently we had stumbled across a hidden village.

"Was that there before?" Osias asked. Thalia shook her head, alarmed by the random shift in the environment.

"I don't get it," Kanoa said with frustration. "We were on a straight path. How the hell could we get lost?"

"Yeah, well, I don't get how a forest could suddenly shorten itself," Cora said with despair, "so I guess we're in the same boat."

I looked into the village and spotted movement. A small crowd had developed at the outskirts of the village, all facing toward us, apparently aware of our presence. I wasn't exactly sure, but from the looks of things, the entire crowd was made of the same person—perfect copies, standing side by side.

"Well, apparently we have a welcoming party," I said with disdain. "Let's just hope that they're friendly."

"Maybe we should just go around," Osias suggested, worry present in his voice. Kanoa walked into the opening and toward the crowd daringly.

"No way, it'll take too long," he objected. "What are they going to do? We have weapons, they don't. I wouldn't worry about a fight, or at least not a good one. Besides Osias, maybe we can get some of your precious answers."

Without any further objections, we all made our way toward the gathering crowd. It was now quite clear what the village and its inhabitants looked like. The huts were built with straw roofs and brick walls, each no more than the size of a classroom back at home. There were two rows of houses, running parallel to one another, with around fifteen huts on each side. White picket fences surrounded each premise, with what appeared to be a mailbox attached to the gates of each hut. An old well was placed at the centre of the village, with a bucket to possibly retrieve their water supply. There was no difference between the huts; they all looked exactly the same. The same could be said of the villagers.

As we approached the crowd, a silence befell them. I stopped in my tracks, as did the rest of my friends, waiting to see their reaction. The group of villagers split into two groups and lined up single file on each side of their homes. They stood quite rigidly, all staring forward and attentively like soldiers. I shot a glance of confusion at the rest of the group, who was reflecting my emotions. The villagers, just as the village itself, all conformed to one specific look. All the villagers were male, muscular and tall. They all had straight, jet-black hair and colourless eyes, as if blind. They all seemed dirty, tired, and overworked. They wore no shirts, and all had a marking branded onto their chests. It was not coloured or tattooed, but rather burned into the flesh. There were four points, all connected with a black line, forming a diamond. In the middle of the diamond was a large, italic capitol M. I had no way of knowing, but I doubted the branding had been by their will.

We hesitantly entered the village with Kanoa in the lead. I wasn't far behind, but the rest of the group had lagged back a bit. My hand fluttered over the weapon on my back, ready to wield it at the slightest hint of an ambush. As Kanoa and I passed by each villager, they knelt at our feet and pressed their heads to the ground in worship. I looked down at them, curious as to what they were doing. Something on their hands caught my eye: they bore the same golden, vein-like markings that I had. Were they kneeling to me?

"Why are they bowing to us?" Adora inquired. Apparently the villagers' submission had made the rest of the group feel more comfortable around them.

"I don't think they're bowing at us," Kanoa replied, his eyes stubbornly shifting back and forth between my hands and the villagers. "I think they're bowing to him."

The group huddled around me, studying my hands and comparing them to that of the villagers. Thalia stared at me intently, marvelling at my apparent influence over the villagers. I wasn't too fond of the implications this discovery brought about. Osias tried questioning them, but they didn't budge. I also tried conversing with them, but I couldn't get them to respond either. They remained glued to the ground, their eyes closed in concentration.

"Why don't they want to talk to you?" Thalia asked, kneeling down and patting one of the villagers on the back. "You'd think they would want to talk to the guy they worship."

"Maybe they're scared," Cora proposed, looking into one of the many huts. "Maybe they think Kail is some kind of god."

"Yeah, well, if they think *he's* a god," Osias said, "then what's with that mark burned onto their chests?"

"You must all hide yourselves quickly," an old yet stern voice demanded. I looked around to see what villager had spoken, but their heads remained down. The rest of the group had also heard the voice, as they too were inspecting the villagers.

"Which one of you said that?" Kanoa asked, running up and down the rows. "You guys heard that, right?"

"It sounded like the man we met," Adora said.

We turned our attention to Adora, and then to Thalia. Thalia shook her head slowly, recalling what she and her sister had heard earlier of the man's voice. Whoever this man was, he seemed to know what was going on in this world.

"Into the forest," the voice said once again, this time louder. It was clear the voice wasn't coming from any of the villagers. The voice was coming from inside my own head. "I will explain myself once the danger is over. Now quickly, heed my words and leave that village before it is too late."

The air around me became heavy and cold. I looked to the sky and saw darkness brewing. Tiny bits of rock and debris rose off the ground and remained suspended in the air. The villagers' blank eyes opened and turned upward. Something was coming. I looked to my friends and saw fear on their faces, and decided it was time to take the old man's advice and run for the trees.

"Guys, I think we should go," I said. At first nobody moved, paralyzed by the incoming threat. I raised my voice to overcome their shock. "Like right now!"

My voice broke their concentration, and they began to move out of the village and into the protection of the thick forest. I hid behind a rather large tree, hoping that its trunk would cover me sufficiently. Unfortunately, our proximity to the village was rather unnerving. I could easily see all the villagers, who were still kneeling and looking to the sky. If we could see them, whatever was coming was going to be able to see us if they tried.

Although we were all scared, none of us dared hide too far into the forest. Something very important was about to happen and I, as well as the rest of the group, was not going to miss it. The dark clouds in the sky began funnelling downward like a tornado. It barrelled down toward the ground with impossible precision, as if being directed by the heavens themselves. The tornado touched down in the very centre of the village, but not even the fragile straw roofs were harmed. The tornado then started to fade away, starting at the top and working its way to the ground. The dark veil completely blew away and revealed something I had not been expecting. Standing exactly where the twister had touched down was a woman. It hadn't been weather at all. It was merely a form of transportation.

"Did you all just see that?" Osias whispered, amazed by the woman's entrance. He was answered with many shushes.

The woman stood tall and majestic, yet eerily ashen and ominous. Her skin was pale, eyes dark and piercing. Her white hair flowed from her head like icicles, striking out in all directions. Her lips were painted dark as her eyes. Despite her foreboding nature, it was impossible to deny her ethereal beauty and grace. A silver tiara floated above her head, bright clear diamonds spinning slowly on its frame. She wore a bright white gown that cut deeply in the front, with black hearts embroidered all the way around the fringes of the gown. She carried no weapon, but a dark orb protruded from her chest just below her neck, its surface swirling with mist. It was a part of her, just as my hand was attached to me. Although she remained bound to the ground, her clothes and hair resisted all demands of gravity, hanging in the air effortlessly. Her presence was draining and overwhelming. She was the type of sight that made you wake up from a dream gasping for air.

"Why do you all kneel?" she asked.

Her daunting voice was serene, yet filled with sorrow and pain. Malice stung her every syllable, yet tenderness rang throughout. She looked around at each villager carefully, and then at each hut. She stopped before a villager and waited patiently. Slowly, each villager stood up uniformly, all facing the woman submissively. She had some resounding power over them.

"I am sorry, your highness," a villager said, apparent apprehension wavering within his voice. I could see him shaking in place, his knees ready to buckle at any moment. The woman stared at him, a smile stretching across her face.

"You didn't answer my question, peasant," she said elegantly, yet the threat was still there in her words. "Why were you all kneeling before I came?"

The villager looked around nervously at his community, who were all trying their best not to flinch. The woman tilted her head, her eyes searing into his skull. He cleared his throat and stammered his response. "There is no reason, your highness."

"No reason, you say," she retorted, quickly pouncing on his words like a predator on its prey. I looked at my friends, wondering why they wouldn't just tell her that we had come by. "I don't like liars, peasant. Must I remind you what happens when a village displeases me?"

The entire village's tone changed instantaneously at her words. Fear entered their wavering stance, and their faces all displayed dread. The villager fell to his knees and brought his hands to her gown, begging for forgiveness.

"Your highness!" he shouted. "We are all that is left beyond the mountains. We have been loyal to you when others have fled or displeased you. We bear your mark with great pride! Please let us live."

She laughed, great pity entwined with her voice. Her hateful laughter made my skin crawl and resonated in my very soul. She bent down, the smile turning to a piercing glare of loathing and fury. The villager leaned backward, tears streaming down his face.

"Let you live?" she asked, as if not understanding the request. "You died the moment you chose to defy me."

With those words, she vanished in a puff of purple smoke. Everything became unnaturally quiet. Shocked expressions filled the faces of the villagers as they scanned the area to see where she could have gone.

Kanoa stood up and began edging his way out of the forest. I looked toward the well and spotted movement. Large, brown skeletal fingers protruded from its depths and tapped eagerly upon the stone base. I grabbed Kanoa's cape and pulled him back. He stared at me with anger, which quickly converted to confusion when he saw the terrified look on my face. I pointed over to the well with a trembling hand.

"Something's here," I whispered.

The villager who had been begging the women was now standing, slowly walking backwards away from where she had been. He was heading directly toward the well and whatever was waiting within it. I almost cried out to save him, but couldn't bring myself to speak. It was too late.

With one swift motion, the hands extended forth and grabbed the villager violently, its fingernails digging deep into his skin. The villager gasped for air for a moment, blood spurting from his lips, and then was sucked straight into the well and was gone. The other villagers quickly realized the disappearance of the man, and some slowly crept toward the well, their legs shaking uncontrollably. There was a moment of silence as they approached, but then a blood-curdling scream emanated from deep within the ground. It echoed and grew louder and louder. All the villagers, my friends, and even I, collectively cupped our hands over our ears to drown out the horrifying shout. The scream warped into laughter. Whatever was inside that well wasn't alone.

I watched as a villager ran into a hut and slammed the door behind him, only for the hut to evaporate into nothing, revealing a deep, dark pit where it had once been. His scream was long and shrill. A figure rose out of the hole in the ground with its arms raised to the air, laughing maniacally. His mouth extended from ear to ear, revealing razor-sharp yellow teeth. His twitchy eyes glowed the same yellow, and his skin was a sickly coloured green. Sharp eyebrows only emphasizing the crazed look in his eyes as he looked around at the scrambling villagers below him. He wore a tall top hat, stripped black and green. Holes had been crudely cut in the hat for his wild, scraggly purple hair to burrow outwards and tickle his dour face. He wore a heavy black trench coat with bright red happy faces littered across it, their eyes crossed out in black. He had dirty, dark silky gloves on his hands—far too large a fit, as they sagged loosely over his scrawny fingers. Long, curled black shoes covered his feet, yet mouldy toes somehow managed to stick out at the end. Laughing was the last thing I felt like doing when I looked at him.

The villagers ran from the hovering entity in all directions, the ones closest to the well actually seeming to have escaped. The stones that made up the well suddenly exploded in all directions, sending villagers hurling to the ground after being struck hard with debris. Bent low to the ground was a figure much larger than that of the other. Whatever it was had somehow created solid ground under his feet, and there was now no indication that a well had existed at all. If I had been scared before, this new presence brought me to a whole new level of fear.

The being's bony fingers pierced the ground, and blood ran down his arms. He wore a badly torn, dark brown hooded robe. The hood had been brought up over his head, leaving his face shrouded in darkness. All that could be seen were intense, glowing red eyes, unmoving and difficult to look at. He stood up, revealing his true massive height, standing as tall as the one of the huts. Silver chains wrapped themselves all along his upper body, creating an almost shirt-like construction. Deep scars were visible under the chains all over his chest. He wore a studded belt, sharp spikes thrusting out all around him. Brown tattered pants and shoes covered his lower body. In his gaunt hands he held two enormous battle axes, connected together with a thick chain that matched his shirt. The axes did not have straight edges like a normal blade, but rather its edge was forged with layer upon layer of tiny barbs and spikes. I couldn't even fathom the pain they could inflict. He swung the weapon above his head threateningly, displaying his power. I hoped this was the closest I would ever come to him.

As the blades spun faster, large hairy spiders fell down from the weapon's coil and bounced on the ground. They were about the size of my face, which sent chills through me at the thought of what was about to happen to the villagers. The insects' features were greatly over-exaggerated. Their many dark eyes gleamed hungrily, and their legs scurried them forward at an alarming rate. They crawled over the hurt villagers, biting at them ferociously. The villagers cried out in terror as they tried pushing the creatures away. There were so many that some people were entirely covered with them. I could only hear their screams.

The man, if he could be called a man at all, turned his attention to one villager in particular who was hiding in a small bush in front of one of the huts. He grabbed the man by the throat and lifted him off the ground effortlessly, staring at him curiously as he struggled for air. A clear glass box filled with water then appeared where the bush had once been. The villager looked down and screamed in terror. His feet skimmed the water's surface as he held onto the large man's arm, trying not to fall into the box.

The man forcefully threw the villager in and closed the lid on top of him. The villager banged on the walls furiously, trying to get out. His eyes brimmed with terror, air bubbles rising from his mouth. He began to gag, and after a few moments he was still, his eyes glassy, wide and vacant.

Some villagers took refuge in huts, trying to hide from the two monsters outside their homes. There was a loud rushing of wind, and I noticed clouds had formed at the far edge of the village. The clouds were spiralling rapidly, growing denser and gaining structure. The clouds burst outward, unveiling a third entity. This one was more majestic than the others had been. He had a certain royal quality to him. Nonetheless, it was still evident he was not here for anything but to bring misery.

Unlike his apparent companions, he did not wear any dark or worn articles of clothing. He wore a sleek chrome jacket that shone, seemingly made out of metal instead of cloth. The untainted jacket flowed down to his feet, with a cut in the front that revealed a white-buttoned dress shirt. The opening extended all the way down, showing off his classy white pants and shoes. His collar was popped, rising high to his cheek bones. His face was slender and almost feminine. His hair was feathered back and grey, his metallic blue eyes completely relaxed. His posture was cool and confident. An almost smug smile formed on his ageless face. In his tightly gloved hands he held what appeared to be a large sword hilt with no blade extending from it. However, rays of light sparkled in front of him in a curved pattern, as if bouncing off a blade. It seemed that the blade was so thin and sharp that only light's reflection gave away its presence. His tranquil composure was intimidating. It made me question not what he could do, but what he couldn't do.

He raised the arm that held the hilt and swiped it across the air in front of him with little exertion, sending a shockwave forth into the huts before him. The force of the blow caused the straw roofs to propel into the air, making the interiors of the houses clearly visible. The villagers who had been hiding were now exposed entirely, the brick walls only reaching as high as their shoulders. The swordsman then lunged forward for a moment, a glint flashing where he stood, and within the blink of an eye he had crossed over each hut and was floating on the other side of the village, his back toward the distance he had just cleared. My eyes fluttered between where he had been and where he now was. He had covered the distance of nearly an entire football field in less than a second. Not even Kanoa had run that fast.

The villagers inside the huts all stared at one another, bewildered. It was unclear to everyone what had just happened. They then slumped lifelessly to the ground in unison. All this had occurred before the straws that had once served as roofs had fallen back to the ground. The swordsman had ended the lives of at least ten people in the time it took me to exhale.

The few remaining villagers seemed to have escaped. They reached the edge of the forest with no known threat around them. A surge of joy spread through me as they entered the trees and were out of sight. My happiness was quickly vanquished, however, as they all re-emerged inside the town boundaries, bound tightly in vines. They writhed in pain as the vines rose into the air above the tree tops, crushing the life out of their victims.

A woman materialized out of the woods. A new threat was now apparent.

She had in her hands a large paint brush. Its wood-constructed green base was splintered, and the bristles were frayed and bent. On her back she held many other brushes of varying quality and hue, protruding outwards like the feathers of a peacock. She wore a painted porcelain mask, yet its features shifted like a normal face. Red rosy blotches were painted on high cheeks, and wavy black eyebrows stood above empty black eyes. Bright red was coloured onto her spread lips, but her mouth remained in a closed smile. Her entire body was made of red and white marble, her robust figure chiselled to human perfection. She was more of a statue than a person, and yet she moved naturally on the tips of her toes, as if her stony build wasn't a hindrance. She was a work of art in motion.

She took her focus away from her restrained victims, placing her weathered brush on her back and replacing it with a red mahogany one. She raised it with one hand and weaved it gently in the air. Fire burst out of its tip and spread through the village, ravaging the bodies and huts. The vines let go of the now-limp villagers, plunging them into the blaze below. The inferno raged on, consuming the entire area in its mass. Heat burned at my face, but no smoke filled my lungs. All I could hear was the nightmarish laughter of the four forces combined from somewhere within the flames. And then it was over.

The fire dissipated, leaving nothing more than charred ground where an entire village had once been. There were no bodies littered on the ground, and no sign of the four fiends. None of us dared move, fearing they were in hiding, waiting for us to reveal our location only to send us to a similar fate as what we had just witnessed. The entire occurrence took no more than a few minutes, and yet the images would last me a lifetime. This dream world had just turned into a nightmare.

"Holy shit," Cora murmured.

Still, nobody left their hiding spots. I surveyed the area, hoping to not find anything out of place. I quickly realized I had no idea what I was looking for. They could be anywhere and anything.

"What were those things?" Osias stammered.

I noticed that Cora had her hand tightly grasped upon my shoulder. Her hand was trembling as much as my heart was. Kanoa had a big smile on his face, which over the years I had come to understand as a sign of fear. Although others would see him smile and think he was happy, I knew what was hiding behind it. That only made things worse for me.

“Your worst nightmares,” the old voice answered. This time, I distinctly knew the voice wasn’t coming from inside my own head. He was right behind us.

The entire group swirled around, weapons raised, ready to fight and panting heavily. A tiny man stood before us, unfazed by our threatening poses. I remembered Thalia’s warning of not staring at the man and couldn’t help but disobey her advice. He was the strangest-looking man I had ever seen.

“I did not mean to startle you,” he said. His soothing voice rang true with wisdom and experience, slow yet deliberate, but nonetheless I was still the last to lower my weapon.

He brought his attention toward me, possibly intrigued by my lack of trust. I couldn’t say that he was looking at me, as the man was missing many key features attributed to a normal person. He had no eyes, no nose, no ears and no mouth. A long white beard grew out from his wrinkled face, and the white hair on his head was brought back into a ponytail. He wore a black robe with red trim that extended all the way to the ground, his sleeved arms crossed behind his back. He stood no taller than my thigh, and yet I sensed great power in his company.

“You do not trust me, Kail,” his voice stated, throwing me off guard for a moment. Was he able to read minds? “I can assure you I am here to assist you, but I suppose the carrier of Hope’s Glow has the right to brandish his weapon as he pleases. And I do not know who Mr. Potato Head is, Osias, but I would rather not have you drawing comparisons between us.”

“Osias, what did I tell you about staring,” I heard Thalia mutter, nudging him hard in the ribs. Osias responded with an innocent shrug.

“Well, sorry but,” he grumbled. “I mean seriously, look at him.”

“I am aware that my appearance is somewhat unsettling,” the man said with a chuckle, his focus remaining firmly upon me, “but I do hope you become accustomed with it.”

“What was that about Kail’s weapon?” Kanoa asked, stepping forward and towering over the small man. The man finally shifted his attention toward Kanoa and tilted his head upwards.

“I am sure you have many questions, Kanoa,” he responded, sounding a little wary of my friend’s tone. “I am sure you all have many questions for me. I will be more than happy to answer all of them, but you will understand that this is probably not the most suitable place for such a conversation.”

He turned away from us and began moving further into the forest. I couldn't see his legs, yet he travelled with ease, gliding over the uneven terrain. None of us followed at first, unsure of where he was leading us to. I was glad I wasn't the only one who wasn't sold that he was here to help, especially after what we had just seen.

"No harm will come to you if you follow me," he assured us, continuing on his path. "But the same cannot be said if you remain here. I know you all want answers, and that is exactly what I plan on giving you, to the best of my ability."

Still, none of us budged. Adora then cleared her throat and spoke up, breaking the awkward silence between us and the strange man.

"Can we at least have your name?" she asked. The old man finally stopped in place, turning slowly to face the question. Although he had no facial features, I could sense amusement in his posture. He felt friendly.

"My name is Alem," he replied with a nod.

CHAPTER 6: THE ANSWER TO DREAMS

"Where are you taking us exactly, Alem?" Osias asked, trying his best to keep up with the old man while stumbling over the thick underbrush.

We had walked deep into the forest, following our small leader with difficulty. He hadn't spoken much since he had led us away from the annihilated village and seemed to be muttering to himself quietly. We were all still pretty shook up, and I was trying my best to erase the memories of what I had seen. I should have known by now that such an activity was an exercise in futility. Memories were trapped within you, whether you wanted them or not. Memories seemed more vivid here. Even the smallest of details stuck.

"I know of a place with many hills that will provide a perfect training ground," he stated.

"A training ground, huh?" Kanoa repeated with added excitement. I could see it wasn't going to be hard for the man to win over Kanoa's trust and favour.

"Yes," Alem replied. "Just beyond these trees lays our destination. There is where I will tell you all you need to know about this place. And hopefully, you will be able to defeat the forces you just witnessed."

"No offence, um, Alem, but I doubt any training you give us is going to be enough to beat those things," I said. He turned around, but still glided ahead. I guess if he didn't need eyes, he didn't need to walk forward, either. "I mean, honestly, did you see what they did back there?"

"They were just having a little fun," he said with a dark laugh. I could tell the man was a little eccentric. I supposed one would have to be in a place like this. "You did not even see Malise join in. Now that would be something to worry about."

"Was she the queen-looking one?" Adora asked with childlike wonder.

"I don't think that was a queen, Adora," Cora objected with a giggle.

"Actually," Alem interjected, turning back around, "she was once the beloved queen of this land."

My pace slowed as I was shocked by this new discovery. How could someone so cruel have once been a praised ruler? Was it possible that this place changed people? Was it going to change me?

"Hold onto your questions, Kail," Alem advised. "We are almost there now."

"Alem, I know you're just trying to help," I barked, annoyed by his invasion of privacy, "but I don't appreciate you snooping around my head like that. If I want you to know something, I'll say it out loud. Is that understood?"

"Yes, Kail, that is understood," he replied. "But I want you to understand that I already know everything about you. Your lack of trust in others, the hardships of your childhood, the hopes you refuse to let go of, your repressed memories... They are as much a part of you as they are of me."

A sudden wave of fear washed over me. Everyone except Alem had stopped walking. I had made it a goal in my life to keep my past closed off from everyone I had ever met. I didn't like that this man, who I had just met, held all my secrets. He could ruin everything I had worked so hard for in an instant. He could be my greatest ally—or my worst enemy.

"So as you can probably understand," he continued, "the fact that your friends are still in the dark about what we both know should tell you that I have no intention of telling your secrets. I am hoping you will do that yourself. You will just have to trust me."

I sighed heavily, grinding my teeth and clenching my jaw. I was aware that all my friends were now staring harshly at me. As mad as I was at Alem knowing my secrets, they were equally upset at the fact that they didn't. They had wanted to know all about me for years, but had given up after realizing I would never answer their questions. My promise was eternal and would never be broken, no matter what it cost me. Now the answers they wanted had been given to someone else.

"So, Kail, how about it?" Kanoa said, his voice veiled in an expectant tone. "Think you'll tell us something for once?"

I avoided their eyes, looking down at my feet stubbornly. There was an awkward silence that wasn't going to go away until someone spoke. It wasn't going to be me.

"Why am I not surprised," Cora said, frustrated and disappointed.

"Give him time, guys," Thalia said. "He'll tell us on his own time."

"Don't count on it," I muttered, turning my back on my friends and walking past Alem.

"The ones you saw are known as The Forgotten Four," Alem revealed, his elderly voice booming through my mind.

His words disarmed my heated exit and stopped me in my tracks. I turned to face the man and he tilted his head toward me. I sensed that he was trying to shift the focus away from me as he nodded his head slightly. I nodded back acceptingly, thanking him for the gesture. Maybe he wasn't so bad after all.

"The Forgotten Four?" Osias repeated, intrigue woven in his words. My friends and I stood before the small man, intently waiting on some answers like kids around a campfire.

"Before I indulge this story of the land, I must make something very clear," he said with a dire and serious tone. "Everything that has occurred in this land is of your creation. I am merely a guide, created by those who constructed these advanced technologies. I am the only thing you will encounter that isn't a part of your imagination, memories or dreams. Other than you six, I am the one constant of this world."

I didn't understand what he meant. Apparently I wasn't alone, as the rest of the group displayed confused looks on their faces. Osias was the only one who seemed to know what the old man was talking about.

"So what you're saying," Osias said slowly, "is that you were designed as our guide in this place. Does that mean the machine extracted our dreams and memories, and created all this out of them? Even The Forgotten Four and Malise?"

"Yes, even them," Alem replied.

"Why the hell would we create those things?" Kanoa growled.

"Perhaps you didn't do it on purpose," Alem replied, continuing to maintain his calm tone with little effort, "but I suppose you should take a deeper look inside yourselves. The darkness inside you all has now been let out and taken form. The only way you are going to ever leave this place is by conquering it."

A look of shame befell our group. I was disgusted at the thought of being the reason those monsters existed in the first place. We were only kids, and yet our lives had produced enough horrors to rule over an entire world. I assumed that plenty of it had come from me, which made me feel all the more responsible.

"So the history of this place," I asked. "We made that too?"

Alem nodded vigorously, excited that we had begun catching on to the rhythm of how dreams worked. "Precisely, Kail. Everything I have told you, and am about to tell you, are creations of your dreams, memories and imaginations. Collectively, they have combined to forge this magical and dangerous place."

"If this is all just our creations," Thalia said, "then how do you know so much about it?"

"As I said," Alem responded, patiently answering each of our questions as they came, "I am but a guide interwoven into the code, designed to help you in your quest. I have done the same for every other person who has entered their own worlds. I have seen things your imaginations are not capable of. I must say, however, this is one of the most beautiful worlds I have ever been in. Ah, the imagination of the young and angry—beautiful in scope, yet horrifying in execution."

“Hey who’re you calling young and angry?” Kanoa said, standing tall over the small man.

“I believe I included you in my description Kanoa,” Alem replied, undeterred by my friend’s aggression. “I know who you are. All those years of disappointment and heartbreak must have been absolute hell. You think this place is your great reward for waiting so patiently, but don’t let your sights be so narrow. You may be a dreamer, but there comes a time when you must wake up before the world passes you by.”

“I think you have me confused with someone who cares what you have to say,” Kanoa snarled.

“Kanoa,” Adora said, swiftly grabbing his cape and pulling him away from Alem. She stared at him with a concerned look on her face, which Kanoa tried to resist. “How about we let Alem tell us his story?”

“Oh, I can assure you that it is not my story,” Alem interrupted with a chuckle. “It is very much your story. After all, you all helped generate it. Shall I begin?”

Our surroundings blurred for a moment, the trees and bushes around us wiggling around in place. Some bushes began changing in colour, from green to orange and blue and pink. The bushes were transforming into our tents back at the campfire. A tree near us fell over; its trunk chopped up into tiny bits, which then rolled their way into the middle of our group. Sparks glittered across their surface before devouring them in flames. We were now standing exactly where we had been early this morning. It felt like a lifetime ago since I had been sleeping soundly in my tent, before Kanoa had stuck his head in and awakened me from my slumber. I had been taken from one dream and thrown into another.

“I think this will do nicely,” Alem said.

“So like, can you do basically anything?” Cora asked, looking around at our creepily familiar environment.

“My abilities are limited to only the things that do not directly interfere with your journey,” Alem stated, looking into the forest. A long stick glided over toward him and hovered before him, as if he was holding it. He then looked to the fire, which the stick prodded, causing the fire to spark and crackle.

“Meaning?” Osias asked, admiring Alem’s psychokinetic powers.

“Meaning that I cannot fight by your side to defeat neither The Forgotten Four nor Malise,” he explained. “The best I can do is train you and give you history lessons, unfortunately. I wish there was more for me to do, but that is just the way things are. These are your dreams, not mine.”

The trees around us began to stretch high into the sky, thickening and fading to grey. The sky darkened and seemed to bend into an arc. The dirt and grass beneath our feet flattened and solidified into a marble floor. The random placement of trees had all aligned in rows, meshing into one another to create two long marble walls. The sky had seemingly hardened, and now served as an arched roof. We were standing in a hallway. In fact, it was the same hallway we had been inside before. We were back in the mysterious castle.

"Oh, not this place again," Osias moaned.

Despite my initial impression, this was not the exact same hallway we had been in before. Everything that had been modern, such as the light switch and elevator doors, were gone. Instead, crystal chandeliers hung from the ceiling, stunning paintings adorned the walls, and a red carpet with golden trim covered the floor. Now it felt more like a real castle instead of an interpretation of one.

"Where are we, Alem?" Adora asked, admiring a particularly realistic portrait of Malise.

I looked down and noticed the fireplace had followed us into the castle. It was becoming clear that we were merely a part of the story Alem was going to tell us. We weren't back inside this castle at all. It was just another figment of our imagination.

"We now stand inside the imperial castle that once ruled over the Kingdom of Drephoria. To be more specific, this is the main hall, open to both the common people and royalty. This is where your story begins."

With those words, two mighty golden thrones rose up at the end of the hallway, opposite the large wooden doorway. The thrones were on level ground with us, although one was much larger than the other. Malise sat in the smaller seat, her face full of life and her clothes a sparkling shade of blue. Her clothes and hair obeyed the force of gravity, and the orb on her chest was of a pure white. Other than that, she looked exactly as we had seen her before; just as beautifully draining. As Alem had said, she wasn't always how she was now.

A white figure sat in the large throne, with no definition or features present. There was only an outline of a person, as if being erased from a page. I presumed the person was supposed to be the king, but wondered why he had been reduced to nothing more than a haze. Malise looked toward the form and smiled, leaning toward him and planting a kiss where a person's face should have been. There was an eerie slowness to her motion, like transitioning between pictures of a slideshow.

"Why can't we see the king?" Thalia asked. Malise laughed, her voice sending warmth to my very heart instead of the dread it had caused before. However, the laughter, just like her movements, was distorted. It sounded very echoic and distant.

"Because I have never seen him," Alem replied, sounding almost disappointed. "Nobody has seen the king since this whole conflict began."

"That doesn't make sense," I said, unsatisfied with his answer. "If everything's just a part of our imagination, that means we created him. We should be able to see him."

Alem looked over to me, his head bobbing up and down, amused by my displeasure. "Not even I have answers to everything, Kail," he said humbly.

Suddenly villagers filled the hallway all around us, cheering and dancing. They all looked the same as the ones we had seen murdered, but they did not have the brands on their chests. There were women this time, whose looks matched that of the men's. There seemed to be a celebration going on.

"Long ago," Alem began in a storytelling voice that reminded me of the teachers I had in school, "there was peace throughout the land. The people all adored their rulers, who in turn treated them with the utmost generosity. Queen Malise and King Morpheus were the first to ever fully unite the land under one rule, ending an untold number of years of conflict. Regular celebrations such as this were held in this hallway. They, unlike their predecessors, promoted equality."

Villagers dressed in white fancy clothing walked around the dancing villagers, offering them fresh fruit and drinks. Laughter and voices of happiness reverberated off the polished walls. Everything still felt slow, and even more dreamlike than they had been back in the dream world. Malise looked over her people with great delight in her eyes, waving and smiling blissfully. What could possibly have happened to disrupt such peace?

"Then one day," Alem continued, "something was brought forth to the King and Queen's attention that changed everything."

As quickly as the party had assembled, they faded away, leaving the hall empty. Malise was now standing in front of her throne. A look of worry had taken over from the carefree look she had earlier. She rubbed her hands together nervously, looking toward us. For a moment I thought she could see us, but I was quickly corrected as a villager ran through me. He passed right through me as if I didn't actually exist, like I was a ghost. The rest of the group stared at me, stupefied by my phantom nature.

"Remember," Alem said, suppressing his laughter, "none of this is real. You cannot control anything you see here. There is a fire pit in the middle of a castle, for goodness' sake."

"Well, excuse me," I retorted, "but this whole place doesn't exactly fit what we call 'real' back home."

"Reality is what you make of it, Kail," Alem stated. "You will come to understand that."

“What’s that supposed to mean?” I asked, unaware of what he was implying.

“Two villagers had stumbled across something on their travels in the mountains,” Alem continued, ignoring my question. “It was unlike anything seen before in this land.”

I turned and saw two villagers carrying a large stone tablet on their backs. The tablet was tied to them, but greatly overshadowed their size. I did not see how it was possible that only two men could carry such a massive object, but decided it probably didn’t matter. They walked right on through my friends and me, kneeling before Malise. Her eyes scanned over the surface and her face became very grave. There was something about it that she didn’t like.

Kanoa walked forward to get a better look, and the rest of us quickly followed. I stood right next to Malise, looking up at her anxiously. It felt so weird to stand beside someone like her, knowing she couldn’t see me. I expected her to reach out and grab me at any moment, but that moment never came. Her eyes remained transfixed by the stone slab. I followed her gaze and was puzzled by what I saw.

Carved deeply into the surface of the shimmering stone was a high cliff with someone standing at its edge, their face overlooking a massive portion of land. All across the entire land stood hundreds upon hundreds of people, staring up at the person with their hands in the air. In the person’s outstretched hand was a magnificently bright object, one that shone out over the land with an ardent glow. He held the sun in the palm of his hand.

Before I had finished soaking in all the details of the image on the tablet, it vanished away with the villagers, although Malise stood still. Her expression had once again changed, this time from grave to distress. Her once-lively face had faded ever so slightly, her orb now off-white.

“Malise had ordered that the stone be hidden away, never to be seen by anyone again,” Alem continued, “but things of value never remain hidden for long. Rumours began circulating throughout the land of what was now being hailed as prophecy. Some villages even went so far as to begin worshipping it as an oracle, disbanding their allegiance with Malise and Morpheus. Most remained loyal, but the minority was very vocal. It is strange to think that strength isn’t always found in numbers, but in determination itself. They said that a god was to descend upon them and lead them into a land of unfathomable joy and riches. You see, the mind can be a very fickle thing. What is new or different has a way of overshadowing what is good, and thus it is taken for granted. There were revolts.”

The quiet hall erupted with shouts and screams. I looked out to where there had been once dancing and singing to find angry villagers shaking their fists against their rulers and gnashing their teeth in rebellion. Malise looked to Morpheus for comfort, but she seemed to receive none. Tears streamed down her face, draining even more colour with them.

"Morpheus himself believed this prophecy had great power and should not be ignored," Alem went on. "Despite Malise's pleas that all conversation of the prophecy be suppressed, Morpheus would not listen. He did not understand why she saw an enemy, when he saw an ally. He said the only thing worse than losing his kingdom's favour would be oppressing it."

The angry mob evaporated and was replaced with Malise and the four that had helped her destroy the last village of the land. Malise was now very pale, as was her clothing, her orb now dark. She was beginning to look like the evil I had seen discard so many lives so easily. I no longer felt any warmth within me when I looked at her. All I felt was cold.

"Malise gathered the four most influential and respected members of the kingdom by her side in order to overthrow the king for his negligence of the uprising," Alem explained. "She used her highly regarded persuasion skills to bring them to her side. Everyone has their price, and Malise bought their loyalty. Together they formed the strongest alliance the land had ever seen."

Everyone in the scene before us seemed to be frozen, other than Malise. She was speaking to the king passionately, yet Morpheus remained passively sitting in his throne. Thalia decided to take Malise's seat next to him, as her legs had grown tired from standing so long. She pretended to be the new queen and actually didn't look half bad in the role. Queen Thalia.

Alem glided over to the alliance and examined them carefully. Their appearances, like their queen's, had changed from what we had been introduced to. They didn't feel like nightmares just yet.

"There was The Illusionist," Alem said, looking up at one of the men standing behind Malise. "He was the one you saw change that hut into a never-ending hole and laughed while he did it."

The Illusionist was quite a different person than what I had seen before. His eyes were a normal white, his mouth in a closed smile, his lips extending no farther than my own. His skin was pale, but not sickly. His hair was cut short and there were no holes in his top hat. His clothes were rather faintly coloured—yellow and brown, but not nearly as dark or grotesque as they had been before. There were no red smiley faces on his coat, and his toes remained inside his shoes. He almost looked like a respectable person instead of a twisted, maniacal monster.

"He was once a master of illusions, supplying the kingdom with wonder and entertainment," Alem explained, circling The Illusionist. "Some said he could even perform miracles to save people from illness or danger. Not everyone in the land enjoyed his company, however. There were those who would corner him in alleys and beat him harshly, citing that his games were merely distractions to the working-class citizen of which he would be given higher wages. He was found by Malise at the castle's front gate, bleeding and on the edge of death. He was employed as the royal entertainment shortly after. These days, he has an uncanny ability to warp his surroundings to any of his twisted whims. Malise is said to have promised him the biggest audience an entertainer could imagine if he joined her. I wouldn't say what he does to villagers nowadays is much fun for them, but as long as he is tricking people, he could not care less. He is not much of a fighter, but he can make you become lost within the complexities of your own mind when in his presence."

As Alem's explanation of The Illusionist ended, I noticed the man finally reveal his sinister smile, his white teeth glinting mischievously.

"Next up on our trip down memory lane," Alem said, walking over to the man standing beside The Illusionist, "is The General. He was the one you saw, or did not see for that matter, kill all those people in the blink of an eye."

There was no change in the man's appearance since we had seen him last. He stood just as elegantly as before, his eyes focused solely on Malise.

"Why does he look the same as before?" Cora asked.

"Well, if you would let me finish," Alem said, cutting her down. Cora shot him a look of aversion, which was met with a laugh. "I am only kidding. The reason he looks the same as when you saw him, Cora, is because he did not join Malise for the same reasons the others did. While the others joined for fame or fortune, things of corruption and greed, The General joined because of his unspoken love for Malise."

"He loved the queen?" Thalia asked. It was a rather surprising development. I now noticed the desire in his eyes as he stared at his zealous queen. He wanted her for himself.

"He was the leader of the Drephorium army. He trained his whole life, partaking in countless battles to keep his queen safe, never once feeling the sting of a blade. The people of the land say he is untouchable, not just by the sword. Many women had approached him for their own, but his focus never faltered, no matter how great the temptation."

"Jeez, I wish I had that problem," Osias muttered, which was once again met with the jabbing of Thalia's elbow into his ribs.

"He ensured that the kingdom never fell once under her rule," Alem went on, "and quickly rose through the ranks and eventually reached the top, where his skill was admired by his fellow soldiers. He never cared, however, as his only goal in life was obtaining her love. He fought for the hope that one day they would be together. He still fights for that purpose, I believe. Unlike the others of the Forgotten Four, his love was pure. For who is there to decide what love truly is but pure? There were even whispers that they were romantically involved."

At that moment, Malise quickly glanced backwards toward The General, who nodded to her coolly. She smiled back at him faintly, her eyes welling up with tears that she fought back, returning her words to the king. The General clenched his jaw and closed his eyes peacefully.

"Nevertheless," Alem continued, "it was no mystery that The General's talents were grand. It is said that no one person who challenges him, does so without the knowledge that it means their doom."

"Oh, that's really encouraging," Osias muttered again.

Thalia turned and gave him a very nasty look. He ran his fingers across his lips, pretending to zip them shut, and then threw away the invisible key with a smile. Thalia looked away and Osias rolled his eyes.

"Oh, don't worry," Alem replied, "they only get worse. That brings me to The Artist, the one who looked like a statue and started the fire."

Alem then walked over to the only female member of The Forgotten Four. She no longer had a mask for a face or stone for a body. She was a real person, just like me. Her face was severe; high cheekbones, a narrow chin and pointed eyes. Although her face wasn't a mask, it definitely reminded me of one. Her brown hair was brought up in a messy bun, held together with small paint brushes. Her body was ideal, busty and well-pronounced. She wore a tight red dress shirt and black tights. Her attire paled in comparison to Malise's or The General's, meaning she was probably not the wealthiest of the group. Despite her seemingly misfit and messy appearance, she fit right into the mismatched cast of characters.

"She had more talent with a brush than words could ever do justice," Alem continued. "Even when she was a child, she would spend hours in front of a canvas, turning them into masterpieces. Unfortunately, her parents were very poor, which meant she would go into forests and spend days finding the perfect material for her brushes, for store-bought brushes were not adequate tools of greatness in her eyes. She was once found inside the royal gardens, destroying plant life for her constructions. She was brought before the King and Queen and told to fill their halls with her paintings, or face the consequences of her crimes. Within a day she had completed the task, to the surprise of Malise and Morpheus. She was hired by the castle shortly after. Any villager who was privileged enough to have their eyes fall upon her paintings became fans instantly."

Adora walked over to an enormous portrait of Malise standing beside an empty white splotch, presumably where Morpheus was supposed to be standing. The level of detail was astounding. Each eyelash of Malise was distinct and lush. The colours were so vibrant that it was almost unbelievable to think it wasn't a high-definition digital photograph. The depth present in the frame gave the illusion that the painting actually extended into the wall. It was the most beautiful painting I had ever seen, and it had been completed in less than a day.

“She painted this?” Adora asked, mystified at its magnificence. The entire hallway was full of equally impressive paintings; some of people, some of the castle and some of the world outside these walls. Every single one was worth laying my eyes upon.

“Yes, she did,” Alem replied, “but she does not paint as she used to.”

“Yeah, she sure has gotten a lot worse,” Kanoa mumbled, standing close to The Artist, his hands passing through her as he tried to touch her face.

“I would not say she has gotten any worse, Kanoa,” Alem countered. “She has the ability to bring her creations to life now. Malise promised her that if she were to join her, she would never have to worry about money or consequences for her creations ever again. Not only that, her talents would grow exponentially.”

“As fun as all that sounds,” Kanoa said, uninterested in Alem’s argument, “I saw what she did in that village, and I would not call that beautiful.”

“It’s a matter of perspective, Kanoa,” Alem persisted, apparently unaware that Kanoa was not paying attention. “Let me give you an example. You tell three artists to paint the sun setting over an ocean near a sandy beach. One focuses on the beach, one focuses on the ocean, and the last focuses on the sun. It isn’t that one painter is right and the others are wrong in what they saw, they all just find beauty different in the world. It is simply unfortunate that she now finds that beauty in misery.”

“Beauty in misery, huh,” Kanoa repeated dreamily. The Artist then sneezed, which caused Kanoa to stumble back in surprise. He laughed nervously and strutted back toward the rest of us.

“Speaking of misery,” Alem said, slowly dragging his focus away from Kanoa and toward the last member of The Forgotten Four. “That brings me the final member of The Forgotten Four. He is known as The Torturer, and for good reason. He was the one you saw conjure the spiders and drown that man in the box.”

The Torturer stood tall among his companions, muscular and rigid. His face was no longer concealed, granting me a look into the monster’s eyes. His dark eyes were cold and unforgiving, and his square jaw shut tight. His brown hair was matted to his skull, unkempt and dirty. Instead of chains on his body, he wore a white sleeveless shirt, revealing his large, scarred frame. He wore thick brown leather pants and black work boots. Although he wasn’t nearly as nerve-wracking as before, there was still a certain air about him, as if he wasn’t helping Malise for any reason but his own. The others, despite their own prowess and abilities, seemed nervous around him. In this case, the enemy of my enemy was certainly not my friend.

“He was tasked with handling the most severe punishments in the kingdom,” Alem explained, “but before the time of the prophecy, his work had been few and far between. The scars you see on his body are self-inflicted, reflections of his own boredom. It is well-known that Malise, in the beginning, only chose him to be a part of her group as a scare tactic, unlike the others who were well liked or highly regarded. The truth was, she was just as afraid of him as her people. She gave him the empty promise that if he were to join her cause, he would be granted all the work he could ever dream of. Unfortunately, she ended up fulfilling her promise to him. Other than Malise herself, he will be the greatest challenge you face. His powers are perilous—delving into your worst nightmares and fears, bringing them to life in horrifying fashion."

"Well, that's okay," Kanoa said, "because I'm not afraid of anything, so let him do his worst."

"Oh, don't worry, Kanoa," Alem replied. "He will. And he will likely teach you a thing or two about yourself while he does it."

A chill crept up my spine as I stared into his dead eyes. He didn't shift his stance, his eyes didn't stir, and he didn't even seem to breathe. He just stood completely still. The horrors that hovered within his head filled me with dread. I wondered what fears he could use against me, and if I would be able to overcome them. My life had certainly given him enough material to work with.

"Malise's request to the king fell on deaf ears," Alem continued. "He would not become the tyrant she wanted him to be. Malise was heartbroken."

Something struck me about Malise's sadness. It hurt me in a way I could only describe as my insides decaying. I didn't know why I felt that way. Perhaps it was because such beauty should not have to feel such pain.

Malise then stopped talking, her eyes filling with black tears, which ran down her face and splashed down on the red carpet. The carpet's colour began to drain, but Malise did not notice as she turned away from her husband and ran toward the doorway. The colour of the entire room began to fade away, spreading like a virus. The Forgotten Four stared at their ruler once more before following after their distraught queen. The schism had been formed, and the path to darkness had begun.

"Malise decided then that Morpheus had lost his mind and was no longer fit to run their kingdom," Alem continued, following after The Forgotten Four and Malise. We stuck close to him as we left the hallway and stood outside its doorway. We were standing outside the castle now, its pristine white walls fading to the darkness we had seen on top of that hill in the real world. Malise's sorrow was spreading through her once-beloved kingdom. "Malise ordered for the doors to be closed forever, locking away her king, her memories, and all that was good within her. It was a betrayal that nobody could have ever seen coming."

Malise shouted out to her cohorts, and they began closing the great wooden doors. The doors slammed shut, echoing loudly. She then drew forth a key from her pocket and walked toward the door, locking it.

"No one except Malise herself knows where the key to the kingdom is hidden," Alem said gravely. Malise turned to face us, her once-troubled face now grim and solemn. She held the key in front of her face. It was shaped as a question mark, symbolizing its mysterious nature, I supposed. It then disintegrated in her fingers, being taken away by the wind. "The castle has not been opened, or seen for that matter, since that dark day."

Our surroundings once again began to shift and churn. We rose high into the sky, leaving Malise and The Forgotten Four far below us. It felt as if I was falling into the sky, my stomach filling with butterflies. We were standing on a cloud, the fireplace still with us on our journey. The cloud's surface felt spongy and bouncy. Adora grabbed at it, but once again was disappointed to discover her hand slide through it. Alem walked to the edge of the cloud and looked down back toward the ground.

"Her reign then began," he said, speaking tenderly, "and Drephoria became quiet, only awakened with the screams of the free. She moved quickly, rendering each village as defenceless as the last."

My friends and I lightly stepped over toward the edge of the cloud to meet Alem's gaze. The atmosphere above us was dark and impenetrable, yet we were the only cloud visible in the sky. I peeked my head over the cloud and was instantly struck by vertigo. I stepped back and took a deep breath to settle my stomach.

"Yeah, you guys can tell me about this later," Osias grumbled, covering his eyes, "I'm not too good with heights."

I tried again to partake in the heavenly view of the land. The mountains we had once passed under when traversing the underwater cave loomed off in the distance, blocking out anything that lay behind them. All that was visible from beneath us was the castle looking over forests, lakes, villages, plains, bridges, and all the other inhabitants of Drephoria. I watched over the land like its guardian, suddenly coming to terms with the idea that I had helped create everything I saw. I was an angel; a god in a cloud admiring his work.

"Malise and The Forgotten Four went to every village," Alem explained, "and demanded their adherence to her rule. Those who refused paid with their lives."

From far below I watched as Malise and her followers decimated village after village, burning their existence from memory in rapid fell swoops. There was no hesitation. Death was brought to those who asked for it. Every time she moved, darkness followed, the land becoming sparse and dead. The people that had once adored their queen were now experiencing her vengeful wrath.

“There were those who pledged their allegiance to their queen,” Alem said, “but they were not spared from agony.”

Malise reached some villages, and instead of flames and screams, there were only screams. She brandished a large metal pole with the diamond marking at its tip. The M that symbolized Malise herself floated in the middle of the diamond. She admired the marking before pressing it into the chests of her loyal supporters, burning her mark upon them. It was either death or eternal cruelty that faced these people. I think I would have preferred death.

“Malise and The Forgotten Four quickly lost sight of their corrupt goal,” Alem continued, a hint of anger in his usual calm tone, “and became consumed with a lust for power. For them, the achievement of power only strengthened their desire for more. This never-ending cycle twisted their bodies, minds and souls. They no longer cared for their people. They only cared for absolute dominance. The land had been torn apart by itself.”

The five fiends below us began to transform into the monsters we had seen firsthand. The Illusionist’s smile stretched across his sickly face, and his clothes became dark. The General remained the same hopeless soul he had been, still running after a love that could never be obtained; looking for a heart that didn’t have room for him. The Artist’s skin hardened, her body turning to stone and her face to porcelain, paint brushes protruding from her back. The Torturer’s shirt extended into chains and consumed his body, his face now hidden within the abyss of his hood. Malise was now the suffocating white queen, her compassion lost. Hatred and pain were what filled her essence now. The whole land before us was devoured, becoming nothing more than a firestorm of death. Cries of pain were engulfed in frenzied laughter. Our peaceful land had been destroyed by nothing more than words. No war had caused this, no depression or land shortage. The killing blows had been delivered by the mouth, not the sword.

“And that is how my story ends,” Alem finished, his tone returning to normal. “Well, your story, actually. What do you think?”

Our cloudy platform faded away, as did the inferno beneath us and the ones who had caused it. We were back standing around our little campfire in the forest, the warm sun dragging out the coldness that had filled me. Peaceful sounds of the forest filled my ears, and the organic smell of plant life entered my nose. It felt as though I had never left this place at all.

Nobody answered Alem’s question, so he let it sink in for a moment, looking around at each of us hopefully. Everyone, myself included, were still stunned by what we had seen. I didn’t even know how to begin analyzing the story; our story.

“Pretty interesting imagination we have, guys,” Thalia said with a nervous laugh.

"Uh, yeah," Osias replied. "I mean, it was a little cliché in parts, but it was flashy and well told. I'd give it about an eight out of ten."

A discomfited wave of laughter washed over our group, lightening the mood considerably. Alem joined in on the fun, but began gliding away from us back toward his path to the supposed training ground.

"Alem, don't ya think you could give us a break?" Cora said, slouching over tiredly. "I don't know about everyone else, but I'm still a little shook up."

"I am aware what I have shown you must have been a little rattling," Alem said patiently, "but the longer we wait around, the more likely it is that Malise will catch on to your presence here. We must make haste."

Cora sighed, standing back up and shrugging submissively. We all began to follow behind Alem once again. I lagged behind for a moment to put out the fire. A quick flash of déjà vu struck me as I remembered myself staying behind at the campsite. I took a second to look around, considering what we would have been doing if Kanoa had never found the castle in the first place. Would we packing up the tents by now? Would we be hiking back into town? Would I be home by now?

"Hey, Alem!" I shouted, running to catch up to the rest of the group. "Did that prophecy ever come true?"

"No, the prophecy was long forgotten," Alem replied, almost sounding as if he was laughing at my question. "Until today, that is."

"Why is today so special?" Adora asked. "Is today some sort of anniversary?"

Alem stopped moving abruptly, causing everyone to bump into one another and allowing me to catch up. "Isn't it obvious by now?" he asked.

My heart began beating rapidly, beginning to realize what he was implying and why he had told us the story in the first place. "Alem," I said slowly, "who was that person in the prophecy supposed to be?"

Alem laughed and turned to me, his head tilted to the side. "Oh, Kail," he said. "Why do you think those villagers kneeled back there? Cramps in their legs?"

"This isn't funny," I said, standing over the man who was embellishing far too much in suspense.

"The person in the prophecy," he answered, stifling his amusement, "the one who was foreseen as saving the land and bringing them to eternal bliss…is you, Kail."

CHAPTER 7: OWN WORST ENEMY

My friends and I followed behind Alem, who had apparently decided not to talk any further until we had reached his destination. Revealing that I was the supposed prophet of the land had left me a little confused and unsettled. I had never been a leader. That was more Kanoa's thing. He was the one obsessed with being a legend, not me. I wasn't sure how well I would perform with that kind of responsibility. I had done such a bad job with looking after my sister, how badly would I do with an entire nation?

Everyone seemed quite fascinated with my newfound status. Everyone except Kanoa. He seemed understandably disappointed that it had been me instead of him.

"And maybe that's why I can't hold your weapon, but you can hold mine," Cora chimed in. Some pieces of this puzzle were starting to fall into place. I looked again at the markings on my hands and remembered their similarity to that of the villagers. I guess I really was the one carved into the stone.

"Yeah, well, it isn't all fun and games," Kanoa sneered. "He might as well have a huge target painted on his head for Malise and her friends to see."

"Kanoa," I said, hanging back for a moment to talk to him. Unlike the rest of my friends who had been admiring my weapon and wanting to know what it felt like to be a hero, Kanoa seemed to not have any interest. "It's not like I chose for this to happen. We all know that you are the leader of this group. Don't worry about it, okay?"

He smiled faintly and nodded his head. "Yeah I know," he said, laughing nonchalantly. "I still have your back if you get into any trouble. I just wish I could use that weapon of yours."

He grabbed it off my back and held it in his hands for a moment, marvelling at its unique design and brilliant colouring. It then slid out of his grasp and fell back into mine. I shrugged my shoulders apologetically, and he huffed angrily.

"Does it ever bother you not having eyes or ears or... basically anything else, Alem? It must suck being old, doesn't it?" I heard Thalia ask with a twinge of annoyance in her voice.

Thalia had always had a kind of anxiety and loathing for all things old, including people. Age annoyed her for some reason that none of her friends could ever figure out. When we asked her why she was so short-fused with old people, or why she threw out her belongings that she deemed "ancient," she would snap at us and say that 'they frustrated her.'

"No it doesn't bother me," he replied without remorse or agitation, possibly understanding my friend's disposition toward age. "I have no need for them, so why should it matter? Being old isn't so bad, either. You'll see one day."

"I better not," she muttered.

"Hey, Alem," Osias interrupted. "Doesn't it get tiring holding your arms behind your back like that? I've only been doing it for the past couple minutes and it's already starting to wear on me."

I noticed that Alem was holding his arms rather high behind his back, and that Osias was copying his behaviour. Alem laughed at the question and without turning around, the sleeves covering his arms pulled back. Hiding beneath the fabric was what looked like a single arm extending all the way across his back. It looked as though his two arms conjoined in the middle where his hands were supposed to be. I guess that's why he never used his hands for anything.

"Well, that's disturbing," Osias muttered, lowering his hands from his back.

"I also don't have any legs or feet, if you were wondering why I can move across this rough terrain so easily," he stated. "I would raise my robe to show you that I am indeed floating, but I think I have frightened you enough for one day."

"Believe me," Cora said, pushing out pained laughter. "Those monsters we saw back at the village have freaked me out a lot more than you probably ever could."

"Perhaps," Alem chuckled, "but that is precisely why I am bringing you to this training ground. To help you overcome those monsters. Speaking of which, we have arrived, my apprentices."

We finally emerged from the forest and entered an open plain. The sky overhead was filled with clouds that fluttered across the sphere of the world like pages of a book passing by in the wind. The clock that represented what I thought to be the sun had stopped for some reason, possibly granting us more time to complete whatever goals Alem had for us. The plain, as Alem had mentioned, was cluttered up with hills. However, the hills were a little bit different than the ones back in the real world. These ground formations were made completely out of mounds of books.

"I thought you said hills, Alem," I said, confused by our new surroundings. "These are piles of books."

"Oh, whatever," Alem replied. "If I wasted my time with details, then we wouldn't get anything done."

The hills popped up as far as my eyes could see, like a graveyard of literature. Their masses varied. Some were no taller than Alem, while others extended far into the sky. The books themselves were all the same: large, leather-bound, with bright white pages. There were probably more books here than I had ever seen in my life. I wondered what they contained, realizing that Alem would soon answer my unspoken question.

"To answer your unspoken question, Kail, Osias and Cora," Alem said, finally standing still and looking forward at the book-beleaguered grassland. "Those books are filled with your memories. All of your memories."

I scanned the landscape again, wondering how only six people could have so much information regarding their lives. It would take lifetimes upon lifetimes for someone to read every page of every book on this field, yet we had managed to store everything in such a short time. I supposed the mind really was the greatest mystery man had never solved.

"All of our memories, huh?" Adora repeated dreamily. None of us had dared to move forward, and even Alem had not walked, or floated, into the books piles. It almost seemed too surreal to be a part of.

"So this is what a field of memories looks like," Thalia said, laughter expressing her amazement. "I always thought our brains had some sort of limit, ya know? Like we would run out of room up there."

"Actually, Thalia," Osias replied. "It has been suggested in the fields of psychology that the mind is an ever-expanding, unlimited storage space. I would love for one of them to see this."

"Yeah, well, this is our world," Kanoa stated. "Nobody can take that away from us."

"Yes, well as much fun as it is listening to you six marvel at what I have seen more times than I care to tell you," Alem said, "I would like it if we actually continued walking and began your training. Pretty please?"

He glided forward into the piles of books and motioned for us to follow. Kanoa was the first, with Adora right behind him. The rest of us followed behind them, running our hands over the fine leather that bound the books. Some mounds towered over us, shading us within their stature. Their number was immeasurable. Every library in the world probably didn't contain this much information.

"So are these organized, Alem?" Adora asked. She had picked a book up and begun reading through it.

"No, I don't think so," Alem replied. "They all seem to have just massed themselves in whichever way they pleased. I thought that maybe each pile was specific to one of you, but you all seem to share so many memories with one another that the books just kind of mesh together."

"Oh," Adora said, reading the book she had picked up intently. "Thalia, I think someone here has a crush on you."

I looked over to Thalia, who began blushing with a curious smile on her face. She skipped over to her sister, who had a big smile on her childlike face, and leaned in to read the book.

"Today was a fairly interesting day. After school, Thalia and I worked on our history project together and there was a moment when we both went to pick up the same pencil. Our hands bumped into each other, and I swear my heart..."

Osias ran over to where the two sisters were reading the book, tore it out of their hands and threw it out over one of the higher piles of books before anyone had time to react. His face was redder than I had ever seen it before, and he was breathing heavily. There was an awkward moment of silence as we all stared at him.

"Ah, that's too bad, I wonder how it ended," he muttered, heatedly turning away from Thalia and Adora, rubbing the back of his neck nervously. Thalia's mouth was wide open in shock, her purple eyes flashed with excitement. Adora giggled and nudged her sister.

Kanoa suppressed his laughter and elbowed me in the side to get my attention, "Yikes," he whispered. "That's not embarrassing at all."

"Yeah, no kidding," I said, also trying to hold back my amusement. "I wonder whose that could have been."

"Read as you go, people," Alem urged of us, turning away from us and continuing on his way. "You may have your fun, but let us not lose sight of our goal here."

"Yeah, and let's show everyone some privacy," I insisted. "Read your own books."

Everyone agreed and began rummaging through the piles of books, looking for interesting pieces of their past while still following closely behind our leader. I sincerely hoped that everyone kept to their word and respected the rules of confidentiality. I doubted that anyone wanted to hear about my past unless I actually told them, anyway. It would be cheating.

I decided not to look for any of my own memories as I didn't feel like accidentally running across something I didn't want to read. Being surrounded by so many things I despised left a sour taste in my mouth. I wished that no books had belonged to me. With my luck, the first book I picked up would be of my darkest moments. And since I had quite a few of them, it was best that I just didn't risk it.

"Wow," Kanoa said in disbelief. "I can't believe I still remember that time I ran over to your house after I had that nightmare. Do you remember that, Kail?"

I laughed and nodded. "You mean the time where you were convinced that an ogre was living in your backyard, and that you needed my help to kill it?"

He laughed loudly and nodded his head. "Yeah, that's the one. It was probably just a raccoon or something, but I was so sure it was an ogre! Aw, man, that's too funny." He looked back at the book and the smile quickly faded from his face, replaced by a look of confusion. "Hey, do you remember what happened after we got back to my house?"

I thought for a moment, and then remembered how the story ended. "Um, yeah I'm pretty sure your parents woke up and found us in your backyard with shovels and butter knives. We got grounded for a solid week. That, and your parents hid the butter knives for a while."

Kanoa sighed and shook his head in frustration. I walked over and looked down into his book. After the part where Kanoa woke up and ran over to my house to retrieve me, there was just a blank page. The story cut off after that.

"I don't remember that at all," he whispered.

I looked up to his frowning face and felt sorry for him for a moment. While I hated my memories, Kanoa felt the exact opposite. These were the types of things that mattered the most to him. My guess was that there weren't very many books belonging to Kanoa regarding theories and equations. These tiny moments, these trivial pieces of his past, were the high points of a frustratingly uneventful life. He probably abhorred the fact that he had let this one memory slip away.

"Don't worry about it, Kanoa," I said with a pat on the back. "I'm sure there are a lot more stories where that came from."

"Yeah." He exhaled slowly, looking at me with determination in his eyes. "I'm sure you're right."

I then noticed that Cora was reading a book with great interest. In fact, she was a little too concentrated on the book, as if she didn't know what was in it. A flare of nervousness shot through my stomach. She had to have been reading from one of my books.

"What's that you've got there, Cora?" I asked on the edges of menace.

She jumped a little, startled by my sudden presence. She quickly closed the book and placed it on the top of a small pile beside her. She looked back at me anxiously and smiled.

"Nothing," she lied. "I was just reading something I had sworn wasn't a part of my memory anymore."

"You're a terrible liar," I spat, picking up the book she had put away and rifled through the pages. I quickly realized that it belonged to me.

"Hey!" she yelled, insulted. "I am normally a fairly decent liar! You just caught me off guard."

"Could have sworn we agreed not to read each other's books, Cora," I said angrily, trying to avoid eye contact and focus on what was in the book. But I couldn't.

"I'm sorry," she said, pulling my hands down away from the book to look me in the eyes. "But I promise I didn't read anything you wouldn't have wanted me to."

I looked in her eyes for any deceit. I had gotten pretty good at reading people through the emotion in their eyes. It was the one thing that was unable to lie to me. I knew the sounds escaping from someone's mouth could be deceiving, a person's actions could be treacherous, and even their intentions falsified. The eyes, on the other hand, just as Cora's were at this moment, were true to their core.

"So what did you read, then?" I asked, subduing my anger.

Her face twitched back to a smile for a moment, but quickly faded away. She seemed embarrassed by whatever it was as she rubbed her hands together nervously. She sighed heavily and looked up with some sort of newfound courage.

"I was just reading about something you did for me a few years ago," she said. "Remember that year I went to band camp for half the summer?"

I remembered it. It was probably the longest time we had ever spent apart. Cora took her singing pretty seriously, as she did with most things that she cared about, but had a bad case of stage fright. The only way she could get up on stage and perform was if she knew she had other people up on stage with her. So she decided to go to band camp and see if she could find some band mates. It didn't work out in the end, and Cora had pretty much given up on singing since then. I would only occasionally hear her voice, and that's when she didn't notice anyone else was around. She had a beautiful voice, one that I wished she had the courage to show to the world.

"Yeah, I remember," I said. "I also remember you giving up on your singing career."

"Yes, well," she said hesitantly, "sometimes people have to grow up and get serious about their lives. Anyway, that isn't what I was talking about."

I never understood why people gave up on their dreams. I always thought it was a waste to have a dream, only to give up on it later. Especially Cora of all people, who never let things just slide away from her. I personally had never really thought about having a dream of my own. The only things I ever wanted out of life were things that I knew could easily be real: finding my sister a loving family, and keeping my friends safe. Unfortunately, life wasn't very kind to me.

"What is it, then?" I asked, making sure we were close enough to the rest of the group to not get lost, but far enough that we were out of earshot.

"Well, before I left for camp," she said, now smiling radiantly, her eyes full of warmth, "do you remember what you did for me? So that if I was ever homesick, I could quickly feel safe?"

"Of course I remember," I nodded with a smile, my cheeks noticeably flushing red. "I made you a CD recording of myself watching your favourite movie. I thought it was so stupid. All you could hear was the movie, and sometimes I would talk over it. I just thought it would be nice to listen to when you went to sleep, is all."

"Kail," she said, her eyes sparkling warmly. "That was the nicest thing anyone has ever done for me. Anytime I felt scared or alone, I would rush back to my lodge and listen to it. It meant a lot to me that you did that."

"But you couldn't even see anything!" I insisted.

"I didn't need to," she replied. "Just because I can't see you, doesn't mean I don't know that you're there for me."

I laughed quietly and shook my head. I didn't understand myself sometimes. How could I have done something like that for someone I supposedly didn't even trust? There was something about this place that made me think more about my life. More specifically, all the things I had done wrong with it. If I could just go back and try again...

"Don't mention it," I said with a shrug, a light mist filling my eyes. "I just thought it would have been something you might have liked."

I began walking away, as I could no longer hold the conversation without getting myself humiliated. I heard her laugh behind me and clear her throat, clearly affected as much as I had been by the exchange.

"What's my favourite movie again, Kail?" I heard her ask, barely audible. Our backs were still turned to one another, but I could feel the weight of an entire friendship's worth of rage and love in her words.

"Eternal Sunshine of the Spotless Mind," I answered instantaneously. "What's mine again?"

"You never told me, remember?" she replied. I stopped walking and tilted my head to the ground in revulsion. How had I not even had the courtesy to tell one of my closest friends my favourite movie?

"Oh," I muttered. "Well, I guess..."

"Would it be possible for you two to continue this conversation when you aren't being hunted down by a murderous queen and her equally unpleasant henchmen?" Alem asked, interrupting me.

"Yeah, I suppose that's all right," Cora responded, quickly brushing past me and following the small man.

I sighed heavily to myself, alone in piles of memories. Memories nobody but I knew about. I looked around, wondering how much I had chosen not to share, and how different my life could have been if I had.

"That means you too, Kail!" I heard Alem call out.

I snapped out of my thoughts and quickly sprinted over to where I had heard his voice. The group had assembled in a relatively symmetrical circle opening within the book piles. Alem stood in the middle and moved his head around, as if scanning our faces, wondering if we were ready for whatever training he had mentioned. He was a very twitchy character.

"Yes, Kail," he said with a laugh. "I believe that you are ready for your training. Not as if you have much of a choice, anyway."

"So spill it," Kanoa said. He clearly didn't enjoy the fact that his time in this place was being wasted on lessons. He wanted to be exploring the world and fulfilling every dream he'd ever had. "What do you want us to do?"

Alem suddenly took great notice of Kanoa and went over to him. He studied my friend intently, tilting his head back and forth. He then spoke softly and slowly. "Do you find that what I am doing here is a waste of your time, Kanoa?"

"Yeah I do, actually," he replied without hesitation. "I should be flying over treetops and fighting things with this sword."

He raised his sword and swung it around in the air above Alem's head. Alem didn't flinch. He simply waited for Kanoa to stop so that he could continue what he was going to say. I was positive that Alem had a point to prove to Kanoa, whether Kanoa wanted to hear it or not.

"Kanoa," Alem began with prudence present in his voice. "Can you tell me what you did when you were in the real world?"

"What do you mean?" Kanoa asked, lowering his sword.

"How did you deal with the real world if you are this... unfocused in this world?" he asked again.

I exchanged glances with the rest of the group to discover we were all wondering the same thing: where was Alem going with this? I hoped he knew what he was doing, as confusing Kanoa wasn't the smartest idea.

Kanoa was silent for a moment. He then cleared his throat and noticeably tried to avoid eye contact with everyone. "I, um... I pretended a lot."

I had always had a feeling that Kanoa only enjoyed some things in our world because it was expected of him. He always seemed distant at parties and in the classroom. It felt like he wished he were somewhere else, and that he was bored with his surroundings. I had caught him on many occasions faking a smile, and I knew I wasn't the only one. Adora was the only one who would actually call him on it, though. If he was pretending, Adora would let him know that she knew.

"But one thing that did hold true with you," Alem said, "was your friends, right? And they are here with you now, Kanoa. So it would appear that you get the best of both worlds."

"I wish this was my world, though," Kanoa muttered.

"And what about me, Kanoa?" Adora asked, her voice wavering ever so slightly. She stood in front of Alem and stared right into Kanoa's distant eyes. This was probably the most upset I had ever seen her. "Am I a part of this new world of yours? You always say that you care about your friends, about me. Was that just pretend, too?"

Kanoa quickly snapped out of his thoughts. He looked right into Adora's eyes and smiled faintly, his face aching with conflict. I knew that he wanted both—his dreams and his friends living in harmony. He bent down a little to meet her eyes, putting his hand on her shoulder.

"Are you kidding?" he said with soft determination in his voice. "You guys are the highlight of my life. Especially you, Adora. Especially you."

"Remember what we promised," she whispered. "If you can't get what you want, you can get me."

I saw Adora flash her ethereal smile and then hug Kanoa quite suddenly. He was surprised for a moment, and his arms remained outstretched. He then smiled and held Adora tight, his face brimming with joy. I smiled too. It was a rare moment of Kanoa enjoying something that wasn't make-believe. She was something real he could hold onto.

"Ah, isn't that sweet," Alem said before quickly changing his tone. "But seriously, we can all join in one big group hug after we stop the ones who would sooner eat you than hug you."

"Okay," Kanoa said, releasing Adora and standing tall. "What's the plan?"

"Excellent," Alem said with a nod. "Yes, the plan. Well, the funny thing about the plan is that there is no real… plan. It isn't as if when you six got here, I had a script to work with. I am just kind of making it up as I go along."

I exchanged some confused looks with the rest of the group. I was hoping that he was joking, or else we were in far more trouble than I had first thought.

"Don't worry, Kail," Alem said, "your faith in me is noted. But do not worry. I have a few tricks up my sleeves that will work quite nicely."

"I could have sworn the only thing I saw up your sleeve was two arms melding into one," Osias muttered, which was met with a look of disgust from Thalia.

"Okay, I've got it," Alem said, 'sitting' down upon the ground and becoming even smaller in stature. "There is really only one way to teach you how to become capable of defeating your foes. Can anyone give me the name of your greatest enemy?"

"I would say that my greatest enemy right now is the guy who can kill people faster than I can blink," Osias replied. "But that's just me."

"No, you are thinking about the question only on its surface," Alem said. "Look deeper within yourselves for the answer."

I thought hard for a moment. I had a feeling Alem was looking for a specific answer, one that pertained to all of us. What was something that challenged me on a daily basis? What was the one thing that kept me from achieving things that I wanted? What was the greatest obstacle in my life, the one thing I would never be able to overcome?

"My greatest enemy is myself," I stated aloud. Alem was already looking at me, aware that I would stumble upon the answer the fastest.

"Very good, Kail," Alem said. "You are your own worst enemy."

With those words, I felt a tingling throughout my entire body. I ran my hands across my chest, feeling a tugging sensation. I noticed the rest of the group had a similar feeling, as they all had looks of perplexity on their faces. It was then I noticed the shadows that we were casting seemed much darker—far too dark for the amount of light present. I looked down at my own shadow and moved my hands slightly to see what was going on. My shadow copied my movements as it normally would, but something was different. My shadow seemed more in tune with me somehow. It was a perfect dark copy of me, no stretches in height and no detail undefined.

My shadow then waved at me, although I had not given it such a command.

I stumbled backwards and fell in surprise, but my shadow did not follow me. It had unattached itself from me and seemed to be pointing and laughing at my fall. I looked over at the rest of the group and discovered they were in similar situations. Our shadows had come to life.

My shadow began pulling at itself. I watched as its arms and chest stretched out of the ground and into the third dimension. It struggled hard against the forces that defined it as a shadow, tugging and writhing like a fly stuck in glue. It wriggled around so that its shoulders, head, and lower body all stood directly in front of me, instead of flatly on the ground. I stood up quickly and brushed the dirt off me, my chains jangling about. I walked toward my shadow, no doubt a look of shock displayed on my face. I reached forward and felt it, and it did the same. I felt it on my fingertips, and it felt me. I didn't pass through it like I believed I would have. It was just as real as me.

"Well, as freaky as this is," I heard Osias say, inspecting his shadow with great caution, "what are we supposed to do with them?"

"Well, that's simple, Osias," Alem responded. "You are to defeat them."

As if choreographed, each of our shadows withdrew their weapons in unison. Their weapons were mirror images of our own. I raised my hands submissively, still not fully understanding what Alem was trying to achieve.

"What?" I asked. "What do you mean, defeat them? I'm not sure if anybody told you, but we don't know how to use our weapons yet."

"Trust me, Kail," Alem said. "If your shadow knows how to use it, so do you."

My shadow suddenly lurched forward with its weapon, only narrowly missing my head due to an instinctive step backwards that I took. I automatically wielded my own weapon and held it at the ready. I looked over and saw that my friends had done the same. They all looked a little nervous, save for Kanoa. He looked indescribably excited.

My shadow swung forward again, and this time I took control. I swiftly stepped backwards and lifted up my weapon, which deflected his back. I was hesitant to actually attack my own shadow. The idea was far too strange for me to comprehend. Or maybe the problem wasn't that simple. Maybe I was too weak to overcome myself. I couldn't handle the thought of not being able to overcome myself. I had been dealing with this problem all my life. What made now so different?

My shadow attacked again, swiping at my feet. I leaped upward and jumped right over his weapon. Everything felt so focused in that moment, like time had slowed down and given me a chance to formulate a plan. I noticed every little detail: the dark chains dangling from his shirt bouncing up and down, his head tilting up to reassess the situation, his arm rising to try to hit me from below. It wasn't going to work. I decided to try and disable him by separating him from his weapon. And that is exactly what I did.

With one fluid motion I kicked down hard at the shadow's wrist, causing him to drop his weapon. I then fell forward and brought my elbow bluntly into his featureless face. I sent my shadow sprawling down to the ground, and his weapon fell behind me. I stood tall and proud from the success I had gained over myself.

I looked over to my friends, who were all having a tough time with their own shadows. Some were keeping the battle rather light, with not more than a few exchanges of weapon against shadow weapon. Kanoa, Cora and, surprisingly, Thalia were having more intense battles, jumping from book pile to book pile, fending off their adversaries. Maybe their shadows were more difficult because of who they were...

I looked back to my shadow, realizing I had let my guard down. His weapon had been brought back into his hands and he looked more poised than ever to defeat me. My fight was far from over.

Blow after blow was received with a well-timed guard, our weapons repelling off one another time after time. I would swing wildly at his head with my weapon and try to follow it up with a kick or punch, but he was too fast. He tried the same moves on me, but I too was fast.

My shadow jumped onto a tall book pile and I ran right up the torn pages after him, my feet treading across their covers, not even giving a second thought to how precise my footsteps would have to be, to climb so quickly.

We were now at the summit of the mound, a somewhat flat surface to battle on. I propelled my weapon upward, flinging a wall of books and memories that temporarily blinded my opponent. I dashed through the distraction and hit him hard with my shoulder, pushing him backwards. He retaliated quickly by sweeping my legs out under me with a speedy kick, sending me sprawling to the ground.

He then tried to bring down his weapon hard upon me. I effortlessly pushed myself up off the ground with one hand, hanging in the air for a moment, and sailed over his attack. I stuck out my arm with my own weapon to try to strike him about the face, but he leaned backwards at the last moment. I landed gracefully back on my feet, facing down my opponent.

I had been so completely enthralled in my battle that I was losing touch with what I was physically capable of, and what I wasn't. I had basically just flung my whole body off the ground and floated in mid-air, something I definitely had not been able to do in the real world. Maybe that was the point of Alem's test: We had to lose ourselves in this world, if we were ever to return to our own. In order to defeat our enemies, I would first have to defeat myself. And it wasn't going to be easy.

My shadow and I swirled endlessly in fierce combat, causing books with memories etched into their pages to spiral around our duel. I leaped over my shadow and tried to hit him from behind, but he twirled around quickly and defended against my strike. We were stuck in an eternal stalemate. Was it even possible to defeat something that was like me in every way? Every blow I tried to deliver was met with resistance. Every swift footstep was matched symmetrically.

Out of my peripheral vision I noticed that my friends were all looking on intently at my battle. Apparently they had finished up with their own struggles and had come to marvel at my own. Why had their shadows been so easy to beat, when my own was giving me such trouble? Was I simply not as strong as my friends?

Frustration mounted within me. I started to attack my shadow without hesitation. I swung madly and ferociously. My increase in momentum was met quickly and equally. There was nothing outside this fight. All other sounds and sights faded away. I guarded strike after strike, our weapons slamming off of one another faster than I could keep track of.

Our weapons then locked up against one another, causing me to push hard against my shadow. Our faces came close to one another, and I looked deep into the darkness of his emptiness; my emptiness. Both of our legs were buckling against the opposing weight we were putting into the push. We were perfectly and evenly matched. No clear victor would be chosen.

I dug within me for an extra bit of strength, something that could help me overcome myself. I thought back to all the times I had felt incompetent, all the times I had let myself down. My thoughts all revolved around me. Maybe I wasn't the solution to my problem...

Then it clicked. The answer to my problems wasn't inside me at all. My shadow was everything that I was. However, I had one thing he didn't. I had my friends to help me.

I let out a mighty yell into the face of darkness. I focused on the smiling faces of my friends and drew from the strength they gave me. I thought about the promise we had made each other: we all stuck together. Every loss and every win was unanimous.

My newfound motivation stunned my shadow momentarily. Its moment of confusion was all I needed. I pushed hard, breaking the bond we had with one another. My shadow stumbled backwards and I charged. He clumsily brought up his weapon, smacking me across the face, which dazed me. I bounced back to the other side of the book pile and took a moment to breathe.

We looked at one another from opposing sides, with my friends looking on. I crouched forward, and my shadow did the same. This was it. I would make one final assault on the darkness within me, and I would be victorious. I swiftly moved toward my shadow, and he launched from his position as well. My feet did not touch any solid surface as I sailed toward him. Was I flying? I closed my eyes and braced for impact. We crossed the pile of broken memories in an instant and collided violently.

I wasn't sure what happened next, but when I next opened my eyes I was soaring through the air away from the battleground, my shadow nowhere in sight.

CHAPTER 8: A MEETING WITH FATE

"So what's for dinner, Kail?" Delphia asked. I sighed heavily and passed her the bowl I had gotten for her.

"What else," I replied. "Cold Kraft Dinner. Seems to be all they ever serve anymore."

I was back in my orphanage. I dwarfed the shoddy table and rickety chair that I was using to eat dinner. It was an eerie sight, seeing a teenager eating with children as if he fit in with them. I wasn't supposed to be here, not like this. I was having another flashback of an event of my childhood. Why was I here this time? What was the point of these memories? They felt so far away, so isolated.

"My favourite," Delphia said.

She ate her disgusting dinner gratefully, as if she was dining at a fancy restaurant. I looked down at my meal and lost my appetite. I wanted to reach out and hold my sister, tell her everything was going to be all right. Change the path that she would eventually go down...

"I heard that someone else is interested in adopting us," I heard myself say. That was the only thing that I talked about while I was in that place: getting out. No matter how happy Delphia was, I never could share those moments with her. I was always the pessimist, the one the darkness chose to speak through. "They're coming later in the week to talk to us. They may be our ticket out."

"Yeah, I've heard that before," she whispered with her mouth full.

"Do you ever actually want to get out of here, Delphia?" I asked. "Or do you want to live in this place forever?"

She looked at me in confusion. I knew it was a silly question to ask, but her passive nature had always upset me. It was as if no matter how hard I tried to find a better place for us, she would be content exactly where she was. I already knew what she was going to say before she said it.

"Why should I care where I am?" she asked with a shrug before going back to her dinner. "I've got you, and that's all that I care about."

My heart sank. The me who was actually in the memory scoffed at the words, but I felt like crying. She was right there, within my grasp. Give her a hug, you jerk! Show her that you love her. She's your sister for goodness' sake...

"Yeah, well," I said, "out there is a whole lot better than in here."

Yeah. Way to go, Kail, that will make her feel better. She remained cheerful however, despite my best effort to bring her down with me. She just kept on eating her Kraft Dinner with a smile on her face. That was my problem: I had put up an impenetrable wall between my emotions and the outer world, so that I would never break down in front of her; never make her question whether I was strong enough to take care of her. I had tried my best never to cry in front of her, and for a while I actually thought myself incapable of crying ever again. I thought that by being hollow, I could offer her more comfort than a sympathetic brother filled with the possibility of doubt. That was a mistake on my part.

"Hey guys, do you want to go down to the pond and skate with us?" I heard a familiar little voice ask from behind me.

That voice would never leave my memory. Although the walls around me were faded, although the little details of the floorboards and the table were obscure, although the memories of the world outside my sister and I were forgotten, that voice remained vivid.

"You know she can't skate," I said without turning around to face him.

I wanted to look him in the face, but I couldn't. That wasn't how things had happened. I couldn't change my memories, but I fought against them regardless. I wasn't going to allow my past to repeat itself, if I could help it. But I couldn't help it. As much as I hated it, they were a part of me as much as anything else.

"Oh, right," the voice said with disappointment, but he didn't leave.

"Well, I can't learn unless I try," Delphia pointed out, looking very excited at the concept of skating.

We had gone over the subject many times, but no matter how many ways I said no, it wasn't enough. I didn't want her on the ice. It was too dangerous, especially due to the fact that none of the 'care-givers' would be supervising. Delphia wanted to skate, and I didn't want her to. It was as simple as that.

"Yeah, well, you don't know how to swim either," I stated. "If you break through the ice... You're just not going skating, okay?"

"Come on, Kail, it'll be fun!" the little voice interrupted. I spun around and faced the voice. He was just as I remembered him: trouble hiding behind innocence.

"I said no, ---!" I shouted as a great pain coursed through me.

A loud twanging noise overwhelmed me in that moment. In real life, I had said his name, but in my memory the name was empty, filled only with searing misery. His name literally caused me physical pain to utter. I writhed in agony inside my body, unable to express how I truly felt. I remained perfectly still, despite the suffering within me. I pushed it all away, focusing on his face. His confused, innocent, dirty, miserable face. My hate for him was only equalled by my love for my sister. A fitting symmetry.

The boy was short and poor-looking, just like the rest of us. His face was very round, as was the rest of his body. He was probably the heaviest person in the orphanage beside the 'care-givers.' I still laughed at the thought of their title. As much as I loathed that little fat boy, he was treated just as badly as the rest of us. He was actually very well liked among the children and was always friendly. Not as if that changed my opinion of him.

"Okay. Sorry, Kail," he said, his chubby cheeks flushing red. His eyes misted a little and he turned away, rubbing the back of his head. I didn't care, not then and not now. He deserved the way I had treated him.

"That wasn't very nice, Kail," Delphia said, frowning at me. "He just wanted to have some fun."

"There are more than enough safe ways to have fun," I explained without remorse, turning back to my undercooked dinner.

I was still recovering from the effects the boy's name had caused in me. The pain had been so intense, so real. I didn't have to wonder why it had happened. Sadly, it made perfect sense to me.

"Why do you always have to talk for me, Kail?" she asked, no longer eating her food.

She was looking straight at me, looking for a direct answer. I remembered this conversation well. If there was ever any proof that my sister was wise beyond her years, it was just about to unfold. It was the first time I began to understand that Delphia was special. Not special in the fact that she was my sister, but as a person. It saddened me to think what she could have accomplished, if only...

"Because I'm your older brother, and I do what's best for you," I explained, apparently not understanding the question.

I hadn't put much thought into my answers for her back then. I wish I could have a real conversation with her now. I wish I could have shown her how much I had changed...But then I thought that perhaps it was best she couldn't see me now. Maybe I was worse now than I had been with her. Maybe it was better that she was...

"When does that stop?" she continued, knowing exactly where she wanted to go with this conversation. As much as I didn't like people having control over the way an argument went, I treasured this moment.

"What do you mean?" I asked.

"When do I start doing what's best for me?" she asked.

She wanted a real answer. I could see it in her eyes. Her mouth twitched subtly and her eyebrows furrowed. It's funny how I didn't realize the little details the first time around; what people really wanted or meant when they talked to me. The emotion hiding behind the words, the deeper meaning just waiting to be found, like a treasure at the end of a maze. It isn't until after everything is said and done that one discovers the true meaning of their life.

"When I think you're ready," I replied. I was like a gardener overwatering his plants. How could I have not seen that she was ready to have her own life? I laughed at the fact that she was more mature than I was. And yet it remained just that: A fact.

"Well, I think I'm ready," she stated. "I just don't think you are."

"What am I not ready for, Delphia?" I asked, apparently annoyed with the way she was talking to me. Little did I know she was about to sum up my entire life, from then until now, with one statement.

"I don't think you're ready to let go, Kail," Delphia stated simply, her eyes glowing into me.

"Kail!" I heard Alem shout out in the distance.

I was lying slumped in a large pile of books, most of which had fallen on top of me. I shook my head and rubbed my eyes for clarity. I couldn't move. I was too deeply lodged in the mound, buried in memories. Alem's voice grew closer and books began peeling off me. Book after book rose away, giving me more room to wiggle about. The last book finally lifted off, revealing Alem standing before me. All the books floated around him, suspended in mid-air. He had been the one to remove them all.

"Thanks," I muttered, stretching my legs.

He tilted his head graciously and the books all fell to the ground gently. I looked down at them and noticed they had fallen in some sort of pattern. I walked over toward them, and realized they had fallen in a way that made them spell out one word: Hope. It was just like when Adora had caught my tear.

"My pleasure," he replied.

"So did I win?" I asked, remembering that my final clash with my shadow was the reason I had been cast out so far from the battlefield.

"Yes," Alem replied, sounding quite proud of my accomplishment. "You were the victor. The rest of the group was quite pleased with your achievement. Unfortunately, their pleasure was short-lived, as we soon after were presented with a visitor."

A shiver went up my spine. "And who would that be?"

He laughed, knowing that I was fully aware of who it was. "Why, Malise, of course! But don't worry. She has promised to be civil. For now, that is."

I suddenly became aware of the fact that Malise had probably been left alone with my friends, possibly being attacked as Alem and I wasted our time talking. I ran past Alem, back in the direction I thought where my friends would be.

"You needn't worry," Alem assured me. "She would not attack them, as they are not the ones who interest her. She came for you."

I came upon many piles of books that diverged into many directions. I was unsure where to go, but I needed to get out of this maze if I was going to help my friends.

"And what if I don't want to talk with her?" I asked Alem, who was floating effortlessly behind me as I feverishly looked for the way back.

"Well then," Alem replied. "She may take it rather personally, and then I would begin to worry about the well-being of my friends, if I were you."

I stopped and turned to face the small man behind me. He looked up at me thoughtfully, and I could feel him urging me to calm down. I realized I was panting and tried to settle myself down before I spoke again.

"Okay," I said slowly. "Lead the way back, then."

He nodded appreciatively. "Remember, Kail," he said, "I am here to help you. I would not abandon your friends so easily."

He then began leading the way back to where I had my battle with my shadow. I reflected on my victory over the darkness within me. Had that been my first step toward accepting this new world? Had it been the first step toward accepting myself?

"Speaking of help," Alem said as we continued walking, "your friend, Kanoa. How well do you know him?"

"Better than anyone," I replied instinctively. "Why?"

"Keep an eye on him," he warned me warily. "I'm serious, and that doesn't happen often, so please think about it. He may prove to be a problem."

"He's a friend," I stated, trying to shut down the doubt clawing at my mind. Alem had a point. I just didn't want to admit it. "And a good one at that. Whatever you think he is, he's not."

"What he isn't," he whispered, "is exactly what frightens me. That also doesn't happen often. Watch him closely, Kail, that's all I ask."

"Okay," I said, trying not to think too deeply on his dark thoughts, lest they start weighing on mine.

Alem kept quiet, probably not wanting to interrupt my thoughts. He wanted what was best for us, and that was good enough for me. I was beginning to like the old man, despite his eccentricities.

"I like you too, Kail," I thought I heard Alem murmur.

"What was that?" I snapped at him.

"Ah, and we have arrived back to our friends," Alem announced. "Well, except for the one. She is not very friendly."

We had returned to the opening among the book piles where we had gathered to battle our shadows. This time, Malise stood in the middle of the group instead of Alem. My friends circled around her, their faces full of anxiety or disdain. She looked over them quietly, apparently refusing to speak. Her presence was just as taxing as it had been the last time. There was something about her that made me feel like I was in a constant free-fall, as if there was nothing beneath my feet but emptiness.

"Oh, thank god you're all right," Cora gasped. The rest of the group looked over to me, trying hard to break their concentration on Malise. Malise remained still. Cora ran over to me and gave me a hug. She leaned in and whispered in my ear. "She's here for you, Kail. Be careful."

"Yeah, Alem told me," I whispered back. "But don't worry about it. I'm not going anywhere I don't want to."

"I have awaited this meeting for a long time, Kail," Malise stated, her morose voice echoing out over the land.

"Yeah, you might even say that it was written in stone," I replied, quickly letting go of Cora and walking up to the malevolent queen. As much as she frightened me, I would never let her know how I felt on the inside. I had gotten pretty good at hiding my emotions.

Her dark, piercing eyes peered directly into my own. I was by no means short, yet she still managed to overwhelm me in stature. Her icy hair hovered around me, as if trying to envelop me in its strands. The dark orb on her chest swirled mysteriously, flaring purple and black. I heard my friends gather behind me, but the gaze I had on Malise remained firm. A slight smile crept across her face. She was terrifying, majestic, devastating and beautiful all at once. There was no one word to suffice for her, yet every word was her own.

"Do I frighten you, Kail?" she asked, her voice ebbing with pride. I wasn't going to fall into any of her traps.

"Judging from what I know of your past," I sneered, "I think you're a little more afraid of me than I am of you."

Her smile grew evermore. She came closer toward me, and I tried my best not to budge. She was pressing me, seeing what she could get away with. I just clenched my jaw and remained steadfast. I wanted to make a lasting impression upon this evil.

“I can assure you that nothing of this world puts fear in me,” she whispered.

“Well, then I guess it’s a good thing I’m not from this world,” I whispered back. “I made this world, Malise.”

Our eyes were now directly in line with each other. I could feel her breath on my face. It was icy and demoralizing. My heart was beating fast, but there was no controlling that. I looked deep into her eyes and saw nothing but despair and sadness. I didn’t know why, but she made me want to weep for her. I wanted to give her a hug at that moment, as if her hostility toward me was instinctive and consequential, not by choice. I felt sorry for her. I quickly shook off the feeling, however, as I realized that my feelings might have been implanted within me, a side effect of her being. This was probably a part of the power she had over others, and why they ended up joining her dark cause. If I couldn’t trust my friends, I sure wasn’t going to trust the darkness I had help create.

“You may have created this world,” she said faintly, her mouth caressing each word as it escaped her lips, “but I have claimed it as my own. You were there when the villagers were punished for their disloyalty, were you not?”

I flinched momentarily at the discovery that she had knowledge of my presence at the village massacre. It frightened me to think that she could have simply looked over, seen us hiding in the forest, and destroyed us with the rest of that village. Her smile faded and she leaned away, once again looming over me. She surveyed my friends behind me, her eyes soaking them in. I didn’t want her to even think about harming my friends, so I brought the focus back to me.

“Yeah, I was there,” I answered with disdain. “They didn’t deserve what you did to them.”

She scoffed, her eyes drawn back toward me. Her hair extended and brushed across my face, chilling me to my very core. Nothing about her contained warmth or life. She was as cold as death itself.

“Of course they deserved their fate,” she stated. “They possessed flaws and were punished as such. I do not tolerate failure.”

I grew angry at her disregard for life. It was almost sickening to hear someone have such little value in something so precious. Her attitude also frightened me. If she had so thoughtlessly ended the lives of those who had once served her, how easy would it be to dispose of her enemies?

“People make mistakes, Malise!” I shouted, frustration evident in my voice. “They’re only human.”

Her hair suddenly stopped moving. The dark orb ceased swirling and her eyes grew wide. The air around me became still, and no sounds could be heard. She bent her head down, her eyes still crazed and intent on looking wrathfully into me. I didn't want to admit it, but I was as scared as I had ever been in my life. My fingers twitched toward my weapon, bracing for an attack. Whatever I had said had not pleased Malise one bit.

"Only human?" she repeated, her voice dripping with hate. "Humans are supposed to be the most intelligent beings to rule over all others. Don't you think such a title should be given to those who deserve it? I'm just preserving the image it so rightfully deserves. Humans cannot afford to make mistakes. You get away with too much, too easily. I'm here to correct those mistakes the only way I know how."

Before I could truly understand the meaning of her words, her attention shifted away from me. She glided past me and toward my friends. I ran after her, but was quickly flung backwards. I slammed up against a pile of books hard, unable to move. I felt a great pressure all over me, but there was nothing to cause it. Malise was the only answer. My friends too had been pushed aside, paralyzed against surrounding book piles. We all struggled against the invisible force, but it was in vain. The only one left standing was Kanoa. He had been able to hold his ground for whatever reason. Malise wandered over to him, but he didn't budge. Apparently, she wanted a word with him as well.

"Kanoa," I heard her say. "I have taken notice of your abilities and desires in this world."

"Is that a question?" he shot back.

I wanted to shout out to him and tell him not to get near her, but my voice remained muted. Despite not having seen what she was capable of in the village, I was now aware she was just as dangerous, if not more so, than her followers.

She laughed, almost warmly. Her manner around Kanoa was much less intimidating than it had been around me. She actually felt...friendly around him. Something wasn't right, and I hoped he was aware of it.

"No, it was not," she answered. "I am simply taking notice of talent when I see it. I also have a keen eye for ambition, something I sense strongly inside you. However, the path you are going down will not lead you to what you truly want. I know the path you desire, and I can help you find it."

Don't do it, Kanoa, I wanted to tell him. It was such an obvious trap to me, but I knew that to him, it was the answer to a dream. Malise, I realized, was a master of coercion. She knew how to get into the hearts of people, and the best way to corrupt them. I hoped that her charms were no match for Kanoa's will. However, I was not my best friend, and could not know how he would handle such an offer. The choice was his, but he had better pick the right option. Not for himself, but for all of us, to preserve his promise.

"That's awfully nice of you," he replied hesitantly, "but you see, I never was the type of guy to take the easy way out. I think I can find my own path just fine."

I expected Malise to unleash her fury upon him, to attack him without mercy. However, this event did not come to fruition. She simply nodded her head compliantly and turned away from him. Her eyes once again flared as they fell upon me. I knew what she was trying to do, and her eyes sensed that knowledge within me. I had taken away her kingdom, her people, even her husband. It was her turn to do the taking.

"Very well, Kanoa," she said with slight disappointment, "but your answer is a naive one. Perhaps once you have spent enough time in this world, you will come to understand the true value of my offer. You will not find what you seek from your friends or the world they come from. This is where you belong, with me. I have patience."

Kanoa seemed conflicted, thinking deeply on her words. I could see that within him, the offer she had made him would weigh greatly. Even after this confrontation concluded, it would long linger in his thoughts. I needed to prove Alem wrong and show him that Kanoa wasn't who he feared him to be.

"I wouldn't hold my breath," Kanoa retorted tautly.

I then fell to the ground hard, released from my stasis. I rubbed at my chest, relieving the pressure. I began coughing as Malise once again came toward me. I looked up at her and saw her looking over me; inspecting me.

"Maybe the prophecy was flawed," she said, talking more to herself than me. "A creature such as you cannot possibly be the one to defeat me."

"I'm no creature, Malise," I spat between coughs, shakily standing. "I'm a human being. And I promise you that while it seems that I have taken everything from you, I'm only getting started."

She lunged forward at me unexpectedly, slamming me once again into the book piles. She grabbed at me violently about the face with her hand, her face inches away from my own. I could see tears in her eyes. Her lips quivered and her breathing became unsteady. I was frightened and baffled by her actions. Her colourless skin reflected off mine. I didn't struggle, as there was no point. I could feel that she was not going to cause any real harm to me—not yet, anyway. She was merely venting untold years of frustration upon me. I would give her this one opportunity, for the next time we became this close, I would surely kill her.

"You don't even know what you are," Malise whispered feverishly, her words trembling as much as her lips. Her eyes fluttered over my face, searching for something within me. "I sense great suffering behind those eyes. Suffering I know all too well...You think that you are human, a living being. You're wrong. You're just a collection of dreams and memories stuck inside walls of flesh and bone. Without your own collection, you are nothing. You might as well be dead. You might as well be me. If I were to tear down those walls, the real you would finally be free. And that is exactly what I plan to do with you. I am going to set you free, Kail."

And with those words, she sealed our meeting with a kiss. Our lips pressed against one another, and we were united. I didn't resist, as a part of me wanted it more than anything. It was filled with pain, sorrow, fear and fury. It was exhilarating and heartbreaking. I lost all touch with the world around me and forgot all problems within my life. Time itself became obsolete, and life irrelevant. I poured everything my existence accumulated to into that one action. All these feelings, and yet the moment was over in the span of the blink of an eye. I opened my eyes and she was gone.

I didn't understand what had happened, but I knew that it was necessary. My skin crawled and my heart faltered, but with each breath I took, I regained my focus. Our meeting had ended and our intentions exchanged. Now our battle could finally begin.

"Kail!" I heard Cora shout.

My feet were back on the ground, and my friends all around me. They all looked concerned, yet something wasn't right. I got the distinct feeling that they hadn't seen what had transpired between Malise and I the moment before she disappeared. I decided I wasn't going to tell them. They probably wouldn't be too pleased that I had shared a kiss with our enemy.

"Where did she go?" Osias asked, nervously looking around for any signs of the enigmatic queen. I knew she was gone, and we would not see her again unless she willed it.

"Did you guys see what happened after she spoke with Kanoa?" I asked, testing to see if the exchange had been blocked somehow by Malise.

"No," Kanoa explained. "After she stopped talking to me, everything just kinda went dark, like I couldn't see anything."

The rest of the group agreed with Kanoa's description. Malise had blinded them to our moment together, possibly to deny them of the knowledge of any weakness she possessed. I knew, however. I knew that she wasn't solid all the way through. The darkness could never completely consume the light.

I then remembered the look on Kanoa's face when Malise had offered him a chance at the freedom he had always wanted. Was he not aware of the unspoken cost of his friends that he would have to pay? Had he forgotten the promise he had made to us?

"You took your sweet time saying no to Malise," I shot at Kanoa.

I was fully aware that I was about to instigate a fight between us. I wanted to make sure he wasn't going to do anything stupid in the future. Unfortunately for me, predicting Kanoa's actions was a very flawed science.

"Excuse me?" he replied. Our friends apparently understood what I was referring to, as none of them looked puzzled by my observation.

"I said that you looked as though you were about to join Malise for a second there," I stated, not backing down despite the menacing advances he was making toward me.

"Yeah, well unless you forgot," he said, "I said no. Whatever you think you saw doesn't matter."

"I want you to promise all of us that you aren't going to let your stupid dreams get in the way of our promise," I ordered. I wasn't going to let this go until I received a satisfying conclusion. By the look on Kanoa's face, I was going to be disappointed.

"I don't have to promise anything like that to you," he muttered, turning away from me with a shrug.

I put my hand on his shoulder to stop him. He quickly spun around and hit me hard with some sort of blast of energy. The shockwave sent me spinning backwards, and I landed hard on my back. Pain circulated through my body on impact. Wait a second...I felt pain? I suddenly became very aware that I had experienced pain inside this dream world. Had I been feeling pain before and not acknowledged it?

Kanoa ran toward me with a look of regret on his face. He then saw the look on my face and became confused.

"What's wrong?" he asked, extending his hand toward me to help me up.

I was still unable to comprehend the feeling of pain. Or was I just too scared to admit it? I decided the only way to make Kanoa, and the rest of my friends, understand my revelation was to give him a taste of his own medicine.

I grabbed his hand hard and pulled forward, quickly pulling up my legs and jamming them into his abdomen. He gasped as I kicked the wind out of him before I pushed my legs forward, hurling him through the air and causing him to crash into the ground, just as I had. He grasped at his stomach and moaned. He then sat up rigidly with a look of horror on his face. My plan had worked.

"Oh shit," I heard him say.

The rest of my friends stood between us, understandably confused at what had just taken place.

"Guys, what is going on?" Thalia asked, staring at Kanoa as he winced in pain. Alem, who I had forgotten all about since Malise had arrived, then walked forward, peeling a large orange in front of him with his mind.

"It would appear that Kail and Kanoa have stumbled upon a most distasteful discovery," Alem said as the orange peels dropped to the ground.

Cora ran up to me and helped me to my feet. "What's he talking about, Kail?" she asked.

"I felt pain." I winced, clutching at my shoulder.

I saw her face shift from uncertainty to dismay. She shook her head in disbelief. I couldn't believe it either. We were in a dream world. How could we feel things here?

"Alem," Osias said, walking toward the old man. "If we can feel pain, what happens when we feel too much pain? I mean...well, what happens if we die here?"

Alem thought about the question for a moment, splitting the orange into its individual slices, which circled in front of him. "There have been occurrences within this world in which those who enter, do not return to the other world."

"I don't think I understand," Osias said. Despite his words, he knew what Alem meant. I knew what Alem meant. We all knew what Alem meant, and none of us could believe it.

Alem took a deep breath. "The body cannot live without the mind. Without your mind, your body is but an empty shell, unable to feel, think or function. If you die in this world, you die in your world."

My breathing ceased and my mouth fell open. What he said made sense, but I couldn't accept it. It was as if we had been dying since we first arrived, and had only now just realized it. I became very aware of my own mortality. Could I really die here, in this world of dreams and memories?

"Now, who wants some orange?" Alem asked.

CHAPTER 9: HOW THINGS SHOULD HAVE BEEN

My group of friends huddled together and began discussing the gravity of our situation. Knowing our actions in Drephoria had a direct effect on our bodies in the real world was not a welcome discovery. I, personally, had never been afraid of death. I had always viewed it as inevitability more than something to fear. However, I was not comfortable with the life of my friends hanging in the balance. Just because I was okay with my own death, didn't mean I was okay with theirs.

"I don't see why everyone's freaking out," Kanoa stated. "We could die in the other world just like in this one, and we weren't scared all the time."

"Yeah, but in the real world we didn't have things with nightmarish powers chasing after us," Osias pointed out.

"I don't see how this changes anything," Cora said. "Either way, we have to find a way out of here. Just because our lives are now on the line doesn't change that fact. If anything, it means we should try that much harder."

"We shouldn't just fight against her blindly," Osias reasoned. "I mean, she came to us. Don't you think that if we attacked now, she might be expecting it? I say we wait her out."

"That thought goes both ways, unfortunately," I countered. "The longer we wait, the more time she has to formulate a plan against us."

We continued arguing over what we should do with the task at hand. Thalia mostly stayed out of it. Situations such as this had a tendency to bring her down. Our course of action was evenly split, and neither side was going to budge. No conclusion seemed to be in reach, but then Adora finally decided to share her opinion.

"We should ask Alem what to do," she said. She reminded me much of my sister at times—always simple yet always effective.

Alem then appeared in the middle of our group without warning, causing me to jump a little in surprise. He really should warn us before making such entrances, I thought to myself.

"Sorry to startle you, but I heard that I was needed," he apologized. "And I do have a suggestion for you all, but I am not sure you will agree with it."

"Well, your opinion certainly wouldn't hurt," Osias said. "Lay it on us, Alem."

"I suggest that you all take a break from the perils of this world," he advised. "This is a dream world! You kids should be out having fun and exploring. My goodness, you are more serious than the adults."

I was unsure if Alem was giving us a serious answer. He certainly seemed to believe that we should take a break from our problems, but I wasn't positive this was the best time to let our guard down. Was it possible that Alem was actually a scout for Malise who was going to get us all killed?

"You have been watching far too many spy movies to think I am some kind of secret agent, Kail," Alem said with a laugh.

"I never said secret agent," I replied. "I said scout. Actually, I didn't say anything. Quit reading my mind. And stay out of our discussions if you're going to make those kinds of suggestions."

"Ya know, I'm starting to like this old guy," Kanoa interrupted, walking forward and patting Alem on the head. "I think we should relax a little and have some fun."

"You would," I said.

Of course Kanoa would agree with a notion to have fun over taking things seriously. Ultimately, I realized, I knew we would end up doing what he wanted. He, like Malise, had the power of persuasion. Not as if he would have to work too hard with the power of a dream world on his side to entice his detractors. Each of my friends expressed their interest in this world and took his side. Even though I would never admit it, I too wanted to see what the dream world had to offer. After all, I helped create it.

"No, this makes sense," Osias said. "If we start this...war all stressed out, then we may not be able to fight at one hundred percent. Plus, maybe the longer we remain here, the more habituated we will become with it."

"Oh, a war, you say," Thalia said. "How very dramatic."

"You know what I mean," Osias moaned, blushing faintly.

"Yeah, I do," Thalia said with a giggle. "And I agree with you! We need to cool off a little before diving back into this fire. Don't you think so too, Adora?"

"Oh yes," Adora agreed, excited at the prospect of adventure. "I think this will be a lot of fun!"

I looked over at Cora for her response. I sighed as I saw her expression: excited and eager. She shrugged with a smile and said, "I guess you know where I stand then, huh?"

"Well then, Kail," Kanoa said with a mischievous grin. "What do you say? Ready to have the best dream of your life?"

I thought over the question for a moment, putting my hands on my hips, pretending to put a lot of thought into my answer. My answer was obvious, though, and Cora pushed me playfully. I nodded my head and said, "Let's go make our dreams come alive."

We walked out of the field of memories and came across a gaping, bottomless pit, only passable by tiny islands of sand scattered across its dark surface. The patches of land floated above the abyss without connection to one another, evenly spread out and just close enough for my friends and I to jump from island to island. I laughed as I noticed that each island Adora had jumped to held her telltale flowers. Unlike the pond Kanoa, Cora and I had walked across, we weren't going to take our chances walking on darkness.

"Maybe we should find a different way across," Osias said, nervously standing at the edge of the pit, refusing to jump to the first small piece of hovering land. "This doesn't look safe at all."

"Osias, exploring was partly your idea," I said, concentrating on making a jump to an island that had grown a random palm tree. "You're now telling me that jumping around on floating islands that hover over an endless chasm, which would no doubt lead to our deaths, isn't fun?"

"Well, when you put it that way," Osias grumbled.

"Come on, Osias!" Thalia shouted from further away. "I made it this far and nothing bad has happened yet. Kanoa is almost all the way across. It's safe, I promise!"

Osias groaned and took a deep breath. "Why couldn't this place have a normal landscape for once?" I heard him mutter.

"I thought normal wasn't good enough for you?" I asked, referencing his constant desire for perfection.

"It isn't," he replied, "but this place is… Never mind, just forget it."

He closed his eyes for a moment in meditation, breathing in and out calmly. He often went into states of deep thought before he did anything that had dire consequences: tests, sneaking out in the middle of the night, traversing across never-ending holes in the ground. This moment was as good as any. He opened his eyes, nodded his head and leapt forward, easily making the jump to the first island. He raised his clutched fists together in the air and congratulated himself for his efforts. Osias always made me laugh.

"Nice job, buddy," I said, turning back to my jumps. "One down and about fifty to go."

Kanoa had made it to the other side with Adora and was impatiently awaiting the rest of us. There was a mountain range in the distance that he wanted to get to, and as this whole escapade was his idea, we all complied in following. I was on one of the last islands and decided to wait for Osias, who was still having trouble getting across the darkness.

"I can't believe we didn't notice that we felt things here," Osias said as he jumped from his tiny island to mine. He bent down and picked up a handful of sand, letting it flow through the cracks in his fingers. "It's funny what you take for granted. I mean, this sand doesn't just feel real ... it is real."

"As real as you think it is, anyway," I said, turning to jump to one of the final islands. I stepped on a seashell as I readied myself, feeling it crack under my foot. I winced slightly, hoping I hadn't broken it. I lifted my foot and, just as I feared, it had been shattered.

"Interesting," Osias muttered, thinking aloud. "Do you think it's possible that we feel things in this place simply because we believe we should?"

I bent down and picked up the pieces of the seashell, feeling sorry for breaking it. It reminded me of Cora, and the moment I forever tainted our friendship. Sadness began to creep into me as I stared at the broken pieces, unable to put them back together. Just like on that day…

"I mean," Osias said, interrupting my thoughts and trying to elaborate on his new thesis, unaware that I hadn't been listening. "Maybe we feel pain and things happen because we think that they should. Alem was talking about mind and body...Is it possible that the pain is in the body, or it is all in the mind? Maybe we could overcome pain or death by not thinking that they exist."

"Yeah," I whispered, still looking at the devastated trinket. "Maybe."

"Hey, Kail!" I heard Kanoa shout from solid land. I looked up and saw him waving to me. I quickly dug a little hole in the sand and placed the seashell inside, burying it away from my thoughts.

"Yeah, yeah, we're almost there," I replied, jumping to the next tiny island with Osias right behind me.

"I couldn't help notice your battle with your shadow back there," he said, his voice rooted in intrigue.

"And I'm guessing you noticed something out of the ordinary?" I asked. "I mean, despite the whole 'fighting-my-shadow' thing."

"Yeah, I noticed you flew for a second," he continued, ignoring my attempt at humour.

I took a moment away from my island hopping to look up at him. He was quite close now, and I recognized the twinkle of excitement in his eyes. I tried to remember at what point in my duel I had flown, but couldn't recall the specific moment. He seemed pretty confident that I had, however.

"I think this place is making you see things," I replied.

I jumped off the last tiny floating island and back onto normal ground. The sheen in Kanoa's eyes flared as I stepped toward him. Seeing as I was good at reading people's eyes, I had a pretty good feeling about what was about to happen: He was going to test out my new ability, whether I had it or not.

I braced for him, but he was too strong. He grabbed me firmly and pulled us both over the edge of the world, into the endless pit of black. I felt a brief moment of vertigo as we crossed the threshold, and then there was only falling. At first I hadn't come to grips with what he had just done. As I looked up and saw my friends looking down on us, screaming our names, I knew that he had really done it. He had killed us both.

"Are you out of your mind?" I yelled, furiously hurling my fists through the empty air at Kanoa.

The darkness quickly consumed everything around us. I could no longer see the sky, my friends or anything else except Kanoa and myself. We were falling forever into untold depths. I had time to let out my anger.

"I don't think we have anything to worry about," he replied, casually putting his hands behind his head as we fell.

His golden hair, baggy silver clothing and flowing cape billowed all around him as we ripped through the emptiness. He looked as though he were just taking a nap on his bed with a fan pointed at him, instead of hurling toward an eternity of nothing.

"Yeah, you're right," I fumed. "We should just chill down here, falling forever, hoping that I gain the ability to fly after a while. Meanwhile, our friends are stranded up top with horrible monsters looking to murder them. What would I possibly have to worry about?"

"Kail," he said. "Could you just shut up for a second and let me hear the sound of silence?"

I was about to start yelling at him again, when I realized that there was no noise other than our voices. Despite the feeling of wind all around me, there was no sound. It was as if I had gone deaf—and if I began looking away from Kanoa, blind too. As a matter of fact, if it wasn't for the effects of the wind on our clothes, I wouldn't have been able to tell we were falling at all. This was the sight and sound of nothing. Was this the feeling of death itself?

"Okay" I said, letting a fair amount of time pass by. "Seriously, how are we going to get out of here?"

He smiled, looking over at me without a care in the world on his mind. "I want you to tell me about a time where I got you into a lot of trouble. Kind of like what's happening now."

His request confused me. Surely this wasn't a time for stories. "Kanoa, we don't have time –"

"If you don't tell me, then we're never going to get out of this," he interrupted. Clearly he had a plan, and unless I went along with him, he wasn't going to let me in on it.

I sighed and thought about a time when Kanoa had gotten us both into trouble. It wasn't hard to do, considering how much material I had to work with.

"Remember the time when we were playing in your kitchen when your parents were remodelling, after they told us not to go near it?" I asked.

He laughed in recognition and nodded. "Of course I remember. You were so scared the whole time that they were just going to burst into the room and we would get in trouble, even after I told you that they were out of town for the day."

"Yeah, well I didn't feel comfortable disobeying my own parents, let alone yours," I retorted. "Anyway, we were in the kitchen and there was an open can of blue paint on the counter. I bumped into it and it spilled all over the floor. The paint went everywhere and there was no way to clean up the mess."

"Man, I thought you were going to cry," he said, shaking his head. "You should have seen the look on your face!"

"I was nervous!" I defended myself, laughing at how silly the situation had been, "I thought for sure they were going to come back and never let me come into your house again. I had no idea how we were going to get out of that one."

"Then what happened?" he pressed on, the glint in his eyes giving me the feeling that I was about to prove a point he had in mind.

"Well, then you said that there was nothing to worry about," I replied. "And then you started painting the entire floor blue. I told you to stop making it worse, but you insisted that it would be fine. I helped you colour the entire kitchen floor with the spilled paint. And then your parents came home..."

"And they loved what we had done," he said, finishing my story for me. He reached out and put his hand on my shoulder. "They said it was like walking on the open sky. Would I ever get you into a serious problem that we couldn't solve?"

I contemplated on all the trouble that Kanoa had gotten me into, trying to conjure up an incident that would have proved him wrong, but I couldn't find one. Sure, he had gotten us into little things that would get us grounded or detention, but never once had he put me into serious peril with lasting consequences. Well, until now, anyway.

"No," I answered half-heartedly, "but where we are now is a little worse than spilt paint. I can't fly, Kanoa! I wasn't even able to walk on water."

He closed his eyes and thought for a moment about what I had said. I hoped he was thinking of a way in which we could get out of here. Maybe he was trying to focus on flying, and then I wouldn't have to worry about it. Unfortunately, none of my hopes were met.

"Maybe you just need the right motivation," he said, his eyes remaining closed.

A deviant smile formed across his face. There was a distant popping noise, and I looked around for its origin. I finally looked down and saw something that I sincerely wished I hadn't. I closed my eyes and opened them again, but the object stuck. Looming far below me was a long patch of land. Land that was growing larger the longer we fell. Unless I learned to fly, and quickly, Kanoa and I were about to have our final argument—just before we slammed into our final resting place.

"Please don't tell me that you put that there," I whispered, my voice cracking in terror.

"Fine, then I won't tell you," Kanoa replied.

"Are you kidding me?" I shouted. "Were you not there when Alem said that we can die?"

"Oh, I was there," he responded. "Which is why I think you should start thinking about flying, instead of yelling at me, right about now."

"Kanoa, stop it," I pleaded, nervously watching our impending doom infringing ever closer. "I can't do it."

"Yes," Kanoa countered. "You can."

"And what if I can't, huh?" I snapped. "Do you really want to deal with the consequences?"

Kanoa grabbed me with great fervour and stared me right in the eyes, hope and confidence present within his. "Don't think about that," he commanded. "You're going to fly us out of here."

"No, I'm not!" I cried out in frustration. "I don't know how! I can't stop thinking about the fact that I'm not supposed to be able to do this."

"Let it all go!" he cried back.

I looked down and saw that the ground was mere seconds away. I grabbed Kanoa and tried with all my might to fly. I didn't know how I was supposed to do it or what it was supposed to feel like, but I tried. I tried so hard to put my entire mind's focus on that one thought; the thought of losing hold on gravity. I looked down again and saw that I was out of time. We were going to hit the ground. I took one last look at the smile on Kanoa's face as we both took our last breath before impact. I closed my eyes and accepted what was to come... But we couldn't die. Not yet. We were going to find a way out of death, and I was going to be the one do it.

The collision never happened. There was no bone-crushing thud or white light at the end of a tunnel. There was darkness, but my eyes were definitely open. I was moving upward, out of the abyss. I was flying. I felt weightless, but I knew I was flying. The wind caressed my face and blew my hair back and whistled through my golden chains. Had I actually hit the ground? Had I actually died?

"I knew you'd do it," I heard Kanoa say.

His presence frightened me, but I quickly realized that he too was flying. We flew together, side by side, through the darkness. I didn't understand what was going on. This was impossible! People couldn't just fly. There were rules... boundaries. Kanoa picked up on my apparent confusion.

"Don't worry, Kail," he said with a chuckle. "We didn't hit the ground, and we aren't dead."

"But," I sputtered, "how are you flying?"

He laughed again and performed a few barrel rolls to show off his newfound talent. "As much as I believe in you, Kail, I wouldn't just try to kill us without a backup plan. You don't give me enough credit sometimes."

"So," I continued, still perplexed. "You can fly too?"

"Of course I can fly!" he shouted, executing perfect flips and spins. "I can walk on water, so why wouldn't I be able to fly?"

I laughed nervously, sighing with a huge sense of relief. Kanoa was often on the edge of craziness, but I was glad he wasn't suicidal. I shook my head, calming myself down and pushing the thoughts of death out of my mind.

"Don't do stuff like that!" I yelled at him.

I swung my fist at him, but he dodged out of the way. I chased after him, flying through the air at ever-accelerating speeds, ascending toward the sky. At first, the velocity and spinning of our motions left me disoriented. I felt queasy, like I was going to throw up. The longer we flew, however, the more accustomed I became to the feeling. It almost felt natural. It felt as though the same gravity that had always kept my feet on the ground had now reversed, that the weight of the world was now the air beneath my feet. We bobbed and weaved around each other, and I couldn't help but notice the absolute joy Kanoa was expressing. I had never seen him that happy in my entire friendship with him. He had found his true place, outside of reality. I felt a little sorry for him as I knew that once we went back to the real world, he would never be this happy again. He had to make the most of this time.

We burst out of the darkness back into the light, swirling and turning around each other. I heard screams from down below and quickly turned my attention away from Kanoa and back to my other friends. It struck me that they probably wouldn't be all that pleased we were laughing when they thought we had died. An understandable reaction, I thought.

"What the hell are you guys doing up there?" Cora cried out at us.

I shot a look at Kanoa, and he gulped nervously. I shrugged and followed him back to the ground where the rest of our friends were looking on at us in amazement. Our sudden appearance was met with both relief and anger. The anger mostly came from Cora.

"Kanoa was just testing something out," I explained, floating somewhat gracefully back to the ground. Kanoa landed gently next to Adora, who was looking at him in pure wonder. I stumbled a little on my landing and would have fallen if Osias hadn't caught me. "We weren't in any danger. Not any real danger, anyway."

"So that was funny to you?" Cora spat, her eyes flaring red and her fiery hair darkening. It crackled in the sunlight. "We thought you were both dead, and instead you're having a good time flying around down there?"

"Cora, it wasn't like that," Kanoa butted in, trying to help me, "I just wanted to see –"

"Shut up! I wasn't talking to you," Cora snapped, her burning stare remaining on me. There was that emotion again; that passion. "You know, Kanoa, it's nice to see all the little talks we had about you being a better person and keeping our collective interests in mind didn't sink in at all."

I looked over at Kanoa as he slowly stepped out of the conversation, mouthing his wishes of good luck toward me. I had a feeling it wasn't going to help.

"Cora, I think you're overreacting here," I replied. As the words escaped my lips, I wondered if I could have said anything that would have pissed her off more. Probably not.

"Yeah, you're probably right," she agreed, mocking me with every syllable. "I'm probably just overreacting. I mean, who am I to worry about you falling into a big, dark pit? Who am I to worry about you leaving the rest of your friends in this place alone? Who am I to worry about you dying …"

Her voice trailed off, but she didn't need to finish. I had never thought of the impact my death would have on others, on my friends. If I were to die, they would have to live on without me. I would be an empty void in their lives and that wasn't the kind of responsibility I felt comfortable with. However, whether I liked it or not, that was the place I filled in their lives, and there was no way around it. These were the people that cared whether I lived or died. My death now had perspective in my life. The worst part of my death wouldn't be the end of my life. It would be the effect it had on my friends.

"Cora, I didn't mean to," I tried explaining, but she turned away from me, her eyes and hair fading back to their normal hue. We both knew I didn't possess the words necessary to make amends for all the things I had done.

"Just because you don't care, doesn't mean I don't," I heard her mutter, her voice cracking under the weight of her frustration. I cringed for a moment, trying my best to not let the guilt of how poorly I had treated her into me. After all, it had always been my choice. Maybe I had lived my life all wrong…

"I'm really sorry, man," Kanoa mumbled softly from behind me. I looked on after Cora as she stomped off, and I knew she was trying her absolute best not to break down.

"No worries," I replied. "How could you have known killing us would have been a bad thing to do?"

I turned to him and engraved the look of disappointment on my face into his mind. I wanted him to know that we couldn't just do that kind of stuff, not after we made a promise to the rest of our friends. Our eyes met, and then he looked down to avoid my stare. I had made my point.

"Now come on," I said, trying to not let my confrontation with Cora affect the rest of the group's morale. "Let's go climb this damn mountain."

The ground leading up to the mountain was very slippery, almost glassy in nature. Kanoa had found it to resemble a skating rink and had transformed the bottom of his shoes into skates. He did the same for Adora, and the two of them were skating around, laughing the whole way to the mountain. The two of them spinning around each other reminded me of the first time that they had met at an elementary school dance, and how they had been the only boy and girl in the whole grade brave enough to do dance together. Drephoria certainly didn't have a shortage of weird sights.

I hesitated before stepping onto this new terrain. The memories flooded back to me and drenched my thoughts in terror. I didn't want my friends to notice I had faltered, so I quickly took a deep breath and stepped onto the slippery surface. With every step I took, my feet felt as though they were becoming heavier. I looked down at them and noticed that my footprints in the ice had left deeper and deeper marks the further I went. I was puzzled and bothered by it, becoming very uncomfortable with my environment. I looked forward to make sure my friends weren't watching. I knelt down cautiously to touch the marks I had made, when Delphia's ghostly face appeared in the ice.

I leapt backwards and slipped on the ice, slamming my elbows into the ground hard. I winced at the pain. Not the pain in my body, but the feeling inside me. Kanoa rushed over to me and helped me up, and asked me what had happened. I told him that I had slipped and nothing more. What was this place doing to me?

"Could you imagine if we saved every lucky penny we ever found?" Thalia wondered out loud. "How rich do you think that would make us?"

We had all familiarized ourselves with Thalia's odd nature. She often wondered out loud and never made much sense. She was entirely capable of holding a serious conversation and was likely my most intelligent friend aside from Osias, but she just didn't like to show off. Osias frequently visited the idea that she possibly had some form of autism known as Asperger's Syndrome, but he was never sure, as she never demonstrated all of the key symptoms.

These were all Osias's ideas, however. I had a theory of my own. I believed Thalia was hiding a darkness that had long haunted her, and her carefree persona was just a façade. Now and then I would catch glimpses of what was hiding beneath, and it was never a pretty sight.

"Well, Thalia, I don't look at the ground very often, so –" Osias began to say, but was unable to finish his thought.

A loud whistling noise became audible. I looked around to find where the sound was coming from, but was startled when the sound found me. A large mound of pennies slammed into the ground next to Thalia, sending shards of ice and pennies soaring into the air. The penny pile sifted around as coins rolled around and spun across the ice. Eventually everything settled, leaving us with one huge mound of pennies, on a skating rink at the base of a mountain made of ice. It all made perfect sense.

"That's a lot of pennies," Thalia stated.

She quickly ran up to the pile and took one, then realized she didn't have any pockets on her silky pants. She shoved the penny into her red boot before rejoining the group with a look of satisfaction on her face.

"You're just taking the one?" Osias asked, still staring nervously at the mass that nearly crushed him.

"For good luck!" she explained.

"Yeah," Osias muttered as we turned back toward the mountain. "We'll definitely need it."

"Okay, well before Thalia spawns a mountain of quarters," Kanoa said, skating over to us gracefully. "I'd love for us to climb this mountain now."

I turned to face the summit Kanoa wished to scale and realized it was much higher than I had thought. So high, in fact, that I doubted we would be able to climb it at all. It wasn't all that steep, but its top extended almost beyond my sight. Other than its height, there was another problem. The mountain, just like the ground, was made of ice. It wasn't just covered in ice; the mountain itself was completely formed of ice, like a solid block waiting to be sculpted. There were no footholds or ledges to grab onto, and it was flat pretty much the whole way up. There was a ridge near the top of the mountain that overlooked the land behind us. I assumed that was where Kanoa wanted to be, overlooking his fantasy world.

"I assume that you understand the laws of friction, Kanoa?" Osias asked, wearily placing his hand on the side of the mountain and demonstrating how slick it was.

"Are you seriously asking me that question?" Kanoa replied.

"Yeah, you're right," Osias muttered. "That was stupid of me."

"How are we supposed to climb this thing, Kanoa?" I asked, slouching in defeat. Why had we come all this way if we weren't even going to be able to achieve what we had set out to do? I knew I shouldn't have said yes to this whole idea.

"Well, I can tell you how I'm going to climb it," Kanoa stated. "But you're going to have to find your own way up. Why don't you just fly?"

I thought about it for a moment, but then I looked over to Cora. The idea of me flying again so soon clearly wasn't a good idea, judging from the spark in her eyes set off by Kanoa's suggestion. I was going to have to find another way to the top, just like everyone else.

"Even if I did fly," I retorted, "that still doesn't account for everyone else. How're they supposed to get to the top?"

Adora had taken off her skates and tried climbing up the mountain. She took about three steps before sliding back down gently. She huffed angrily and walked away from the mountain, defeated.

"Well, now that we've ruled out walking up the icy vertical slope," Osias said, restraining himself from being cruel to Adora, "now what?"

There was a moment of silence as we all pondered over the possible ways to climb the incline. I mulled over the idea of Kanoa and me possibly carrying the rest of our friends to the top, but I wasn't sure if they would be willing to try such a suggestion. Just as I was about to voice my idea anyway, I heard a noise that resembled the flapping of wings, only much louder and more fierce. I looked at my friends to see if they too had noticed the sound. Judging from their faces, they had.

"What the hell is that?" Cora asked, looking to the sky for an answer. I too looked up to try and discover the whereabouts of the sound, which was getting closer and closer.

Out of the corner of my eye I saw Thalia staring at the top of the mountain, mesmerized by whatever she saw. I traced her line of sight and spotted the source of the disturbance. My mouth dropped open as my eyes reached the peak of the mountain. It looked down upon us with unknown intent, its frame massive and pitch black. Its powerful wings shook violently, its amethyst eyes ferocious and focused. The thing sitting atop the icy mountain could only be described by something from fantasy: it was a dragon.

"That cannot be what I think it is," Osias whispered, clearly as stunned as the rest of us.

The dragon flicked its large, spiked tail around, chipping pieces of the mountain away. Its long, dark talons gripped deeply into the icy surface of the peak, its scales glittering from the reflection of the ice. It was both breathtaking and petrifying with its presence. Then again, how could a real-life dragon not be thrilling...but then, this wasn't real life. Was it?

"I suggest we find a different mountain to climb," I murmured, not letting my eyes drift away from the creature atop the mountain. Although it was staring at our group with high interest, there seemed to be something specific it was focused on. Perhaps it was friendly...

The dragon lifted off the mountain, sending large chunks of shattered ice cascading down below. It spread its enormous wings and soared down the side of the mountain directly toward us. Despite how large the monster actually was, it flew so gracefully and quickly. It let out a mighty roar. The sound barrelled down the mountain faster than it could fly. The thunderous vibrations nearly pushed me off my feet. It was just the motivation I needed to start running.

"I think now's a good time to start running!" I shouted, stirring the group away from the descending monster.

I tried my best to run away, but the slippery surface under my feet caused me to do more sliding than sprinting. I looked over to see Kanoa skating as best as he could as he held Adora's hand in his. I turned to face Cora, who was also struggling to get away. I could feel the dragon right behind us, its breath thick and pungent. The pounding of its wings was close enough to ruffle my hair and clothing.

"Kail, just fly away!" Cora shouted to me over the roaring creature.

I looked back and saw it was gaining ground on us quickly, its front legs outstretched, claws ready to dig deep. I could see the glint in its eyes and the sheen on his teeth. I couldn't leave my friends. I couldn't break my promise.

"Forget it!" I shouted, pulling my weapon from my back. "I'm not going anywhere without you."

I turned to face the creature, sliding backwards on the icy ground. Cora cried out at my sudden stop, but I had to protect my friends. I had to protect her. I then noticed that Thalia had stopped running long ago, and it seemed as though she was trying to stand up to the dragon. She gawked at him as he bore down upon her. I had always known that Thalia was a little strange, but I never expected her to be straight-up insane. The rest of the group picked up on the fact that Thalia and I had stopped. I started running back to grab her, but quickly realized it would be too late. The winged monster would reach my friend long before I did, and then it was going to come after the rest of us.

"Thalia!" I heard Adora shout out from behind me as I rushed to save her sister.

What I was doing was ridiculously foolish. I was running headlong into an enemy that could rip me to shreds an in instant. The dragon had landed on the ground and was lumbering toward Thalia, ice shards springing from the ground with every step. It growled and snarled hungrily, towering over my friend. I shouted out Thalia's name, but she wouldn't move.

"Thalia, get away from there, it's going to—" I yelled at her, but she put up her arm toward me as if issuing silence.

She looked up at the dragon as it approached, unflinching despite its dangerous nature. It lunged forward, its claws scratching deeply into the ice as its whole colossal body lifted into the air. I heard shouting all around me as the monster descended down upon my friend like a dark cloud. It all seemed to happen in slow motion, and yet there was nothing I could do to save her.

I slipped, not paying proper attention to what I was doing. There was a loud thud, but I wasn't sure if I had caused it or the dragon. I fell hard on my back and slid all the way up to Thalia. I grabbed at the ice to slow myself down, but failed to get a proper hold on anything. I would have slid farther if she hadn't caught me. I would have slid right into the dragon's grasp. I closed my eyes, partly from the pain that I had brought on myself, and partly from the fact that I was about to be eaten by a mythical creature. But only the former pain actually came to fruition. Had it already eaten me?

"You can open your eyes now, Kail," I heard Thalia say with a giggle.

I anxiously opened my eyes and temporarily believed I had gone blind. I quickly realized the darkness I was looking into was actually the thick neck of the dragon itself. My breath choked up and I scurried to my feet, nearly falling back to the ground. The dragon huffed, but did not move. I stood shakily, my weapon clutched tightly in my hands. I looked over to Thalia for some sort of explanation, but the smile on her face only confused me further.

I looked back to the monstrous creature before me and took in all its little details. It stood over us like some kind of guardian. Its body was not made of scales, but rather its skin seemed to twist, with tiny ridges protruding all over. Its long neck and musky scent reminded me of something, but I couldn't recall what it was. Its trunk-like tail skittered across the ice, swaying back and forth patiently. Its four legs were stumpy, but serviceable. I was sure it relied on its gigantic wings for travel anyway. The wings themselves seemed to be made out of a waxy substance that didn't quite resemble skin, more like plastic packaging. Its piercing purple eyes seemed peaceful. I sincerely hoped it was on our side.

“Is it safe?” Osias whispered loudly from behind us, keeping his distance and trying not to upset the mighty beast.

The dragon yawned, displaying its shiny black teeth. Thalia nodded confidently and walked closer to the creature. She put her hand on one of its thick legs, but it did not stir. It actually appeared to smile at her touch.

“Thalia, do you really think that’s a good idea?” I asked quietly, still not sure if loud noises would disturb the monster.

“I don’t see what harm it can do to us,” she replied.

I shook my head in frustration. Of course Thalia wouldn’t see any harm in a flying animal that could swallow us all with one gulp. Despite the fact that the creature seemed to have calmed down, I still wasn’t sure what to make of it. It was a dragon, after all.

“Did you make this, Thalia?” Adora asked.

The rest of my friends now stood in front of the giant being. I shot a glance at her to see if she was kidding, but she wasn’t. Was it truly possible that we could create anything we could think of in this world?

“Well, we were trying to think of a way to get to the top of the mountain,” she answered, the dragon now bending its head down to Thalia submissively. “So I thought I would help.”

“Well, that’s one way to solve the problem,” Osias said. “What is that smell? It smells like...black liquorice or something.”

I instantly remembered what the dragon’s smell and skin makeup reminded me of: black liquorice. The creature huffed once again, sending a wave of the candy smell washing over the entire group. I didn’t particularly like black liquorice.

“Yummy, my favourite,” Thalia said.

“So...wait,” Osias said, walking up to Thalia and trying his best not to look nervous around the epic creature. “While we were thinking of ways to get to the top of this mountain, your obvious solution was to conjure a giant dragon made completely out of black liquorice?”

“His name is Salvador,” she stated, happily looking on with awe into the eyes of her creation.

Osias stared at her with his mouth half open, trying hard to think of something intelligent to say to the whole situation. He sighed heavily in resignation.

“Ya know,” he said. “A girl like you could be dangerous in a place like this.”

She turned towards Osias with a sly look on her face. “Well, it’s a good thing I am on your side, then,” she said with a playful wink.

Osias turned away from Thalia with his face flushed and eyebrows raised. "That girl scares me sometimes," he whispered to me.

"I hadn't noticed," I said with a laugh.

"So are you going to get on it or what?" Kanoa asked, apparently not impressed with the sight of the dragon. "That's why you made it, right? So you could get up the mountain?"

We all looked over nervously at the monstrous creature Thalia had decided to name Salvador. It seemed tame enough, but the thought of using such an animal as a pet was a little too far-fetched for me to accept. Then again, before I had come into this dream world, the thought of ever even seeing a dragon seemed too far-fetched.

"I'm right behind you, Thalia," Adora stated. She enthusiastically hopped over to her sister and put her hands on the dragon's side. Salvador didn't seem to mind her touch either. Maybe the dragon was safe after all.

"No, I don't think so, Adora," Thalia said, firmly pushing her sister away from the creature. "You're not risking your life flying this thing."

"But you can?" she asked. Thalia started to say something, but the words were caught in her throat. She didn't have a valid answer. "Cora, what do you think?"

"Well," Cora said, but looked to Thalia and stopped herself. "You should probably discuss this with your sister."

Adora turned her attention back to Thalia, following Cora's suggestion. "If you are planning on doing something as dangerous as this, you can count me in, too. We survive in this world together."

Thalia stared at her sister, conflicted with her judgement. "I'm supposed to keep you safe, Adora," she said.

Adora put her hands on her sister's shoulders, looking right into her eyes, and smiled. "As long as I have you and you have me," she said "we will be safe. Promise?"

Thalia's eyes fluttered, thinking deeply on the responsibility she had as an older sister. The two sisters hadn't been out of each other's sight since we got here, which was undoubtedly the same thing I would have done had Delphia been here. Thalia was very protective of her sister. She and I were the only ones that understood what it was like to carry the weight of a sibling wherever we went. I had failed in my task, but I knew Thalia was much better suited for it. I had faith in her, and I hoped she had faith in herself.

"I promise," she finally responded, hugging her sister closely to seal the deal.

The dragon growled impatiently as we took our time mounting it.

"Oh I'm sorry," Osias said, putting his hands on his hips and looking angrily at the beast. "Are we boring you?"

It twisted its neck and bent down, bumping Osias in the chest with its enormous snout. He cowered back behind me, and the dragon smiled again.

"Shutting up now," Osias whimpered.

"Hey, I wonder if Adora's flowers will start growing on the dragon," Cora whispered to me with a laugh, temporarily forgetting the fight we had just had. She looked down at the flowers at her feet. "Have you ever seen flowers grow out of ice before, Kail?"

I looked down quickly to see that it was true: Adora's signature flowers had indeed grown out of nothing but the icy surface beneath my toes. "Have you ever seen a dragon before?" I countered.

"That's a good point," she muttered.

Thalia was the first one to mount the dragon. She used the twirls in its hide for hand and foot holdings, clumsily climbing her way on top of the creature. He didn't seem the least bit caring of the matter. She then crawled her way toward the front of its back, throwing her legs over the neck of the monster for support. It looked as though she was riding a horse.

"There's plenty of room up here for all of us!" she stated. "I promise he won't bite."

"Biting is one of the many concerns I have about this creature," Osias moaned. He quickly entered a moment of meditation, and then began grabbing onto the dragon's side. "But I suppose there's no point in listing them all off."

"And as delicious as he may seem," Thalia said as Osias helped Adora up onto the back of the dragon, "please refrain from eating Salvador, as I'm sure he would not appreciate it very much."

"Oh, I can guarantee you," Osias replied, strenuously pulling Adora up to sit level with him and her sister, "he will be taking a bite out of me long before I take one out of him."

Osias and Thalia exchanged a quick glance and smiled at one another. I often enjoyed the playful banter the two partook in. It always lightened the mood and soothed any stress anyone in the group may have had. I knew that I would never acquire the traits necessary for such lax and snappy conversations, but it was nice to have others close to me that did. To me, that was one of my favourite parts of having best friends. I was close enough to them to not just live my life, but their lives too. Sometimes, living the lives of others were the best moments of my own.

I quickly leapt up onto the creature's back. The dragon's thick hide was very stiff, as if the liquorice had been hardened over time. The skin was a little greasy, however, and Cora almost fell as she attempted to climb up to join me.

I grabbed her arm and helped her up. She thanked me and we exchanged a moment of our own, albeit far more awkward than Osias and Thalia's. I hoped that we could all become a united group again before we decided to take on the horrors of this world. We were going to have to be at our best if we wanted to defeat our foes.

"Is something wrong, Kanoa?" Adora asked.

I looked over and noticed that Kanoa had not joined us on the dragon, and didn't seem to have any intention of doing so. He was standing below the rest of us with his arms crossed, staring into the eyes of the beast.

"No, I think I'll find my own way to the top," he told us. "Dragons aren't exactly my style."

"How can dragons not be someone's style?" Osias muttered.

"What was that, Osias?" Kanoa asked.

"I asked how you're planning on getting to the top if you aren't going to accompany us on the dragon," he replied quickly.

Osias's quick thinking paid off, as Kanoa began thinking deeply instead of climbing up and making Osias think twice before poking fun at him. I saw a devilish twinge at the sides of Kanoa's lips as he thought. Apparently he had a plan.

"I have an idea," he said with a mischievous grin. "Why don't we have a little race to the top of the mountain?"

The question hung in the air for a moment, waiting for an answer to snatch it up. He looked up at us expectantly, like a dog hoping for a treat. I looked for someone to object to his request, but I honestly saw no reason why we couldn't partake in a race—other than the fact that we didn't know how to actually control the dragon.

"We don't even know how to give this thing directions yet, Kanoa," I said, voicing my concern. "Maybe we should wait a little longer before any races?"

"He is not a thing, Kail," Thalia said. "His name is Salvador."

"Right," I said. "We don't know how to control Salvador yet."

"Well, then I guess you'd better learn," Kanoa replied. With those words, he was off and skating. He tore past us toward the mountain on his blades, cutting sharply and serenely across the ice like an Olympic champion.

"Well then, I guess he wins," Osias said with a shrug, "because until we actually know –"

Thalia yelled loudly and kicked at the sides of Salvador's neck. The enormous creature sprung to motion and lifted off the ground with tremendous force. For a moment I was entirely in the air before immediately slamming back down onto the dragon's back. My heart jumped into my throat, and I hung on for my life. Its massive wings stretched out and raised high above us. It spun around quickly to face where Kanoa had dashed off to and followed after him. I pushed myself as close to the dragon's hide as I could, the strength of the creature's wings incredible and frightening.

Wind tore past me, causing an almost deafening whistling sound. I held on as hard as I could, but it still felt as though I was going to slide off, due to its slippery skin. Cora let out a scream as she began to glide down the monster's back, losing her grip. I pulled one hand away from my grasp on the dark dragon and felt myself being dragged away, bringing myself closer to Cora. I ripped my weapon away from my back and held it out for her. She bounced a little as the dragon tilted upward to begin scaling the mountain, just the redirection we had needed. She held out her hand and clumsily snagged the weapon before completely falling away from me.

I held on tightly and dug my feet firmly into Salvador's tail, skidding a bit further before finding a good foot-hold. It was then that I noticed I had been mere feet away from sliding off the creature myself. Close one.

"This is insane!" Osias shouted, holding onto the dragon as hard as he could with his legs wrapped around its sides.

"No way!" Thalia protested, using one arm to hold on loosely to the dragon's neck and her other arm to hold onto her sister. "This is way too fun to be insane!"

I awkwardly pulled Cora back up to safety, but her polearm kept getting in the way of an easy rescue. I quickly shot a glance to the top of the mountain and was surprised to see that we were rapidly catching up to Kanoa, despite his head start. Then again, we were riding a dragon and he was only skating, so perhaps our gained ground was understandable. We were fairly low to the ground, and if we weren't careful, we were going to end up crushing Kanoa.

"Thanks, Kail," Cora said. "You're always saving me."

"Oh, no problem," I said absent-mindedly, still fixated on Kanoa's position. "We're just lucky that nobody fell, or else – "

"Look out!" I heard Adora shout, one of the few times I ever heard her raise her voice.

We were right on top of Kanoa and, for a moment, I could no longer see him. I was afraid that Salvador had smeared him into the side of the mountain. Thalia somehow managed to steer her dragon to the left in a last-minute attempt to avoid the collision. The rapid redirection caused me to lose my balance. I tried grabbing onto something, but there was nothing to hold on to.

Cora reached out to grab me, her eyes wide, but our fingertips only grazed one another. The moment hung in the air, our eyes meeting, hers terrified and full of sadness and mine but an empty reflection. There was no noise as I fell backwards because a part of me knew that I had come to my end. There was only the look in her eyes. I swung my arms around wildly to try and catch my balance, but it was too late.

I still had Hope's Glow in my arms and wasn't prepared to let it go. I completely fell off the winged creature's back and began to free fall. Its long legs and tail reached out far behind the monster, and I made one final attempt to latch onto something. As I fell past the muscular leg of the dragon, I thrust out my weapon and, amazingly, got it stuck around the gnarled toes of the beast. The sudden snag of my weapon wrenched at my arms and felt as though they would rip out of their sockets. I hadn't careened down the side of the icy mountain to my doom, but my problems were far from over.

The dragon's leg flailed, repulsed by the foreign weight I had added to its toes. I slammed up and down onto the side of the mountain violently, causing shots of pain to course through my body. Its tail fell up and down against the mountain, spraying ice shards all around it. Its massive wings produced loud, thumping echoes against the icy surface below, sending miniature shock waves of sound my way. I wasn't sure what I would have preferred: gaining more altitude to stop hitting the ground with the risk of falling to my death, or staying low to the ground and enduring the beating. I simply held on as tightly as I could, wondering how long until we finally reached the summit.

"Kail!" I heard a voice shout nearby.

I spun my head around as much as I could to try to see where the voice had come from as cold wind tore at my ears and face. I noticed that Kanoa was skating far behind the dragon, avoiding its dangerous tail as best he could. Somehow he had averted being trampled by the out-of-control creature and had been forced to stay behind us. It didn't matter how he had done it, I was just glad to see he was all right. Unfortunately for me, his face bore something I feared more than most things I could imagine: a smile.

"Let go!" he shouted. "I'll grab you as you slide by!"

"That sounds like a terrible idea!" I shouted back, smacking down onto the hard, icy surface of the mountain once again. "Got any other ones?"

The dragon's tail once again swept across the side of the mountain like a great windshield wiper, threatening to collide with Kanoa. Instead, he effortlessly jumped clean over the massive tail and began powering his way toward me. His agility and prowess was stunning, almost to the point where everything around him appeared sluggish. Each stride he took brought him many metres closer, despite the incredible speed with which the dragon was carrying me, which then led me to wonder just how high this mountain truly was.

"Kail, you have to let go!" he shouted again. "I promise that I'll catch you!"

"I can't let go!" I cried, my pants skittering across the now-jagged surface of the mountain side.

My chains jangled loudly against the battering force of the wind. I wasn't going to fail my responsibility by letting go of Hope's Glow, letting go of the one thing I had been granted in this world.

I heard Kanoa curse my stubbornness and attempt to get closer to me. He extended his arm toward me, but remained just out of reach. The dragon wriggled around for a moment and almost sideswiped my friend right off the narrowing face of the mountain. We had to be getting close to the top. I hoped that Thalia would find a way to stop her creation before he took us into the stratosphere.

"Give me your hand!" Kanoa demanded, his own just out of reach.

I took a deep breath and freed one hand from my weapon. I was almost certain my grip wasn't going to hold and I would instantly lose Hope's Glow, but to my surprise, I held on. I extended my arm as far as I could toward Kanoa, our fingertips mere centimetres from each other. I gasped and strained to grab hold of him, but we just weren't close enough. Kanoa's face quickly turned from determination to sheer dread. His focus seemed to have shifted from me to something behind me. I turned my head uncomfortably to see what had caused his distress, and then quickly joined him in his worry. The top of the mountain was fast approaching.

"Now would be a really good time to let go, Kail!" Kanoa barked at me.

"I'm not letting go!" I yelled in frustration. Our fingers grazed one another, but it wasn't enough. I cried out in anger at my predicament, for it was the only thing I could really do. "I just can't. I'm sorry, but I just can't do it!"

"Damn it, Kail," he grumbled.

He swiftly pulled his blade forward and held it in front of him. I wasn't sure what he was doing, but as I looked back at the ever-enclosing summit, I wished he would do it quickly. For a moment I thought he was going to cut off my arm, which was probably the only way I would let go. However, to my pleasant surprise, when he swung, he didn't aim at my arm. He brought his long sword into Hope's Glow in a fast upward motion, unlatching it from the hold it had on the dragon's foot. There was a loud clanging noise as his blade collided with my weapon, and the wrenching pain on my arms ceased. I had broken free—but my troubles, once again, were far from over.

The dragon peeled away from us as I fell into Kanoa's outstretched arms. I slammed into him hard and he caught me clumsily, which although painful, was a far better fate than sliding all the way back down the mountainside. Kanoa had not braced for the impact, unfortunately, and quickly lost balance, his skates cutting away at the mountain and trying to regain control.

I put my feet back onto the ground to try and slow us down, which apparently wasn't the smart thing to do. I promptly fell on my back. Kanoa, still moving forward at a high speed, tripped over me and his skates came dangerously close to slicing open my face. I pushed his feet away from me as we slid up the top of the mountain. I scratched at the icy surface, trying to slow down before I overshot the top and fell to my doom.

Suddenly, Kanoa and I were in the air, but had not yet reached the tip of the mountain. Our arms and legs flailed wildly as we soared. We landed painfully on a flat plane and skidded a little, due to the slick surface. I remembered the ridge that I had seen overlooking the land while in the mountain's shadow. I could finally breathe easy. The soreness in my arms and legs caused me to groan, which was met with the laughter of my friend. I looked over to him as we lay at the top of the world, thinking about the many reasons we had not to laugh, and not caring about any of them. I joined my friend and laughed with him.

"Now if that wasn't legendary," I heard him say between coughs and laughter, "I don't even want to know what is."

"You," I choked out, still looking up at the blank sky. "You're a little crazy, you know that?"

"Yeah, well," he responded between deep breaths, "everyone's a little crazy, and knowing that is the only thing that keeps me sane."

There was a loud thud nearby, and I instantly sat upright. Thalia's pet dragon had landed at the other side of the ridge, looking rather anxious. The remainder of my friends that had been able to hold onto the creature quickly jumped off his back one by one, before it spread its wings and took flight. After Salvador had dumped off my friends like it was a bus unloading children, it let out a mighty roar in mid-air and flew out of sight. As abruptly as it had entered our dreams, the monster was gone.

"Damn dragons," Osias grunted. "Hope I never have to see one of those again."

"Are you guys okay?" Cora shouted, slipping and sliding her way toward us.

Thalia, Adora and Osias slowly made their way over, looking out toward the land the mountain oversaw. It was cold enough at the top of the mountain to see my breath escape my lips. I waved over to them to show that we were fine. Kanoa stood up and staggered toward the edge of the ridge.

"Can you believe your eyes, Kail?" I heard Kanoa whisper gently, wonder and awe possessing his question.

"Yeah, right," I said, shakily getting to my feet. "My eyes are among the last things I would trust in this place."

I looked out over the world and was amazed with what I saw. The icy surface of the mountain's base below remained the same, but beyond its cold grasp laid a churning, restless land of colour and motion. Nothing stayed the same for long, as each mountain flattened into plains, each lake evaporated into trees, and each patch of snow melted into sand. The land was waging a never-ending battle against itself in a chaotic struggle to find peace. Just like in dreams, nothing was ever constant. If I looked away from something for a moment, it was gone. I couldn't even be sure if Kanoa was seeing the same things I was. It wasn't just my imagination creating this place after all.

"It's like," he whispered, sounding nearly on the verge of tears. "It's like I've been homesick my entire life for some place I'd never been. And now I'm here. I've finally found my home."

"It's something, all right," I muttered, trying not to take his moment away from him. "You won't see anything like it anywhere else."

"See, this is my problem," Kanoa fumed, an unsettling amount of rage in his voice. "Our world didn't have enough mysteries. It was always about science reducing wonders into facts. I'd love for those teachers at home to get a look at this and tell me they understand it. Lie to my face like I lied to theirs. They'd never understand this like I do."

I stared at him briefly, wondering what was going through his head at that moment. What compelled him to say something like that? I understood that Kanoa always had frustrations about the mundane nature of life back home, but I always assumed it was just something he would grow to accept. I quickly looked away from him and back out over the land, not wanting to think about the potential damage a sight like this was doing to his psyche.

"I wonder if this is what Alice felt like," Adora said, sounding distant.

I looked around dazedly and realized that the six of us, The Inseparable Six, were now standing side by side, all looking out over our very own wonderland. Something about the whole scene just felt right. I didn't want to be anywhere else with anyone else. I knew, for once, that I was exactly where I wanted to be. The feeling was one I was not accustomed to. It was a feeling I was afraid of. Was my life always leading up to this place?

"Oh, man, look at the sky!" Osias shouted out excitedly.

I looked to the sky and quickly realized that we were in outer space. Apparently the mountain had risen higher than I thought, but the land still remained visible below us. There was no blue sky, but the darkness of space. Besides the many twinkling lights of distant planets and stars, I saw a myriad of different things: spaceships possibly out of science fiction properties, meteors streaking across the sky, the clock that watched over time in this world, and most notably, two large moons off in the distance that seemed to be moving toward one another.

"There goes the Starship Enterprise!" Osias exclaimed in euphoria-like joy. "And the Millennium Falcon! And The SSV Normandy! And the – "

"We get it, Osias," Kanoa interrupted. "There are a lot of space ships, and you're a big enough nerd to know all their names."

With the weight of the universe above us and the gravity of our dreams below, I felt like I had been caught in the middle of something very special, something I had never felt back at home. I suddenly felt very aware of my being. I knew that I held a place in space and time. There was no wind here, no air to breathe, only me. When I was back at home, I always knew I was alive, but not like this. It is one thing to hear about what is out there in the giant expanse of the galaxy, but when everything is laid out in front of your eyes and you actually know it's there... It's like the distance between you and God no longer exists. You are God.

"See, Cora," Kanoa said. "This is what I always saw when I closed my eyes. This is what I always wanted to show you, but never could."

"I'll admit," she replied, sounding as if she was conceding to a long-standing argument. "Your imagination was always something I admired, Kanoa. I don't always agree where it leads you, but this is pretty amazing."

"Thanks," he said, taking the compliment humbly.

"I guess this is a new one for The Inseparable Six, huh?" Cora asked. I looked over to her and realized that she had been standing next to me the entire time.

"Yeah, I guess so," I said with a distant laugh, still looking out, wanting the image before me to never end. The two looming moons out in the distance were clearly on a collision path with one another. I hoped their massive impact wouldn't affect us.

"What do you think of this place?" she asked, somehow managing to break her gaze from what was before us to look at me. I only noticed out of the corner of my peripheral vision, as I dared not look away, lest it vanish away from me like a mirage.

"I don't think anything needs to be said," I responded, my voice sounding distant to me. "Putting words to it would just ... ruin it."

"Nothing is ever easy with you, is it, Kail?" she muttered in frustration. "Well, not with you and I, anyway."

I felt guilty for the way I had treated her. Not just in that moment, but for everything I had done to her since we had entered this world, and even before that. I put all my effort into tearing my eyes away from their trance and focused them upon her, my best friend. I saw the glimmer in her eyes and the fire in her stare and smiled.

"Come on, Cora," I said, playfully nudging her shoulder. "We both know it's the friction between us that causes that spark in your eyes."

The flame in her eyes simmered with moisture, and she smiled back at me. We both quickly looked back at our creation and I knew that without her, this place would be different. But I also knew that I didn't want it to be different. It was perfect the way it was.

"Hey, Cora," I said. "What would you want out of a perfect world?"

"That's kind of a random question, don't you think?" she replied.

"Have you seen where we are?" I asked with a laugh. "I think this is as good a time as any to ask that question."

She laughed and nodded her head in acceptance. She looked down for a moment, and I knew that the answer had always been on the tip of her tongue. She had just been waiting for someone to ask her. I bet she was glad it had been me.

"Well, I guess that in my perfect world," she began, choosing her words wisely as to not miss her chance, "I would want people to have the courage and the freedom to sing out loud, at the top of their lungs. Everyone always has music going through them in one way or another, so why don't they just express it? Everyone has a voice... and I want to hear them all."

The answer hung in the air for a moment, letting me visualize their meaning and judge what she dreamed for. All she really wanted was for people to have the same passion in what they did as she did. Unfortunately for her, I knew her perfect world was impossible. People just weren't the way she wanted them to be. Some people just didn't have voices.

"But it's just a stupid dream of mine…" she said, interpreting my silence as a sign of my disproval.

"I don't think it's stupid at all, Cora," I replied with sincerity. "I think it sounds beautiful."

"I think so too," she said with an embarrassed smile, looking back out over the ridge. "And what about you, Kail? What's your perfect world?"

Therein was the problem with asking complicated questions: people usually reciprocated. Sometimes I just wished that people would answer questions and not feel obligated to 'return to sender'. And yet at the same time...with this particular question, I had it already answered in my head. I was exactly where I wanted to be—with her and the rest my friends on this mountaintop peering into our wildest imaginings. This, right now, was my perfect world, I wanted to say. So why couldn't I tell her? Why couldn't I let someone into my thoughts when they were looking directly at them?

"I..." I stuttered. "I'd rather not say."

"But I thought you said now is as good a time as any?" she complained, confused.

The hurt look in her eyes was almost too much for me to handle without wanting to just leap right over the ledge. There was literally nothing holding me back from emptying myself out to her, except myself. My life had taught me that the more I invested myself in others, the harder they would end up hurting me, even if they didn't mean to. It was just a part of who I was now, whether I liked it or not...and for the record, I hated it.

"I know, but," I muttered, completely and hopelessly conflicted. I fought through the pain of her gaze and looked right into her eyes with determination. "One day...I'll tell you, Cora. I'll tell you ... everything. I promise."

"Oh, Kail," she said, sighing heavily. She looked away from me with tears in her eyes and pain in her voice. "I've been your friend for as long as I can remember, and I still don't know a damn thing about you."

I followed her gaze back out into the void that held everything. It held all the dreams, memories, imaginations and lives of six people, and yet I still wondered whether it held the answers to my problems. At that moment, I felt very alone.

"You're such a mystery to me," she continued, "and I hate that about you."

The two moons out in the distance finally completed their destined course into one another. They met not with sound, but light. From their impact sprung the tiniest, brightest light I had ever laid my eyes on. The light caused my eyes to cringe and repelled them away. The crushing force the two had on one another began to mould their two foundations into one. The light spread, as did their transformation into a single entity. Those two worlds...our two worlds had finally collided into one another at the speed of light.

"I know you hate what you don't know about me," I said, barely above a whisper. "But I'm glad you stick around for what you do know. For that, I'm thankful."

She was silent for a moment, and then spoke the last words I heard before we could no longer see each other. "I can't believe that we're dreaming."

"We are dreaming," I responded, the light sucking the words from my lips. "We're dreaming with our eyes open."

The light that had once been no larger than a pinhead on the horizon was now growing all around us. What had once been two round moons had now melded into one; one that I could had sworn resembled nothing other than a heart made of rock. If someone had been watching, they would have seen six friends standing over their lives, under the emptiness of the unknown, facing the heart of all things. And as the white light washed over us, consuming us in what may have been our ends, my hand brushed against hers and they too, became one. My life in her hand, and her life in mine, was the last things I felt before all had vanished before my eyes.

CHAPTER 10: AND SO IT BEGINS

"Kail, I'm scared," Delphia whispered, fidgeting in place beside me.

She held her favourite blue gloves in her hands tightly, scrunching them up to relieve stress. Over the years, they had been used so many times to comfort her that the material had torn and frayed. I began to wonder if they had ever actually been used to keep her hands warm.

"Don't be scared," I whispered back, keeping my eyes on our doorway and listening intently for any footsteps. "They'll be really nice and like us, and then we can go away with them."

"You say that every time," she muttered, probably reminiscing about all the other times I had told her such things. How many times I had lied to her...

I snapped out of my memory and once again realized I was back in the orphanage. It was getting more difficult to pull myself out of the memory and remember that I was actually still dreaming. It just all felt so real, like I was living it for the first time and just happened to know what was coming next. It was a little unnerving going through the motions of my life, knowing what was around the corner without being able to change anything. If I wasn't able to change anything as I wanted to, then why did this keep happening to me?

"I think I hear someone," Delphia said, excitement and anxiety in her voice.

She hastily shoved her gloves into her pocket and grabbed my hand with hers. I could feel her warmth in my hand. It was the first time I had been able to hold my sister in over ten years. My heart felt as though it would burst through my chest. I wanted to scream or cry or laugh, but I didn't know what to do. It was like finding something precious that I had thought lost so very long ago, and hoping that I would never let go of it again.

"Now, remember," I told her quietly and calmly. "Just be yourself, and they'll like you."

"What if they don't like me?" she asked, sadly looking down at the floor.

"Well, then at least I'll still like you," I replied without missing a beat. That was nice of me to say, I thought to myself.

"Yeah, but you're my brother," she whispered. I looked down at her and she looked up at me simultaneously. Our eyes met and produced a smile on both of our faces. Yeah, I thought to myself, and I still am. Always will be.

The footsteps stopped right outside our door, snapping our attention away from each other. Even though I knew what would come of this meeting, it was still an odd feeling to witness the first encounter I had with people I would know for the rest of my life. If I could only find a way to alter this moment, I would perhaps be able to change what would inevitably...

The door creaked open slowly, inch by inch, revealing who was behind it. The people that had just entered my life were a young couple who were fairly wealthy, judging by their clothing. The woman had long dark hair and glasses that shielded her bright green eyes. The man had short, feathered blonde hair and a pair of deep blue eyes. They looked perfect together. Both of them had on luminous smiles, not like the impressionable ones I am sure my sister and I currently had.

These two people were holding hands and clearly in love with one another. These two people would eventually go on to take me away from this place I refused to call home. These two people would come to love me like they would a son, a love I would never return. These two people were the reason I would never see Delphia again. These two people were my future adopting parents.

"Kail and Delphia?" the woman asked, her voice laced with the condescension that was difficult to pick up on as a young child, but once you are old enough to use it for yourself, you know what it sounds like. The woman meant well, but it is always hard talking to kids without making them seem stupid.

We both nodded our heads nervously, the pained smiles still on our hopeful faces. At this point in our childhood, we put on this act of being the happiest children in the world many times. They wanted us to act like kids who had merely grown tired of living in an orphanage and decided that now was a good time to explore the possibility of living with a family we could call our own. In reality, however, we lived in a terribly depressing place that made us constantly feel like used toys at a garage sale, looking for new owners. And every time I hoped that it would be our last act, our final showing...

"My name is Keeley, and this is Garnet," she explained, motioning to the man standing beside her. "How are you today?"

Oh, we're fantastic, I thought to myself maliciously, filled with both the hatred of the events that had now been put in motion and the frustration of not being able to change them. If I could just reach out and close the door so that they would leave and never come back. Yes, these people were responsible for the upgraded way of life I would lead for the next decade, and for that I was grateful. However, they were also indirectly responsible for the moment in my life that would forever haunt me more than any other. Would I trade my life in reserved happiness for one of whole sadness? Yes I would, every time.

"So this is your room, huh?" Garnet, my future father, asked timidly. It appeared that he was almost as nervous as we were. "May we come in?"

Without saying a word, Delphia grabbed me to her side and motioned them graciously to enter our room. They came in leisurely and looked over our belongings, and just as I was unsure at the time this meeting took place so many years ago, I was once again uncertain as to whether they were genuinely looking through our belongings or merely acting their part. Just as I had walked through museums with only marginal interest as to what I was viewing despite its priceless value to others, I felt as though they did not show as much care as they should have. This was our sad excuse for a home, and they probably thought it was pathetic. Yet the welcoming faces they had when I first saw them remained upon their faces. Perhaps still part of the act, or authentic interest?

"That's our bunk bed," Delphia said, excitedly pointing over to where we slept.

I was impressed with the courage she displayed, for if she had not pushed me away from the door, I would not have moved at all. The truth of the matter was that I had been terrified of our guests. For all the prepping I did, and all the advice I gave my sister in order to impress our potential parents, she was the only one between us to actually utilize my words.

"You two sleep right here?" Keeley asked animatedly, a typical parent overreaction to such a small and obvious revelation.

"Yup," Delphia said, nodding almost spastically. "I sleep on the bottom and my brother sleeps on the top. He says that I roll around in my dreams, and it's too dangerous for me to sleep so high up."

I could feel that the two adults in the room both had shifted their focus to me, and I knew that in that moment I was blushing. I had never been a big fan of bringing attention to myself. It was always more Kanoa's thing, which reminded me that at this moment in my life, I had not yet met Kanoa. For the time being, I had my sister to thank for any attention thrust upon me.

"So you look out for your little sister, huh?" My mom...Keeley asked, rather impressed, making her way over to where I was standing.

"Uh, yeah," I replied hesitantly, startled both by hearing my voice without calling for it, and by the newfound interest in me by the two adults. "She's my little sister and I look out for her. That's what big brothers are for."

Why am I talking about it like it's a job? I thought to myself begrudgingly. Although I was not pleased with what I had said, the two adults seemed rather impressed with my awareness of liability. I knew what they saw in me: a sense of maturity and responsibility. But they were not conscientious of the fact that it was misplaced. These traits they found in me were not innate to my personality. They only applied to Delphia. I was not universally caring or thoughtful, as they wanted me to be. They would later find this out when we became separated from one another.

"Do you like it here?" Garnet pressed on, putting me through some sort of pre-planned gauntlet of questions the two had prepared. It was then I began to notice they had forgotten all about Delphia.

"We," I began, walking over to my sister and bringing her back to their attention, "don't care where we are, as long as we have each other. We have as much fun as we can but we want a real home."

"Yeah," my sister added, "my friends here are nice and I like to play with them, but I want to go where my brother goes."

"Do you have a lot of friends here?" Keeley asked my sister, bending down to meet her at eye level.

My mom... She looked a lot younger then. Eight years does a lot to a person, no matter who you are. Nobody lives that amount of time without getting a few wrinkles they would like to forget. I wondered about all the ones I had undoubtedly created.

"Yes," my sister replied. She happily rested her head on her shoulder and displayed her childish smile, made authentic by a few missing teeth. Any sign of anxiety she once had was gone, and she was very excited to indulge in her life for our possible adopters. "I like to play hide-and-seek in the forest with my friends. I have this hiding spot in a tree trunk that nobody has ever found me in!"

"And the adults, um, old people here take good care of you?" she pressed on with a big smile, laughing at my sister's story.

I wanted to wipe that smile off her face, for I knew she wasn't asking these questions because she wanted my sister to display her wonderful, innocent personality. She was asking these questions for her own secret reasoning; the true reason they had come here.

"They're nice to me," she answered, less enthusiastically than her previous response. "But my brother doesn't like them very much."

This shifted the focus back to me, for her answer was truthful. This further intrigued the man and woman.

"Why don't you like them, Kail?" Garnet asked. It wasn't for a sinister reason, such as child abuse, as he was probably thinking.

"I just don't like them," I replied, now warming up to the hopeful parents and being more honest. "They treat everyone here like they're their parents, and they're not."

"What if we were your parents?" Keeley asked.

This question caught me completely off-guard, as it had the first time it had been asked. My heart soared into my head and filled it with all the conceptions I had as a child of love and having parents who cared for me. At this point in our lives, my sister and I no longer really cared about the quality of our adoptive parents. As long as they put a roof over our heads and fed us regularly, we would be content. We just wanted a place to call home.

My sister and I exchanged wide-eyed stares, and I could see the very definition of child-like wonder. I could see the dreams she had been having since the beginning, dreams I had put in her head, coming to life in those small yet hopeful eyes of hers. Little did either of us know at the time that her dreams would never come true, which meant that neither would mine.

“Well then, I would like you,” I stated with an uneasy sigh of laughter.

There was a sudden, jarring, loud burst of static that erupted over the memory in front of me. Keeley and Garnet were now gone, our door was closed, and Delphia was lying down on her bed. It was as if time had fast-forwarded, or an entire scene from a movie had been spliced out. I was once again disoriented to my surroundings, confused as to what had just happened and why. Were the missing pieces simply not important enough to be included, or I had actually forgotten about that part of my life?

“Maybe they have bunk beds at their house,” my sister thought out loud, still showing the dazed look on her face she had right before time had shifted.

Once again not through my will, I leapt up onto the top bed and sat there with my legs over the side. My legs were almost long enough to touch the ground from atop the tiny bunk bed, reminding me that I was still a foreign presence in my old memories.

“Well, I hope that they’re comfier,” I complained, grabbing the stiff mattress with both hands in displeasure.

“Maybe they have a pool, too!” she continued, letting the imaginings of our possible new home get the better of her.

“You don’t know how to swim,” I stated with a laugh.

“Yeah, but I could learn with a pool,” she countered, undoubtedly pretending to swim in her bed, although I couldn’t see what she was doing. It was often frustrating not being able to control what I was doing in these memories.

“Our room is going to be bigger than this one,” she stated confidently.

I could hear her bouncing around excitedly. I dropped my head down to look at her and saw her at her most joyful. It was like Christmas morning, her birthday, the last day of school, and every other happy thing she could think of, all rolled into one moment.

“Hey, we aren’t out of here yet,” I reminded her, wincing at the subtle yet terrible foreshadowing in my words. No, we certainly were not out of here yet, I repeated disdainfully in my head.

“Yeah, I know,” she conceded, calming down and lying back onto her pillow.

There was a moment of silence between us that I enjoyed thoroughly. I was just staring at my sister in her bed, like I had done so many times before. I almost wanted to give in to the pull of my memory and just forget the fact that none of this was real. Yet it was real, it just wasn't real anymore.

"Do you think Mom and Dad would be happy for us?" she asked, not really caring to hear my answer, just making the question known to me.

I thought it over for a moment, both then and now. What did it matter whether they did or not, I thought. They weren't around anymore. Our lives were out of their hands now.

"I don't know," I responded truthfully. "I don't really care."

"Why don't you care?" she asked, looking up at me intently.

I only vaguely remembered how this conversation played out, as I had still been focusing on the prospect of finally escaping our stay in the orphanage. I remembered remaining transfixed by that thought for days afterward, constantly telling other children that they would soon never see me again. I hadn't been lying to them, as it turned out, but the truth would come about itself in a way I hadn't been expecting.

"They left us here," I replied through clenched teeth. "Why would they care? It's not like I even know what they look like, and they probably don't know what we look like. You can't love someone when you don't know what they look like."

Was that true? I thought to myself. What does it take to love someone? Do you have to know what someone looks like to love them? If that was true, then how could Delphia love me, or I love her, if we no longer knew what each other looked like anymore? I never really even pretended to understand what love was, because to me it was just a word. I felt that it was a word I could apply to Delphia, and possibly my friends—but it was still a word, no different from any other. It was a word that everyone was guilty of throwing around without knowing the weight of it, myself included. It was a word that people used when they didn't understand how else they felt about someone. A word with a different meaning to everyone was hard to take seriously.

"Just because Mom and Dad don't know what we look like," she said, "doesn't mean they don't exist, or that they don't love us, Kail."

"Kail, there you are," Osias said with a sigh of relief as he offered his hand to pick me up off the ground. "We all got separated after the sky kind of exploded on us."

I realized we were no longer on top of the mountain, and that I was lying in an open field, covered with trimmed red grass, looking up at the sky. There were no longer any moons or stars or spaceships, but the wild clouds and the giant clock were back in their respective places. Among the clouds, I could have sworn the word "Hope" was etched across the sky.

“Are you okay?” he asked with concern, his hand still outstretched toward me.

I looked back at him and away from the clouds, a look of severe confusion unquestionably upon my face. I decided it was best not to worry my friend or fill his head with the thoughts pouring out of mine.

“Yeah, I’m fine,” I replied, swiftly taking his hand and getting back onto my feet.

“Well that’s good,” he said, “because Alem’s back, and he wants us to begin our little adventure now. Why the hell is the grass red here? You know, that sight up on the mountain got me thinking. What if we’re all having separate dreams?”

“What do you mean?” I asked, looking around for where the rest of our friends were, paying little attention to Osias’s ramblings.

“I mean,” he explained, “we all got hooked up into separate machines. What if what I’m dreaming about and what you’re dreaming about are different? What you see of me right now isn’t real, or what I see of you isn’t real, and we’re all in our own unique dreams? What if I’m actually still asleep in my tent, and this whole thing is just one big dream? What if all my life has just been some kind of dream?”

“You know what I think?” I said, looking over at him and watching him feverishly pace back and forth. “I think you’re just over-thinking everything, like you always do.”

“Yeah, maybe,” he replied, noticeably unconvinced. “Or you aren’t thinking about this nearly enough.”

“How about we go back to our friends, see what Alem has to say, take out these bad guys, and then we can start talking about your craziness?” I said, patting him on the shoulder to try and snap him out of his fortress of a mind. He tended to ramble when he was engrossed in a topic of his interest. Or when he was scared.

“Hmph,” he grunted, still wrapped up in his theories. “That would be one long conversation.”

My friend and I walked across the red field, heading back to where he had stumbled upon the rest of my friends and the venerable old man whom we had accepted as our guide to this mystifying place. According to Osias, Alem insisted that we should begin our journey, so that we might find our way back into the real world. I didn’t think it sounded like such a bad idea.

“Ah, it would appear Osias has found him,” I heard Alem’s prudent voice emanate through my head. “They shouldn’t be long now.”

“You can hear that, right?” Osias asked.

"You mean Alem's voice?" I asked, knowing what he was referring to and nodding in response.

"Yeah," he said with a heavy sigh. "He keeps asking me 'what am I going to do with all those various talents I possess' and I keep telling him that I have no idea. I have no idea how he knows of my intelligence anyway, because I certainly haven't been able to use it here. This...whole place is a little out of my jurisdiction ya know? I'm only eighteen, for goodness' sake. I mean, I always thought of being a writer, but my parents say that I would be squandering my potential. I don't know, they're probably right."

"Well, if you want to be a writer," I said, "then do it. You shouldn't be what other people want you to be. You only live once, ya know?"

"Yeah, but you only die once," he countered, sounding defeated. I assumed he had discussion with himself often, possibly every day. "I'd rather not disappoint anyone or waste the one chance I get at life. I don't like letting people down."

"I thought you didn't like counting on other people?" I teased, referencing the many times Osias would insist to perform a task himself instead of giving anyone else a chance. They 'simply wouldn't do it as well as I can,' as he would put it.

"I don't like that, either," he retorted. "You know me, Kail. I work better on my own. Life's given me plenty of practise."

"You're not on your own right now," I said, trying to console him. It was best to jump on Osias's self-doubts before they spiralled out of control and sent him into a deep depression.

"Ah, here comes Frodo and Sam!" I heard Thalia shout. "Nice of you two to join us."

Osias turned to me with a humble smile on his face. "Don't look at me," he said. "You would definitely be Sam."

"At least I don't get molested by a spider," I pointed out, putting my hand softly on the back of his neck and pretending to be a spider. He shuddered and pulled away from me.

"I'm not a big fan of spiders," he stated, apprehensively rubbing the back of his neck.

"Don't say that too loud," I advised him. "The Torturer might hear you."

"He will not be the first step in your path to victory," I heard Alem say. "The Illusionist will likely be the first of your fearsome foes."

"That was some cute alliteration," Osias said, taking his place in the circle that had formed between my friends and our new ally.

Kanoa looked very excited about the task at hand, bouncing up and down between his toes and heels. Adora and Thalia whispered to each other, possibly discussing what they should do if they were to become separated. Cora seemed rather distant, looking down at the red grass beneath her, her eyes glinting ever so softly. It was good to see that all my friends had survived the event that had taken place on the mountaintop.

"I can assure you," Alem said, "that The Illusionist is far from cute. He is cunning, manipulative, twisted, and most importantly of all, relentless in his treachery. When in his presence, whether you realize it or not, you are not to believe anything you see or hear. As his name implies, he specializes in illusion."

"He doesn't seem like he would put up much of a fight," Kanoa said with a shrug, once again displaying his foolish courage.

"Why must you fight everything that moves?" Osias asked, agitatedly raising a disapproving eyebrow at our reckless friend.

"Not everything that moves," Kanoa corrected with a smile. "Just anything that gets in my way."

"Don't substitute valour for lack of appreciation for your own mortality," Osias warned him.

"Hide behind your big words for as long as you can," Kanoa sneered. "Sooner or later, you're going to have to fight just as hard as I am."

Adora poked Kanoa in the ribs with her elbow and gave him the sternest look she could muster, which wasn't all that imposing, and he was silent. Osias shook his head in frustration and chose not to speak any further either. Alem looked back and forth between the two, as if sensing something between them deeper than the argument that had just taken place.

"Ignore them," Adora said, "and continue with what you were saying."

"Yes," Alem replied, still studying my friends thoroughly. "As I was saying about the Illusionist and his… ways. Your greatest strength will lie not with your fists or weapons, but with your wits. He is a very clever fellow who can, and will, use your uncertainty with this world against you. As a matter of fact, I would say that your best chance of victory will be achieved through none other than Kail here."

"And why's that?" I asked, irritated with the fact that once again everyone was looking to me for some kind of answer. First I was the unwilling oracle of this world, and now I was the best bet of defeating our first challenge. I was beginning to wonder if anyone else was going to get a turn in the spotlight.

"Why do you think?" Cora asked, clenching her jaw with a disheartened tone in her voice.

With Cora's words, it then became clear to me why I would be so valuable in this first fight. I had gotten pretty good at questioning everything in my life, including this whole dream. Why wouldn't I do well in a battle where the only way to win was to not believe anything to be true?

"Kail's lack of trust in this world," Alem explained, "will be of great use to you all. I cannot say for sure how long it will be in your journey before you come across The Illusionist, but as long as you have him close to you, Kail will steer you clear of any dangers you may face."

"Hold on a second," Osias interrupted, causing Kanoa to roll his eyes. "I have a question. Does everyone that comes into this program, or whatever it is, have to complete quests and defeat villains like we do?"

"No, this was all made especially difficult for you six, just for the fun of it," Alem teased, to which Osias squinted his eyes in displeasure. "I have told you already that no single person has the same kind of memories, or dreams or imaginations as another, never mind the fact that there are six of you here all at once!"

"What if Malise shows up?" Adora asked.

"Then you have me," Kanoa assured with a pat on her shoulder.

"Actually," Alem butted in, "once again, Kail will be the only one to vanquish her for good. He possesses Hope's Glow and, as that prophecy foretold, it is the only thing that will bring peace to this land. Luckily, he did not lose it on your adventurous dragon ride. "

I suddenly felt the weight of the weapon on my back and the responsibility that came with it. I knew that it wasn't real, and the only reason it was so precious was because this dream world said it was, and yet I couldn't help but feel somewhat significant and pressured because of it. If I gave this power the recognition that was desired of me, it would be like I was back in the orphanage, looking after my little sister and hoping that something good would come of all my effort. Could I really take on that kind of duty again? Could I handle failure again?

"So I have to use this thing to defeat her, huh?" I asked, pulling the weapon off my back to view it for myself. Its sheen reflected myself back at me, a look of cautious realization in my eyes.

"Yes. Other than your very own imaginations, Hope's Glow is the most powerful weapon at your disposal," he replied, marvelling at my weapon and I united together. It shone ever so slightly as I felt the courage within me swell. "You should see when that thing lights up. It is quite the spectacle."

"Yeah, yeah, Kail's the chosen one, blah blah blah," Kanoa cut in, breaking up the moment of self-revelation I was having. "Can we get on with all this already?"

"You may leave immediately," Alem stated, his voice sending a chill through my body. "But I must warn you, this is not a matter that any of you will leave from unscathed. This is the most dangerous environment you will ever encounter in your lives. It's odd, isn't it? That something you carry around every day of your lives, something you take for granted, is now here to haunt you. These are your imaginations, and they will leave a mark."

"Jeez, don't overwhelm us with confidence or anything," Osias muttered, looking noticeably shaken. "What the hell are you doing scaring us like that before sending us off?"

"Would you have preferred me not to warn you of what lies ahead, and have sent you into a maze blindfolded?" the old man replied, not seeming the least bit apologetic.

"Kind of," Osias muttered, looking down at his feet tensely.

Alem's warning left us all visibly worried. Even Kanoa was a little on edge. Dark clouds began circling above our heads where a clear sky had been moments ago. None of us had any idea what to expect, had no idea what any of our imaginations were capable of. I had enough problems to fill this world myself, and I dreaded to think what my friends had to add. For once, I wished I had very dull and safe friends. I had known these people long enough to know that this new world of ours was going to be perilous. Right now, my friends were my worst enemies.

"Well, then," Kanoa said, breaking the eerie silence that had befallen us. "I guess we'd better get going."

"We don't even know where we're going," I spat, annoyed with his willingness to plunge into the great unknown without the slightest clue of how to get back out again. His impulsivity was the reason we were in this predicament in the first place.

"It doesn't matter," Alem said. "There are no paths or tunnels or lairs to find. As you all undoubtedly saw atop that mountain, the land of Drephoria isn't exactly a stable one. Go in any direction you like. I can assure you that they will all lead to the same destination."

"So after we defeat The Illusionist, The General, The Artist, The Torturer, and Malise herself," Thalia said, listing off our adversaries in a strangely calm manner, "then what happens?"

"Well, assuming you get that far," Alem replied, "hopefully all goes well and you all can return to your own world. I heard you six are inseparable, after all, so hopefully that stays true."

"Hopefully," Osias muttered, shaking his head. "Well then, like Kanoa said, I guess we better get going and hopefully make it home in one piece, which seems rather unlikely by the sound of it."

"Sounds good to me!" Thalia chimed in, trying to spread cheer to our gloomy group of friends.

"Okay," Osias said with a sigh, shaking off the weight of the events bogging down his thoughts. "Just point us to that yellow brick road, and we'll be on our way."

The menacing clouds overhead began to evaporate as smiles made their way across our faces. I realized, and I hoped the rest of my friends did too, that we simply had to accept what we were up against. The position we were in was like no other in execution, but conceptually, I was sure that everyone had to make a choice of this nature at some point. Just like in our normal lives, we had to do things that were difficult, and things we didn't want to have to do, and this was no different. The events in each person's life may be different, but that doesn't change the idea of life: it's a test filled with multiple choice questions and no wrong answers. The point is to be strong enough to actually pick an answer.

Without another word, Kanoa waved good-bye to Alem and began to walk away from the group. We all looked on after him and to my surprise, I wanted to follow him. I took a deep breath and turned to the small old man, who was already facing me. He nodded to me, and I got the feeling that he was proud of me; that I was who he thought I would be all along. I wasn't convinced just yet, but waving good-bye to him and walking after my friend was as good a start as any.

"What the hell are we doing?" I asked Kanoa with a laugh, still in disbelief that I was taking a task as serious as this without having my feet firmly on the ground. I hated surprises.

"Why do you find it so hard to accept what this world has to offer?" he asked, his eyes still looking out into the horizon. When Kanoa was committed to something, there was no slowing down or looking back. It was all forward for him from now on.

"Why do you find it so easy?" I asked, not really understanding the question itself or the reasoning behind it. I had a million different answers that probably wouldn't get to the heart of what he was thinking.

"Because the moment I start to doubt any of this is the moment everything falls apart," he replied. He didn't look at me, but the sparkle in his eyes was bright enough to shine like diamonds. "If you found the meaning to your life in your own backyard, would you really start asking questions?"

"This is the meaning to your life, right here?" I asked, frustrated that he had still not gotten rid of his obsession with Drephoria. I understood that this world could be a dream come true for someone like Kanoa, but I was getting worried about the foreboding implications it posed. Would Kanoa be able to let go of this place when the time came?

“You don’t get it,” he replied, shaking his head in disappointment. “Maybe I’m acting the way I am because someone in this group needs to be brave enough to keep pushing forward.”

“Yeah, or maybe you actually believe half the insanity coming out of your mouth,” I said with the kind of anger that was shrouded in worry. I felt like I was fighting a battle I knew I couldn’t win, and worse yet, a battle that he didn’t even see a point in fighting. “Are you doing this for us, or for you?”

Kanoa half-turned to me with wild eyes and a guilty countenance. I had caught him and he knew it, but there was nothing I could do. It was like telling someone to put out a fire they’d started once it had already gotten out of control. It was too late. He had already started the fire, and scolding him about it wasn’t going to fix the damage done.

“Here we go,” I heard Adora say close behind, causing Kanoa to turn away from me.

The moment between us passed and we found the rest of our friends now following us, just like they always did. The six of us had left our mentor behind and were walking through the world alone. Like so many times before, Kanoa and I led our friends into another chapter of our lives together. This time, however, I had the distinct feeling that we were knowingly leading them into the white light without a way back. Worse yet, the two of us were heading in different directions. Maybe if we all just kept telling ourselves that it was just a dream, everything would seem okay. I realized that I had always thought of our lives together without ever thinking of what would happen at the end. I supposed that if we lived our lives together, we might as well end them together.

CHAPTER 11: MAZE THROUGH THE MIND

"Anyone else notice that Alem didn't exactly tell us how we are supposed to defeat this Illusionist person?" Osias asked. "He just kind of said, 'Good luck to you, children, don't get killed too quickly!' I swear, I have more questions than answers every time we talk with him. What if we just walk around forever and never find anything?"

"Well then, I guess we get to hear you complaining for a long time," Thalia teased. "We're in a dream. Stop trying to use that big brain of yours to figure everything out."

I knew that wouldn't sit well with Osias. We were still walking aimlessly in the red grass-covered field. It was probably the longest our surroundings had ever remained the same. There was a slight breeze, and no sounds other than the rustling of grass beneath our feet. I kind of enjoyed the fact that our environment wasn't altering drastically every few minutes. It was rather peaceful.

"Remember the way that guy turned that whole house into a big hole?" Kanoa asked, referencing our first encounter with The Forgotten Four. "We have to look out for anything that seems out of place."

"Kind of hard to tell what's out of place around here," I pointed out.

"Well, what about that?" Adora asked, pointing out into the distance.

We all looked over to what Adora had found and were amazed at we saw. On the horizon was what only could be described as a floating maze, hovering in place high in the sky. Tangled roots and large, unruly clumps of dirt hung from below the chunk of land-like stalactites hanging from a cave. It was a simple patch of land, literally overflowing with wall after wall of the labyrinth. Sporadically, an entire piece of the maze would fall off the sides of the landmass and plummet freely towards the ground, evaporating along the way before it crashed into the ground below.

There was something about the walls that seemed extraordinarily reflective. They were like walls made of mirrors. Leading up to the strange territory was a golden path that appeared transparent, as if made from some kind of gas or cloud. Despite its unworldly nature and random appearance, the whole thing was inviting, begging to be explored. I doubted that if I tried my absolute hardest, I'd be able think up a better trap created by The Illusionist than what was before us.

"Perhaps we should just ignore that and continue on our way," Osias muttered, transfixed by the wonder on the horizon.

"Well, if we wanted to know where to find The Illusionist," Cora whispered, "I think we just found him."

"He doesn't hide himself nearly as well as Waldo," Thalia added.

"So, are we going up there or what?" Kanoa asked, cutting straight to the issue at hand.

On the one hand, it seemed imprudent to simply barge into what was clearly an ambush and expect to walk out alive. However, this was our purpose, and skirting around it was only delaying the inevitable. We either faced the first of our worst nightmares, or ran away from something that would quickly catch up with us, possibly when we were unprepared. Then again, how could I know if we would ever be prepared or not?

"The way I see it," Osias said, "is that if we go in there, we face him on his terms and in his territory. We would be walking into a perfect situation for him, not us."

"What says that he can't make everywhere his territory?" I countered. "For all we know, if we walk away from this he can just make us walk around in circles until we go in anyway. He's a magician, after all."

"You guys talk too much," Kanoa interrupted. "Why can't you guys ever just do something without psyching yourself out about it?"

"Unless you've already forgotten," I snapped, still upset with him. "The reason we're having this discussion is because you threw us into this world in the first place."

"Why do you keep making this world out to be a bad thing?" he shouted back, his eyes twinkling not with the sparkle of wonder, but with the tears of aggravation. This sudden change in his emotions caught us all off-guard, myself included. "You know how much I've wanted this, Kail, you know better than anyone!"

"Of course I do, but—" I said, but was quickly cut off again.

"Then why are you shitting all over it?" he asked, pushing me back a little. "Why are you ruining this for me?"

"I didn't mean to upset you, man," I replied, retracting my earlier temperament. "I'm just saying that we have to be realistic here. I know this is a world of dreams, but we have to treat it like the real world in matters like this. I mean, this is life or death here. It doesn't get any more serious than this."

"Kail," he replied, a zealous flame igniting in his eyes. "This is meant to be something more. We don't have to worry about disappointments or holding back or not getting what we want. We don't have to think about 'realism' at all anymore. We aren't supposed to treat this place like the real world, because it isn't! We're getting a chance at something that nobody we know will ever get. This is an experience!"

"What are you experiencing?" I asked in a whisper, not wanting to know the answer.

"This is pure life," he stated, believing every word he said.

"What does that even mean?" I asked, dumbfounded and terrified at how quickly this world had consumed him. I knew that the rest of my friends were staring at us, wanting to know what the conclusion of this argument meant for them. Would Kanoa be the reason none of us got to go back home? "You have dreams every night in the real world, Kanoa, and anything that takes place in them is just as insignificant as whatever takes place here. Except that here, you can die. You want to throw your life away for something that isn't even real?"

"Real? What does that even mean?" he asked, seemingly contemplating some kind of answer. Instead he just shook his head. "How is this not real? You said yourself we can die here, so why can't we live here? This is all real. It's the people living their lies in the other world, that world filled with broken dreams, that aren't real."

"Don't do this," I pleaded one last time. "You're going to get yourself killed filling your head with thoughts like that."

"Death is the big sleep I've always dreamed about," he replied without missing a beat.

There was an emptiness in his words that burrowed to the very core of his being. Every once in a while, someone close says something with a certain level of detachment that makes me realize what they're saying is innate to their being. This was Kanoa in his most basic form. He wanted to live a life away from the weight of reality, and now he had been given his chance. We had stumbled upon his version of heaven.

"You're a fucking psychopath," I stated, no longer wanting to continue the conversation. "If I'd known who you really were going to be in this place, I never would have followed you here. This was all a huge mistake."

"Kail, I didn't mean –" he tried to explain, but I put up my hand to silence him.

He had already let his true intentions be known. Whether he meant to or not was secondary. I shook my head and walked away, toward the path that had been built for us. If he wanted to get himself killed, we had might as well get it over with.

"What the hell is going on?" Cora whispered, hurriedly walking backwards in front of me.

I could see the fire in her eyes, and I knew it would keep on burning until I gave her an answer. I knew that she was aware of Kanoa's eccentricities, but had no idea how far they could go. Well, now she knew.

"We shouldn't have let him convince us to come here," I vented to her, my head still shaking in disgust. "We literally gave him the shovel he would use to dig all of our graves for us."

"Yeah, well, I could've told you that," she muttered, looking back to Kanoa. "I've been telling you for years, but you –"

"Not now, Cora," I snapped.

"Okay, well if you're so upset, then why're we walking into that ambush now?" she asked, surprisingly calm considering the situation. "Shouldn't we wait until everyone cools off before we fight...whatever it is that is up there?"

"I figure I might as well channel this aggression into something productive," I stated.

"Kail," she said, putting her hands on my chest to slow me down. There was deep anguish in her character at that moment that stopped me in my fiery tracks. "I don't want this to be the way things end for us."

"I'm not mad at you," I replied, confused as to what she was referring to.

She smiled affectionately and sighed. "Not between us. I mean that I don't want any of us to break the promise we made at the beginning. I'm not worried what our parents will think if we don't make it back to them. I'm worried about what will happen to the six of us in here."

It was always a frustrating feeling, having to make decisions not based solely on what was best for me, but what was best for everyone in my life. This was a frustration our group of friends rarely had to experience. We had each other, and that was all that mattered. However, even in our tightly knit group, occasions arose where the good of the few was sacrificed for the good of the many.

"I'll tell you what," I said, settling myself down a little. "I'll look after everyone just as closely as you do. I've clearly lost my wingman in this journey, and would really like it if you could take his place. Would you do that for me?"

She looked at me with crimson delight in her eyes. I had finally loosened up a little and given her the recognition as a friend that she had always wanted; had always deserved. Not having Kanoa to help me through this was going to be a difficult adjustment to make, but I knew that Cora was the best replacement I could ask for.

"Of course I will," she responded.

“Lovely,” I heard an irritated Osias mutter. “We follow someone into madness, and discover he himself is mad. Does that make us crazier than he is?”

Osias and Thalia had moved away from Kanoa, who now only had Adora by his side. She seemed to be consoling him, but he remained motionless and distant. Adora was always first in line to stand by Kanoa. She would even follow him into places I would not dare venture, and that really meant something. I wasn’t sure if that made her a better friend than I was, or she just was too naive to understand the difference between being supportive and being an enabler.

“My sister sure knows how to pick them, huh?” Thalia asked, playfully jabbing Osias in the ribs.

“Says the girl who once dated a guy with a motorcycle,” Osias taunted, his jealousy doing a poor job at hiding itself.

“I enjoyed his energy, and his means of transportation was an expression of that,” she retorted, never particularly proud of her past romantic exploits.

“You were both fifteen,” he said, shaking his head. “That’s not even legal.”

Kanoa began making his way toward the rest of us with Adora in tow. He paused for a moment as he passed by and looked up at me. Some kind of apology attempted to creep out of his mouth. He searched for the words, I could see it in his eyes, but he couldn’t find them. He only let out a deep sigh and kept on walking. He knew his words had broken something that they didn’t have the capability to fix. It probably didn’t help that my eyes held a stare with daggers that could cut his words to pieces.

“You didn’t have to be so hard on him,” Adora said softly, but firmly.

I looked over to her and noticed that she was staring right at me. There was something about her passive temperament that was oddly unsettling. It made me feel that whatever I said didn’t matter to her, that whatever she said was true, and I was merely shooting blindly at the truth.

“Doesn’t it worry you that the one time you would hope he’s pretending is the one time he isn’t?” I asked this with the full intention of getting into an argument. Arguments with Adora were fairly pointless, but I was mad enough to try anyway.

“It is good to see Kanoa not pretend for once,” she responded, her earnest eyes appearing to reflect on all the times she had caught him in a lie. “You should be happy to see your friend so free, so real for the first time in a long time.”

“Don’t try to defend him,” I replied, annoyed with her defence of something that was so clearly wrong. “I don’t know what you think you know, but his...obsession with this place is going to get us all into a lot of trouble.”

"I don't care," she continued, ignoring my reasoning. "He is still your friend, and you didn't have to be so hard on him. This is his dream you're talking about here. You know what that means as well as I do."

"His dream is going to get us all killed," I replied, hoping that Kanoa hadn't poisoned her mind as well. "At what cost is he willing to go to fulfill it?"

"At what cost are you willing to go to fulfill yours?" she asked of me before turning to the rest of my friends. "What would any of you be willing to go through to see your dreams come true?"

So many different answers attempted to rush out of my mouth at once that they ended up getting clogged in my throat. I had no response to her question. My dreams were private, and what I would do to get to them would probably be just as extreme as what Kanoa would do for his. People's dreams are what they live and die for. I swallowed my responses and nodded my head in compliance. She had made her point, even if I didn't like it.

"Now, let's get on with this, shall we?" she asked, airily passing by me toward the golden path before us.

We walked together toward the looming land above us, and with every step of the way, I began formulating some kind of plan to use against The Illusionist. Perhaps we could lure him out of the strange maze and get him out in the open. Or maybe we could work together in making some kind of trap for him. Was there a way to trick a master of trickery?

"Is it just me, or is this path made out of...sunlight?" Thalia asked.

Her question pulled me away from my plans, and I realized that the path before us was translucent. It was more a ray of sunlight than a solid pathway to walk on. The trail was very bright and made up of millions of tiny shards of the sun, all floating at the tips of our toes. There was an untouchable quality to the whole thing, like we weren't fit enough to walk on its shimmering surface.

"Hey, look!" Thalia shouted, running up to the path and jumping on it without hesitation. To my surprise, and likely to the surprise of everyone else, she didn't fall through. She did a little dance in celebration. Apparently the path was for walking on, after all. "I'm walking on sunshine!"

"And don't you feel good!" Adora shouted back, thrilled by her sister's joyous discovery. Everyone burst out laughing.

"This place sure has a thing for making metaphors come to life, huh?" Osias asked.

One by one, we all cautiously stepped upon the extraordinary road that led us up to the strange fortress in the sky. The once-distant walls that plummeted below were now monstrous in size, and we could hear a faint shattering noise as each one fell. The horizon in every direction I looked to appeared empty, as if there was nothing beyond where we were now. I was thankful that I was not afraid of heights, as the path was relatively long and narrow, and very high up. Osias was having a tough time not having a panic attack.

"I'm trying so hard not to freak out right now," he muttered, refusing to look anywhere but directly in front of him, his body stiff as a board and his hands clenched tight.

"That's your problem, Osias," Thalia said. "You try too hard."

While I did agree that Osias did try awfully hard at pretty much everything in his life, everything from his scholastic work to his relationships with everyone around him, I didn't think he was trying too hard at resisting a panic attack. He genuinely seemed as though he was about to have one.

"If I wasn't trying as hard as I am right now," he responded, "then I'd probably be hyperventilating and running back to solid ground."

"Are those walls made of mirrors?" Cora asked.

We were past halfway up the winding road, and everything ahead of us had become quite clear. The reason the walls had appeared reflective from far away is because they actually were reflective. They were entirely made of mirrors. The entire maze was one big reflection of itself.

"Oh, that's just great," Osias said with a sulky sigh. "I get rewarded for getting through this terrible ordeal with something even worse."

"I don't see what the problem is," Kanoa said with confusion in his voice.

"Even if we manage to find The Illusionist in there," I explained, "it'll look like there are a thousand copies of him. It'll be impossible to find anything in there."

"Well, don't look now," Thalia interrupted, "but I don't think we'll be able to go back, even if we wanted to."

I quickly turned around to see what she was talking about. The beginning of the path had disappeared, and the fading began creeping its way up to us. I thought of leaping off the path and flying away, but remembered that Kanoa and I were still the only ones able to do so. I wasn't even sure I could do it on command. The only thing we could do at that moment was flee to the forest of mirrors and escape a deadly fall. The trap had been set, and we had fallen into it—right on schedule.

"What's she talking about? Someone please tell me what she's talking about!" Osias yelped.

"She's not talking about anything," I lied, putting my hand on his shoulder and pushing him forward. "We just have to run now."

Kanoa lifted up off the ground, hovering in place in response to the discovery of the disappearing platform. Everyone now knew of what they had to do, except Kanoa, who refused to take his eyes off the land in front of him. For such a dire situation, the air around us remained unnervingly calm.

"Why is he flying?" Osias asked again, even more frightened now. "What's going on back there? Why are you pushing me?"

"Just start running," I repeated, raising my voice. "And don't stop until we get onto solid ground!"

"Well, then we should just turn around!" he shouted, still unaware of our encroaching doom. Everyone had begun running to the top at this point, but I stayed back to ensure my friend wouldn't be left behind. "Because there's no way I'm going in the—"

"Osias!" I yelled, staring him right in the eyes to let him know how serious the situation had become. "Run!"

I dug my fingers into his arm and practically dragged him behind me as I bolted toward safety. I didn't dare turn back, anticipating the ground beneath me to disappear at any moment and send my friend hurtling toward his end. I had the reassurance of flight at my disposal. At least, I hoped I did.

"We're not going to make it!" Osias gasped between deep panting and grunting noises.

I was afraid that he would pass out before we reached our destination. My heart was pounding furiously, but slowed ever so slightly at the sight of my friends jumping off the fading path and onto the floating, but mercifully solid, ground ahead of me. We were so close...

"Kail, you're not going to make it!" Cora screamed as she turned back to face me.

Apparently I was the only one that believed I would make it. I turned to see how close the path had come to vanishing out from under us and nearly gave up running in that instant. It was right on Osias's heels, and unless I did something drastic, we actually weren't going to make it.

"Just leave me," Osias mumbled, his defeated eyes unable to meet mine. He had given up hope and wanted me to leave him to fall. "I don't want to be a burden."

"Oh for goodness' sake," I wheezed, laughing at what I had just decided to do. "You really should have more faith in your friends."

I grabbed him with both hands, and with all the strength I could find in myself, lifted him right up off his feet. There was a look of terrified astonishment in his eyes at my sudden power, which I returned with a smile. I saw that the path was just about to disappear out from under us, and focused all my energy in getting my friend to safety. I spun around and with great force, threw him toward the rest of my friends in hope that he would clear the distance between us.

I felt my feet lose grip on the ground and closed my eyes, hoping that I would be able to once again do the impossible. Luckily for me, impossible was a word that was becoming as ambiguous as love.

I heard the faint thumping noise of Osias crashing into my desired target, and the cheer and applause of my friends. I slowly opened my eyes to the sight of my friends all in one piece as I hovered effortlessly over the red field below. It looked like a crimson ocean from high up. More and more of the walls fell off the floating land mass in front of me and disintegrated into tiny daggers below. I got a chill thinking of what awaited us inside the eerie creation. We were out of the frying pan, and into the first level of hell of our imagination.

"We're not out of the woods yet," I heard Osias state glumly as I uneasily made my way over to the rest of my friends. He was tending to his shoulder, which he had apparently landed on. I shrugged an apology to him that he accepted with a wincing nod.

"No, we just got into the woods, actually," Thalia said. "Well, I guess it's more of a maze, isn't it?"

I noticed that Kanoa was looking at me admiringly as I planted my feet back on the ground. I shot him a small smile and swiftly looked away, not wanting my thoughts to linger on a frustrating topic at a time like this.

"You had me worried there for a second or two," Cora said, trying her best to suppress a smile she didn't want me to see.

"Well, I'm glad it was only a second or two," I replied. "I don't like it when people worry about me."

"You'd better get used to it if you're going to pull stunts like that," she shot back, turning her attention away from me and into the many reflections around us.

"I must say," Thalia said, admiring her image reflected in the mirror. "I do like how young this place makes me look."

"You're not even twenty years old yet," Osias said, looking over himself in the mirror. This was likely the first time anyone outside of Kanoa and I had seen their new appearances. "How could you possibly look old?"

"I don't keep track of time," she replied with disdain. "But it sure keeps track of me."

Although wall after wall fell away to their destruction, the sheer amount of tightly packed mirrors never dwindled. Reflections of ourselves reverberated from every wall and echoed on images of ourselves eternally. Even the ground itself had a reflective surface. Some mirrors were bent, giving a distorted view of the figures it imitated, but none were cracked or broken. They all appeared in pristine condition. The walls towered over us, so that there was no escape for our eyes being fooled.

I could hear Thalia's breathing become slightly more apprehensive, brought on by our claustrophobic surroundings. Our reflections were so clear, so lifelike, that they could easily be mistaken for our real selves. So many images were reflected from so many different angles that merely standing in place was disorienting. We hadn't taken one step into the maze, and it felt like we were already lost.

"I'm getting dizzy just standing here," Osias grumbled.

"It looks like there's infinite of me," Adora said, pointing out the fact that when she stood between two mirrors, her reflections bounced off one another forever.

She walked up to the mirror and gently put her hand on it. She fell forward, right through the mirror, which caused Thalia to shriek in fear. Adora quickly reappeared behind where she had previously been standing, having teleported through one mirror and out the other. She quickly turned around and tried to comprehend what she had just done.

"Well, that was odd," she whispered.

"Adora, don't do that," Thalia whimpered, her voice cracking as she rushed over and hugged her sister tightly. "Don't go somewhere I can't follow you."

"I only passed through that mirror," she stated. "I am sure you can do it, too."

Kanoa, taking Adora's supposition, quickly ran at one of the mirrors in front of him—and just like Adora had done, popped out of a mirror that had been behind him. He didn't slow down, though, and ran through the mirror again, and again, and again in a never-ending loop. He dug his feet in the ground and skidded to a halt, smiling profusely.

"Yeah," he said with a laugh. "I can warp through mirrors, too. No big deal."

"Maybe we can use this little ability to help us against The Illusionist?" Osias proposed.

His proposition was met with a burst of maniacal laughter. Laughter that was unfortunately familiar. There was no way of telling where the chilling noise came from. It seemed to ricochet off all the mirrors around us, and only seemed to get louder the longer it lasted. My friends and I all readied our weapons for what was to come, for we knew that The Illusionist couldn't be far off. Hope's Glow shone faintly, a slight warmth seeping into my hands. We formed a circle, our backs all facing one another, so that there was no angle he could strike us at that we wouldn't see coming. Our first challenge was about to begin.

The laughter stopped abruptly and an unsettling silence befell the air around us, adding an unnerving weight to our already troubled minds. The only sound that filled my ears was that of the tremulous breathing of my friends. My eyes swiftly shifted back and forth, scrutinizing everything they looked upon. The anticipation was made worse with each passing moment, constantly feeding the gluttonous fear now present. My legs were anxiously recoiling up and down, waiting to leap up in the air at the smallest hint of danger. What would happen when he got here? Or was he already here...

I caught a glimpse of something out of the corner of my watchful eyes. I looked up to what I thought I saw, but found nothing but the ever-present mirrors. Were my eyes playing tricks on me, or was it the work of The Illusionist? Again, I thought I saw a dark flash pass by, but again my eyes were too slow in catching the movement. I looked to my friends to see if they had seen anything, but their eyes were not as active as my own. I turned my attention back to the flashes I had seen in the mirrors and waited intently for another. I picked up on another flash, and then another. They happened faster and faster, but I remained unable to gain a lock on it.

It then occurred to me what was happening, and the revelation tore the air right out of my lungs. I weakly whispered my warning and hoped my friends would hear me:

"He's in the mirrors."

The Illusionist suddenly appeared before me, in all of his grotesque glory. I could smell the foul breath that oozed out of his gaping mouth. I could feel the gaze of his jaundiced eyes, and see every little detail of his ravenous outfit, down to the crosses stitched into each of the bright red happy faces' eyes. He was close enough that the untamed purple hair leaking out of the holes in his mangy top hat threatened to tickle my face, and the mouldy toes that poked out of his long, curled black shoes nearly grazed my feet. Being this close to the creature was cause enough for me to vomit.

Just as quickly as he had appeared, he vanished, and the moment was over. I heard Cora let out a scream that ripped me away from the repulsive sensations The Illusionist had left me with. I turned around to see that the mirrors around us had begun to shift around in place, drastically altering our surroundings. Our group was no longer in a tightly packed circle. Thalia was missing. Before I was even able to comprehend what to do, a mirror swiftly swivelled, trapping Cora on the other side. I ran over to the mirror and punched its surface to try and knock it over, but it was too late. She was gone.

The mirrors continued to twist and churn all around the four of us left, emitting terrible screeching noises as they moved. I tried to get over to Kanoa before he too was lost. He simply turned to me with the signature sparkle in his eyes and a playful sneer on his face. Before I could reach out to him, a mirror blocked my path and he was gone, a reflection of myself taking his place. I turned around to try and get to either Osias or Adora, but the mirrors had shifted behind me, and they too were gone.

They were all gone. All that was left was the endless reflections of my lost and scared face. We were now playing The Illusionist's game without knowing the rules, and the worst part of it was that we were all alone. His show, the show he had been likely planning since we first arrived in Drephoria, had finally begun.

I thought of calling out to my friends, but realized that I would have heard my friends calling out for me if we were able to hear one another. I assumed that whatever The Illusionist had done had caused us to be as far away from each other as possible. What were we supposed to do? Were we supposed to look for each other, or find a way out of this trap on our own? I decided there was no use thinking in one place, and supposed I would bring my questions along as I wandered aimlessly around my new environment.

The first thing I noticed when I turned to face the lonely road ahead of me was a strange figure pinned to one of the mirrors that was now serving as a kind of wall in a hallway. Whatever it was, it appeared fairly small and was at my eye level. The closer I came, the more I began to believe it was an animal of some kind. I was viewing the mysterious object diagonally, so I was only able to see its silhouette, but it appeared to be compacted at its base, with a smaller sphere located on top. Jutting out of the top sphere was a long and pointed cylinder, reminiscent of a beak, perhaps. I was beginning to believe that the creature was quite possibly a duck.

The animal had its head turned to me in such a way that it appeared as though its head was spun completely around. The duck seemed harmless enough, having a normal beak instead of the razor-sharp teeth I would have expected from The Illusionist. I could only see one of its small, glassy eyes staring at me, almost mournfully. The thing I believed to be a beak protruded outward from its head and remained closed. I did not approach the animal, assuming it was an obvious trap set for me. Its feet were stuck underneath its body, jammed up against the mirror's surface. As I slowly approached the animal, I was very sure that it was indeed a duck, not unlike those found back in the real world, other than it appeared to have... fur instead of feathers.

It was then what I had claimed to be a duck jauntily hopped up the mirror. Its large ears, which I had mistaken for a beak, bobbed up and down as it bounced away. It scaled the entire height of the mirror, completely defying any kind of physics, before bounding over the top and out of my sight. I tilted my head sideways, and realized that I had only thought it to be a duck due to the angle I had been staring at it from. Its legs hadn't been on its back at all, and it hadn't been turned to look at me. It was just a normal rabbit, with ears that had looked like a beak.

I rubbed my eyes again to ensure that it was in fact a rabbit I had seen. I had been so sure that it was a duck, but it was only because of my perception, not the reality of the situation, that I had been proven wrong. My mind reeled from my discovery, but more importantly, I was also concerned what this first encounter meant for my future here. I knew what I was up against: the whole place was going to be filled with optical illusions and other creations that would distort my view on reality. The whole place was going to be a living, breathing paradox.

I took a deep breath and cracked my knuckles, mentally preparing myself for the tasks ahead that would undoubtedly test me intellectually. I reminded myself that I had always been good at reading a situation, and that talent would be of great use in my current predicament. I thought of my friends and how they would fare without me at their disposal. What if they got stuck in this place forever? What if The Illusionist got to them before I did? I decided dwelling on their well-being was an exercise in futility, as I wouldn't be able to help them if I myself was unable to find my way out.

I saw that at the end of the long hallway of mirrors, there was a large metal gate. There was no roof above me, so I decided that instead of risking venturing beyond the gate, I would simply fly my way out. I lifted off the ground easily, now well accustomed to the feeling of flight, and began gaining altitude.

Unfortunately for me, The Illusionist appeared to have anticipated what I would do, and my easy way out wasn't so easy after all. No matter how high I flew, the mirrors all around me stretched into the sky further and further, like silly putty. I flew so long and so high up that I could no longer see the ground beneath me, yet the mirrors entrapped me still. I heard the frenzied laughter of The Illusionist far off in the distance, mocking my vain attempt at escape. I sighed in defeat and made my way back down to where I had started. This was going to be just as complicated as I had feared.

The gate lay before me, at the very end of the long, stretching hallway. I cautiously walked toward it, keeping an eye out for anything suspicious, which was rather difficult to do considering my environment was entirely suspicious. I had been walking for a while and noticed that the gate was actually becoming further away than it had been when I had begun walking. My casual walk turned into a jog, which then escalated to a full-blown run, and yet the gate only rocketed faster away from me. It was like trying to stick two positive magnets together. The harder I tried the more they repelled.

I stopped in place and looked behind me to see how far I had travelled. To my confusion, the hallway extended endlessly behind me, leaving me completely stranded and frustrated. Once again, The Illusionist's barking laugh filled the air around me. I looked back toward the gate and began running at a relentless pace. However, the more I ran, the bigger the gap became between my goal and I became. If I wanted to overcome these tasks, I was going to have to start thinking outside not just the box, but the entire world the box was in.

I closed my eyes and thought about the situation carefully, knowing that worrying about the fact that I may never get out wouldn't lead to an answer. I tried my absolute best to throw away what the real world had taught me and didn't focus on what was possible, but what was possible here. The facts of the matter were that the more I pushed myself toward the end, the further I became from achieving what I wanted. There was no turning back, because there was nothing to turn back to. I had to keep my eyes forward. The answer was on the brink of my mind, but it was just out of reach. It was so frustrating, knowing an answer but not being able to express it. If I could just pull back and get to the root of the problem...

It was then that it dawned on me. It was like waiting all night for the morning, and finally being rewarded with the sun. My eyes burst open through the darkness and shone with the blinding revelation of discovery. I was filled with the excitement only attained through the greatest of accomplishment. I stared at that unreachable gate and smiled triumphantly. Its secret was now known.

I positioned myself directly in the middle of the hallway and stood as still as a statue. I then moved one foot backwards, and the other followed. The gate didn't budge. Again I stepped back. I began walking backwards, slowly at first, and then more quickly. Faster and faster, trying my absolute best not to stumble and fall, which was much easier said than done. This time, there was no laughter from The Illusionist. The only laughter that could be heard was my own—for the distance between the gate and I had begun to shrink, just as I had hoped.

After a long while of running backwards, the gate finally rested in front of me. I looked over it carefully, searching for any oddities that struck me as suspicious. It was a fairly plain gate. Its bars were black and made of metal and the handle polished gold. The words 'Lucky Guess' were etched across its surface, which made me smirk. I decided there was nothing else to do than to go through it.

I turned away from the mirror image of the gate in front of me and put my hand on the real lever that opened the real gate. What I had been running toward the entire time had only been a mirror image—I had been running away from the real gate. I wondered if I had simply turned around at the beginning, if the gate would have been there and I could have saved myself the hassle of so much running. It was probably best for me not to dwell on such things.

Past the gate, I found myself in a completely circular room, with mirrors once again acting as the walls. There appeared to be no exit to the room, so I turned back toward the gate. To my disappointment, the gate had disappeared and I now stood in a round room with no way out. I walked around the entire room, lightly dragging my hand across the icy, smooth surface of the mirrors, looking for some indication of a door. After ending up back where I had started, I realized I was quickly running out of ideas about how to get out of this new predicament I found myself in. Had I angered The Illusionist enough by solving his last puzzle that he had punished me by leaving me here? I was beginning to think he was a bit of a sore loser.

Something popped the bubble of silence that had formed around me since I had entered the room. I looked above to see what the noise was, wary of what new wicked treachery The Illusionist was capable of. I was surprised to see that it was none other than Kanoa, who was descending upon me, waving to me enthusiastically. It was understandable that if it I were to find anyone still alive in this place, it would have been him. I waved back, happy to see a familiar face in this strange place.

"Am I glad to see you," I stated, giving him a warm high-five as he planted his feet on the ground. He looked rather excited, but I was unsure if the reason was due to discovering me, or some adventure he had gotten himself in since we had been separated. It was likely a mixture of both.

"Yeah, you're the first one I've seen since we all split up," he said, looking around the room curiously. "How did you get in here?"

"There was this strange hallway," I explained, "and after I got to the end of it, there was a gateway. I opened it and passed through, it disappeared behind me, and now I'm kinda stuck here. Have you had to deal with anything like this?"

"Nope," he replied, still looking around the reflecting room. "I was just flying around trying to find you guys. I don't think there's a way out, because no matter how far I flew, this place just went on and on forever."

"Damn it," I muttered. "Well, at least we found each other. About earlier—"

"Don't mention it," he said with a wink. "I crossed the line, and I'm sorry about that. It won't happen again."

It wasn't like Kanoa to back down and apologize so easily. Something caught my eye as I looked at Kanoa's reflection in the mirrors: despite his overly familiar, excited disposition, there was no twinkle in his eyes. It was probably nothing, but I had just become so accustomed to seeing that glint when he was excited...

"How were you able to fly here?" I asked, joining him in looking around the room.

"What?" he responded, clearly confused. "Did you forget how to do it already?"

"No, I've gotten pretty good at flying," I replied. "I just meant... When I was stuck in that hallway earlier, I tried flying my way out, but no matter how high I flew I could never get out. The mirrored walls just grew taller and taller, the higher I went. I was just wondering how you did it."

"Oh," he said hesitantly, very subtly disarmed by my question. "That's weird. I don't know. I guess The Illusionist has different plans for each of us."

"What does that mean?" I asked, swiftly jumping upon his words without pause.

"What?" he replied, turning to face me with genuine confusion. "Why're you so jumpy all of a sudden?"

"Why are you lying to me?" I asked, boldly standing toe-to-toe with my best friend, giving him no room to walk away from my question.

"What am I lying about, exactly?" he asked almost mockingly, putting his hands on his hips. "I don't have to lie anymore, Kail. I can be real here."

"In the real world," I said, wanting him to know what I was referring to. "Had you always felt how you feel here? You said that this was your dream come true, so what was it like living in a world where your dream could never come true? Were you ever happy? Or was it all just a lie?"

Kanoa didn't budge. The smile left his face and his eyes grew dim, darkened by the answer formulating in his thoughts. I knew that by asking these types of questions, I was opening Pandora's Box. These types of questions would reveal the truth about Kanoa, and once I knew them, there was no turning back.

"People lie to themselves," he replied indifferently, as if he was reciting a well-known speech. "That's just a simple fact. Perhaps it's because they're unhappy or bored with the way things are. So they make up things to make their lives seem more exciting than they actually are. They lie to themselves enough, and suddenly the difference between fact and fiction gets real blurry. Suddenly those lies they told themselves are the way things really are. After all, life is just a four-letter word for lie. So why not stay here, and make your lie one worth telling?"

I stared at him for some while, unwillingly admiring his little speech. It was a feeling of respect at the cost of loathing—giving credit to something not because I wanted to, but because I had to. And that's when it struck me: I had never once known Kanoa to be gifted with words.

"That was pretty good," I whispered, "but if you had done your homework properly, you would know that what you just said is more likely to come out of my mouth than his. And never once have I heard Kanoa say the word 'fiction' properly. Kanoa simply does what he can never find the words to say."

He opened his mouth to say something, but his jaw merely hung open, apparently forgetting what it had set out to do. He squinted his isolated eyes and sighed with laughter, defeated.

"So does that mean you simply say what you could never find the courage to do?" he asked.

"Now that sounds more like something the real Kanoa would say," I said, subtly moving one of my hands to my weapon.

"Well, I do know one thing about him," he said, the sly grin on his face creeping from ear to ear as he reached for his weapon. "He always was a bit of a hothead."

His smile, then split across his entire face, making a sickening slicing noise as blood dripped from his lips. His teeth turned sharp and his eyes sour. I watched in horror as the skin on his face began melting, and spots of his bare skull became visible. Flames poured from his disintegrating face, peeling away more and more layers of tissue and muscle. His hair caught on fire too, and was soon burnt away to nothing, leaving a foul stench in the air.

The heat became so unbearable I was forced to pull away, just as his eyes turned to liquid and oozed down his now-skeletal face. Where my best friend had once stood was what could only be described as a demon—a fiend whose skeletal head was surrounded by the aura of a hellish firestorm. It let out a howling shriek of laughter which was instantly recognizable to me. This imposter of Kanoa had been The Illusionist the whole time.

I tried to get close enough to vanquish The Illusionist, but the blaze emitting from him had become too strong. The louder he laughed, the more the flames grew, and I quickly became aware of the fact that I needed to find a way to escape the room, which was now akin to a furnace. The fire spread everywhere and The Illusionist was nowhere to be found, yet his chilling laughter remained present. It pained me to think the last thing I would ever hear would be that terrible noise.

The flames grew tall and formed a blanket over me, making it impossible to fly my way out of what would soon become my fiery tomb. The smoke clogged my throat and my thoughts. I was running out of time and of options.

I could barely see anything anymore, and my eyes stung just from opening them, but I decided that what I needed to do didn't require sight. I held my weapon in front of me with both hands and held my breath against the smoke, which had begun to burn my lungs. I charged blindly through the flames, feeling them lick their hot tongues at my heels. The hot air around me pressed down from all directions, and even though I had such a small distance to run, I felt as though I would pass out before I reached the end. I had always thought that drowning would be the worst way to die, but I was now reassessing my choice.

My weapon suddenly crashed into the glass wall of the room, and it shattered all around me. The laughter of The Illusionist ceased as tiny pieces of the mirror fell to the ground. Thankfully, I fell on top of my weapon instead of cutting myself on the shards beneath me. The fire behind me vanished in an instant, and all the sensations of heat and suffocation I had previously felt were gone.

I lay there for a moment, greedily breathing in every mouthful of untainted oxygen I could find. Smoke lazily lifted off of me, taking away any evidence of what had just happened to me with it. I had survived another test of The Illusionist, this time a little less skilfully than the last. To him, this was all just a game; a show for him to demonstrate his abilities. And we were his unwilling audience.

After panting heavily long enough to comfortably retrieve my composure, I clumsily got to my feet and slung my weapon back in its place. At first I believed that the way before me was another dead end, with seemingly nowhere to go but back. However, the mirror in front of me did not stretch into the heavens, but rather only stood marginally taller than I was. I jumped to see what was beyond the mirror, and found what appeared to be another hallway. Unfortunately for me, the hallway appeared upside down. The ground above my head acted as a ceiling, and the open skies were at my feet. I stopped jumping and looked directly above me into my reflection, which was staring back at me, just as confused as I was. What was I supposed to do this time?

My first thought was to simply fly up and over the wall in front of me, and move along the hallway without my feet actually on the ground. But my plan was quickly flipped on its head, because the moment I lifted off and began ascending was the moment my head slammed into the ground where my feet had been. I laid there for a moment, crumpled on the ground, my head filled with both physical and intellectual pain. Apparently flying was out of the question, as the world would simply invert itself if I tried. I flipped myself over and looked back up to the ceiling, my reflection above in as much pain as I was below. The Illusionist's laughter shortly followed.

Through all the pain that filled my head surfaced the memory of Adora, passing through the mirrors like some kind of portal. The only difference here was that when I passed through the mirror, I would have to remember to somehow shift gravity, so that what was upside down would become right side up. I imagined that it would be just as difficult as it sounded, and equally as painful if I didn't do it correctly.

I closed my eyes and vividly envisioned myself sticking to the ceiling above me, as though it were the floor beneath me. I tried to make it sound much less complicated than it actually was, hoping that if I thought it was simple, it would be. I pushed all other thoughts out of my head and focused solely on this one idea; the idea that I wasn't really where I was, and that I was in fact where I wanted to be.

I opened my eyes quickly and felt myself fall backwards, the ground beneath me giving way to the ceiling above me. A sharp feeling of vertigo threatened to rip me apart as I felt my centre of gravity shift backwards into the mirror, then forward to the ground below me, and then back to the ceiling I was now lying on. My hands shot out and gripped the ceiling beneath me, worried that I would plummet back to the hard ground where I had once been. I dared not breathe, concerned that any unnecessary form of movement would correct the physics I was currently breaking.

After a few trembling moments, I was sure that my plan had worked and that everything was now inverted for good. What had once been up was now down, and with that, another one of The Illusionist's tricks had been foiled. I thought

I heard a low, disapproving growl, but it had probably just been my imagination.

Now that I had successfully flipped the world on its head, I awkwardly got to my shaky feet. I looked out to the end of the hallway and saw what appeared to be a spiralling downward staircase, undoubtedly another one of The Illusionist's challenges in waiting. Walking along this inverted hallway was highly disorienting. Looking up into the open sky was actually a view of the red grassy field, now far below me, from where we had begun this wild adventure.

I wondered what kinds of strange sights my friends were currently seeing. I wondered if they had been able to overcome whatever obstacles they had faced with ease, or if they were in trouble. I wondered if any of them had gotten hurt…or worse. I wondered a lot of things, and the more questions I asked, the more grave the answers became. I was never known to be much of an optimist.

"Hello?" I heard a voice shout from far away.

I stopped for a moment to try and pick up the voice again. My patience was rewarded with another shout, reinforcing my theory that Osias had been the one I was hearing. He sounded as though he was located at the end of the hallway below the staircase, so I swiftly closed the gap between us, excited by the fact that I had found a friend. The loneliness that was slowly creeping its way into me was quickly banished. It then occurred to me that this could be another trap set by The Illusionist, just as he had done with Kanoa. I pledged myself to be careful.

I reached the end of the hallway and came upon the spiralling staircase, now certain that Osias's voice was emitting from further below me. The staircase was located inside a type of stairwell. The mirrored walls extended down the length of the steps, with no other landings along the way. The staircase had no railings, and each step appeared to hover in the air without anything keeping it in place. The whole thing just hung in the air motionless.

Another strange thing about it was that it ended abruptly. The staircase looked as though it had only been completed halfway, and then abandoned, never able to touch the ground beneath it. As dangerous as it looked, I was more concerned with where it led and, more specifically, whose voice was emitting from the bottom of it. I needed to find a way to ensure that the user of the voice was its true owner.

"I bet Osias is too stupid to get up those stairs!" I stated, loud enough so that he could hear me. It was a simple test, but one that only Osias would be able to complete properly.

"Excuse me?" he shouted back, clearly shocked and vexed by what I had said. "Kanoa, is that you? I'll have you know that I can't reach the stairs, or I would easily be able to scale them! I bet you haven't been able to solve all of the puzzles you've encountered—while I, on the other hand, have completed each

I have come across with ease. As a matter of fact, I would go so far as to say that The Illusionist stole many of his ideas for this place from me!"

I slowly poked my head over edge of the stairs and saw Osias standing below the staircase, a heated scowl on his face. I waved to him apologetically with a relieved smile on my face.

"Hey, Osias," I said. "Good to see you again."

"Kail!" he shouted, waving back at me happily. "Did you hear Kanoa a second ago?"

"No, that was me," I explained with a laugh. "I had to make sure you weren't The Illusionist."

"What do you mean?" he asked.

"I'll explain everything when I get down there," I said, intently looking over the precarious stairs I was about to climb down. "But first, I'm going to have to figure out a way to do that."

"Why don't you just fly down?" he proposed.

"Yeah, flying doesn't work so well here," I answered, still looking over the stairs and wondering what their trick could be.

I cautiously put my foot on one of the steps and kept my other foot on solid ground. Nothing weird happened, so I shifted the majority of my weight to the foot on the floating step. I was rather content with the progress I had made and began descending the spiralling staircase confidently. However, after only a few steps, I realized that I had somehow backtracked to the top of the stairs—as if I had been going up the stairs instead of down. I looked back at the staircase and noticed no difference in their construction.

I tried several more times to descend the steps, more slowly and vigilantly each time, and each time it appeared as though I had ascended them. The fourth step seemed to be the culprit of my confusion. As if on cue, The Illusionist's ever-annoying laughter filled my tiring ears.

"What are you doing up there?" Osias asked, apparently not hearing anything of The Illusionist and his taunting.

"I seem to be having a little trouble going down," I replied, beyond befuddled as to what to do. "Every time I try to go down the steps, I wind up back at the top. Maybe you have some ideas?"

I saw Osias close his eyes and enter into deep thought. He paced back and forth, waving his hands occasionally as if sifting through mental images, looking for the correct answer. I waited for a few moments, giving him as much time as he needed. He often reminded everyone that you couldn't rush the process of being a genius. Patience with Osias was the key to unlocking his mind. He muttered to himself briefly, stopped pacing, and opened his eyes. He looked to one of the mirrors next to him that was adjacent to the floating steps. He put his hand on the mirror and smiled proudly. I could almost see the light bulb turn on over his head.

"Try going down the steps again," he ordered, his eyes remaining transfixed on the mirror.

I shrugged my shoulders and obeyed his command, only to be once again denied the ability to descend the steps of the spiralling staircase by the rogue fourth step.

"Nope," I called to him. "Nothing changed."

"Now turn around and look in the mirror," he continued, unfazed by my failure.

I furrowed my brow, confused with what he was trying to accomplish. Despite my hesitation, I did as he asked and looked in the mirror. At first, I saw nothing out of the ordinary. The image in the mirror was merely a reflection of the world I was in.

"Now raise your right hand," he directed, excitement present in his voice. I did what he asked and informed him as such. "What hand are you holding up?"

"My right hand," I responded wearily. "I don't see—"

"Shh!" he hissed, uninterested in my doubts. "What hand is your reflection holding up?"

"Well, it's holding up..." I replied, slowly beginning to understand where he was leading me. "The left hand."

"The mirror world is an exact reflection of what is in the real world," Osias explained. "So those steps that are spiralling downward in a counter-clockwise motion are actually spiralling downward clockwise. Try going down the steps while looking at their reflections, not at the actual steps."

It was so abstract and yet so straightforward a solution, one that I never would have thought of without Osias there to guide me. I was glad that I had found him when I did, or I might have been stuck at that staircase for an eternity.

"I knew I was your friend for a good reason," I said, making my way toward the staircase to test out Osias's idea.

"Thanks, that means a lot to me," he replied, keenly awaiting the result of his hypothesis.

I positioned myself in front of the stairs, but instead of looking at them, I looked at their reflection in the mirror next to me. I tried to mute the sights creeping in from my peripherals and focused solely on the mirror image. I walked the first three steps without hesitation and stopped just short of that fabled fourth step to stare at it indignantly, as if it embodied all of The Illusionist's treachery and infuriation in its very being.

I took the next step like it was my first ever in life: carefully, cautiously and courageously. My foot landed on the floating step, and I felt like I had just been transported into Neil Armstrong's shoes when he touched down on the moon. I felt the weight of success. I heard Osias let out a momentous cry of accomplishment. Together we had bested our foe's latest illusion.

As I walked down the staircase, I noticed that the word 'Cheater' bubbled out of the surface of each step before me. I smiled and decided to inform Osias of our victory.

"Hey, Osias," I called out. "I think The Illusionist isn't too impressed with us. All these steps have the word 'cheater' on them."

"Oh, he's mad," he said with a laugh.

I was just about to join my friend in uniform laughter, when the steps beneath my feet vanished without warning.

Luckily, I had traversed halfway down when my free-fall began, and didn't fall as far as I could have. Unluckily, there was still quite a ways to drop, especially considering that the staircase never reached the ground in the first place. I crumpled on the ground next to Osias without any form of cushioning to soften the impact. My groans of agony were met with more laughter, this time belonging to The Illusionist.

"Are you okay?" Osias asked, frantically running over to attend to my pain. "What happened?"

I waved him off so that he didn't harm me further in his hysterical state. "He can be a bit of a poor sport, that Illusionist," I whimpered.

I struggled back to my feet with Osias now surveying our surroundings. We were located in an L-shaped hallway, with two possible directions for us to travel. I assumed that Osias had come from one direction when he had discovered the stairs and luckily called out. If he had just continued on his way, we may have missed each other.

"So, what have you come up against since we were separated?" Osias asked, excited to delve into the particular wonders of this illusory land. I decided we didn't have that kind of time to waste and answered his question unsatisfactorily.

"Oh, just some frustrating puzzles here and there," I replied. "The only thing really worth mentioning was a run-in with an imposter Kanoa. Apparently The Illusionist can copy our forms, which is why I needed to make sure you were really you."

"How interesting," Osias said, marvelling at The Illusionist's ingenuity. "We'll have to keep an eye out for any further trickery of that manner. I myself got stuck walking on a set of stairs that seemed to just go around in circles for an eternity. I believe they're known as -- "

"I really think we should be going, Osias," I interrupted, stopping him while he was still able to be stopped. "There's no telling what could be happening to our friends right now."

"Oh, yes, of course," he stuttered. "All I'll say is that this staff can be quite the nuisance when manoeuvring around tight spaces. I would imagine Cora is having equal amounts of annoyance with her weapon."

"I'm sure Cora is doing just fine," I said, not just to comfort him, but myself as well. "Now, which way did you come?"

Osias pointed to the hallway to our left, so I began walking down the one to our right. The reunion between us temporarily put my worries at ease. Hopefully, I would find the rest of my friends in the condition I had found Osias. This was only our first challenge, and according to Alem, it was supposedly our easiest. Failing this early in our quest would be very disheartening.

"So, do you think that once we defeat The Forgotten Four, destroy Malise, free the land, and all the rest of that easy stuff, that we'll just wake up?" Osias asked as we made our way down the hallway.

"I don't see any other way," I replied, focusing on my reflection in the mirror at the end of the hallway.

There was a look of determination in my eyes that caught me by surprise for a moment. I wasn't exactly accustomed to what I looked like when my mind was so thoroughly involved in something as important as the well-being of my friends. The passion in my eyes would have impressed even Cora, had she been with me to see it.

"And what if we die?" he continued on, pulling me away from my reflection and pushing me to turn the corner. "Do you think we wake up then?"

"Alem said that we would die in the real world, too," I reminded him. "I'm not going to be the one to try and prove him wrong."

After we turned the corner, what lay before us slowed our steps to a halt. There was a severance in the mirrored hallway, a gap that was filled with three evenly spaced platforms that attempted to bridge one side with the other. There were no other ways across the gap for as far as my eyes could see in either direction. The three silver planks floated, not unlike the steps I had traversed earlier, but were all at an even height and evenly spaced. They were all bound together on their sides, which made them resemble the letter 'E.'

It appeared that all that was required of Osias and I was to hop across the three platforms. However, we were dealing with a creation of The Illusionist, so I was hesitant to apply the word 'easy' to this new obstacle. If we missed one jump, we would have a long time to figure out what had gone wrong before we struck the ground far below.

"So, do we just start jumping across or what?" Osias asked somewhat apprehensively.

I remained uncertain as to what aspect of this new complication held the trick that would catch us off-guard. I was more worried about what would happen if Osias were to fall, as I would be able to fly if an incident arose. At least, I hoped I would be able to fly if I fell.

Before I was able to share my concerns with Osias, I heard voices from across the gap. Osias's head perked up as he, too, heard the ever-nearing voices. We both placed our weapons in our nervy hands and prepared for battle. The voices were unfortunately too distorted to discern, and only worried us further. I looked over to my friend, who looked quite nervous.

"Do you even know how to use that thing?" I asked him.

"I suppose we shall soon find out," he replied with a notable gulp.

The voices emerged into view and revealed themselves to be the welcome sight of Thalia and Adora. The sisters' laughter turned into shrills of joy once their eyes fell upon Osias and me. The echoes from the hallway mirrors must have twisted their voices into unrecognizable sounds. Either that, or The Illusionist had just been having a little fun. With their appearance, our group had been brought back almost to completion.

"Thalia? Adora? Is that you?" Osias asked. I then remembered I had told him about my confrontation with the doppelganger Kanoa, and decided it was best to test their identities.

"No, it's the other twin sisters you went into a dream world with," Thalia responded.

"Osias can be a little strange sometimes," Adora stated.

"This is true," her sister replied with a nod. "But I am too, and I find we complement each other's strangeness quite well."

The two girls laughed giddily, apparently unfazed by whatever trials they had faced thus far in The Illusionist's puzzling lair. Osias looked over to me, his cheeks subtly flushing red and his eyebrows raised.

"I think I can speak for both of us when I say those two are definitely Adora and Thalia," he muttered.

"You'll get no objections from me, my friend," I agreed, patting him on the shoulder.

"Come on over, you two!" Thalia shouted. "I'd rather not have to raise my voice to have a conversation with you."

I nodded in agreement and turned to Osias. "Do you want me to go first, to see – "

"Oh, nonsense," he said, shaking his head and backing away from the ledge. "I'll show you how it's done."

I looked back to Thalia, who was tapping her foot in anticipation. I realized that Osias's newfound courage had probably surfaced out of a desire to impress her—a desire that, in my mind, would undoubtedly end poorly.

"Okay. I don't mind you going first," I said, trying to make him appreciate that running into a trap would probably be far more costly than walking into one. "I just think that it might be better if we discussed this a little –"

"Move aside, Kail," he ordered, prepping himself for the act ahead of him. "I've been able to complete even the most complex of The Illusionist's tests. This one looks to be his easiest one yet. Meet you on the other side."

Without another word of opposition, Osias bolted off at a run, heading straight toward the hovering platforms. I rushed after him in an attempt to stop him, but it was too late. He leapt off the edge of the hallway and cleared the distance between him and the first platform quite easily. For a moment I was impressed with his ability, and thought that my distress had been for naught. However, after effortlessly clearing the first jump, something occurred on the second jump that nobody—especially not Osias—had expected.

He hung in the air for a moment after his second bound, and then plummeted downward in a free-fall.

He let out a surprised gasp of fear, which gave me my cue to begin chasing after him. Without taking any precautions, I hastily jumped off the edge of the hallway and reached the first platform with the same ease as my friend. It was then I discovered the cause for Osias's misjudgement: the second platform had not been on the same level as the first or third platform at all. It was located far below its two companions, and the angle in which we had been viewing them had led us to believe they had all been on the same altitude.

Osias's screams were drowned out by the skin-crawling laughter of The Illusionist as he revelled in claiming his first victim.

I clumsily skidded to a halt before I met the same fate as my friend. Only the tips of my toes slid off the edge of the platform. My skin crawled at the thought of how close I had been to joining Osias in free-falling. He had to think of something quickly, because I feared that even if I were to begin flying after him, it would be too late.

As he fell, with the platform quickly approaching him, he grabbed his staff and held it out in front of him, attempting to hit the platform. His staff slammed into the platform, and he brought up his other arm with lightning speed and grabbed the opposite end of his weapon. With his head just narrowly avoiding impact with the platform, he fell below it and held onto his staff with all his might. Thankfully, my friend's weight did not cause the staff to break, but instead the momentum of the drop caused the staff to bounce upon the platform's surface, smashing Osias's head into the bottom. Despite the loud cracking noise the collision created, he hung on tightly—for if he let go, he would surely fall to his doom.

"Osias!" I shouted out to him while he dangled perilously below me. "Stop moving around, or your staff is going to slide off the edge!"

"You gotta be kidding me," I heard him whimper. He continued to readjust where his hands were on his staff for a better grip, but in doing so the staff jiggled around ever so slightly, bringing it closer and closer to the edge of oblivion.

"Can you pull yourself up?" I called out to him, noticing that Adora and Thalia were looking on in horror, unable to conjure any words to apply to the situation.

"Can you fly down here and pick me up?" he countered with a tone of frightened agitation.

I felt the sweat begin to push through my skin as I mulled over how to solve the situation. If I flew down and attempted to pick him up, I might accidentally cause more harm than help by pushing him off the edge—and that was if The Illusionist would even allow me to fly at all. However, if I just let him try to pull himself up, he might fall anyway, and I wouldn't be able to catch him in time. The more I thought about what to do, the closer he came to making my decision for me by falling into the red sea of grass below. Indecision, I thought, would be the worst decision possible.

I got to my feet and prepared myself for the plunge to save my friend. I looked to Thalia and Adora one last time and nodded to them, to assure them that it would be okay. The looks on their faces didn't exactly fill me with confidence, as they seemed on the verge of tears. I closed my eyes and focused solely on the action of swooping down and grabbing Osias before he fell, tuning out all external distractions. However, a distant howling noise caught in the inner realms of my hearing forced my eyes open. The hollering grew louder, and with it my recognition of whom the sound belonged to: it was Kanoa.

With unfathomable speed and pinpoint accuracy, Kanoa—or rather, a white streak that I assumed was Kanoa—ripped Osias away from the platform he had been hanging from, staff and all. The impact knocked the wind right out of Osias's lungs, and he began coughing relentlessly as he was whisked from his precarious ordeal and placed gently down beside Thalia and Adora. The whole action had occurred so quickly that I had barely any time to process it.

Kanoa looked over to me and threw an over-exaggerated wave in my direction, his familiar twinkle sparkling in his eyes. This was definitely the real Kanoa, as the tormenting cackling of The Illusionist had once again fallen silent.

"Where the hell have you been?" I asked, relieved to have almost the entire group back in one place. I worried momentarily for Cora, but assured myself that she would soon rejoin the rest of us. The Illusionist's traps were becoming easier to overcome with each addition to our group, and once we became whole again, we would be unstoppable.

"Oh, you know," he replied. "I was just flying around and getting a feel for the place. There are some pretty interesting sights to be seen, I'll tell you that."

After a few leaps and bounds, I cleared the latest, and hopefully last, trap set by The Illusionist and stood once again next to my friends. The fear I had seen in the eyes of my friends from our previous predicament had vanished. Everyone once again appeared to be at ease.

"Jeez, if I had a dollar for every time I saved your ass," Kanoa teased, circling Osias, "I'd have enough money to make one of these dream machines myself!"

"That wasn't necessary," Osias stated, indignantly brushing himself off and shooting contemptuous looks in Kanoa's direction. "I could have saved myself, you know."

"Excuse me?" Kanoa replied, taking a step toward Osias. Adora instinctively floated in between the two calmly, as if she didn't realize the storm brewing around her. "It looked to me like you could've used my help."

"Yeah, well if this place has taught me anything, it's that looks can be deceiving," Osias countered. "And I definitely didn't need your help. In fact, if it weren't for you, I wouldn't be in any form of danger right now. Instead I have to worry about dragons, falling to my death, this never-ending maze, and The Illusionist, who is probably just as messed up in the head as you."

"Well, excuse me for actually bringing you outside of your perfect little comfort zone," he retorted, seething with rage. "Sorry to tell you that the whole world isn't just one big classroom that you can hide in. You're just scared that in this world, using your brain isn't enough to get by. The world was meant to be more than having our noses stuck in textbooks for our whole lives. In reality there are a lot more things to worry about than studying for a test, and failure is a matter of life and death!"

"If you hadn't gotten it through that thick head of yours," Osias replied, his voice steadily rising, "this isn't the real world! Just because this is the only place where you get to feel like you're worth something, doesn't change the fact that this place isn't worth anything. You're always so wrapped up in your own little fantasy world, and now that we've walked into it, you suddenly think we'll accept it like you already have. As if that somehow that makes it more valid. Well, let me tell you this. A lie is a lie, no matter how well it's told or how many times you tell it. I agree with Kail. You're crazy, and the only one that needs help here is you."

"You ungrateful little –" Kanoa grunted between clenched teeth, but Adora stood her ground and put her hand on his.

"That's enough," she ordered, her voice rising ever so slightly with the elevation of anxiety.

I could see the wounded rage spilling out of Kanoa's glistening eyes as he tried his absolute best not to lose out to his emotions. Osias seemed to be in some sort of trance, staring at the damage he had done with his words, not looking particularly proud of what he had said. As rough as I had been with my best friend earlier, Osias had certainly taken hurtful truth to a new level that perhaps should never be ventured to.

"You know what would be great?" Thalia muttered in frustration. "If we didn't get into an argument every time one of us opens our mouths. I mean, we are in a dream world, so this is probably as good a time as any for something impossible to happen."

"To be fair," Adora interjected, her eyes still firmly set upon Kanoa. "I doubt any group of friends has had to deal with what we are currently up against. But as long as we remain together, it won't matter what we are up against. Right?"

Although I wasn't sure who she was speaking to, we all nodded in agreement. Kanoa was the last to consent, still too wrapped up in his aggression to be able to concede to harmony. I saw Adora squeeze his hand, which unravelled him completely, his eyes darting back to her. He took a deep breath and sighed heavily, the negative emotions escaping with it.

"I'm sorry," he said, no louder than a whisper. "I wasn't listening."

"Just tell me that you will just keep on helping us in whatever way you can," she replied, looking up at him with her angelic eyes. Kanoa never looked more at peace than when looking at Adora. She was the sun he could always count on after the storm.

"I'll get us out of here any way I can," he replied, not once taking his eyes off her. It was like he was referring only to the two of them when he spoke, as if the rest of us weren't around them at that moment. I hoped he remembered all of his friends when he deployed his master plan.

"Okay, now that we have that settled," I interrupted. "Can we please find Cora, kill The Illusionist, and get the hell out of here? Does that sound like a good plan? Good, sweet, let's go."

Everyone agreed, and after I asked Thalia which way they had come, we set out in the opposite direction to find our final missing friend. I kept trying to think of anything but the possibility of Cora being injured in any way, but the more I struggled against my imagination, the more futile the battle became. I decided that talking to someone would probably be best for me.

“Sorry if it seems like we’re attacking you from all sides,” I murmured to Kanoa, quietly enough so that no one around us could hear. The hallway we were currently in was taking many turns, so we stayed close enough together not to get separated again, but far enough to have our own private conversations.

“Yeah, I figured you were the one who told him to go on that little rant back there,” he teased, sounding surprisingly lighthearted considering what had just transpired.

“I know it seems like I’m hard on you sometimes, but,” I stuttered, fumbling around in my head for the right words. “I’m harsh because I care, you know? If you were just like anyone else in my life, I would let you get away with stuff that bothered me, but you’re not. You’re supposed to be my best friend, and I expect more from you. You can tell me that’s unfair if you want, but that’s just how I feel about it. I’m sorry if that causes any pain, though.”

“You think I don’t know that by now, after everything we’ve been through?” he replied with a disbelieving smirk on his face. “If I couldn’t take your judgement, then I wouldn’t have stuck around. Part of what makes it fun being your best friend is trying to prove myself to you. I like the challenge. The worst thing I could do is fail you. I’ve given you plenty of reasons to bail on me over the years, but the fact that you’re still here…That’s worth the pain.”

I stared at him with confused admiration. I began to wonder how it was that I had caught The Illusionist in his act for speaking so eloquently, when the real Kanoa had just proved himself more than capable. Either this Kanoa before me was just another copy of the real thing, or the real thing was far more complex than I had assumed him to be.

What was the real Kanoa like? He was just as big a mystery as I was, except he had nothing to hide. It was a strange feeling, having someone I thought I had labelled shake that label any chance they got. It made me think that maybe I didn’t really know him at all; that he only showed me what he wanted me to see.

“You really are crazy, you know that?” I said with nervous laughter.

“I know you think I’m crazy, but I want you to know that no matter how bad things seem, I will get you out of here,” he stated with no sense of doubt in his words. If I had ever seen Kanoa more determined, then I certainly didn’t remember what it looked like.

“You know that’s kind of like a crazy person promising that they aren’t crazy, right?” I said, somewhat off put by his daunting aura of resolve.

There was this way in which he walked, like he wouldn’t have even bothered taking any steps forward if he didn’t have utter confidence in what he said. I wondered if everyone was as lucky as I was to have such a person in their lives.

He stopped and looked at me, a power present in his eyes that I almost felt unworthy to match by meeting his gaze. "Yeah, well, what if that crazy person was your best friend? That's what I am, Kail. It's what I'll always be, crazy or not. Don't you ever forget that."

I didn't even have to respond. The conviction in his voice demonstrated his commitment, not only to me, but to everything we stood for. He could have been anything. Insane, ordinary, stupid, intelligent, depressed, happy, strong, weak, confident, arrogant, or whatever other trait I was uncertain about. But there was one thing I was certain about—he was my best friend.

"Famous last words?" I asked. It was the only thing I could think of.

Before he could respond, a chilling scream burst through the hallway and stung my ears like ice pellets. Everyone stopped and turned to one another in fear of what realizations the sound brought with it. Three things concerned me greatly about the shriek. The noise itself was exceedingly painful, it sounded extremely close—but most importantly, it unquestionably originated from Cora.

"I certainly hope not," Kanoa muttered.

We all readied our weapons for whatever perils were laying in wait. We stuck close together so we wouldn't become separated again, like we had in the beginning of our journey through the maze. I kept my eyes in diligent search for anything that seemed out of place, thinking that what we might be heading into was just another trap. Regardless, I assured myself in that moment that I would do whatever it took to make sure Cora was retrieved safely, even if that meant my life for hers.

"Remember, everyone," I said as we ran toward our uncertain destination. "Don't believe everything you see, and be prepared for anything."

"I can promise you that you cannot prepare yourself for what is next," a solemn, sinister voice echoed through my head.

The voice nearly caused my knees to buckle right out from under me and sucked the air right out of my lungs. It was sudden and completely unexpected, but unmistakeable. The voice belonged to Malise.

With much of my momentum stolen from me, I struggled to keep up with my friends as we ran through the twisting and turning hallway to reach Cora. My mind was in a total stalemate of thought. A part of me thought to warn my friends of what I had heard, but the other part urged me to get to Cora in spite of possible danger. Question after question assaulted me, making me feel more vulnerable with every step I took. What had Malise's words meant? Was she nearby and preparing for some sort of ambush? But none of them pressed on me as much as the question of what exactly we had gotten ourselves into.

Before I could come to a conclusion on even one of my self-enquiries, the hallway ended abruptly, and everyone came to a sudden halt. All the previous commotion of my friends running and my churning mind ceased in an instant. Before us was a large square room. The walls were not made up of four large mirrors, but hundreds upon hundreds of panelled mirrors lined up side by side. There was no ceiling to the room, so the familiar floating clock was clearly visible overhead. The world around us seemed unusually calm. None of these things mattered, however, because in the centre of the room was the only thing worth noting. Cora sat at the heart of it all, completely tied up.

"Oh, thank goodness you guys are here," she said with a relieved sigh while struggling to release herself from her bindings. "The Illusionist captured me after we all got separated, tied me up, and left me here. I've been calling out ever since."

It sounded and looked like Cora, but I couldn't be certain if it was actually her. Her fire-red hair was the same, as was her puffy pink dress, but I was yet to be convinced. Although we were relatively far away from her, I could still see the inferno in her eyes as she wrestled with the straps that constricted her. Unlike my encounter with the doppelganger Kanoa, if I wanted to test the legitimacy of Cora's person, I was going to have to rely on something other than appearances alone. If The Illusionist wanted to pick someone that I would be most prone to save, he sure made the right decision.

Kanoa took a step forward, but I put my arm in front of him to block his path. "What's the matter?" he asked.

Without immediately answering him, I meticulous searched the room, looking for anything that would shatter the illusion of safety. I could feel my friends becoming restless, wondering exactly what I was doing. Unfortunately for them, even I couldn't give them an answer. Something just didn't feel right.

"Kail, what are you doing?" Cora asked in frustration, still trying to break free. "I need help here. These straps really hurt."

Her pleas stung me a little, and I thought about the possibility that the person in front of me really was my best friend, a best friend I had hurt enough as it was. After I decided that nothing in the room seemed overly suspicious, I shifted my attention back to Cora herself. I began formulating a plan on how to guarantee her genuineness.

"We can't be sure that's actually Cora," I whispered to my friends, knowing that only Osias was aware of the possibility that The Illusionist had taken her form. "The Illusionist has the ability to copy us almost perfectly."

"How do you know that?" Kanoa asked, understandably perplexed by my words.

"Because I saw him do it," I explained. "He pretended to be you."

"Shit," he whispered, sounding impressed either by The Illusionist's ability or my accomplishment of seeing through it. "So how do we check if Cora is really Cora?"

"What're you guys whispering over there?" Cora groaned, becoming increasing uncomfortable with our hesitation. "Is something wrong? Kail, what's going on?"

"Cora, let me ask you something," I said, thinking quickly. I put away my weapon to make the ordeal seem less menacing than it likely was. I took a few steps toward her, but motioned for the rest of my friends to stay back and out of potential danger. I didn't want them near if things turned sour. "Why don't I trust anybody?"

The air in the room suddenly became eerily stagnant and heavy, as if I had just walked into an area with more gravity. I looked back to my friends and saw the anxiety in their faces, their weapons at the ready. I looked back to Cora and saw her face scrunch in confusion, mulling over my question.

"What do you mean?" she asked.

"Why don't I trust anybody?" I repeated slowly, trying to make the question as obvious as possible without giving away the reason I was asking it in the first place.

Her eyes darted back and forth, as if she was looking for the answer somewhere in the room. "I don't know," she replied, noticeably perplexed. "You never told me."

I paused in place for a moment to consider her answer. The look of misunderstanding remained upon her face. She was undoubtedly wondering why I wasn't rushing over to help her. With every cautious step I took toward her, I could more clearly see the pain in her eyes—not just from the bindings around her ankles and wrists, but from the betrayal she felt in me. Although I was content with her answer, I pressed on, hoping that my coldness to her was not in vain.

"What happened to my sister?" I asked with less determination in my words, the question stinging my tongue as it left my mouth. I didn't like having to bring up such a painful memory, but I felt it was necessary.

Cora appeared to be obtaining a better grasp on the situation and the reasoning behind my questioning. "I don't know," she replied once again, but with more conviction. "You never told me."

With every moment, the distance between the rest of my friends and I grew, but the space between Cora and I lessened. Once again she had answered the question to my satisfaction, but I realized my questions were too broad. If I truly wanted to gain the faith I strived for, I would have to go deeper, make things more personal. I had to ask something that nobody outside of Cora and myself would know; would want to know.

"Why," I said, my voice barely registering in the outside world. I cleared my throat and took a deep breath, trying my best to exhale the insecurity inside me. My words were still no more than an unsteady whisper when I asked, "Why did I leave you that day on the beach?"

"I don't know," she replied without falter, the pain in her words now as easy to see as it was in her eyes. "You never told me."

I was close enough that I could see her lower lip trembling, but she fought back against the pain defiantly, just as I knew Cora would have done. I could see the shimmering flame in her eyes, the very essence of all that she was, and yet I still didn't want to believe. Was it The Illusionist's fault that I didn't trust her, or was it my own?

I stopped, now close enough to reach my hands out and save her. We stared at each other for a moment, each of us wanting to know what was going on in the other's head. I heard movement behind me but put my hand up in warning, knowing that Kanoa thought the coast was clear. There was one final thing I wanted to know, one final test to put her through. I had sent her through hell and back for me, and yet I needed to ask her one more thing.

"What's my favourite movie?" I asked, my voice now as calm and peaceful as the world around me.

She smiled, pained laughter bursting forth from her wavering lips. She nodded and broke eye contact for a moment, knowing her answer before she spoke it. She looked back up at me, tilted her head to move her crimson hair out of her crimson eyes, and said, "You sent me that tape when I was in summer camp of you watching it. It was the nicest thing that anyone ever did for me. It kept me safe and made me feel that no matter how far away I was, I would always have the memory of you right by my side. You would always be in my mind, and I in yours, and that was all that mattered. It's Eternal Sunshine of the Spotless Mind."

A smile fluttered across my face, disappearing as quickly as it appeared. Her answer sunk in and I looked down at the ground below me, weighed down by the events that had just unfolded. I looked back up at her and nodded my head, seeing her blissful expression staring back at me. It killed me to see her so happy, and yet I was so relieved to hear those words. I got back to my feet and began shaking my head.

"I'm sorry," I said, sighing in resignation. I placed one hand behind my back, on my weapon. "But I never told you that either. Cora's favourite movie is Eternal Sunshine of the Spotless Mind. Not mine."

Cora's expression slowly turned from joy to shock. She opened her mouth as if to say something, but her voice remained silent. She squirmed around nervously, wrapped up in the lies she was telling. She furrowed her eyebrows, her eyes bearing into me, but this time they did no harm. I knew that the eyes that I was looking into had no power over me, and at that moment she knew it too. She suddenly stopped moving around, and her face went blank. I had caught The Illusionist once again—and this time I had my friends with me.

“Ugh,” she growled. “I hate trick questions.”

She promptly jumped to her feet, the ropes around her wrists and ankles tearing apart at the seams and setting her free. Her beautiful appearance quickly began to devolve into a grotesque spectacle. Her perfect skin bubbled and turned a sickening green. Her feminine frame morphed into a contorted atrocity. Her delicate dress ripped to shreds and changed into black, filthy garments.

The transformation from friend to foe was swift, gut-wrenching, disturbing and utterly mystifying. It was a perfect summation of The Illusionist, who now stood before me. We had reached the climax of his twisted performance, and I knew that it was going to be an unforgettable one.

“Now!” I shouted to my friends, signalling them to initiate the long-awaited battle.

I withdrew my weapon and forcefully brought it forward, hoping to land the first blow on The Illusionist. Before the blow could connect, he disappeared without warning. I heard chuckling behind me before I could even comprehend what had just happened. I felt a great amount of pain as I was struck in the back and sent sprawling forward.

I turned to face my enemy as he stood triumphantly over me, taunting me with laughter. His rotting teeth and wild eyes bore down on me with all their revolting might, trying their best to strike fear in me, and doing a pretty good job of it. It was clear that there was no running this time. The Illusionist was set on finishing his act.

Before he could cause any more significant damage to me, my friends, with their weapons drawn, interrupted the private altercation and entered the battle with full force. Without any hint of effort, he disappeared out of sight and away from danger. It was now rather evident that The Illusionist’s aim was first and foremost to get rid of me for Malise, thus ruining the prophecy. My friends were merely obstacles to his cause. Kanoa quickly helped me to my feet and placed my weapon back in my hands, his dreadful smile plainly visible.

“I guess you were right,” he whispered. “I kinda wish you weren’t.”

My friends and I all formed a circle with our backs facing one another, to have a clear view of the entire room. Our circle felt tighter than usual, the absence of Cora resounding through our ranks. I scanned the room, feeling The Illusionist’s presence and knowing for certain that he hadn’t gone too far.

Silence befell the air, only disrupted by the uneasy breathing among the five of us. Osias tried entering his meditation, but Thalia pushed him to keep his eyes open. The pain still coursed through my back and I was unable to stand up straight, hunching over to ease the aching. I could hear someone begin tapping their foot impatiently and someone else tapping their fingers across the face of their weapon. This was the calm before the storm, but the problem was that we had no idea what kind of storm we were preparing for, or what kind of toll it would exact from us.

Suddenly, the panels upon panels of mirrors outlining the room began to shake and pop out of their frames. The once-square room around us began to break apart at the seams, rapidly restructuring before our eyes. We no longer stood in a room, but on a hovering platform high in the sky with no borders to prevent us from going over the edge.

The mirrors began erratically zooming around the platform without any pattern, only narrowly dodging one another, causing an incredibly disorienting sensation of reflection. Even standing caused me to lose my sense of direction. The mirrors were exceedingly thin, making them difficult to spot, especially considering how fast they danced around the platform. It was as if we had walked into the middle of an enormous ballet of mirrors.

"What do we do?" Osias asked, clearly as overwhelmed as I was.

A mirror bumped into my arm and pushed me forward, causing me to slam into another oncoming mirror. I stumbled and attempted to regain my footing when I was struck again, this time much harder than by the mirrors. I began to panic, looking around for my friends. I was launched into the air without warning and crashed through one of the mirrors, sending shattered glass scattering in all directions around me. The landing was painful, but not nearly as excruciating as what I had landed in. I looked to my shaking hands and saw blood trickling out of the open wounds the glass had cut.

Laughter howled from my pain, and I realized my greatest fear: The Illusionist wasn't in the mirrors. He was the mirrors.

I stood back up and saw The Illusionist with his back facing me. I assumed that he had perhaps lost sight of me in the scuffle, so I snuck up behind him in an attempt to catch him off-guard. When I felt I was close enough to do the maximum amount of damage, I brought my weapon forward and into his back.

He quickly spun around, his devilish smile wide and his laughter filled with frenzy. It was then I realized that what I had been sneaking up on was in fact a mirror, and as Hope's Glow crashed through the glass, I plunged through its falling pieces like a curtain as another blow was dealt into my back. I spun across the ground, bumping into mirrors along the way, until I finally came to a rest, becoming increasingly entrenched with the agony of defeat.

I gingerly lifted myself off the ground and looked around, the spinning mirrors completely encircling me. I began devising a plan, thinking of a way, any way, that we would be able to defeat The Illusionist in his own element. I heard more breaking glass and lost my thoughts for a moment, now wondering what he was doing to my friends.

I tried moving in the direction I heard the noises, but the movement of the mirrors was too unpredictable. I was extraordinarily frustrated with my current circumstances—frustrated with the fact that we still hadn't found Cora, frustrated that we had fallen into The Illusionist's trap, and most of all, frustrated that there was nothing I could do.

"Destroy the mirrors!" I heard Osias shout from somewhere out of my sight.

Without needing any further persuasion, I held my weapon tight, fought through the pain in my hands, and sent it careening forward, hoping to slam into a mirror. Luckily, there were so many mirrors travelling so quickly that my sloppy strike was met with the destruction of another one. Glass shards sprawled in all directions and chimed as they glistened across the floor. With one less mirror to worry about, the space around me became a tiny bit more manageable. If I counted the mirror I had fallen through, I had obliterated two—and only had about a hundred to go before the room was mirror-free.

Thalia suddenly appeared in front of me, slicing her way through a couple of mirrors in the process. Her two scimitars glistened as she cut through the clear glass, causing what appeared to be millions upon millions of tiny fragments to explode around her. It was like seeing sunlight filter through water; shimmering diamonds in a sea of glass. Her face had a few cuts and scratches on it. I was surprised that I had yet to suffer any gashes to the face.

"All these mirrors were making me claustrophobic," Thalia explained quickly, continuing to breathlessly carve her way through the ever-enclosing mirrors. "I thought I'd redecorate the place a little, if you don't mind?"

"Fine by me," I replied, focusing on decimating a few mirrors of my own.

A mirror spun in front of me, and I prepared to smash it down. Before I could, The Illusionist himself appeared in the frame and leaped out effortlessly, phasing between the mirror's surface and the space in front of me sooner than I could react. His sudden reappearance left me stunned and unable to warn Thalia of our impending predicament. The world around me felt slow as he inched his way toward me, his nauseating breath billowing across my face. The tiny space between us was thankfully divided by one of Thalia's blades as she attempted to cut The Illusionist's face clean off. It almost succeeded, but almost wasn't nearly enough.

The Illusionist quickly turned his attention away from me, swiping the blade out of his face and nearly out of Thalia's grasp. Caught off-guard, Thalia stood no chance of defending herself against his next attack. She gasped slightly and stared deep into the eyes of her enemy as he pulled her in close to laugh in her face. He hastily brought his fist into her stomach, propelling her into the air and out of sight as the mirrors continued twisting and turning about the room.

Before I was able to check on my injured friend, he snapped his focus back to me, revelling in the fact that we were once again alone. I readied my weapon, determined not to hold back.

He swung his fist to the left of my face, not even coming close to contacting. Before I could understand why he had missed so drastically, a fist connected on the right side of my face and nearly knocked me off my feet. I swung wildly in the direction the blow had come from, only managing to demolish a mirror in the process.

Another mirror bumped into me, pushing me backwards and into another strike aimed at the back of my knee. I fell to the ground for a moment and tried getting back up, but was struck in the chest, sending me skidding across the platform's smooth surface. I crashed through a couple more mirrors, their pieces cascading down upon me like frozen rain.

I laid still, soaking in the pain and frustration The Illusionist's invisible attacks were inflicting upon me. If I wanted to have a fair fight with him, I was going to have to start destroying all of the mirrors he was using to hide in.

I jumped to my feet and starting spinning around in circles, my weapon cutting through the middle of more mirrors than I could count. I held on tight and spun as fast as I could, letting out an involuntary shout as I rotated. The effect of my action was a golden whirlwind of broken glass. The reflection of Hope's Glow shined all around me. The more I revolved, the more I began to notice how sparse the mirror population became. A smile formed upon my face as I celebrated my progress.

Out of the corner of my eye, I spotted the reflection of The Illusionist in the surface of the floor, meaning he was descending on me from above. I stopped spinning, the final pieces of glass falling to the ground, and raised my weapon to the sky to block the impact. I was bewildered to find no sign of him above me, and quickly looked back to the floor.

The shattered pieces of glass that littered the floor sprung up into the air as The Illusionist flew out of the ground and landed a jarring uppercut, right into my chin.

The sudden impact seemed to slow down time and erase sound from my ears. Tears stung my eyes and caused the bits of glass around me to shimmer ever so brightly. Each little piece seemed to emanate what little light they could in all directions as they spun aimlessly through the air with me. I remained suspended in midair for a few moments with the tiny beacons of radiance around me, and if it weren't for the fact that I was in so much pain, I might have been able to enjoy their beauty to the fullest.

But the moment passed as suddenly as it began and I plummeted back to the ground, crashing into the platform with no means of cushioning. I was now bleeding quite profusely from all the little gashes I had sustained from the broken glass. However, worse than the bruises, worse than the blood and all the pain I had endured, was the disappointment that coursed through my veins. I was supposed to live up to so many expectations. The expectation of defeating the evil present in the land, the expectation of freeing its people, the expectation of keeping my friends safe and getting them all out of here. Yet I was coming up short in every category. I was failing everyone by lying on the floor, bleeding and broken. And that feeling was enough to make me want to get back to my feet.

I rose unsteadily to my feet and wiped the blood out my eyes, trying my best to regain what composure I had left to make one final stand against my enemy. The number of mirrors that traversed the room had greatly reduced. I was actually able to catch glimpses of my friends. To my confusion, I witnessed each of them locked in heated combat, and yet they were all separated from one another. Their enemies, however, were all the same. The Illusionist had generated copies of himself to keep everyone preoccupied in their own personal battles.

Each of my friends struggled with their opponent, none able to gain an upper hand, not even Kanoa. Hope's Glow faded as the optimism within me began to falter, for even defeating one of them would barely put a dent into our seemingly bulletproof problem. Whatever help I needed wasn't coming to me.

A maniacal laughter resonated from behind me, indicating that my time for resting was over. I sloppily turned around with my weapon raised, but I was completely ill-equipped to defend myself from the force of the contact. The Illusionist hit me with such a great momentum that if I hadn't used my weapon as a barricade, I would surely have been broken in two.

I was lifted clean off my feet and sent flying through the air, legs and arms flailing uncontrollably. Before I was able to make my landing, I was fiercely caught by the throat, which ripped the oxygen straight out of me. His fingers tore into my neck and my attempts at freeing myself were in vain, as his grip was far too strong. I squirmed around, my feet unable to touch the platform beneath them. Hope's Glow was still in my hand and I used what little strength I had left to try and hit him, possibly liberating myself from his vice-like hold on me.

He simply laughed wildly at my feeble efforts, with spittle running down his cracked lips. He and I both knew he had gotten the best of me. This is how I would meet my end: at the hands of a monster created by my nightmares.

"Well, what are you waiting for?" I asked, my voice caught between his fingers. "An invitation?"

His low giggles erupted into a fit of psychotic laughter, his whole body convulsing in the act. Although his head was shaking as he cackled, his crazed sallow eyes never broke hold from me. The level of insanity in them could not be overstated. The look in his eyes made me question what he saw in the world, if what he saw even closely resembled what I saw. Was everything he saw just as twisted as he was? Did he see anything at all, or had the corruption that had poisoned him so long ago made him completely blind?

Something about me caught his attention and his laughter died in an instant, the ever-present grin remaining on his foul face. An eerie silence befell the two of us as we simply stared at one another, accepting what was to come next. As he brought his free hand into the air to deal his final blow to me, the only thought that continued to cross through my mind was the wish for another chance—not just at a specific thing, but at everything.

The Illusionist suddenly jolted forward, a strange expression of disbelief and horror upon his face. His grasp upon me loosened and I slumped weakly to the ground, my legs unable to support the weight. I choked and coughed, clutching my neck to try and soothe the acute pain I felt.

I looked up and watched as The Illusionist's trembling hands made their way toward his torso. A blade protruded from his chest where his heart would have been, if he had one. His eyes slowly trailed down to the impalement, and I heard a slight whimper as they rested upon the cause of his death.

The shock of realization brought him to his knees with a thud. He quickly looked away, apparently ignoring what he had just seen, and began shifting his head from side to side, opening his mouth and then closing it, as if trying to find a way to escape his fate. His eyes then finally returned to me, and although they were still feral and his rotting teeth were stuck in a smile, I saw fear in him.

He chuckled quietly to himself and nodded his head, understanding the irony in his current predicament. The Illusionist then began to fade into purple smoke, his body evaporating all around him. He didn't resist, but instead peacefully accepted his erasure from the dream world he had been a part of, until all that was left of him was the sound of his soft, demonic laughter.

The weapon that had ended his life dropped to the ground and bounced around a little until it rested in place. I stared at it, still alive and breathing because of it. I heard footsteps approaching to retrieve the polearm and looked up to thank its owner.

"I guess it was about time I saved you for once, huh?"

"About time you showed up," I replied, wearily getting back onto my feet. I noticed that although I was still bleeding, the agonizing amounts of pain I had been experiencing moments ago rapidly subsided. I assumed that pain itself didn't last very long in dreams, so it made sense that the same rules applied to Drephoria. "I owe you big-time, Cora."

"Don't mention it," she said with a playful shrug, enjoying her heroic moment as she bent down to pick up her weapon. "Seems as though I made it just in time, by the looks of you. Are you okay?"

I looked out across the battlefield and realized that although I had just witnessed The Illusionist die firsthand, or at least one version of him, there were still multiple copies engaged in combat with the rest of my friends. After the great relief I had experienced watching The Illusionist fall, knowing that truly vanquishing him was far from a guarantee was rather disconcerting. Even though the fight felt as though it had ended, in reality it seemed to have just begun. Luckily, we now outnumbered him.

“I’ll feel a lot better when there isn’t a single Illusionist left in this world,” I replied.

As if my words were some sort of cue, four of the remaining mirrors made a beeline toward us. Cora placed her back against mine to prepare for whatever assault was thrown at us. I made sure not to step on her wavy pink dress. Her heart was pounding so hard and so fast, I could feel it against me. I squeezed her hand quickly to remind her that I was there with her. I needed her to stay strong, like I knew she was, if we were going to get out of this alive.

Two mirrors stopped directly in front of us and two to our sides, completely boxing us in. I had a feeling I knew what was to come next, and attempted to pre-emptively stop The Illusionist’s plan before it had time to begin. Unfortunately, my strike was blocked as The Illusionist bounded out of the mirror only for a moment, and then sunk back into its surface.

I turned quickly to the mirror on my right and swung at it, but that too was deflected by a dark flash that barely registered in my mind before disappearing again. Knowing his agility was one of his strongest attributes, I was going to have to work together with Cora to break out of this box.

“Cora, aim for the mirrors and hit as fast as you can,” I whispered, trying to keep my plan secret from our enemy.

With no further explanation, I began lashing out without falter, relentlessly toggling between striking the mirror in front of me and the one to my right. Conversely, Cora tried stabbing at the mirror in front of her and the one to her right. The two of us went on the offense without slowing down, our blows averted almost faster than we could deal them. Every motion was a blur, as if I was moving automatically and not of my own accord. Our movements almost looked rehearsed as we effortlessly weaved back and forth in a choreographed flurry of steel.

The clanging of metal and the grunting of futility continued without pause, but through it all I never once felt Cora leave my back. Regardless of how unattainable our victory appeared, we held our ground together.

The only response from The Illusionist was his now-ingrained laughter. It no longer bore the sadness I’d heard in it earlier during his demise. Whatever sympathy I had felt in that time was now gone, replaced by the irritation he caused by his incessant warping. There was no stop to this stalemate in sight, because I couldn’t see him to begin with. He was everywhere and yet nowhere all at once.

"He's too fast!" Cora cried out. "If there was a way to hit all four mirrors at once, we might be –"

"Cora, I need you to jump as high as you can!" I interrupted, formulating a plan faster than she could finish her sentence.

"What?" she responded, surprised by my random request.

"Just jump!" I ordered.

She swung her long polearm once more, gaining enough momentum in the process to lift herself off her feet and high into the air. As I heard her lift off, I thrust Hope's Glow with as much force as I could muster, sending it careening away from me like a Frisbee.

The next few moments passed by sluggishly, as if too much was going on for time to appropriately measure, so it was forced to slow down to accommodate it all. I watched my weapon crash through the first mirror to my left, sending its pieces splashing to the ground. The Illusionist had planned to lunge from that mirror next, so he was forced to alter his path to the next mirror. Before he could pass through that one, however, my weapon slammed into it, and I saw the look of confusion in his eyes as the surface he inhabited came crashing down around him.

By the time Hope's Glow reached the third mirror, the one to my right that he attempted to spawn from, the laughter had stopped, but the smile remained. I had turned my weapon into a boomerang, and just as I had planned, it would return to me—but not before destroying the last mirror.

Cora still hung in the air above me as Hope's Glow reached its final destination. The Illusionist made one ultimate effort to escape his jail beyond the mirror's facade. While running, his hand rose forward, reaching out to touch the world I occupied, his eyes wider than ever before. As my weapon collided with his frame, effectively splitting him in two, he stopped dead in his tracks, letting out a silent howl that was drowned out by the shattering of glass.

Hope's Glow returned to my hand, and The Illusionist fell apart into a million little pieces, each of them dark and stained. This time I hadn't just watched him die—he had died by my hand. I took a certain amount of comfort in that fact.

Cora finally landed her lofty jump right on top of The Illusionist's shattered body, the bits of glass cracking beneath her feet. She had an astonished look on her face, either caused by the length of her leap or the fact that my plan had actually worked. Either way, I undoubtedly shared her expression.

"Well, that was something else," she said, exhaling deeply.

I looked behind her and realized that our other four friends had eliminated all of The Illusionist's replicas but one. I assumed that this last duplicate was the real deal, for he seemed to be putting up more of a fight than they had left in them. Cora and I would have to add to their cause and hope that six would be able to overwhelm one.

“What do you say we make the first member of The Forgotten Four truly forgotten?” I asked her, now feeling almost no pain and beginning to return to peak condition.

“Well, other than the fact that what you just said was extremely cheesy,” she teased, flicking the hair out of her eyes to reveal the burning embers in them, “I think I can handle that.”

We rushed over to assist our friends. The terrain was now easy to journey across, with the lack of mirrors blocking our path. We watched as Kanoa, Osias, and Thalia each tried their best to land a successful hit upon their foe, while Adora looked on rather helplessly. She appeared to be standing in a small, translucent bubble, swaying her arms around gently. I wasn’t sure if it was because she was injured, or perhaps because she didn’t have a real weapon of her own, or possibly because her sister forbade her from entering combat, but she did not appear to be a part of the battle.

“Adora!” I shouted as I approached. She turned to look at me and smiled to see Cora and I still alive. She didn’t take a step outside of her little sanctuary, so I had to walk right up to her in order to find out what had happened since we had been separated.

“Kail, you’re bleeding,” she said, trying to tend to my wounds. “Are you all right?”

“Yeah, nothing I won’t recover from,” I replied, nodding to Cora as she ran off to join the rest of our friends in the duel. “What’s going on here? Is everyone okay?”

“Well, The Illusionist appeared and started making copies of himself,” she explained slowly, apparently uninterested in the time-sensitive nature of our conversation. “Thalia told Kanoa to keep me safe if something were to happen to her. Kanoa killed two of them, and my sister killed another. I was rather impressed. When there was only one of him left and things started to get serious, Osias placed this bubble around me to keep me out of danger. I kind of like it, but I think I’d rather be helping you guys. Good thing you two showed up, though, as this last one seems to be giving them all kinds of trouble.”

“Okay, you just stay here and keep safe,” I told her, turning around and running toward the rest of my friends.

“If you say so,” she said, not budging from her little haven.

Kanoa was deep in conflict with The Illusionist when I arrived, dodging out of the way of potentially lethal blows and then dealing some of his own with his large sword. I noticed that his cape had suffered some damage. There were rips running up and down his back. He performed acrobatic actions that would have been impossible for him to do in the real world.

The Illusionist swung at Kanoa's head, to which Kanoa responded by ducking to the ground and executing a one-handed cartwheel, all in one smooth motion. He used his free hand to swipe at The Illusionist's feet, but unfortunately he jumped clean over it. The two of them landed back on their feet simultaneously and continued their fight without missing a beat.

The rest of my friends, on the other hand, appeared to be catching their breaths, slumped over and panting heavily. I took this opportunity to prepare a strategy.

"Guys, we need a plan—" I said, but was quickly interrupted when The Illusionist turned his attention to me. He darted straight toward me without a second thought. I should have known my presence would upset the balance of the battle. He was here for me, something I couldn't keep affording to forget.

"Glad to have you back, Kail!" Kanoa shouted as he chased after his foe. "But now really isn't the time for talking!"

I braced for the impact bearing down upon me, but was thankfully relieved when Osias jumped in front of me with his magnificent staff raised. He created some kind of force-field that quickly assembled itself around us. The Illusionist slammed into it with a sickening thud and was sent flying back into Kanoa's direction. Although he had little time for recovery, The Illusionist composed himself and hit the ground in fighting form, defending himself against Kanoa's onslaught of strikes.

Osias looked back to me and saw the amazed expression on my face. "Yeah, that's what I do," he explained with a shrug.

I nodded my approval and patted him on the back. "Thanks," I said. "Now let's see what we can do together, shall we?"

I felt the adrenaline pump through my body as I stepped around Osias and dashed toward Kanoa and The Illusionist. The Illusionist was fresh out of traps to spring on us. He was being forced out of element, and it was beginning to show. Osias had already landed a critical hit upon him, and Kanoa was becoming increasingly close to landing a fatal blow. It was only a matter of time before he slipped up for good.

The thought of pushing him into a corner frightened me. Had he really run out of tricks, or was something far more sinister up his sleeve?

Kanoa heard me coming and without a word being spoken between us, stopped himself mid-swing and ducked down. I leaped over him with my legs outstretched, kicking The Illusionist square in the chest, repaying one of the many hits I owed him. I was going to refund them with interest.

He slid backwards as I landed on my feet, and before he could retaliate, his focus was shifted elsewhere. A pathway made of ice shredded through the air around him, icicles dangling from its sides as it materialized out of thin air. Thalia then whizzed past me, gliding along the icy trail as if she was snowboarding. I turned to see where the path had come from and noticed its origins forming at the tip of Osias's staff. As Thalia passed by, she shot a wink in my direction before continuing on her way to her intended target.

She aimed one of her scimitars directly at The Illusionist's head, bending down to make sure he couldn't duck out of her way. He quickly fell to the ground, effectively dodging her strike, but not before her blade cut right through his dark top hat, fully exposing his mangled jungle of purple hair. If Thalia had bowed down any lower, I would have surely been looking at the decapitated remains of The Illusionist. We were getting closer.

He let out a short burst of laughter before smashing the frozen path out from underneath Thalia, sending her hurtling to the ground. She quickly got back to her feet, reciprocating The Illusionist's laughter with her own. I could almost see the likeness between the two, in an uncanny sort of way.

"I almost Sleepy Hollowed him," she grumbled as she shook the shards off her.

We all circled him, just as he had once circled us with his mirrors. He was now the one that was cornered without any place to go or hide. His eyes darted back and forth like a wild animal about to lash out, but we were all ready for him. We inched closer and closer, tightening the perimeter with each step. He raised his hands defensively. Our weapons were so close that he began tapping them away, an ugly smile lingering upon his face.

"I kind of feel bad, all of us ganging up on him like this," Thalia said with a laugh.

We all began laughing, nervously at first, but then comfortably. Our cacophony of laughter rose, but it was nothing like his, and the sound washed over him like a poison. For once I saw the disgust in his eyes as we laughed, and for the first time, his signature smile turned into a displeased frown. Now he knew what it felt like to hate something that someone took pleasure in.

Cora's polearm drew too close for his comfort, and with one swift motion he grabbed it from her and slammed the handle deep into her stomach. She fell to the ground clenching where her weapon had made contact, gasping for breath. We all looked to our friend instinctively, which was exactly the distraction he had hoped to create.

With our focus diverted, he disappeared from the circle we had formed—and rematerialized making a run toward Adora.

Everything happened so fast that I barely had time to comprehend what had occurred, let alone figure out what to do about it. Thalia let out a scream and froze in fear, unable to run to help her sister. Her reaction inflicted déjà vu upon me. Luckily, I did not react in the same manner this time.

I began running as fast as I could after The Illusionist, quickly realizing that he would beat me to her no matter how fast I ran. His laugh was more sinister than I had ever heard before, appropriately reflecting the unspeakable intentions that were unquestionably bubbling in his mind. Running wasn't going to cut it, and in the real world I would have probably been out of options.

Fortunately, this wasn't the real world, and here I wasn't confined to simply running.

I launched myself through the air, diving forward with Hope's Glow at the end of my outstretched arms. I noticed it lighting up more brilliantly than I had seen before, almost assuring me that what I was doing would work out in the end.

I came back down short of The Illusionist, just as I had expected. I plunged my weapon into the surface of the ground and pushed off again, performing a wide, arching front-flip that would hopefully put me right where I wanted to be. As I soared through the air, my head now upside down and facing where my friends were, I noticed that Kanoa had flown after me. He had thrown his enormous sword in a haphazard attempt to save Adora. I just prayed that it landed on foe, not friend.

I reached the apex of my flip and began descending right on top of The Illusionist. In that moment, factoring in the structure of my weapon, my trajectory upon my opponent, and Kanoa's impending blade, I recognized an opportunity that was too perfect to pass up. I adjusted Hope's Glow in my hands to make sure it would befall my adversary suitably, fitting the idea that had just surfaced in my mind. If we weren't in Drephoria, my scheme might have been insane, but insanity is exactly what thrived here. And understanding that was what I finally had come to accept.

I brought Hope's Glow down upon The Illusionist from behind, forcefully wedging him between two of the spires that shot from the base of my weapon. Although my feet had yet to touch the ground, I pushed down hard to ensure his absolute constriction. His run abruptly came to a halt, and he almost tripped from the burden I had thrust upon him. Remembering Kanoa's blade, I used all the power I could summon in my arms to fling myself up and over my enemy, gracefully landing in front of him. I faced Adora and ducked down on one knee to clear myself out of jeopardy.

My head snapped down from the force of the landing, but I was still able to hear the sound of ripping flesh behind me. I waited for the telling thump of him hitting the ground, but no such noise came to be.

I slowly turned my head upward and saw Adora standing above me with a triumphant smile upon her face. She didn't say anything, only gave me the thumbs-up. It was all the congratulations I could have wanted.

I got to my feet and turned to watch the final Illusionist stumble backward, Kanoa's blade skewered right through him and my weapon wrapped tightly around him. Whether this was the true Illusionist, or whether he had been killed earlier, wasn't a concern of mine. All that mattered to me as he lurched back and forth, his life waning, was that I would never have to hear that laugh or see that smile of his again.

He took one last deep breath, presented me with an inelegant bow that he held for a few moments, and then sagged forward to the ground. As he evaporated into purple smoke, I knew that I had just witnessed his final performance, and there would be no encore. The curtains had finally closed on The Illusionist.

I heard Thalia begin clapping, but I was uncertain whether she was clapping at our victory or The Illusionist's grand exit. Kanoa's blade and my chakram lay where The Illusionist had fallen, but while Kanoa actually had to go retrieve his weapon, mine simply soared through the air and back into my hands. It was a handy little feature that I greatly appreciated.

Kanoa reached for his sword and performed a mocking little bow of his own as be bent down to pick it up. I laughed, thankful after all that he had chosen to throw it, but more importantly thankful that he had been there at all. When all was said and done, he had been the one to defeat three versions of The Illusionist. And when all was said and done, he was right: he may be crazy, but he was my best friend.

"Now that was legend--wait for it!" he exclaimed, pausing for a moment before completing his sentence. I nodded my head, knowing what was to follow. "Dary!"

The Illusionist suddenly reappeared behind Kanoa, his arms outstretched and his smile extending from ear to ear.

Just like the rest of us, Kanoa had no time to react. All we could do was look on in horror as The Illusionist draped his arms firmly around my best friend and enveloped him in his darkness. Kanoa's eyes opened wide and he tried to shout something out, but his voice was never heard. He was gone. The Illusionist uttered the first real word I had heard from him with a voice dripping in rasp and malevolence.

"Gotcha."

With that single word, he detonated into a cloud of purple smoke, stealing him and Kanoa away from my sight.

Time stopped. The world froze and all was still. Even the gigantic clock that floated above our heads had ceased. No matter how much I wanted to, I couldn't bring myself to move. I couldn't even breathe. I had no clue what had just happened, but what I knew for certain was that we had all been deceived. I didn't know why yet, but I felt it deep in my gut. He had fooled us all along. He wasn't after me—he was after Kanoa. It was his final and by far most impressive trick of all.

The impenetrable cloud swirled for a moment. There was something inside causing the disturbance. Malise herself emerged out of its depths. Whatever overwhelming dread that filled me in the moment of Kanoa's departure was instantly multiplied a hundred times over, and now threatened to consume me entirely.

She floated toward me, her presence too much for me to stand. My knees would have buckled had I still the capability to move, but everything had become idle and lifeless. I didn't know what had become of my friends, but I knew that it didn't matter. Malise and I were alone, just as she wanted.

She floated around me, taunting me with her mobility. "I told you that you were not prepared for what was to come," she reiterated, her voice unnaturally serene, stressing each syllable to its limits. "But I was not referring to this. This was only the beginning, but what comes next is the end."

She stopped circling and hovered directly in front of me, our eyes locking. She pulled in real close and paused for a moment, her face completely devoid of all emotions. "Let me ask you," she whispered eerily. "Are you remembering a dream, or dreaming of a memory?"

CHAPTER 12: THE TRUTH REVEALED

With that, she vanished, and so did the rest of the world. As her mysterious words chilled me like a winter's breeze, darkness fell over my eyes, leaving me blinded by the abyss around me. The darkness pressed in on me, crushing me with its overwhelming emptiness. I was able to move, but there was nowhere to go. I was nowhere, inhabiting space without a destination. I heard a faint voice calling my name.

Unable to see where I was going, I wandered around aimlessly, my arms extended from me and searching for the source. The voice grew louder and louder, pulsating like a heartbeat, but I wasn't getting any closer to it. It was getting closer to me. The voice began saying my name in quicker succession, until the repetitions became so fast they overlapped one another.

I stopped looking for the voice, for it had found me—and the louder it became, the more it began to sting my ears. It repeated over and over again without end, escalating in volume to an unbearable level. It consumed my mind, causing me to fall to the ground and scream out in agony, but all that could be heard was the voice.

The voice that called out my name belonged to my sister, Delphia.

My eyes opened the instant her voice stopped, and I immediately realized I was no longer covered in darkness. Where I resided was far worse than nowhere. It was the last somewhere in the world I wanted to be. I was back in my room in the orphanage, back inside the prison that held my childhood. I was sitting on my bed, looking out the window. I was only able to see the sun's rays filtering into the dark room, revealing the tiny specks of dust floating directionless through the air. I sat there alone. All was quiet. Although my past memories contained sketchy details and blurred textures, this one was entirely vivid, as if I was experiencing it all for the first time. This memory was fresh in my mind, fresh as a recently opened wound.

The day I had stumbled upon was not just any ordinary day, but a very particular day, and in that moment I realized what my flashbacks had been hinting at since the beginning. They weren't just some random selections of events that my mind had chosen to take interest in. They had all been leading up to this. I knew the purpose for these instances and feared more than ever what was to come. Had I truly been so blind as to not have seen this coming? Or had I merely forced myself to not believe it was possible? Whatever the reasoning, whatever the purpose, Malise had been right: I was not prepared for what was to come next.

"Kail, there you are!" Delphia shouted as she burst through the door, slamming it behind her as she jumped up and down in front of me. She spun around continuously, but I could still see the toothy smile displayed across her childish face.

I wanted nothing more than to reach out and alter what was about to occur, to somehow change the past. This was my second chance. This was how I altered my memories. I fought against my stationary body with all the rage and hatred that I found in this memory, desperately struggling not to let everything unfold as it once did. I put all the will of my being into breaking free from my stasis—but for all my intense rebellion and unsaturated loathing for the past, there was no hope for redemption. I was as intertwined with my past, just as anyone else was, and there was no escaping it; not then, and not now.

"Delphia, calm down. You're making me sick with all that spinning you're doing," I muttered, putting up my hand to issue my command. In reality, the only spinning that was making me sick was a single sentence that kept rushing through my head: Please make this stop.

"I'm too excited," she replied, ignoring my pleas. "They're back! They're back and today's the day! Today's the day, I just know it!"

I abruptly stood, the motion causing me to momentarily lose hold on my awareness of the memory. I was becoming so involved that I was beginning to forget it wasn't real, or rather that it was real, but wasn't actually taking place. But it was actually taking place...

"What are you talking about?" I asked, sternly grabbing her by the arms to get a straight look into her wondrous little eyes.

This was the closest we had been in any of the memories, and yet I couldn't feel any further away. The moment would pass and I would never be able to relive it, not as I did now. Even knowing this fact, I was still unable to simply enjoy the second chance I had been given because I didn't see it as a gift, but instead a curse.

"Keeley and Garnet are here," she explained, making sure I fully understood her, "and they want to adopt us."

I reeled back, absolutely stunned by the news. It was something I had been waiting for before I could even remember. It was the only thing ever on my mind, the only wish I had ever made, the only dream I had ever had, and it was actually coming true. I could feel tears of joy flood the barrier I had built to hide my true emotions from Delphia, finally revealing that just like her, I was able to cry.

"I've never seen you cry before," she stated, gently brushing the tears from my face, "but I'm glad you did."

"Oh wow," I whispered, taking a deep breath and shaking away the melodrama. "Sorry you had to see that. Promise it won't happen again. Well, I guess it won't have to happen again, now that we have real parents."

The words sounded strange as they left my mouth. I was beginning to think that I may never have been able to say them truthfully. To have real parents again—I snapped out of my thoughts, forcing myself to remember that I was in a memory. I had always felt the tug of my memories on my consciousness in my previous visits to my past, but never stronger than it was now. I was becoming completely synchronized with my memory, losing grip on reality. I was going to experience this day just I had done all those years ago, in all of its bittersweet glory.

"I told you everything would be okay," she said as she gave me a warm hug, her arms too short to circle my waist.

She was so small, so fragile. I wished for my memory to end there, for I was in a perfect state of bliss. Why did I have to remember the bad stuff? Why couldn't memories only form from the good? Why did we have to hold on to what we didn't want to remember? I couldn't answer any of those questions, but I did return my sister's hug, and as my arms gently wrapped around her with the sunlight pouring over us, I knew that what I was holding onto was something special. The moment could have lasted forever and it wouldn't have been long enough.

"Kail?" I heard a voice whisper from the hallway outside my room. "Are you in there? It's Keeley."

My sister and I turned our heads toward the doorway and saw Keeley and Garnet standing just outside the doorframe, pained smiles upon their faces. It must have been an odd sight to behold, a brother now aged far beyond the memory's record, holding his little sister in a darkly lit room, only illuminated by trickling sunlight and the radiance of their smiles. But I didn't care what it looked like, because the truth was that it put me at ease. It made me feel whole again.

I turned back to my sister and she turned back to me, and then she let go. Maybe it was out of embarrassment, or perhaps excitement, or maybe she simply thought our time for hugging was over. But as she let go, I felt cheated. I didn't care that we had company or that she thought the hug was over. I wasn't ready to let go.

"Can we talk to you for a moment, Kail?" Garnet asked. "In private?"

My head was once again ripped away from the sight of my sister against my will and back to the adults outside my room; our room.

"What for?" I asked, wary of the request.

"We just want to talk," Keeley replied. "I promise it will be quick, and then you can come right back here to your sister."

It was the biggest lie I had ever been told, and the truth of it would go on to preoccupy my thoughts every day for the rest of my life. If I had been old enough to understand that adults were just as deceitful as children, then I might have been able to see their ulterior motives. But I was just a kid and believed every word they said as the purest of truths. I realized that this day would go on to shape the person I would become in so many ways that the time before this day seemed almost irrelevant. The person I was died that day, and along with it the countless wishes and dreams that would never come true.

I turned back to Delphia and saw that she was nodding her head enthusiastically, simultaneously clapping her tiny hands in excitement. She didn't care what they had to say to me, all she knew for sure in that moment was that I was happy, which made her happy. However happy she had been when I was miserable paled in comparison to what I saw then. I had been holding her back from true happiness all this time, and I'd been too selfish to realize it.

All our years together, and I thought I had been holding her back, feeding off her joy and giving nothing in return. I never understood why she chose not to give up on me. Now I understood that she wouldn't have been better off without me. She had just been waiting to be as happy as she could be, and that required me. Our happiness was bound together. It was within this moment of comprehension that whatever strands holding my mind within the fabric of reality finally snapped. I was at the mercy of my memory.

"Yeah, okay," I replied. "I guess so."

The two adults walked out of the doorway to give my sister and I some privacy. I knelt down and grabbed her by the hands, which were covered up by her blue gloves.

"I'll be really quick," I explained. "You stay right here and don't talk to anyone."

She ran her fingers across her lips like a zipper, expressing her compliance. "I'll be right here when you get back," she promised.

I stood up and waved to my sister. I followed Keeley and Garnet out of my room, taking one final glance back at my Delphia, who was alone in our gloomy room. She was fidgeting with her blue gloves, but it was an excited fiddling, not a fretful one. As I closed the door, she tilted her head sideways, her shimmering blond pigtails bobbing slightly, and waved back with an endearing smile upon her beautiful face. And that was the last I saw of her.

"So tell me, Kail," Keeley said, beginning to walk down the hallway and toward one of the exit doors that led to the front of the building. "Do you think we would make good parents for you?"

I nodded quickly, not really caring about whether or not they would be a suitable fit for my sister and me. All I cared about was getting the two of us out of this place before another year went by. Christmastime was fast approaching, which meant it was likely that no other potential parents would come back until after the New Year. I absolutely hated Christmas in the orphanage. It may have been selfish of me, but it felt like everyone in the world was experiencing the greatest day of all, and I had been left out.

"And you would like to come home with us, if we wanted you to?" she asked, the anticipation of my answer manifesting in her words.

I saw Matthias avert his eyes as he walked past me, holding a pair of ice skates in his hand. I kind of felt bad for the last time we had spoken. I hadn't exactly been nice to him. I would have to make an apology before I left, just to get him off my conscience.

"Hey, Matthias," I said, temporarily ignoring her question. "Do you think you could watch my sister while I'm gone?"

His head popped up, surprised to hear me speak to him in such a civil tone. He looked around for a moment before giving me a response.

"Yeah. Sure, Kail," he said.

"I'm sorry about before," I apologized. "I just get worried about her sometimes."

"It's okay," he said, nodding his head. "Don't worry about it."

"Okay," I nodded, happy that he had accepted my request. "I'm trusting you with her, okay? So don't let me down and keep her safe."

"You can count on me," he stated. He eagerly rushed off toward my room, and I felt much better knowing that she would be looked after.

"That was really sweet of you," Keeley said, looking over to her husband with an enthusiastic smile on her face. My plan to make myself seem kind-hearted had worked perfectly.

"Now, about you coming home with us—" Garnet pressed on, not wanting me to lose sight of the conversation.

"Of course," I replied, not needing him to repeat the question. I looked up to their smiling faces to assure her I was being honest. "Of course I'd come home with you."

"How soon would you like to be out of here?" Garnet asked, opening the door for his wife and I, causing the bright reflection of the snow to burn my eyes.

I shielded them for a moment to allow them to adjust, until I was able to see the parking lot and trees that were situated at the front of the building. The orphanage was almost completely surrounded by trees. The infrequently travelled road that led into the parking lot was the only connection we had to the outside world.

"As soon as I can," I replied, reminiscing on how unpleasant my life had been in isolation.

"And how much do you," Keeley stuttered. Her voice was low, causing me to realize that they hadn't moved beyond the doorway. "How much do you love your sister?"

"Delphia?" I uttered, turning to face them and noticing the seriousness present in their expressions. I didn't understand the question at all. I furrowed my brow and tried giving them a simple response, but my mouth only formed words without actually saying them. How much did I love my sister? Surely they knew.... but then, why else would they ask it? I began to feel extremely pressured in that moment, and very insecure about what they were asking of me. "What do you mean?"

"We don't want to make things harder than they already are for you," she persisted, ignoring my question. "We want to make you happy, and—"

"It's just that," Garnet interrupted, "we can see how close you two are, and we wanted to make sure that when we adopted you, that nothing would really change."

"Us," I said, correcting him. My eyes trailed down to my feet. "You mean when you adopt us."

There was a moment of silence that hung in the air, swaying over us with haunting implications. Every ounce of joy I had amassed earlier between my sister and I began to leak out of me. I was deflating. I began breathing heavily, trying to persuade myself with the possibility that I was interpreting the situation all wrong. But with each breath I took, I came closer and closer to the truth; the truth I didn't want to hear.

"Kail," Keeley whispered, finally breaking the spell silence had cast on us. "I thought we had made it clear that we're here only for you."

I began shaking my head vigorously, refusing to accept what I had just heard. I clenched my jaw, refusing to let the emotions rising within me to explode into the world. I was basically hyperventilating, unable to even fathom the consequences of a life without Delphia. They had no idea. No one did. She kept me balanced, she kept me alive. Without her I had no one to turn to, no one to rely on. Without her I could barely exist at all.

"No," I managed to choke out. "You don't mean that."

"Kail, it isn't as bad as you think," Garnet insisted, running over to me and kneeling by my side. "I mean, she would still be your sister, and you would get to see her anytime you wanted."

"Why can't she just be with me?" I whimpered, my words crumbling as they left my lips. "Why can't we just be brother and sister at your house, and you be our parents, just like I dreamed of? This isn't how this was supposed to happen.... I'm not leaving without her."

"Kail, listen," he said, trying his best to remain reasonable and caring. "We simply can't afford two children. And you're perfect! You're what we always wanted in a son. You're strong, independent, and smart. You're everything a parent would want. Nothing will change, I promise! Please, Kail, please understand."

"I'm not leaving without her," I repeated, refusing to look at either of them.

I wasn't independent. I needed my sister by my side. They thought they knew who I was, but who I was wasn't the same person without Delphia. They had tricked both Delphia and I into believing in them, believing in an unfulfilled future, believing in deceptive hope, and believing in unobtainable dreams.

"Kail," Keeley whispered, trying to melt away my aggression. The fury and frustration mounted within me, burning away whatever restraint I had in me, until the heat became so unbearable I finally lost my temper.

"I hate you both," I stated, looking them both in the eyes as I said it to make sure they knew I was serious. "I'll never be your son."

Before I could fully gauge their reactions to my unforgiving statement, I ran past them, clumsily bumping into both of them as I passed by. I heard one say to the other that I just needed time, but that wasn't what I needed at all. What I needed was a world where Delphia and I could live together no matter what, even if that meant staying in the orphanage all of our lives. It would be a better life than one spent apart.

Tears formed in my eyes and threatened to evaporate from the fiery rage I felt within. I rushed through the hallway and back to my room, wanting nothing more than to slam the door and shut out a world filled with deception. Delphia was the only one I could count on to be straight with me. She hadn't been tainted by our world's evil.

As I approached the door, I noticed that it had been left open, even though I was overly certain I had seen Matthias close it behind him. Thinking that he had possibly not closed it properly, I stuck my head inside, but neither saw nor heard anyone. An unsettling emptiness filled the room. The sun no longer discharged its light through the window. My eyes twitched as I came to the realization that she was gone.

For a moment I was confused as to where Delphia could have run off to. My temper temporarily extinguished itself. I tentatively entered the dark room, wandering around its vacant space, searching hopelessly for some clue as to where my sister had gone. It was then that Matthias' presence in the hallway, holding the ice skates, resurfaced into my mind.

I froze. Surely I hadn't been gone long enough for them to have—but even thinking about it was only wasting precious time. I ran out of my room, leaving it alone and empty, just as it had been when I walked into it.

If I had stressed to my sister how important it was to stay in her room, perhaps this may not have happened. If I had stopped Matthias in the hallway and told him not to go out of the room, perhaps this may not have happened. But it was happening, and I now had to deal with it. I trusted him... How could I have been so stupid as to trust someone else with my sister's safety?

I bolted through the orphanage as terrible thoughts bubbled into my boiling brain. She didn't know how to skate. What if she had tripped and cut her legs on the sharp, cold ice, or the skates themselves? She had no helmet. What if she had fallen and severely injured her head? These were the calibre of questions rifling through my head, and no matter how fast I pumped my legs, I just didn't seem to be running fast enough.

I crashed through the back doors of the orphanage, nearly ripping them clean off their hinges. I sprinted into the thick forest that flanked the building, stumbling through snow that came up to my thighs. The ground slanted downward the further I went, making way for the river located at the bottom on which kids often skated. I had a long way to go, but I didn't care.

I pushed past each tree as if it were an obstacle, almost colliding with several of them in the process. If only it had been summertime, or if I had been able to fly, I would be able reach them so much faster. I promised myself to not take out my aggravation on Delphia, but instead save the brunt of it for Matthias. Delphia was going to have a rough enough time as it was when I had to explain to her that we would be spending another Christmas without a family of our own.

It was a very cold day, and I was under-dressed for the weather conditions. Branches cut away at my dry flesh as I boldly pressed on through the thickets of bushes and trees. Snow filled my shoes and liquefied, soaking into my feet. The wind scraped past my exposed ears and shot into my eyes, making the journey all the more difficult without my senses. With every aching step I took, my anger grew, and I began to feel genuinely sorry for Matthias. For when I found him, I would let him know just how bad a day I was having.

I heard a distant shouting emanate from deep within the woods. I stopped for a moment to ensure who the voice belonged to, praying that it was Delphia, and where it was coming from. I concluded that the voice unfortunately belonged to Matthias, but I was definitely getting closer. I set my course for where I believed he would emerge from and quickened my pace considerably. He had no idea the wrath that was about to befall him, and whether he deserved it or not was not up to me to decide.

I saw his fat form bob into my frame of vision, yelling about something that I took no interest in. He saw me racing his way and put his arms in front of him, telling me to stop what I was doing. He must have been terrified of me, judging from the scared look on his face.

I paid no attention to his pleas and lunged at him with full force. I toppled him onto his back and began drilling my fist into his chest and face. He tried grabbing my arms and pushing me off him, but the sheer energy I was using against him was overwhelming. Luckily for him, he not only had his own blubber to protect him, but was wearing padded, winter-appropriate clothing. These details only gave me the incentive to hit harder and harder.

Blood began to pool in the snow around him, leaking from his face and pouring out of my hands. He tried sputtering out some kind of treaty, but I refused to listen. I heard a muffled snapping noise, possibly the breaking of his nose, but I continued on. With each successive punch I felt relieved, which only made me want to hit him more and more. He was the conduit for my aggression to stream from.

I should have felt the intense pain pulsing through my hand as I delivered blow after blow, but I didn't. I had become numb to everything around me. All I felt was my own supernatural ferocity and ravaging hatred as I vented every frustration I possessed into him without clemency. If the world would show me no mercy, I would give none in return.

"We need to get help," he finally choked out as blood gushed from his mouth. His words only temporarily halted my assault.

"You're not going to find any help out here," I panted, restarting the beating.

"No," he gurgled, pushing my fists out of his face. "For Delphia!"

I immediately ceased at the mention of my sister's name. His words jolted me with a surge of alarm. His disfigured mess of a face looked up at me, and despite the agony and fear written all over it, there was another, more subtle expression: sadness.

"What did you just say?" I murmured, unsure I had heard him correctly. He began fumbling beneath me, once again trying to escape my grasp. I grabbed him by the neck of his coat and brought him in close, not cringing in the least as he coughed blood in my face. This time I shouted my question. "What did you just say?"

"I need to get help for Delphia," he stammered, barely able to articulate anymore.

My whole body locked up. I had to manually remind myself to breathe, for no thoughts entered my mind. My eyes wandered around the vacant forest, hoping that she would maybe walk into view and into my arms. What did he mean by help? I began fearing the worst without even being sure what he meant. I only had to stare into his eyes to know that something terrible had happened, and I was too late to fix it.

“Where is she?” was all that I was able to ask.

He pointed off into the distance, toward the river.

Without any need for further confirmation, I shoved him to the ground and bounded onto my feet, hurdling through the forest faster than I had ever run before. I didn’t care what state I had left Matthias in, or even if he would be able to make it back to the orphanage in his condition. Terror fuelled me, gripping me completely and pushing me to my limits.

I tripped and fell numerous times, cursing my failure with every fall. I was covered in snow, blood and sweat. I felt the weight of each little piece of them dragging me down. I could feel the planet fading into oblivion behind me, no longer holding consequence over my actions. Please let this not be happening, I repeated over and over in my head, please let her be okay, please let this all be a dream.

Images began flashing through my head, some of which I remembered and some of which I didn’t understand, perhaps a result of the cold finally setting in. I saw Delphia, in all of her pure glory, walking into our room and comforting me after being denied one of countless times. I saw her standing in a vivid forest I didn’t recognize, and her face reflecting up at me from an icy surface. I saw her eating her dinner with her signature smile, playing with her blue gloves when she was nervous, sleeping softly in her bed as I tucked her in, jumping up and down excitedly, us hugging one another…

All of these tiny, seemingly insignificant moments coalesced together to create a whole picture. It was the picture of my sister—the most wonderful, spirited, innocent and momentous person to ever grace my life, exactly how I would always remember her to be.

The trees grew sparse, allowing me to trudge through the snow more easily and see further. The ground was very lopsided now, and I had to be very careful to ensure I didn’t fall. I saw the river that trailed behind the orphanage, covered in gleaming ice. It was a beautifully sunny day, the sun reflecting radiantly off the river’s frozen surface. I called out Delphia’s name, but was met with no response.

I scanned all over my side of the river, looking for where she could be. As I cleared the final trees that made up the edge of the forest, I lost my footing and tumbled down the last remaining feet separating me from the river. I was so tired from all the running and fighting I had done that if it weren’t for my sister, I doubt I would have gotten back up. But I did, and when I looked back over the frozen river, I wished that I hadn’t.

There were many cracks in the ice, but none as noteworthy or severe as the ones extending from one very specific place far out in the middle of the river. They all converged on a single location, one that had several markings surrounding it, possibly caused by the blades of an ice skate. A tiny pair of wet blue gloves was strewn to the side, noticeably torn apart. In the center of the spot lay a great hole, a place where the ice had fallen through and opened up to the black, chilly waters beneath. All of this was secondary, however, to what rested beside this black hole in the middle of this glistening, frozen river.

Delphia was lying face up with her eyes open, staring blankly at the sky. Her hair was no longer in pigtails, but spread out all around her head, frozen to the surface of the ice. Her face was colourless and her lips blue, as blue as the tiny gloves next to her. But the most haunting detail of the whole scene was the fact that she just did not move. She was simply motionless, absolutely still.

History stopped unfolding, time had ceased, and the world no longer spun. With her death, I witnessed the end of all things. It was the largest event imaginable on the smallest scale conceivable.

I fell to my knees, unable to breathe, blink, or even think. I just knelt there, not capable of conjuring enough energy to even go check on her. I sat there frozen in helplessness. I felt devastation fall down upon me, smothering me in despair and grief.

For all the sorrow that spawned within me, I couldn't bring myself to cry. I wanted so badly to cry, but I just couldn't bring myself to do it. The world around me was too quiet, quiet enough that even if I were to cry, it would just be swallowed up before the sound reached my own ears. I wondered if there was a single living thing left other than me. It was as if the world had ended, and God had forgotten to turn out the lights.

The sight was too painful to stand, but my eyes were pulled against their will to my sister's lifeless body. There was an inner resistance within me that rose and rose, threatening to rip me apart from the inside. I thought that maybe I too was about to die, and maybe that wouldn't have been such a bad thing if it meant seeing Delphia alive again. And then I desynchronized, repossessing control over my body and consciousness. I let out the most ferocious, pain-encrusted scream I could.

I thrashed around in misery, cursing how powerless I had been to change what had happened. I had been crying out in anguish, from the moment I had seen Matthias in that hallway to the moment I had begun beating him to near death, and yet I still had been incapable of doing anything. I had been a slave to my memories all along, never once being strong enough to break out of their chains and live a better life. Just as this day had made Delphia a prisoner of death, it had condemned me to life. And those two paths were ones that would never cross again.

This was the exact moment that had shaped the rest of my life. This is where it all began, and in the same moment, ended. It wasn't just a piece of me that was lost that day, but an entire half.

Losing Delphia imbalanced me and wholly pushed me off my axis. I no longer saw the bright side in things, no longer cared for the sunrise after the storm. There was no good or justice anymore, just the void she had left. It was the worst feeling I could fathom, and it never went away. I locked myself in the recesses of my mind, never wanting to add any more pain or suffering to what was already there. Delphia's death marked on impact on me that could not be understated. Two people died that day, not just one.

I didn't know what else I was supposed to do. In all my other flashbacks, they had simply ended and I had been sent back to Drephoria. This time I remained stuck in a type of purgatory, wallowing in my wretched memory for what would probably be an eternity. What was the difference, after all? I had always been stuck here. This was the reason I shut myself off from other people, so that I would never have to experience something like it again. Maybe it didn't matter if I was ever taken away from this place. Maybe it was where I belonged after all.

There was a sudden flash of light, and Delphia teleported into my arms. Her tiny frame easily fit within my arms and yet she still felt so heavy. My whole body shook uncontrollably. I shuddered, my face contorting in shock and horror. This certainly had not taken place in my memory, and the sight of her in her state this close was too much for me to handle. I moved my hand over to her eyes to cover them, their inert gaze tearing my heart out. What had I done to deserve this amount of torture?

As my palm rested on her face, something unexpected happened: her eyes turned to face me.

"Kail," she whispered, sounding as if she had just awoken from a deep sleep.

I was rendered speechless. This abrupt alteration of my memory was more than just jarring. It was completely uncanny, denying my certainty of anything I had learned in life. Fearing that I may have imagined it, I slowly tested what I believed to have seen.

"Delphia?"

"Kail," she repeated. "Why do you look so sad?"

I burst out in a hushed, depressed laugh, my eyes watering with joy. There was no doubt in my mind now that it was Delphia I was speaking with.

"I'm sorry," I apologized, trying my best to keep composed. "I thought you died."

She looked puzzled for a moment.

"I did die," she said.

I nodded reluctantly at her words, on the verge of losing all sense of control. The only thing keeping me together was the fear that this opportunity might be over sooner than later, and I was not about to waste it on tears.

"I know," I muttered. "How much time do we have?"

"I don't know," she answered, perhaps not fully understanding the question. "Does it matter?"

That was my sister: always content with the time granted to her. Even though she had died so young, she had probably still been satisfied with the simple fact that she had me as a brother through it all.

"No," I replied. "It doesn't matter."

"You look so different," she said, reaching up to my face. "So old."

"You look just as I remember," I said, pushing stray strands of hair out of her face. "Perfect."

"You look scared," she whispered, raising an eyebrow.

"I don't know," I said with a shrug. "I guess I've always just been afraid that you would eventually see what I had become, and... I thought you wouldn't like me anymore."

"That's silly," she said, dismissing me with her tiny yet unforgettable laugh. "You're my brother, Kail. I'll always like you."

We stared into each other's eyes in silence, enjoying each passing second to its fullest. I believed that, given the chance, I could have spent the rest of my life that way: on the side of that frozen river with only the desolate world and my revived sister. But I knew that this would not last forever, and it was for that reason that I wanted to spend our limited time together talking about something. Anything at all. I spoke whatever came through my mind, not caring whether or not it had purpose or coherence.

"I want to cry, I want to scream, I want to die," I prattled on, "but I can't stop smiling. Having you in my arms again is the best and worst thing that could ever happen to me. It's like death itself, I guess. Having to let go of everything I once knew, with the hope that something better is waiting on the other side. But there's nothing better on the other side, is there? This is as good as things get. And it isn't even real. This hollow portrait of happiness is the best I can hope for. I don't know what's worse, never being given this opportunity or knowing I'm just going to have to let you go again."

She squirmed around in my arms, making herself more comfortable. "Death isn't so bad once you've had someone worth living for."

I wasn't sure if she was feeding off my consciousness, or if she had learned more complex vocabulary in the afterlife, but her current diction far surpassed what it used to be. I didn't mind, however, as I always knew that Delphia would have grown up to teach me a thing or two using nothing more than her words. Even in death I was learning valuable lessons from her, which made me long for the life I could have had with her by my side even more.

"You have no idea what this did to me," I lamented. "I just lost hold of everything after you left. I shut myself off and never even gave the world a chance. It was like no matter what, this still happened, and I could never just forget that fact in order to be happy. Any joy I felt was only temporary, but this...this lasts to the day. This is permanent."

"Why do you feel that way?" she asked, becoming more concerned the more I explained.

"I don't know. It's just—" I struggled to find the appropriate words to describe how I had been living my life. "Ever since you left...nothing feels right. Like when you left, the world was knocked off its axis. There was just so much of me that reminded me of you, and I had that with me every day. No matter how good things seemed, there is this void between me and happiness. I promised myself that from this day forward I would never find myself in this position again, that I would never find myself losing someone I had become so attached to. I promised myself that I would never feel this kind of loss again, and by not letting anyone see the real me... I succeeded in that goal. The more I let people in, the easier it is for them to tear me apart."

"You've never been happy since this day?" she asked. "You haven't smiled or laughed at all?"

I winced at how bad it sounded out loud, but it was the truth nonetheless.

"Nah," I groaned, forcing myself to look away from her as I admitted my most embarrassing truth. "It's not the same. It's just pretend. They're just melancholy smiles."

She put her hand up to touch my face, to ease the pain she felt in me. Her warm touch caused me to feel whole again. I closed my eyes to absorb the sensation, one I hadn't felt in a long time. She dropped her hand away from me, but I raised my hand and placed it on hers, making sure neither of us let go of one another. What was the point of memories if the only pleasure I could experience came from the new, not the old? No memory, for me, could ever dream of reaching the euphoric impression of a current moment, not a past one.

"I hate my memories," I stated, keeping my eyes closed. "All they do is remind me what I've done wrong with my life, and how things could have been. My memories are nothing more than a curse that I live with every day. I wish...I wish I could forget everything. Start anew with a clean slate and wash away what I remember. Whatever hope there is in my life lies in my future, not my past."

"How could you say that?" she whimpered, with pain present in her voice. "I'm only a part of your memories now. Am I a curse?"

"Delphia, that isn't what I—" I said, but was interrupted by a sharp slap to the cheek. My eyelids snapped open to reveal my sister with a very upset look on her face.

"You can't keep living like this!" she yelled. Her voice sounded much older. "You're supposed to learn and grow as a person from your memories. If you just forgot everything all the time, there will never be a foundation to construct your future on. This isn't how people are supposed to live. You can't just hide from the world, Kail. It's where you live. You're a part of it, not me."

She was making me feel as if I was the child in the conversation, and she was the adult. I was rather taken aback, but valued her opinion greatly. We likely would have gotten into the best arguments if she had made it as far as I had. There were so many 'what ifs' running through my head... What if we had both been adopted? What if we had both gone to the same school, made the same friends? What if Delphia had been with us in Drephoria? I didn't know how it would have turned out. How I could have flourished with her guidance...

"I'm sorry," I said, ashamed of my egocentric ideals. "I just meant that... I've been through so much, you know? Sometimes I think it would be better if the burden of memories wasn't so much to carry."

"Kail, even if you did forget everything that you've been through," she explained, calming down and resting back into my arms, "it wouldn't mean that it didn't happen. That's the point of memories: to remember what your life has been up to the present. All the things you've seen, everything you've been taught? That's all part of your memory. If you didn't have memories, you wouldn't have me. What you've learned and what matters the most to you...That's not something you want to wash away. That's what makes you who you are."

I pondered over her words for some time, thinking of their inferences and applications to my life. It was true. I hadn't been growing or learning as a person. I had just been holding on to something that had happened years ago, without letting anyone know the cause for my stasis. Even though I was approaching my twenties, I was still just a kid. A kid who had lost himself in the world he had chosen to hate.

"So what was I supposed to learn from all of this, then?" I asked, frustrated that I always had to turn to Delphia for the answers.

"Isn't it obvious?" she asked, tilting her head slightly. "Why do you think we're here in the first place? You did more than just hold on to this memory. You obsessed over it. You based your entire life on the outcome of this single moment. I remember telling you this before, but I guess I can tell you it again...You don't know when to let go, Kail."

So that's what this was all about: my inability to just put things to rest. It was a part of who I was, even before this day had come to pass. I protected Delphia to the extreme, out of fear of one day having to let her go. I blamed my adoptive parents for her death and never truly forgave them, because I just couldn't let it go. I caused countless fights among my friends because of my incapacity to stop holding on to what I believed. And what I believed was that the world was far too dangerous a place for me to go and get attached to objects and people. Delphia's death had taught me that.

"Yeah, I guess you're right," I admitted, defeated by my own stubbornness. It was my moment to familiarize myself with the act of epiphany. "I just don't know when it's time to move on. It's funny, you know...wanting nothing more than to forget the past, but at the same time always living in it. I guess you never really realize how messed up your beliefs are until someone lays them out in front of you."

"Now you're getting it!" she said with a congratulatory laugh.

I laughed too. We shared my first genuine moment of bliss in years, finally shedding the shackles that bound me to my past. I noticed that the golden chains that had been dangling off my arms since I first arrived in Drephoria had fallen off. They laid in a tangled mess at my feet, no longer sharing any ties with me. The feeling of freedom was more than just gratifying. It was life-affirming.

"So, do you know who I am?" I asked, at a loss for the answer myself.

She looked up to me with a sympathetic smile and nodded. "Yes, I do," she replied with confidence. "You're my brother. You're someone who needs to let go."

Her words were cryptic to me, but as the world around us began to dim, I knew what she had meant. Our time together was coming to an end, just as untimely as it had the first time. Just as I had suspected, the impending forced severance we would soon undergo cut my spirits in two. I wasn't losing her again—not this time.

"Delphia, no. Don't do this," I pleaded, my mood shifting for the worse. I held her tightly, thinking that if I kept her close enough, she would be unable to fade away from me. This memory was going to have to take me with it, if it wanted her. "Don't leave me again."

"I have no choice," she replied, sadness evident in her voice. "This is the way things must be."

"But why do they have to be this way!" I cried out, panicking as the encircling trees began to disappear. "What says that you have to die, and I have to live?"

All that remained was my sister and I, and the darkness surrounding us. I could feel the warmth of her body beginning to cool, the weight in my arms lessening. I was losing her all over again and was just as helpless as before.

“Nothing says this is the way things needed to be,” she stated. “It’s just the way things are. But regardless of why things are the way they are, you need to accept them and move along.”

I watched as her feet began to drift off into the shadows, twinkling away from her like stardust. I grabbed at them in futility, attempting to catch them in my hands. If I could hold on to just one piece of her, maybe I could remain whole. She pulled my hands close to her, not allowing me to fall into the same broken cycle I had been living for most of my life. She stared into my eyes defiantly, resisting my tugging and wriggling. She wanted me to accept what she already had, but I just didn’t know if I had it in me.

“I’m losing you again,” I stammered, watching as her legs vanished into nothing. “Just like last time. What am I supposed to do?”

“You look me in the eyes,” she replied, “and you tell me that you aren’t going to walk away from this like last time. You stay here and accept it. This time you learn to let go, Kail.”

Tears streamed down my face and dripped onto hers. I could now barely feel her in my arms, but she began weighing down my mind. She was all I could think about, just like before, and yet... I knew that she was gone. I knew that she was a part of my memories, and nothing more. There were no second chances with Delphia and me. Our end had already come and gone. There was no hope for her ever coming back... but that is exactly what I needed to understand. This wasn’t a moment to grieve over, but to rejoice. The power of this realization poured out of me, and I could see in her eyes that she knew it, too. I was finally letting go.

“I didn’t cry last time,” I said, pointing to my eyes. “But I can cry this time. See?”

“It means that you’re actually feeling the pain of loss,” she explained, no more than her arms, chest and head left in existence. “Now, let me hear you say it.”

My heart pounded with such strength that every beat threatened to force the words right out of me. She nodded her head, encouraging me to make the biggest breakthrough of my life. That was my sister. Even at the end, she was there in the beginning of something new. The belief that I needed to say it began to transform into something else: the want to say it.

“I’m going to let you go now, Delphia,” I whispered faintly. I cleared my throat and took a deep breath, correcting my lack of confidence. “I’m going to let you go now.”

She pumped a feeble but triumphant fist in the air. It wasn’t just my triumph, but ours. She put her hand to my face one last time and blessed me with her imperfect, ethereal smile for the last time.

“That’s my brother,” she said. “Always doing what’s best for me.”

And with that, I released my grip on her and watched what was left of her dissolve to darkness. She was gone, and I was alone. It was just as it should have been all along. It was a catharsis I never knew I needed. My eyes had finally opened to the error of my ways, allowing me to live the life I wanted, not the one created for me from my past. Delphia had come from my memories to show to me that they were not the curse I perceived them to be, but a gift. She was gone, but she would live on forever in my memory, nervously fidgeting with her blue gloves, blessing me with her flawed smile, and giving me lessons to share with the rest of the world.

The darkness lifted, placing me back where I had witnessed The Illusionist steal away my best friend—and for the first time, the grave situation had my full attention. I was no longer distracted by thoughts of Delphia or the rest of my past, for I knew that what had happened, happened for a reason. The only thing I had control of was the future, and I intended to make it one worth living.

Before time resumed and the rest of the group was able to react to the events that had just unfolded, I looked down and noticed that the wounds I had sustained during the fight were freshly opened, my blood seeping out and onto the floor. At first I felt faint seeing so much of my blood outside my body, but then I realized that they formed a familiar pattern, one that made sense to me now. Spelled out in my blood were two simple words that I took great comfort in, thanks to my sister's wisdom. They were her final parting gift to me. These two words were ones that perhaps no one else would be able to appreciate: No Hope.

Truer words have never been bled.

CHAPTER 13: BROKEN PROMISES

"Kanoa!" Adora screamed, jump-starting motion back to the dream world.

She ran past me toward where he had been taken by The Illusionist, but was never able to reach her destination. Her scream shook the glass platform beneath our feet, and the floor began to rumble dramatically. There was a great shattering noise as what was holding us high above the red terrain far below gave way. There was no gradual destruction of the stage. It simply exploded away from below us. We all hovered in the air for a moment, just long enough for me to see the looks upon the faces of my friends. They all believed that they were plummeting to their deaths, and for a moment I believed it too.

But it wasn't the time to believe that there was no hope for us. It was my moment to demonstrate that I was a different person.

As we fell, the horrible cries of my friends uniting with the sound of breaking glass, I chose to shut out everything that was going wrong and focus on what I could do to make it right again. Kanoa was gone, so I could no longer rely on him to assist me. It was up to me, and me alone, to save my friends now. The promise he had made before this journey had even begun, the promise to stick together to the end, had been broken. Not by choice, but broken nonetheless. I would have to begin anew and create a new plan over the old that adapted to our new circumstances. No matter what, I was going to stay true to our promise and get my friends out of here alive.

I broke out of my free-fall and floated in the air, watching as my friends were unable to do the same. Unless I did something drastic, and quickly, they would crash into the world under me with the abundant pieces of glass as their cushioning. The question that ran through my mind wasn't what I could do to save them, but what I couldn't do to save them. And instead of being limited by what I couldn't do, I was liberated by it. I now finally understood what Kanoa had seen in this world and felt disappointed that I wouldn't be able to share his insight with him. Instead, staying true to my friend's memory, I would simply show what I had learned.

Fully expecting that my plan would work and leaving no room for doubt, I reached out to the falling glass below my friends and altered its course. I brought every tiny piece to a halt, demanding them to defy the pull of gravity. I restructured their disbanded formation into a kind of blanket, waiting to catch my friends in its frame. As they contacted, I bent the individual pieces into a bowl shape to accommodate their fall, so they wouldn't feel the full force of the collision. Their fall came to a gentle stop. It was like catching floating leaves in a basket.

The layer of safety then dispersed from underneath them, flooding over the red field below, covering the entirety of the landscape in broken glass. The gap between where my friends had been and the ground below had been filled up entirely. There had been nowhere near enough pieces to produce such a reformation of the land, but it had happened all the same. All that mattered to me was that my friends were safely resting on the ground far below. I exhaled in reprieve, thankful that my first bold step in my new life had been a successful one. I knew that both Delphia and Kanoa would have been proud.

I descended back down to the ground, quickly realizing the events that had just unfolded had affected them deeply. Only Adora had risen to her feet, running around aimlessly and calling out for Kanoa. She had found his blade after the fall and was keeping it handy, just in case she was to find him. The rest of my friends were still lying on the glassy ground, blankly staring up into the sky.

I decided that it was perhaps best not to relay to them what had transpired after Kanoa's capture, figuring that it would take too much explanation. Not to mention that by the looks of it, they had enough on their minds as it was.

"Kanoa!" Adora called out repeatedly, not seeming to understand that he wouldn't respond to her call.

I noticed the true effect my previous action had caused. Each individual blade of grass was made up of splinters of glass. The few trees that now populated the vast terrain were made whole by fragments of glass. Everything glinted from the light, but the pieces were too small to reflect anything properly. As far as my eyes could see, the world was just one big, broken construction.

"He's gone," Thalia stated. Her voice was uncharacteristically depressed. It reminded me of how she used to sound. "There's nothing we can do."

"What do you mean, there's nothing we can do?" Cora snapped, getting uneasily to her feet and shaking bits of glass off her. "The Illusionist took him, so we're going to go get him back."

"How?" she asked, not moving from her back. "You say that like he's just going to give him back. We failed, simple as that. We lost."

"What's gotten into you?" Cora asked, becoming frustrated with Thalia's inability to think positively. Although my friends all seemed to be unaware of my presence, I still watched intently, seeing the flame kindling in Cora's eyes. "We haven't lost anything yet. We're still here, and as long as even one of us remains, we can't give up trying. We fight back until there isn't a single one of us, or them, left."

"You think we can get him back?" Adora asked, discarding her sister's cynicism.

Cora shifted her eyes around uneasily as Adora's hopeful, expectant face turned to her. I knew Cora secretly expected the worst for Kanoa's fate, but she couldn't devastate such optimism. Not at a time like this.

"We're going to try our best, Adora," Cora said with a nod. Adora smiled and continued to call out Kanoa's name.

"I thought the whole point of a dream was to escape from the worries of real life," Thalia rambled on, speaking more to herself than anyone else. Looking at her was like looking back in time, to a darker time. "When you fall asleep, there's this unspoken promise that exists, you know? All your worries are washed away by the unknowable darkness of the dream. I guess that's just another broken promise. Because here we are, in a dream, and I'm more worried than I've ever been in my life. So now what's the difference between dreams and reality?"

"This place doesn't exist outside of us," Osias replied, jumping into the conversation. "Without us, none of this would even be here."

"Would the other world exist without us being there?" she asked. Something about Kanoa's exodus had left a mark on her and shaken her to her core. I noticed that her once-blue hair had darkened to a deep violet, the white streaks fading to black. "How do you know the real world exists anymore, now that we're here? What if this is the real world, and we were all dreaming before this? What if we're awake and this is our reality?"

"All right. I think that's enough of this conversation," he grumbled, resigning from speaking any further on the subject. "You're starting to sound a little too similar to Kanoa for my liking."

"I didn't even get to say good-bye," Adora whimpered, finally giving up on searching for any sign of her best friend.

"You didn't have to say good-bye," Cora told her, desperately attempting to maintain the last glimmer of hope in the group. "We'll find him, and he'll be fine. Everything will just be fine if we--"

"You don't know that," Thalia interrupted, looking off into the distance. "You shouldn't lie to her just to try to make her feel better. She's a big girl. She knows things aren't okay."

"Come on, Thalia," Cora said, trying to soothe the anxiety her friend felt. "You always keep your cool in any situation we get ourselves in. You're the strongest girl I know. You can't let your sister get upset over this."

"Oh, I'm not upset," Adora explained, carefully running her hands up and down the face of Kanoa's blade. "Just worried. For me, there is no point in getting worked up over things. It isn't like it's the end of the world. And even if it were the end of the world, what could I really do to stop it?"

Cora let out a disbelieving burst of laughter, clearly discouraged by everyone's bleak outlook.

"Thalia, back me up here," she pleaded, kneeling down beside her for some support. Thalia had now sat up, pulling her knees up to her chest. "You're usually the one I can turn to for some spiritual uplifting."

"I don't think so," she replied, her eyes blank. "Not this time."

Something had changed among my friends. The dynamics had shifted. When Kanoa left, for the first time, they had to cope with the fact that it was very possible that we wouldn't have each other for the rest of our lives. They had always known it in their minds, ever since Adora had given us a scare a few years back, but this was the first time it had become an actuality. Our first taste of reality had been spoon-fed to us by our dream world.

"Things are just...spiralling out of control, aren't they?" Osias asked of no one in particular, kicking with despair at the glassy grass.

"No, not really," Thalia replied, lightly rocking back and forth. "Because that would mean that we had things under control at some point."

"Guys, don't be ridiculous," Cora said, reapplying herself in a search for solidarity. "We can't just give up because we hit one little bump in the road."

"One little bump?" Osias restated, the tension rising in his voice. "Kanoa's gone, Kail seems to have completely lost his mind again, we have no idea where Alem is, and we didn't even manage to destroy The Illusionist. If that's a little bump, I would hate to see what a pothole feels like."

That was the first time I had been acknowledged. I had become a kind of spectator as my friends took turns speaking with one another. I would have voiced my opinion if I had one, but at the moment I remained speechless, waiting for a more appropriate time to speak my mind. I couldn't let myself remain a bystander in my own life anymore.

"I'm just trying to make things seem a little less fucked than they actually are, all right?" Cora yelled, quickly escalating the mood to its breaking point. "I'm not the kind of person who just sits around and wallows in my own grief, feeling helpless, hoping that everything fixes itself. If I just keep telling myself that everything will be all right, and actually try to make everything all right, then what's there to stop me?"

"Um, how about the fact that things may not be all right?" he replied, never one to back down from an argument. "If you don't actually believe that everything will be all right, then why are you lying to yourself? Just because we can't lie to ourselves as well as you can, doesn't mean we aren't trying!"

It was then, just as my friends began to turn on one another, that I finally settled on what I wanted to say to them. They had left me out of the discussion, for they believed that I had nothing to add. To them, I had always been an outsider looking in. I was going to have to trust that they would accept me, and trust wasn't something that came easy for me. It was time to let them know that I was just as big a part of the group as any one of them. It was time for them to realize I wasn't just a bystander, but a friend. It was time for them to know who I really was.

"My sister is dead," I said, no louder than a whisper. My friends had become too enthralled in their grief and frustration to hear me.

"What's the point in trying, if we know we're going to fail?" Thalia asked, diverting Osias's original meaning and warping it to her own despair. "When everything seems to be at the edge of disaster, thinking about the good just doesn't seem enough. It all seems so hopeless."

"My sister is dead," I stated more loudly than before. When I said it, the words began transcending their meaning for my friends, and started sinking in for me as well. Still, it wasn't enough, and they continued to overlook what I was giving to them.

"The moment my sister loses hope," Adora said, rushing over to be at Thalia's side, "is the moment I lose it, too."

"My sister is dead," I gasped, knowing that they would be unable to hear my voice.

Saying it out loud was just as difficult as it was to accept the fact in the first place. By saying it, I was not only accepting the truth of my words, but also forever breaking the promise I had made to myself to never let anyone in. Unlike Kanoa's promise or the promise of dreams, however, mine was one worth breaking.

"This cannot be happening," Cora growled, vexation causing her to cover her face with her hands.

"My sister is dead!" I shouted, my voice echoing out over the turmoil and disarray.

I caught my breath and grabbed at my heart, which was now beating hard enough to burst through my chest. I had done it. I had opened myself up to the world. I could now finally say that I didn't just have friends, but that they had me too. Where they had lost Kanoa, I could now replace him. A relieved smile lifted my face. I observed my friends staring at me with shock and awe displayed on theirs. They could now see me just as plainly as I had always seen them.

"What are you—" Cora stammered, but couldn't bring herself to finish her sentence. They all just watched me as I stood in rapture, as if at any moment I would sprout wings and fly away. I certainly felt as if I could.

"Delphia," I began, staggering into the centre of my friends. "She's dead. Has been for a long time. She died right in front of me, and there was nothing I could do. I know the feeling of being helpless...I've felt it ever since then. When you're helpless you can actually feel the world turning around you, and yet you stand perfectly motionless. You're just a pawn waiting for its turn, knowing that it may never come. You can feel time pass through you, like you aren't even there... This isn't a moment I have that feeling. This isn't a moment that we lay down and accept defeat. This is a moment we stand together and carry on. Everything may seem broken and hopeless, but we have the power to fix this."

Understanding that I had probably just dropped a considerable bomb of revelation upon them, I patiently awaited someone's response. The strain that I had felt between my friends began to loosen, making room for the tiniest shreds of hope. Hope's Glow had been gleaming ever since I had returned to Drephoria from my flashback, but now more than ever, its light shone bright. I could now see what the prophecy this land had foretold saw in me, and felt ready to take on its responsibility.

"Where do we even start?" Cora asked. I could feel that my change in disposition startled her more than anyone. This was her dream coming true, which seemed to be more than she was willing to believe. "We don't know where Kanoa is, or even if there's a way to get out of here. How can we be sure we can fix this?"

Seeing as it was a difficult question to give a definitive answer for, I once again turned to my sister for direction. I thought about not only what she had taught me, but what it now meant for me. Sometimes lessons were taught at the wrong time, and it wasn't until long after that I realized their meaning. Luckily for me, she had given me lots to think about in her limited time granted, so I quickly found an appropriate message to give.

"My sister once told me," I explained with a smile, "that just because I couldn't remember what our parents looked like, didn't mean that they didn't exist, or that they didn't love us. She was seven years old when she said that. It's taken me almost a decade to understand what she meant. Maybe we can't be sure there is a good solution to come from all this, but that isn't what's important. Sometimes the idea of something is more important than having the real thing. Sometimes the real thing just can't compete with the beautiful power of the idea. Sometimes the idea is all that you have left. And at the end of the day, sometimes that is all you need."

Just as I finished my speech, Alem appeared beside me, already nodding in agreement. Although surprised at first, everyone was glad to see him again. It was comforting just to have him with us, knowing that perhaps he would be able to set us back on track.

"Well, you all sure know how to put on a spectacle," he praised, purposefully ignorant of the rather murky mood he had come into. His temperament was a little jarring, but I still found it welcome. "And if you think that is as luminous as Hope's Glow gets, Kail, you are sure in for a treat!"

"So, are we like the biggest failures you've ever seen, or what?" Osias grumbled, embarrassed by our less than satisfactory success.

"Oh, it didn't go so badly," he said before quickly reassessing his answer. "Well...yes it did, but it could have been a whole lot worse."

"How could that have possibly gone any worse?" Osias asked, unconvinced that he hadn't failed as critically as he believed. That was the thing with Osias: he either achieved great success or total failure. There was no middle ground.

"Well, all six of you are alive, are you not?" Alem replied, not understanding the cause for my friend's negativity. "That must count for something."

"How can you know that?" Adora asked, picking up on the possibility of Kanoa's survival. "I mean, how can you be sure? The Illusionist grabbed him and then he was gone."

"Trust me," he reassured her. "If Kanoa were dead, you would notice. All of Drephoria would become unstable. It would begin ripping itself apart. If one of you is lost, so is the balance of this world. The effect one of your deaths would cause on this land would be... cataclysmic. From the looks of things, everything is all in order—or disorder, depending on how you look at it. In other words, everything is as it should be. As I said before, things could have been a lot worse."

With this news, Adora became ecstatic and jumped up and down excitedly. She reminded me of my sister more and more every day. There was something that she brought to the group that eased my mind, and I could tell that her return to form instantly lightened whatever darkness still loomed over my friends. We were well on our way to a full recovery.

"So, how do we get back to The Illusionist?" I asked, wanting to be sure that all of our effort against him had not been a lost cause.

"Oh, I wouldn't worry about him anymore," he replied. "Malise is not going to be very pleased that he was only able to capture Kanoa, and not defeat a single one of you. I doubt you will see him again."

"So we did it?" Thalia asked, physically shaking in anticipation.

"Yeah, you did it," he stated, not understanding how there had been confusion over the matter.

We all looked at one another with exhilaration in our eyes. We jumped for joy and closed together, embracing in one big group hug. We involved Alem in our embrace despite his obvious discomfort. Whatever dread lingered from our time spent in uncertainty had completely dissolved. True hope was able to resurface on the horizon. This was the group of people I had grown to know over the years and named my best friends. As long as we never lost sight of the feeling of unity, we would be able to take on this world and walk away with a story to tell.

"I guess things aren't so bad after all," Osias conceded as we released our hold on one another. We were all still smiling. "I kind of wish I could have done more, but it's good to know I'll get the chance to redeem myself.

"So, who's up for your next challenge?" Alem asked, looking around for any takers.

"Oh, fuck off," Cora declined with a giggle.

"Oh yeah, that's right," Osias whined. "He was only the first of our problems. I literally cannot wait to see how much fun we have with the other members of The Forgotten Four, or Malise herself for that matter."

"Well, maybe The Illusionist was the hardest to defeat and the worst is behind us?" Thalia proposed, her bright optimism returning to her.

"Yeah, right," Osias said while scoffing. "Because that's how these types of things usually work out. They send the toughest enemy first, and save the easiest stuff for last. Darth Vader should have been the first enemy Luke fought. That would have gotten rid of the need for an entire saga."

We all stared at him, disapproving of his returning cynicism. He quickly realized his misdoing and hung his head. "Sorry," he said.

"No reason to be sorry," Alem said. "You're right. Things are only going to become tougher from here on out, and you will be tested to your absolute limits. I believe that you all have grown as individuals and will be able to at least put up a decent fight. Especially you, Kail."

My friends all turned to me, recognizing me as the leader I was supposed to be. I honestly felt as though I had matured since our journey had begun, but seeing the same level of confidence in the eyes of my friends only strengthened my resolve. Their trust in me—and my newfound trust in them—was paying off.

I looked to Cora, who I held in the highest consideration with regard to what kind of person I was. She was always the first to let me know when I treated others poorly, and always the first to tell me I was going about my life all wrong. But the look I saw in her glowing eyes in that moment told me I was exactly who she wanted me to be. I was who she needed me to be. I was finally ready to be a true leader.

"I'm ready," I promised, my eyes firmly locked on my friends, letting them know they were my primary concern from now on.

I was no longer going to hold them back. Instead, I would put them ahead with an advantage. They could count on me as much as I had always counted on them. We were in this together. I knew that for certain.

"So, what do you think our chances are on all this, Alem?" Osias asked, cutting right to the chase. He wanted to get the most informed opinion at our disposal.

"Well," he replied, "my guess is that things are going to get bad... and then they're going to get worse."

Although his lack of faith did put a damper on our spirits, he was only being honest. I couldn't see how things were going to get better, but I did know that we weren't going to quit just because things got hard. That was something the old me would have done. He would have lost hope before even putting in any effort. But the old me was now just like my sister: nothing more than a memory.

"You're not the optimistic type, are you?" I teased, keeping things light. Our period of poignancy was over.

"No," he replied, sensing my playfulness. "I always considered myself the realistic type. That's probably why I float around and have no eyes."

"So I guess we should head out and search for some more trouble, huh?" Thalia asked, punching the air in front of her like a boxer.

"Oh, I'm sure trouble will come searching for you," Alem declared, his words vaguely ominous.

Thalia dropped her arms to her sides and nodded her head in acceptance. The foresight of our looming future began to settle in, and with it came all the questions any future brought. Where would each of our paths lead? What awaited us beyond the short reaches of certainty? Would everything turn out for the best in the end? Who would still be there? The future was an odd thing to think about, for it was always present, but could never be reached. It wasn't until something came to an end that the future was knowable, and that was because it no longer existed.

"Well, all good things do come to an end," Thalia stated, recollecting our previously blissful moment and parting with it, knowing that such things were only brief treasures. We had to move along if we wanted to save Kanoa, even if that meant abandoning joy's fortune.

"So does that mean the bad things last forever?" her sister asked.

Despite all of her innocence, she was still competent in delivering profundity. It was like she was from another planet—insightful in a way that no one else was capable of, and yet never meaning to be as thought-provoking as she was.

She looked to our faces and realized she had upset the order we had been re-establishing.

"Sorry," she said.

Her sister patted her on the head and held her close. I could feel my friends becoming restless, no longer wanting to just sit around and dwell on what was to come. It was time to follow Kanoa's lead and rise to action. I looked around to see where we should continue our adventure, but saw nothing but emptiness on the horizon. Alem was right. There was no use in searching for what was only going to be found when we least expected it.

"Where should we go?" I asked, thinking that perhaps he knew better than I about the next logical step to take.

"Anywhere your feet can take you," he replied, following my gaze off into the wide region of our dream world.

"I remember reading a book called *Madame Bovary*," Osias whispered, looking on with the rest of us. "There was this one line in particular that I've been thinking about ever since we got here. It went along the lines of, 'My mind travels more freely on this limitless expanse and I am given ideas of the infinite, beyond the bounds of reality.'"

"You memorized that?" Thalia asked, impressed and affected by his recitation.

She too looked out into the infinite scope of possibilities that awaited us, each as enigmatic and enticing as they had always been. Seeing such an open plane, and knowing that divine horrors and unspeakable joy were only a matter of time and place, really made me appreciate the totality of life.

"No, I think I'm remembering it wrong," he admitted, not looking away from our vast surroundings. "And it isn't even referring to dreams, anyway. It just feels...appropriate."

"Well, it sounds good regardless," she said, more concerned with how the words applied to our setting than their accuracy.

We were now free to set our own paths, and our potential was only restricted by our imaginations. As long as my mind extended far beyond the reaches of my sight, out into the arcane atmosphere, I would be able to accomplish anything. All I needed were my friends to follow me into our great unknown.

I walked away from the circle, following in what would have been Kanoa's footsteps, but instead they were my own. I would no longer follow others. Others would follow me.

At first the wavering silence of indecision deterred my bold initiative, but then I remembered something Kanoa had always done that had alienated me during his leadership. He never waited for others. It was this recollection that caused me to turn back to my friends, lingering for their approval. They looked back at me with doubtful faces, but all I asked for was an opportunity. It was a lot to ask for in a time such as the one we were in.

I wasn't surprised when Cora was the first to step forward. She was the one who would follow me to the ends of this dream world, even if I led us there blindfolded.

"What are you doing?" she asked, running to my side as I turned back to face the monumental obelisk of the indefinite before me. Although nothing was truly in front of me, I saw the promise of everything.

"Leading," I stated, inspiring confidence in my stride. "I worried about you back there, you know? Before you arrived to save me from The Illusionist, I mean."

"Why? What happened?" she asked.

I explained the entirety of what had occurred before her arrival on the scene, and as I spoke, the rest of my friends bid Alem good-bye. They promised him that we would all meet again. Her face lit up, and then diminished when I told her of how I had used our lack of communication with one another as the ultimate weapon to expose him as a fraud. Her steps slowed the more I went on, losing the desire to follow someone she realized that she barely knew. Despite being glad that my plan had worked, I could see that my means had come at the sacrifice of our lacklustre friendship.

"That was a nice little trick with the movie question," she said, her voice trailing off. "He would have had you all fooled if it weren't for that."

I decided that it was time to reward Cora for all I had done wrong against her. While letting go had been my ticket to salvation, her inability to do as much granted her the greatest result. Call it undying loyalty or sheer stupidity, but she treated me like more than just a friend with her devotion. I didn't know why she had stuck by me all these years, but she was with me now at a turning point in my life, the one she had always been waiting for. All the passion she had abortively poured into our link with one another in the past was finally about to pay off.

"Yeah, I guess so," I said, "but I feel really bad. I mean, I'm glad he thought he knew the answer to the final question, but by not knowing the answers to any of the previous questions, he knew as much as anybody else in my life. My friends should know more about me than my enemies. You especially. You should know more than anyone else."

She stared at me tentatively, not wanting to believe that I had finally seen my faults and was so quickly correcting them. She knew what was coming and she wasn't prepared, but I finally was.

"I agree," she blurted, "but—"

"It's Memento," I said, cutting her free from her refrain. "My favourite movie is Memento."

There was no need for a big dramatic embrace or voiced expression of gratitude. My simple revelation and her illuminating smile were more than words or actions could ever accomplish. We made our breakthrough, transitioning from close strangers to hopelessly dedicated friends. Eyes opened or closed, no matter where we were in the world, we were there for each other now and forever after. We could now move forward amicably, knowing that in spite of being in a dream world, what we had was real.

"Wow," she whispered, still riveted to my disclosure. "How fitting. I've got to say, I don't know what's gotten into you, but I'm a big fan of this new Kail."

"Yeah, well," I said, "you can get used to him, because he'll be around from now on. You and I can both thank my sister for that."

I thought back on all that had transpired since we had first arrived in our mind's heart. Our first shaky steps as we familiarized ourselves with the rules and regulations that so greatly differed from what we were used to. My awakening in the forest, Kanoa teaching me how to fly, and our view over all things were the memories that stuck out the most.

Memories: the intangible objects I had used to defeat my shadow in the field of memories. The timeless items that had brought me back into my past, reliving moments I now cherished instead of trying to forget. Although the time may come when I would eventually regret entering this world, for now, I was glad taken a chance.

The rest of my friends caught up with Cora and I, all five of us forming a line that carved into the face of Drephoria. We had cleared our first hurdle, and paid the price of such a difficult obstacle with one of our own. We had experienced the might of our dreams and imagination working in unison, threatening to consume us with their promises of a better life, but we had resisted their temptations. We had felt the void left by the fading of hope as all seemed lost, but had persevered through the darkness.

But only I had felt the formidable curse set down upon me by my memories, and although they had taken their toll, I now appreciated their lessons. With me at the forefront of our endeavour, I would lead us in the search back home, strengthened by the parting words of the one who meant the most to me.

Out of the broken promises, hope, and curses rose the beacon of all desire: the gift of another chance.

CPSIA information can be obtained at www.ICGtesting.com
Printed in the USA
LVOW081155130613

338408LV00001B/221/P

9 781621 372783